Praise for *Heir to the Duke*

"Ashford makes a strong start to her Duke's Sons Regency series with a story that affirms the value of being yourself and having fun in the process."

—*Publishers Weekly*

"Ashford launches her new series on a high note with an engaging tale about love and marriage that showcases her usual Georgette Heyeresque flair for characterization and impeccably realized historical setting."

—*Booklist*

"With her keen knowledge of the Regency era, Ashford…tempts the reader with engaging characters, plenty of passion, and a devastating secret in this nicely written, heartwarming, and compelling read."

—*RT Book Reviews,* 4 Stars

"Graced with lively wit, excellent period detail, and appealing protagonists, this fetching romp enthusiastically launches Ashford's new series."

—*Library Journal*

"Delightful…engaging and fun."

—*Smart Bitches, Trashy Books*

"A fabulous romance with wonderful characters… I couldn't put this book down."

—*Night Owl Reviews,* Reviewer Top Pick!

Also by Jane Ashford

About the Author

Jane Ashford discovered Georgette Heyer in junior high school and was captivated by the glittering world and witty language of Regency England. That delight was part of what led her to study English literature and travel widely in Britain and Europe. She has written historical and contemporary romances, and her books have been published in Sweden, Italy, England, Denmark, France, Russia, Latvia, the Czech Republic, Slovakia, and Spain, as well as the United States. Twenty-six of her new and backlist Regency romances are being published by Sourcebooks. Jane has been nominated for a Career Achievement Award by *RT Book Reviews*. She is currently rather nomadic. Find her on the web at www.janeashford.com and on Facebook.

On the far side of the large room, her mother sat at a cluttered desk, pen in hand. Georgina watched her scribble on the page before her. It couldn't be denied that, as people often observed, Mama looked rather like her dogs, particularly when she was vexed, as she apparently was now, her lips turned down in her round face. A small, plump woman, with glossy brown hair and prominent eyes—though her eyes were blue, not brown—she had the same bustling curiosity. Sometimes, the similarity made Georgina smile. Today, it raised her protective instincts.

Mama's desk was the only conventional piece of furniture in the spacious chamber. Everything else catered to her dogs. There were rafts of colorful pillows where they could lounge, piles of sticks for them to chew, and scattered heaps of other toys. Hearths at each end kept the room warm in winter, and small, hinged flaps in two of the long windows gave the animals access to their own walled garden. There was a tiled area where they were fed and a large tub in the corner where they were bathed. The pugs were kept scrupulously clean, though their sheer numbers meant that the place still smelled just a bit of dog. "Sebastian has arrived, Mama," said Georgina. "You must come and say hello."

What the
DUKE
DOESN'T KNOW

JANE
ASHFORD

sourcebooks
casablanca

Published by Sourcebooks Casablanca, an imprint of Sourcebooks, Inc.
P.O. Box 4410, Naperville, Illinois 60567–4410
(630) 961–3900
Fax: (630) 961–2168
www.sourcebooks.com

Printed and bound in Canada.
MBP 10 9 8 7 6 5 4 3 2 1

One

Lord James Gresham gazed at the spires of Oxford University, visible above the trees at the edge of his brother's garden; at the early summer flowers in curving beds; at the fifteen people standing about chatting and drinking lemonade. It was a pretty scene, the sort of thing one dreamed of when tossed by a five-day tempest seven hundred miles from shore, or when repairing the ravages of a broadside that near as nothing took down the mainmast. Some poet had a bit about a lovely summer's day. Probably Shakespeare. Nine times out of ten it was Shakespeare. If Randolph was here, and not stuck in his parish in the far north, he'd know the lines, for certain. Randolph had been mad for poetry before he became a vicar, always spouting some sonnet or other. Well, he probably still did. No reason a parson couldn't, and he had a whole congregation for a captive audience now.

James had forgotten all the poetry they'd tried to make him memorize at school. He'd never taken to any subjects except those that would help him onto a ship. For as long as he could remember, he'd been mad for the sea, haring off at sixteen to a midshipman's berth on a man-of-war. How green he'd been, and how thrilled. All he'd ever wanted to do was captain a navy ship.

And now he'd lost his vessel, only two years after he'd been given a command at last. The *Charis* had been small, yes, and years of war had left her battered and limping into port, but he still couldn't believe the Admiralty had decommissioned her. All their blathering about reduced requirements, with Napoleon beaten for good and all, and more efficient designs coming along in the shipyards, was just so much noise as far as he was concerned. Like condolences at a family funeral, the words hadn't penetrated his sorrow. But they'd towed the *Charis* off to some backwater and abandoned her. And after ten years of service, they'd shaken his hand, given him a medal, and told him to enjoy a bit of a well-deserved rest.

So here he was, stuck on shore, waiting for a new posting, like who knew how many other navy men. The most likely berth would be second or third officer on a bigger ship, and more years to wait for another command.

The prospect depressed his spirits. It had made him consider, seriously, whether it wasn't time to leave the navy and settle down. Had he, perhaps, had his fill of the sea? Which had brought him here, to this covey of chattering guests in their civilian clothes.

James eyed his hosts, his youngest brother, Alan, and Ariel, Alan's lively and lovely new wife. According to family gossip, Ariel was a wizard at promoting perfect matches. She'd greased the wheels of Nathaniel's marriage and helped Sebastian win a dazzling heiress. He hadn't been able to resist asking her to see what she could come up with for him. With his prize money from the war, he certainly had the means to support a wife.

James strolled over to a table under a spreading oak and helped himself to a couple of small sandwiches. When he'd left the *Charis* for the last time, and had the leisure to consider his future, he'd fully absorbed the fact that, although many senior naval officers were married, they didn't see their wives and families for years at a time. A tour of duty could take you halfway 'round the world, where even mail packets rarely reached. You were back for a few weeks or months, then off again. Such a life would be nothing like his parents' close partnership. And in that instant, he'd realized that his model for marital happiness was his father, the duke, and his beloved duchess.

Thus had begun the conflict within him, his love for the sea fighting his desire for the kinship he had observed—and lived—in his youth. As a boy, he'd been surrounded by a horde of brothers and cousins and aunts.

At times, the back and forth seemed almost like a true battle, ringing with the echo of gun barrages and beset by swinging cutlasses. He couldn't see a way to have both, and yet he wasn't prepared to give up either.

As he usually did at this point, James turned away from the inner argument. He'd never been one to brood, and he didn't intend to start now. He went to join a cluster of his brother's guests.

"*Chelonia mydas*," said an older man in the center of

the group, "maintains the balance of its body fluids by excreting the excess salt from seawater."

A woman on James's left tittered with embarrassment, earning censorious glances from the others.

"*Chel*—what?" asked James, his interest caught by the mention of the sea.

"The green sea turtle," replied the professorial type.

In fact, he most likely is a professor, James thought. Alan's friends came from the Oxford faculties. His brother was very much at home here, performing his arcane experiments on the nature of light. And if James knew what that meant, he'd be…well, quite another sort of person. "You mean these turtles can drink down seawater and then…be rid of the salt, er, naturally?"

The older man nodded.

"There's many a sailor who would be glad of a skill like that," James said.

The woman tittered again, her hand in front of her mouth. The professor gave her a condescending glance, as if she was an errant child. "It is one of the elements that allows the species to live their lives far from land," he added.

James noticed Ariel approaching with a very pretty blond in tow, and he examined her with interest. Although his brother's wife had made it abundantly clear that he couldn't order up a bride to any particular specifications, there was no harm in wanting a handsome one, was there? It seemed to him that the woman one was going to be looking at for the rest of one's life ought to be easy on the eyes, and this girl certainly was.

He stepped forward to meet the two ladies and was

distracted by a flicker of movement at the edge of his vision. He turned in time to see a slight figure emerge from the shrubbery at the bottom of the garden and stride toward him. In one raking glance, James noted a loose, shabby coat over worn trousers, a rough scarf pulled well up over the face, a slouching cloth cap shading it, and, riveting his attention, a pistol in the fellow's right hand. It was primed and cocked and aimed right at him.

With reflexes honed by years of war, James was instantly in motion. He lunged low, his speed taking the assailant by surprise. He caught the intruder's gun hand in a crushing grip and forced it upward. The pistol went off harmlessly into the sky, the sound alarmingly loud in the peaceful garden, even as the weight of James's body smashed the lad to the ground.

The party erupted into a babble of screams and shouts and questions. Some people ran toward the house; some froze in place. Glasses of lemonade dropped to the grass. Sandwiches went flying. James scarcely noticed. He was preoccupied by the fact that the body under him was definitely not that of a stripling. There were tantalizing curves under his hands. The intruder was a woman, not a boy.

"Thief, murderer!" she cried, flailing at him with her free hand.

Blows landed on his shoulder, his cheek. "What? Stop it. Ow!" He tried to grab her other wrist and missed.

"Let me go!"

She landed another good hit, making James wonder if she'd blacked his eye. He managed to get hold of her free arm, and pinned it above her head. Her body

arched and writhed beneath him in the most distracting way. "Let go of the pistol first," he said, tightening
his grip on that wrist.

With a sound like a growl, she released the gun.
Using her imprisoned hand, James managed to shove
it out of her reach on the grass.

"What have you done now, James?" said his
brother's voice from above. James craned his neck
and discovered a circle of faces—appalled, curious,
frightened, amazed—staring down at them.

"He's a thief and a murderer," repeated the shooter.
"A blackguard of the worst stripe."

The eyes in the circle of observers focused on
James. They were not universally filled with righteous
indignation at the attack, he noticed. Indeed, a couple
of the women gazed at him reproachfully. The professor was starting to scowl. It was a scene out of one
of those nightmares where you faced an examination
all unprepared.

Incensed, and bewildered, James gathered himself
and jumped up, keeping a secure hold on the girl's
arms and pulling her along with him. Before she could
get a solid footing on the lawn, he bent, threw her over
his shoulder, and carried her off toward the house.

Her fists rained blows on his back. She kicked and
squirmed like an eel in his grasp. She called him all
sorts of names. It was like trying to carry a sack of
maddened cats, and he nearly lost his footing a time or
two. She must be some sort of lunatic, he decided. But
why the devil had she set her disordered sights on him?

As he maneuvered his shouting burden through
the open French doors at the rear of the house, he

heard one of the guests say, "Your parties are always so invigorating, my dear."

But James couldn't spare a moment to wonder about the eccentricities of Ariel's hospitality. The girl had started to claw at his neck above his shirt collar, and it felt as if she might be drawing blood. He hurried into the back parlor and dumped her unceremoniously onto a sofa. The cap fell from her head as she landed, releasing a cascade of raven-black hair. "What the hell are you shouting about?" he asked.

"Thief! Murderer!"

"Will you stop?"

"Never!" Dark eyes burned in a face smudged with dirt and half obscured by swathes of dark hair. "I swore to make you pay, if nothing else!" Her hands crooked into claws.

She looked ready to fly at him and scratch his eyes out. James took a step backward. "Pay for what?"

"You know very well what you've done!"

"On the contrary, I have no idea who you are or what the devil you're talking about."

"Liar! Thief!"

"Why do you keep saying—?"

Ariel walked through the French doors, looking surprisingly composed. "Alan is seeing the guests out. What's this all about?"

"I think she must be an escaped lunatic," said James. "Is there a bedlam house near here?"

The girl sprang up from the sofa. She extended an arm to point at him, a picture of outraged virtue, if you were devoted to bad melodrama. "I came here for justice," she declared.

Ariel looked at James. "I have no idea what she's talking about," he said.

"Ha!" said their visitor, her full lower lip curling.

"Will you stop?" said James again. "If you're not mad, then you've made some sort of mistake. Got the wrong man."

The girl shook her head, fists and jaw clenched. But as they simply stared at her, her shoulders slumped a little.

"You're tired," said Ariel. "Are you hungry?"

Tears started in the girl's eyes. She blinked them away angrily.

"Come with me," Ariel went on. "We'll get you something—"

"Hold on there," James protested. "She tried to put a bullet in me!"

Ariel paused on her way to the inner doorway. "Do you have another pistol?" she asked the girl.

The intruder slumped a little more. She bent her head, and wings of raven hair fell over her cheeks. "No," she said. She did sound exhausted.

Ariel gave James a look that seemed to say, "See?" She went over and took the girl's arm. "Come."

"Get Mary to help you," said Alan from the doorway. "Eliza, too. She did fire a pistol in our garden."

With a wave of acknowledgment, Ariel took the stranger away.

"Are you just going to let her go off with that... assassin?" asked James.

Alan shrugged. "Once Ariel gets an idea in her head... But that's why I mentioned the housemaids. She'll have them with her."

"Oh, maids. That's all right then." When his brother ignored the sarcasm, James shook his head. "Where's the pistol?"

Alan took it from his coat pocket. "It's practically a relic, and not well cared for. I think it went off by accident, when you jostled her hand."

"Jostled?" James couldn't believe what he was hearing. "I saved your garden party from an armed attack. And do I get so much as a 'thank you'?"

"Thank you," Alan replied. "You were quite impressive. I've never seen anyone move so fast." He started to put the pistol back in his pocket.

"Shouldn't you lock that away somewhere?" James asked, somewhat mollified.

His brother looked at the shabby gun, nodded. "I will. Later. It's empty now." He slipped it away. "So what did you do to her?"

"What?"

"Why is she after you?"

"I've never seen her before in my life." James gazed at his brother, deeply aggrieved. "Why do you assume I did something?"

Alan raised an eyebrow. "A girl rushes in, waving a gun, calling you a—"

"And you believe *her*—clearly a lunatic—over me?"

"No, but…" Alan shrugged. "You tend to be the one of us who goes just that step too far, James," he said. "You locked Nathaniel's valet in the garden shed on the day of his wedding."

"I thought that was part of the prank!" James protested. "Sebastian took his clothes. Robert cut the bell rope."

Alan conceded with a nod. "That jape did get rather out of hand."

"And the shed did the fellow no harm," James pointed out. "It was all part of a joke, nothing like this…female calling me a thief and murderer."

"And you're sure you don't know why?"

"I swear I have no idea who she is or what she's talking about."

"How…odd."

"You are a master of understatement," James replied.

The two brothers stood, perplexed, in the comfortable parlor, shafts of afternoon sun illuminating pale cream walls and blue-and-yellow chintz. Somewhere in the house a bell rang. Female voices were audible for a moment, then were cut off by the sound of a closing door. "Perhaps a glass of wine?" Alan suggested.

"Excellent idea."

The men had drunk their wine and run through a number of improbable theories about the uninvited guest before Ariel at last returned. They sprang up when she entered the room, and James opened his mouth to ask a question. Then he caught sight of the figure behind her.

His brother's wife was a lovely woman—small and curvy, with glossy brown hair, skin like ripe peaches, and entrancing hazel eyes. But this newcomer very nearly cast her in the shade. She was certainly a far different, far more unusual type.

The cascade of jet-black hair had been tied back with a blue ribbon. It tumbled down the back of a simple blue gown, one of Ariel's, James assumed, and framed an absolutely exquisite face. Broad forehead, jutting cheekbones, a pointed chin, full lips as pink as rose petals, skin the color of honey. Huge dark eyes with sooty lashes stared at him, burning with the fire of an avenging angel. No wonder she'd smudged herself with dirt and hidden her features with a scarf and cap. She'd have been mobbed otherwise, and God knew what else.

"This is Kawena," said Ariel.

James realized his mouth was hanging open. He closed it.

"I promised that she would have the chance to tell her story," his brother's wife went on. "She believes that James—"

"He killed my father!" the girl interrupted.

"That's rot," said James. "I've never killed any… or…was he a French sailor?"

"No! My father was an English gentleman!" She glared at him.

"Then I didn't kill him. Unless he'd signed onto one of Boney's fighting ships. And if he did, then he deserved—"

"You stole everything he had and broke his spirit so that he died," Kawena accused.

"I did no such thing." James had never been more certain. "You have the wrong man."

"Liar!"

It seemed as if she would fly at him again. Who would think that dark eyes could burn like that?

"We're getting nowhere," said Alan, with a crisp authority that made Ariel smile. "We must begin at the beginning if we are to untangle this riddle.

You…Miss…Kawena, sit there." He pointed to the sofa. "James, over there." He indicated an armchair well out of reach, then drew Ariel to a pair of seats between them. "Now, give us your tale."

"It's not a 'tale,'" the girl responded. "It's the truth!"

"He only meant your story," Ariel put in. "What happened to bring you here."

The visitor sat back. James thought she might be trembling, but she was doing all she could to hide it.

"I come from the island of Valatu, very far from here."

"Far? That's on the other side of the world," James interjected.

"You admit you know it!" Kawena accused.

"My ship called there for supplies once or twice," he replied. "It's in the middle of the Pacific Ocean," he told Alan and Ariel. "Or, well, not the middle, but a thousand miles or more from the coast of Australia." He turned back to Kawena. "But I never saw you—"

"My father never let me near the harbor when ships were in."

James could easily see the wisdom of that. "Your father, the English gentleman," he said. "I don't remember meeting any—"

"He didn't work in the trade house. He was not a shopkeeper!"

"The beginning," Alan reminded her. "And if you could stop interrupting, James."

"Me? I'm not the one who—"

Alan held up a hand to silence him. James subsided with a frown.

Under three pairs of eyes, Kawena hesitated briefly. Then she put back her shoulders, seeming to gather herself, and said, "My father was the son of a rich English merchant. When he was young, he was sent out on a long voyage, so that he could learn how the trading was done. But when his ship was blown off course by a great storm, and he came to Valatu, he was…much taken with the place. And he met my mother. And so he chose not to go on with his ship, but to stay there."

Her voice had a wonderful lilt, James thought. She didn't sound like anyone else he knew.

"He understood what ships needed so far away from their homes," Kawena continued. "And so he made a place where they could trade for island things. Fruit and other food, fresh water, things that people on the island made. He took in trade items desired by other ships. Rope and metalwork and sailcloth. My father was very wise and…and canny. He built a fortune in this way." Sadness in her face shifted to anger. "And then you stole it from him!" she said to James.

"No. I didn't. You've made a mistake."

"Your ship was the last to come before it went missing. None other stopped in our harbor until the one I left on. We searched the whole island, with great…thoroughness."

Everyone turned to look at James. "I remember stopping there," he said. "I did speak with the man at the trading post. We loaded fruit and fresh water and a trinket or two. But I know nothing of your father, or his fortune."

"You took it, and when my father found it was gone, he had a fit and died!"

"I did not!" He grimaced. "I'm sorry about your father, but I did not steal anything from him."

The trouble was, Kawena was starting to believe him. This large, handsome man was not what she'd expected to find. He didn't have the tone or the look of a liar. His blue eyes were direct and clear; there was nothing evasive in his stance or his manner. He seemed honestly revolted by her accusations. And being here in this house—the small, pretty woman had been so kind to her, chatting openly about who lived here and her daily life. She gazed at the two brothers with their deep auburn hair that curled slightly, their square jaws and easy grace. No one here felt like a thief. She had no sense of deception.

But if this James Gresham knew nothing of her father's treasure, then she didn't know what to do next.

With that thought, the exhaustion and fear and uncertainty that had been hovering under the surface of her consciousness came surging upward. She'd been shoving it all down and ignoring it as she hunted her quarry across the world. Until this moment, there had always been a next step to take, another trace of James Gresham's path to follow. Now...what was left?

Despite the generous aid of a ship's captain friend of her father's—giving her free passage and helping to hide her true identity—she'd spent all her money on this long journey. Aside from the shabby clothes she'd arrived in, she had only a few coins and the ancient pistol she'd bought near the London docks, which she had *never* meant to fire! That shot was James Gresham's fault entirely. She'd meant to frighten, not injure.

But if Gresham was not the thief, if she could not

immediately recover her father's fortune… Kawena endured a moment of something very like terror. Everyone she knew, everything familiar, was half a world away. And she had no notion how she would get back to them. In all her twenty years, she had never felt so alone.

Silently, Kawena struggled for control. She would not reveal her plight to the three strangers gazing at her, waiting for her to speak when she had no idea what else to say.

"Are you all right?" asked the young woman. Ariel, she had said to call her Ariel.

Kawena nodded, trying to keep her expression blank. On top of everything else, England made her feel quite disoriented. Everywhere she went in this land, something reminded her of her father. Intonations, mannerisms, habits that she had thought unique to him turned out to be quite common in his home country. It was unsettling, to say the least, and yet fascinating, too. How she would have loved seeing it in his company, sharing each small observation, each start of recognition.

The sharp pain of loss lanced through her again. With her father's death, she had lost more than a parent. He had been the one person who accepted her wholeheartedly, as she was. With him she didn't feel the conflicting tides of her dual heritage so strongly. To sit with him in his cluttered workroom was to be at home. She'd listened to all his stories, spoken his language, absorbed the quaint vagaries of English manners as he described them.

Kawena plucked at the blue fabric of the gown

Ariel had lent her. She'd worn such dresses, brought from far across the sea, to please him. Other times, she'd slipped on the easier garb of her mother's people, to show kinship with her family there. Both and neither were fully hers, she often felt. She was warmly welcomed everywhere on her island, yet always just a bit of an outsider. And when her father was gone…he had been her anchor, and now she was adrift.

"Kawena?" said Ariel.

What was there to say except the truth? "No other ship stopped in our harbor after yours," she said to James Gresham. "And my father always insisted that the captain of each ship be the one to come ashore and trade. No one else."

"I did trade. But no more than that. Someone on the island must have stolen your treasure. The man in the trading post had a shifty look, as I recall."

"That was my half brother," replied Kawena. "I would trust him with my life." The three children of her mother's first marriage were as close to her as true siblings. "And I have told you, we searched. There are not so many places to look on the island. And people there all know each other's business. They would see that there was no way to use my father's fortune without being exposed. Anyway, someone would have seen, told."

"But couldn't it have been one of the ship's crew?" asked Ariel.

They all turned to look at her. "Are you siding with her?" demanded James.

"No. It's just…if your ship was the only one…"

"They don't let sailors wander about on Valatu.

No shore leave allowed." James Gresham looked at Kawena. "I suppose I see why… The thing is, I was the only one who—"

"Had the chance to steal it," finished Kawena.

James frowned at her.

"Still," said Ariel, "someone could have sneaked off the ship at night."

"They would not know where to look," said Kawena. Although…could a very cunning man have found his way into the trading center? A big part of her problem was that she didn't know precisely where her father had kept his hoard. He'd tried to tell her something as he lay dying, but… She swallowed another wave of sorrow.

"My crewmen were not thieves," said James.

Kawena straightened. "My father told me that Royal Navy crews are the dregs of press gangs and criminals."

James started to speak, stopped, then said, "My crew wasn't."

"None of them?" asked Alan. "If a man is faced with the temptation of, what, a chest full of gold?" He looked at Kawena.

"My father put his fortune in…small things."

"What kind of things?" James asked.

Kawena's conviction that this man had stolen her father's cache of jewels finally died under the simple curiosity of his gaze. He simply couldn't look and feel so guileless and be guilty. Another wave of despair swept over her. If it wasn't him, if her long, long chase had been misguided, what was she to do?

She tried to rally her spirits. She couldn't give up. She just couldn't. Perhaps a very cunning thief might have slipped past the watches her father set on trading ships. There was a chance that such a man could have discovered the jewels. What other explanation was there? "Someone from your ship robbed me," she declared, wishing she felt as certain as she had when she first arrived. "And the captain is responsible for the acts of his crew."

"I..." James Gresham didn't deny the principle. "My ship's been decommissioned, the crew dispersed to other vessels, or mustered out, even. There's nothing I can do—"

"We must find them, and question them," Kawena said. She tried to sound as if there could be no doubt about the matter. "It is your duty to make this right." She saw that this latter idea reached him, which only increased her conviction that he was not the thief.

"It might not be so difficult," mused the other man, the brother. "Such a man would be spending more lavishly than made any sense, I suppose."

Kawena cast him a grateful look.

James scowled. "None of you understand what a large task this is," he said. "It would take a deal of time, and pulling some strings at the Admiralty. Which I'm not sure how to do, if you want the truth."

Ariel leaned forward in her chair. "Well, you can both stay with us until it's all straightened out."

Kawena tried to hide her relief.

"I didn't agree to do any 'straightening,'" James objected.

Ariel looked at him. His brother looked at him. Kawena focused a steady, expectant gaze on his face. She wasn't pleading. She wouldn't stoop to plead. But she was…anticipating. She had a feeling that a silent appeal for justice would make a difference to this man.

"Oh, very well," James Gresham muttered under the combined onslaught. "I'll see what I can do."

Two

"DO YOU THINK IT WISE TO HAVE OFFERED HOSPITALITY to a total stranger?" Lord Alan Gresham asked his wife. Ariel, nestled against his shoulder on the parlor sofa, fixed him with her entrancing hazel gaze. As they were alone—their unexpected guest ensconced in the last spare bedchamber and James off brooding in his own room—he pulled her closer.

Ariel smiled her approval of this move. "Probably not wise," she said.

"Then...?"

"If wise means cautious and cool and unwilling to inconvenience oneself to help," she added. "But I believed her story. Didn't you?"

Alan considered all that he'd heard earlier, then nodded.

"And I know what it's like—what it feels like—to be alone in the world, with nowhere to turn. Kawena had that look. I could *not* turn her out into the street."

Her hands clenched into delicate fists. Her expression was fierce. Remembering the day he'd found her all alone in her mother's dark house, deserted by parent and servants, yet refusing to be cowed, Alan was flooded with love for his spirited wife. He had to kiss her.

Ariel laced her arms around his neck and kissed him back with such enthusiasm that neither had any further interest in conversation for quite some time. Indeed, their rising ardor dictated a delicious retreat to their own chamber in the waning hours of the afternoon.

However, after dinner that evening, Ariel led her husband and guests back to the pleasant room off the garden and decreed that they must make a plan.

"She's going to have to tell me what I'm looking for first," James responded. His period of solitary reflection had not improved his mood.

Kawena hesitated, reluctant to reveal any of her secrets. But if she didn't trust these people, what was her other choice? Even if she gave up, acknowledged her voyage a failure, she didn't have the money to pay her passage home. And she was not giving up! She refused!

She took a breath and made up her mind. It felt like stepping off the cliff on the north side of her island home and plunging into the deep green water below it. "My father kept his fortune in jewels," she said. "He always traded for gems when he could. He knew how to value them, and he said they were the most portable kind of wealth." She held out cupped hands. "They were in a cloth bag about this big."

Alan raised his eyebrows. "A fortune indeed." He turned to James. "It should be easier to find a sailor selling jewels than one merely spending coin."

His brother nodded, but didn't look happier. "I've

been thinking about this tangle," he said. "We're going to need an admiral. At least."

"What for?" asked Kawena.

James sighed. "I can't just march into the Admiralty with a list of my former crewmen and demand to know where they are. Or, I could, but I wouldn't get anywhere. The clerks will want explanations and authorizations. Particularly authorizations. I suspect I would need approvals just to get a load of forms to fill in. And submitting forms to the navy is like…tossing sovereigns in a wishing well. Only it takes a lot longer. Just about as likely to do any good, though."

The others considered this. "But an admiral could find the men?" said Ariel.

"He could use back channels, get me in to see the proper person, unofficially. If he wanted to."

"Then you must ask an admiral for help," said Kawena. The conclusion seemed obvious. She didn't see the problem.

"Right," replied James. "The thing is, I'm not acquainted with any admirals."

"But you are in the navy. Surely you know an admiral."

"I've stood on a deck near one or two of them. Shook hands with another at a reception in Sydney."

"Well, perhaps he would remember you," said Kawena.

"Possibly." James's voice was very dry. "But he has no reason to do me any favors."

"I don't believe you even want to try to help me."

"Oh, no, only too happy to risk my career to find your baubles," he muttered.

"If you mentioned Papa?" said Alan diffidently.

"I've always made my way on my own merits," James replied.

Alan nodded as if he understood perfectly. Kawena looked from one brother to the other, confused. "You might ask Nathaniel," Alan suggested.

"What has he to do with anything?"

"Who is Nathaniel?" asked Kawena.

"He's their oldest brother," Ariel told her as the men conferred quietly. "There are six of them, altogether."

A picture formed in Kawena's mind—six tall, handsome, auburn-haired men with piercing blue eyes. The image was rather dazzling.

"Nathaniel is Viscount Hightower," Ariel finished.

"Viscount?" Kawena knew this was a noble title. She'd heard of such names from her father. But it wasn't the sort of rank she'd associated with this comfortable but small house.

"Alan and James, all of them, are sons of the Duke of Langford."

"Duke!" The word came out so loud that the other three stared at Kawena for a moment. When she said nothing more, they continued their deliberations.

"Nathaniel has a knack for solving problems," Alan said. "And he's discreet. You can talk to him about matters you don't want to…burden Papa with."

"Burden?" James looked at him, wondering what escapades his studious youngest brother could have had to cover up. But he understood the notion completely. The trouble with going to their father wasn't fear. The duke was no domestic tyrant. Quite the opposite, really. The thing was, you didn't want to disappoint him. Ever. It didn't bear thinking of. And then, other times, matters that seemed to carry the weight of the world just amused him too much.

"We should write Nathaniel," Alan said. "He'll know how to find a useful admiral."

"He's on his honeymoon," Ariel objected.

"No, they've left the country house and gone to Brighton."

Ariel gave her husband a look that Kawena couldn't quite interpret. Perhaps she was amused.

"Are you sure?" James said.

"Quite," replied Alan.

"Well, I suppose he can always say no." James rose. "I'll give it a try."

He went off to his room to write the letter. Kawena's hosts said their good nights soon after, leaving her alone in the parlor. She sat there for some minutes, bemused by the evening's revelations. A duke! Her father had told her about England's king and parliament and the different classes of English society. She understood that a duke was near the very top of it. But she'd never expected to encounter such an august personage. She tried to picture a duke in her mind. Would he wear a coat and breeches just like any other man? Would he carry some sign of his noble title? It was too bad that she'd probably never meet the man. She would have liked to see. On the other hand, his sons seemed quite down-to-earth, so perhaps there was no particular marker of duke…hood.

It occurred to Kawena then that it was a stroke of great good fortune that the man she had pursued—wrongly, it seemed—for theft had such powerful connections. And that he was willing—grudgingly—to use them to help her. All the fears and warnings that her mother had poured into her ears when she left their island ran through her brain. Things might have turned out so much worse.

She brushed a hand over the fabric of the dress Ariel had lent her. She owed this James Gresham more thanks than she had expressed, Kawena concluded. She rose. She would thank him now, before this day was done. It was only right.

At the writing desk in his bedchamber, James wrestled with the wording of his letter. Alan seemed to think it a commonplace thing to ask Nathaniel for a favor, but it wasn't so for James. He'd scarcely seen his eldest brother—well, any of his family—for the last ten years. This was the life of a navy man. Brief shore leaves, letters exchanged across leagues of ocean, had been his family life for all that time. He felt the sting of it yet again as he tried to frame sentences to address his brother. There were times when he didn't even feel part of the Gresham clan any longer.

James sat back, melancholy. He put down the pen. Surely Nathaniel had better things to do than find him an admiral. Why would he bother? Why should he? And with that final question, a memory from more than twenty years ago popped into James's mind.

He'd sneaked off from the nursery at Langford, as he did every chance he got, yielding to the temptation of a perfect summer day with a brisk wind. He'd taken advantage of the cover offered by the shrubbery and made his way to the fountain in the rose garden, an irresistible, forbidden spot. He even remembered his five-year-old reasoning. The fountain wasn't the lake, was it? He didn't try to go down to the lake alone anymore, after the terrible dustup with Nurse the last time. The fountain was a poor substitute for those broad waters—except that he could sail his model ship across the basin and retrieve it on the opposite side for another go. Voyages launched into the lake often ended with a lost vessel. And it was increasingly difficult to persuade his parents to replace the little ships. They didn't seem ready to acknowledge that his existence was empty without one.

So, he'd rigged up his toy boat, retrieved from its garden-shed hiding place, and sent it out into the fountain waters. He'd been so engrossed in maneuvers that he hadn't realized anyone had seen him until Nathaniel appeared at his side.

The eight years that separated them in age made Nathaniel a rather awe-inspiring figure. He was also seldom seen about Langford, as he was mostly away at school. Gazing up at his tall eldest brother, James had expected a scold and to be sent back to his minders. But Nathaniel had watched the little ship scud across the fountain and said, "Where did you get sailcloth?"

James had hunched a bit at the question. But he had to tell the truth. "I cut up one of Father's shirts," he admitted. Quickly, he offered his excuse. "I would have used my own, but it wasn't big enough for the mainsail."

To his surprise, and delight, Nathaniel had laughed. And they'd spent the next hour sailing his ship together, back and forth across the fountain. The jets of water from the dolphins in the center had done double duty as hazards of the sea. They capsized once or twice, and Nathaniel had even taken off his shoes and waded into the fountain on a rescue mission. When Nurse finally caught up with him, the scold was not nearly so bad because Nathaniel was there.

With a lingering smile, James picked up his pen. He could write to that Nathaniel. It would be all right.

He'd just started to do so when there was a knock at the door. "Come in," he called without looking up.

He heard the door open, and a lilting voice say, "Hello."

James turned in his chair. Kawena stepped through his bedchamber door, shut it, walked over, and sat down in the armchair by the empty fireplace. "I wanted to thank you," she began.

"You can't sit here," James said.

She looked down at the comfortable chair, back up at him. "Why not?"

"This is my bedroom." The moment he said it, he became acutely conscious of the bed just a few feet away.

"I know. I came up to thank—"

"It isn't proper," he blurted out.

"But you are taking some trouble to help me. When you don't really wish to. I can see that, you know. It is only right that I thank—"

"Not that. You shouldn't be in a man's bed-chamber. Alone. With him. Me." He heard himself stammering like a callow youth, and was revolted. She was just so very beautiful. Utterly alluring, really. The effect seemed multiplied here in his private quarters.

And she appeared so at ease—as if they knew each other far better than they actually did. James could almost imagine her coming over to him, offering a hand to pull him to his feet, and closer… No, this line of thought was unacceptable. He stood and moved toward the door instead. "It isn't done," he added. "Young ladies do not visit gentlemen in their bedchambers." Well, some did, if what he'd heard about country house parties was true, but that was irrelevant to this discussion.

"We must speak only downstairs?" wondered Kawena. "Is that an English rule?"

Her honest bewilderment was rather charming. "If a man and a woman are alone in a bedchamber, people assume they're…up to something improper," James explained.

"Getting into bed together, you mean?" Kawena replied, without a trace of embarrassment. She gazed at the wide four-poster as if it was on exhibit.

James felt his cheeks redden. Years at sea might have left him unused to polite female company, but even his brother, Robert, the town beau, would have been confounded by this quite unusual young woman. "Er, yes."

"But we are not."

"No… Not in this case. However—"

"And no people know that I'm here," she pointed out. "I told no one I was coming up."

"You can never tell when there's a servant about," James replied. The staff at Langford always seemed well aware of everyone's movements.

"Do they hide and watch?" said Kawena, looking surprised.

James choked back a laugh, and then wondered if maybe they did. How else would that housemaid have seen Sebastian with the frogs…? But that was beside the point. He needed to remove a lovely young woman from his bedchamber—didn't he? Yes, yes. And wasn't that a problem he'd never imagined having? When had it become his job to preach the proprieties? He felt like a fool even trying. But if she didn't go soon, he might not be able to resist… James decided to shift the onus off onto someone else. "This is my brother's house. I wouldn't wish to upset him, or his wife."

Kawena cocked her head. "Your brother and Ariel would not approve of my being here?"

James assumed so. No, of course they wouldn't. And that was beside the point. He nodded.

To his relief, Kawena rose at once. "I would not wish to offend them. They have been very kind to me." She shrugged as she moved toward the door. "My father always says…" She paused, swallowed. "Said that it is rude to disregard others' customs when it does you no harm to observe them."

"Pr-precisely." She passed quite close to him on her way out. Her long fall of black hair swayed seductively with each step. Was he really throwing her out of his room? Her initial words came floating back. She'd come up to thank him. Perhaps with something warmer than words? Some marvelous island custom? No. She hadn't meant that. Clearly, obviously. No sign whatsoever of any such thing, despite her unembarrassed mention of bedding. Besides, it would be an awkward complication, as they were living together in his brother's house. Not together. As fellow guests. Strangers, in fact.

"Good night," said Kawena.

"Good night," James replied, shutting the door firmly behind her.

He leaned against it, listening to her soft footsteps retreat along the corridor. Perhaps helping her wasn't quite such a burden. It would give him a chance to become better acquainted with one of the loveliest, and most unusual, girls he'd ever encountered. Her courage and fire drew him—now that she'd stopped calling him names. How many women, how many people, would have done as she had, sailing halfway around the world to find justice? *Very few, hardly any, really*, he thought. She'd looked positively intrepid, stepping out of the shrubbery with her gun. And under his hands, on the turf, she'd felt… James fell into a pleasant reverie. It was some time before he returned to his letter.

❦

Kawena was wakened the next morning by a young maid bringing her a cup of tea and pushing back the draperies on the windows. Kawena didn't really like tea, but she took a polite sip and suppressed a grimace at the bitterness. Her father, who had been inordinately fond of the dark beverage, claimed it was much more palatable with milk added, but milk had never agreed with Kawena's digestive system. When the maid went out, she set the cup aside.

Sunshine streamed through the windows. Apparently it did not rain all the time in England, as she'd been told. She could see a corner of the garden below, bright with unfamiliar flowers. It was a comfortable house, the largest she'd ever been inside. And her hostess, Ariel, seemed very far from hidebound and prim. Had her father been prejudiced by his decision to abandon his home country? Immediately, Kawena felt disloyal. Ariel Gresham was probably not a typical Englishwoman.

Surely James Gresham must be an odd sort of Englishman. Mustn't he? Last night, in his room, he'd been clucking over her behavior like the circle of watchful old women at home on the island. In her experience, young men did quite the opposite. They were always on the lookout for ways to circumvent rules and get you to go off alone with them into the trees. Were they so different here on the other side of the world?

Kawena stretched and threw back the bedcovers. No doubt she had much to learn about her father's homeland. She only hoped it would all end well.

Dressed in her borrowed gown once more, Kawena found Ariel and James at the breakfast table in a bright room at the back of the house. "I've made a list of the crew from my ship," James was saying.

"But there's no sense doing more until we see if Nathaniel knows an admiral," Ariel replied.

As Kawena sat down, James nodded.

Ariel picked up the teapot and gestured toward the cup beside Kawena's plate. "No, thank you," Kawena said.

"Would you like coffee? Cook could make some."

Kawena shook her head. Coffee was even more

bitter than tea. She didn't see how anyone could stand to drink it.

"You must be used to quite different foods," Ariel added, setting down the pot. "Perhaps I could order—"

"I am in England. I will eat English food." Kawena smiled to show that it was no hardship. She was deeply grateful for their hospitality.

"Fruit," said James.

Both ladies turned to look at him.

"They eat a deal of fruit on the Pacific islands."

Ariel smiled and nodded. Kawena examined the man, wondering why he seemed uneasy. Then she gave up wondering and went to fill a plate with the items on the side table. The eggs were familiar, and she had eaten sausages in the course of her travels. Some she had found palatable, others revolting, with no way that she could see to tell the difference beforehand. Bread was safe. She liked bread, though they did not eat it on Valatu. And jam—jam was a welcome addition to her life indeed. This on the table was raspberry, her newly discovered favorite.

Silence fell as they ate. They were, after all, three strangers thrown together by family ties and circumstance. "Have you been to Oxford before?" Ariel asked James after a while.

"No. Never had the occasion to come."

"You should look around. There are a great many lovely buildings. You could take Kawena about," she suggested. "Show her something of her father's country."

"You'd be a far better guide," James answered. "And Alan best of all."

"He's gone off to his laboratory. And I have an appointment this morning. I'll come with you another day, but you should go out exploring."

James shrugged. "I don't know anything about the colleges, but I could use a bit of exercise."

"I'd like to see this place," Kawena agreed. And so the matter was settled.

Three

Lord Alan Gresham kept no personal carriage, preferring to hire a vehicle if he needed one and save the expense. James and Kawena found this no hardship when they set out on foot a little while later. Less than half a mile down the green lane, they came to a place where three roads met at a bridge across the River Cherwell. On the other side, they were immediately among Oxford colleges. "I don't know the names of any of these places," James said. "They're hundreds of years old, most of them. And, er, architectural." He was very conscious of her vibrant presence by his side, though she didn't take his arm as an English girl might have. He'd offered it as they'd left the house, but she obviously hadn't understood the gesture. She'd marched off like an explorer on an expedition instead.

He watched her gaze at the intricate stonework and leaded windows that surrounded them. She was far more fascinating than any fusty carvings. And it wasn't just her unfamiliar style of beauty that made it so difficult to tear his eyes away. He'd thought that was it, of course. She *was* one of the loveliest creatures he'd ever seen. Then, as they walked and talked, he'd started to notice an air, a manner, unlike anything in his previous experience. Kawena's lively presence brimmed with…the unexpected, with an exhilarating whiff of adventure.

Some of the buildings loomed as large as mountains to Kawena, and as unlike her island home as anything could be. She felt squeezed by narrow passageways under heavy arches. "I've never seen anything so old," she said. "Not built things, I mean." Beaches and oceans and cliffs were far older, she noted. And yet not oppressive at all. "Your brother went to school here, but you did not?"

"No. I couldn't wait to escape the classroom. The idea of going on to university…" James shook his head. "Never in the cards. There are two kinds of Gresham brothers, you see. Randolph and Alan, and Nathaniel a bit, took to their books like fish to water. Sebastian and Robert and I could hardly sit still long enough to turn a page. We'd far rather be doing other things."

For no good reason at all, the phrase reminded Kawena of their recent conversation in his bedroom, and all the "other things" a man and woman might do together, besides walking under great burdens of stone. Her errant mind offered up the moment when he'd thrown her over his shoulder and carried her off.

Of course, that had been outrageous. She'd been angry—and rightly so! She wasn't the least bit sorry that she'd pummeled him. And yet… Briefly, Kawena lost herself in his vivid blue eyes. Everyone she'd grown up with, even her father, had had brown eyes.

She'd glimpsed other hues on her travels, while keeping her head well down. Now that she no longer had to duck under the brim of a cloth cap, she could look her fill. There was something particularly compelling about this man's gaze. Each time she met it, she felt an odd little shock.

Kawena realized that the silence had stretched too long. What had he said? Oh yes. "What other things?" she said.

"What…?" He blinked. "Oh. Ah, for me, captaining a sailing ship. Riding and cultivating his sidewhiskers and waving his saber about for Sebastian. He's a cavalryman, you know. Robert's addicted to high society, cares more about the cut of his waistcoats than the written word." James paused, then added, "Though I hear that may have changed lately. Which is dashed odd."

Kawena didn't understand all of this, but she let it pass. It was tiresome to be questioning every unfamiliar phrase. And this was not the time to be staring into a man's eyes. She had important things to accomplish. She walked on, feeling a tiny twinge of gratification when he automatically followed.

"What about you? How were you…educated? Is there a school on Valatu?" James acknowledged that he knew nothing about the place, beyond the quality of its fruit. He'd thought ten years ago that he would explore the far corners of the world when he went to sea. But the navy gave you little time to look about the countries where you stopped, unless you counted the dockside establishments designed to separate sailors from their money, which he did not.

Kawena strode past another massive stone structure. "My father and mother taught me. As did others, sometimes, if they had some skill I wished to know. That is the way we learned."

Thinking of his formidable parents, James decided that the exigencies of Eton hadn't been so very bad.

"My father taught me English things. Like how to read and write."

"Your...people on the island don't read?"

"There is nothing to read in our language. And no reason to." Kawena smiled at the confusion on his face. "We can all talk to each other."

"But if you want to send a message...?"

She shrugged. "We can ask a child to run and find someone. Or just wait. The English don't like to wait, I think."

"No Latin, or thrice-damned Greek," James mused. How cheerfully he would have skipped those onerous subjects. "What did your mother teach you?" he asked, curious.

A tremor of loneliness shook Kawena. She missed her mother and her home. It was harder than she'd imagined to be so far away from every person she knew. "Useful things," she said. "How to plait palm leaves and make bark cloth and gut a pig."

"You can gut a pig?" he wondered.

"Of course." She didn't see why this should be surprising. "And how to judge people's words by the look in their eyes and the way they move. How to hear the silence. How to care for your...property."

"Property?" It seemed a grand word for the village he'd seen on the island.

Kawena didn't seem satisfied with it either. "The homes and gardens on Valatu belong to the women. They tend the earth. I know it is not so here. My father told me. Island men own their boats. They take the canoes out to fish and sometimes make long voyages to trade or explore. Women hold the trust of the land."

"What do you mean?"

"Well…" It was true that the idea didn't sound right in English. This happened to her so often, and the other way around as well. Kawena considered how to explain. "Years ago, when I was small, my father wanted to build a bigger trading center out of timber, to impress the foreigners who anchored in our harbor. He said they would respect such a building more than one made of palm and bamboo. And my mother asked, 'What if it is blown down in a storm?' As it would have been, of course, sooner or later. Nothing can stand against the great storms. And my father said, in that case, he would rebuild it. My mother asked about the next storm and the next. He got impatient then, as if she was being stupid, and said he would rebuild each time. 'And when the trees are gone?' my mother asked. 'For storms come faster than trees can grow.' And so, we do not have a trading center made of timber."

James puzzled over this tale. It took him a while to work it out, rather like one of those parables vicars liked to pose. "Bamboo grows more quickly," he concluded finally.

"Much."

"Sounds like your mother knows her own mind," he said then.

"Oh yes," replied Kawena, with feeling. "She's wise and funny and very smart."

He was much struck by her choice of words. "Mine's like that, too."

"When I'm with her I often feel four years old again. It seems she can see right through me."

"Exactly." How odd that two people from opposite sides of the globe, and completely different families, should feel just the same, he thought. It was like meeting an old friend in the street, and yet not like that at all.

"She didn't want me to come here," Kawena continued. "Because it was dangerous, of course. But I think sometimes she's afraid of my outlander half."

"Outlander?"

She looked up at him, her dark eyes fathomless under the brim of a borrowed bonnet. Ariel had gotten her to wind her cascade of black hair into a braided knot at the nape of her neck. James found he missed that shining fall. It suited her so much better.

"I have an island part, her part, and an English part from my father. They fight each other sometimes." She pressed the palms of her hands together and pushed back and forth. "I think my mother was afraid that the English part would win me over if I traveled here," she added. "But the strange thing is, I feel the pull of all she taught me far more from this great distance. I miss her," she finished, her voice melancholy.

James didn't know how to respond to the sadness in her expression. Long naval voyages gave one very little opportunity to talk to young ladies about personal subjects. Or any subjects, really. But he was driven by a desire to comfort her. "You'll inherit her house, though," he tried finally. And cursed himself for a clumsy idiot. How was that helpful, to make her think of her one remaining parent's death?

Kawena shook her head. "It will go to my half sister. My mother had a husband who died before my father came to the island. I will always have a place in my sister's home, of course, but... That is why my father promised to provide for me." Kawena had forgotten her problems for a while as she saw new sights and spoke with this interesting man. Now they came rushing back. "England is so large," she said. "Perhaps I was a fool to think I could recover his fortune."

The mournfulness of her words, in her face, shook James. "If someone on my ship stole those jewels, we'll find them," he responded. His former reluctance had somehow evaporated. The grateful look she threw him sealed the change.

They came out of a twisting lane into a more open space, with a wider sky above. In the center of a square stood a circular domed structure, embellished with columns and balconies. "I do recognize that building," James said in an effort to lift the mood. "Alan's mentioned it. It's the Radcliffe Camera."

"Camera?" wondered Kawena.

"It means 'room' in Latin. Scholarly types love their Latin. This one's not as old as some of the other places we've passed. A fellow—Radcliffe, I suppose—left them money to build it about sixty years ago. It's a library." They stood gazing at the ornamented brick and stone. "Would you like to go in and see the books?" James dutifully asked. Alan had raved about the collection, declaring it was not to be missed.

Kawena shrugged. "I would rather walk. The building is pretty, though."

James laughed with delight.

Kawena turned to blink at him.

"You don't have the least interest in staring at a bunch of loaded shelves, do you?" James said.

She looked vaguely guilty. "I'm sorry, did you want to look…?"

"No more than you. Less, perhaps. Alan's dragged me through a library before. And I can tell you they're deadly dull. Just leather spines and flaking gilt and dust."

"But why did you laugh?"

"Because you made no bones about it," he answered.

"Bones? What do bones have to do with it?" Kawena appeared quite bewildered.

"It's an expression." James thought about it. "It's a deuced odd expression, isn't it? What *do* bones have to do with…anything, really? And who 'makes' bones? Butchers? No, that can't be it."

"I don't understand," said Kawena.

She was gazing at him dubiously. "Can't blame you," James responded. "Nor do I. But what I meant was, you don't pretend to be interested in things when you're not."

"Why would I?"

"There's a question." In James's limited experience, polite society did little else, as well as pretending *not* to be interested in what actually fascinated them. He'd always had a devil of a time navigating the resulting shoals.

"Are you feeling quite well?"

James couldn't help laughing again. "Actually, I

am. Very well indeed. Shall we abandon our pursuit of architecture?"

Still frowning at him, Kawena nodded.

He led her up Catte Street, then turned down Holywell toward the deer park. The route would loop them back toward Alan's house, with a look-in at the water meadows on the way.

As Kawena walked, she tried to decide if he'd been laughing at her in that strange exchange about books and bones. All in all, she thought not. There'd been no mockery or contempt in his voice. She'd experienced instances of both on her travels and had come to know the tone. Still, it was hard having so little common ground. Here in England, she felt as if she were floating on the surface of things. She knew just enough to be aware that she had no understanding of the depths. Every so often, things popped up to startle and confuse her. Her natural assumptions were often wrong. It could be quite tiresome. And perhaps more. She realized that she felt a strong desire to understand James Gresham. He was so far from what she had expected when she set out to find him, and the more she learned, the more attractive he appeared.

They crossed another bridge. The little river made a soft gurgle below, nothing like the surge and hiss of waves. "Do you miss the sea?" Kawena said. "I've never been away from it for so long."

"I do," admitted James. "It's been ten years since I was ashore more than a couple of weeks."

"And more than the sound," she went on, her voice gone dreamy, "the sea is a...presence. On my island, it's all around, in all the colors of blue, stretching out forever, full of life and…mystery. You should see some of the strange things that have washed up on the beaches."

"And its dark moods can take you down like the flick of a giant's finger," he replied.

Kawena stopped and looked up at him. "It's told that in the days of my mother's grandmother, a wave as high as a mountain rose out of the sea and swept the island. The old people say there was a roar like thunder, and then water crashing over everything, breaking houses like so many twigs. Many people were killed."

James nodded. "I've watched my ship ride up waves higher than the main mast, rising so fast your breath catches. A moment on top of the world, then you're plunging just as far into the trough, falling, it seems, into the very maw of the sea. You can't imagine you'll ever come out again. Then it starts all over again."

They stood at the entry to the deer park, gazing at each other, conscious of a kinship not shared by others in this university town. A wealth of knowledge and experience seemed to vibrate between them, framed by memories of the world's greatest ocean. It was a recognition and a bond.

Then the moment was gone. They were strangers again, though standing quite close together. The merest movement would bring them into an embrace.

Kawena took a step back. She looked around as if startled by her surroundings.

James gathered his scattered faculties. "Shall we walk back beside the river?" he said, pointing across the meadow.

"That tame little bit of water is called a river here?" Kawena replied.

"Even the Cherwell has been known to flood."

They headed across the grass to the line of willows that marked the stream, more self-conscious now than they'd been when they first set off. Conversation on the remainder of their walk was limited to observations about the landscape. Oddly, though nothing in the terrain suggested it, James found himself recalling a time when he'd pushed his way out of a tangle of undergrowth on an unknown shore and very nearly shot over a precipice, just inches from his feet.

Back in her bedchamber at the house, Kawena took off her borrowed bonnet, which she'd been told she must wear whenever she went out, even if the day was quite fine. Her reflection looked back at her from the mirror above the dressing table, a likeness more perfect than any quiet pool could render. Her face looked very bare, with her hair braided and twisted into a knot. The style created an odd combination of heaviness at the back of her neck and absence everywhere else. She longed to pull out the pins and let it tumble down her back, to appear more like herself. Her cheeks were flushed from exercise, or perhaps from that breathless moment on the walk when they'd spoken of the sea. Remembering it, she felt again that tug of connection. Was he what her mother called a kindred spirit? Her parents had been such, she'd been told—drawn together despite their many differences.

Recalling the way some of those differences had

echoed through their household, Kawena shook her head. She'd come all this long way to find her father's jewel hoard. She'd intended nothing more. That task had to come first. All else depended on it.

She put the bonnet down, and wriggled a bit inside constricting undergarments. She hadn't worn English dress for such long periods before. There was no choice here, but… Kawena fingered the blue cloth of her gown. Every single thing she wore belonged to Ariel, and she would have to have more clothing while she stayed here to search for the crew of the ship. There would be other expenses as well. There were bound to be. And her money was all gone. Her father had always said that where there was take, there also must be give. She needed to find a way to earn these things.

Kawena found her hostess in the parlor that opened onto the garden. Unfamiliar birdsong and the scent of exotic flowers wafted in from outdoors. Ariel was bent over a book, but looked up with a smile when Kawena entered. "I'm reading the funniest old play," she informed her. "It's full of lost babies who turn out to be royalty, even more than usual, and secret meetings that go wrong, and lovers who overcome the most astonishing obstacles to be married in the end."

Kawena knew what a play was. Her father had made her read several from a great fat book he cherished. This sounded rather like Shakespeare, though she couldn't have said which story. She'd never been able to keep all of them straight.

"First a prince, then a princess. Everyone seems to be someone they're not."

"Because they are in disguise?"

"Exactly." Ariel smiled in sudden delight. "Like you in your boy's clothes, jumping out of the bushes. Why, your great journey might be a splendid play."

"They would have to leave out a lot. Hanging over the ship's rail to relieve yourself in a storm, for instance." No story she'd read among her father's books had included such information. And it might have been useful to know.

Ariel looked startled, then rather intrigued. "Did you really...?"

Kawena nodded. "There was a little canvas cubby, held up by ropes. It had a board with a hole in it."

The other woman gazed at her, hazel eyes wide, a slight smile curving her lips. "I don't think anyone else would tell me that."

She shouldn't have, Kawena realized. The English had many rules about what was proper to say, and this subject was not acceptable. "Is the play Shakespeare?" she asked quickly.

Ariel smiled as if she'd followed some of Kawena's thoughts. "No, the author is John Dryden. It's called *Marriage à la Mode*."

"Mode? I have not heard that word."

"It's French," Ariel told her. "The title, I mean. The play is English."

Kawena had heard of French—France. Her father had imported a globe to show her the world he came from. Just as he had made her study a dictionary. And yet she continually found that to know the definitions of words didn't necessarily mean that you grasped their sense when they were strung together. "What does it mean?"

"Well…" Ariel tapped a finger to her lips. "Fashionable marriage, I suppose."

Kawena puzzled over this. Did English marriage have fashions, like clothing? Did they change with the passing years? She put the idea aside with a shrug. "You have been very generous to me," she said to Ariel, holding out a fold of her gown. "I thought there might be some work I could do for you in return."

"There's no need—"

"I do not like to take so much without giving," Kawena interrupted. "Surely there's something I could do around the house?" She realized that she knew little of English housekeeping. She'd seen a woman presiding over the basement kitchen, and two younger ones fetching and tidying upstairs. There was a boy also. She hadn't been here long enough to get to know them, and they seemed to live separately from Ariel and her husband.

Her hostess gazed at her. "You could keep me company."

"Company?"

"Indeed." Ariel smiled again, as if quite taken by the idea. "It's pleasant to have you here, to talk to. Alan is very busy in his lab just now. His experiments are at a crucial point."

"Experiments?" This meant trying some operation, as a test, Kawena remembered. But she couldn't form any picture of what that might be.

"He studies the nature of light."

Kawena examined this sentence, made up of simple words and yet conveying absolutely nothing. She looked at the sunlight streaming in through the French doors. "Nature?"

Ariel laughed. "I know. I was just the same when he first told me. How do you study something that is just there, all around us? But it turns out that you can bend light, and separate it."

"Separate?" Kawena had thought that her grasp on English was fairly solid. Now she began to doubt.

Ariel closed her book and rose. "I'll show you." She went over to a writing desk in the corner and picked up something small. Returning, she held up a transparent stone in the shaft of light from the outer doors. Color sprang up on the wall opposite—red, orange, green, blue.

"You can make rainbows?" Kawena exclaimed, astonished and delighted.

Ariel laughed. "A prism can. By picking out the...elements of the light. Alan intends to demonstrate that light is a wave, rather than a corpuscle, and you needn't ask me what that means, because I don't know."

Watching the play of colors on the wall, Kawena marveled. "Can I see it?"

"Of course." Ariel handed over the stone.

Kawena tried various angles until she called up the colors on the wall again. "I have only seen rainbows in the sky," she marveled.

Her hostess nodded. "They are made when water, raindrops, act as prisms. Or so Alan has told me. He could explain it better than I."

"It's amazing." She moved the stone, made the colors shimmer.

Ariel let her play with the display for some time. Then she said, "So, will you keep me company?"

Kawena turned to her. She was by no means averse, but she still didn't understand the request. "You have many friends here." She'd seen the garden full of guests.

"Acquaintances," Ariel corrected. "Friends of Alan's. He has lived in Oxford for years, but I moved here just a few months ago. And the people I've met…" She paused, frowned. "Most of them seem to think that a young woman, if she is at all…pretty, must be stupid."

Kawena pondered this idea. "That makes no sense," she said.

Ariel nodded. "Except that girls are not well educated here, as these Oxford types think of education. Even many of their own daughters."

"So they do not teach them, and then they blame them for not knowing?"

"Exactly!" Ariel seemed delighted at her immediate grasp of the point. "Even though some of them are quite bookish."

"Bookish?" Here was another word she didn't know.

"They love books, and have taught themselves a great deal." Ariel looked briefly guilty. "I read mostly plays, however."

Kawena didn't see why she shouldn't, if that was what she wished to do.

"And so, many of them treat me like a…pet, or an appendage of Alan's. It seems as if some of the older professors can't even hear me when I speak. As if my voice was too high-pitched for their ears. Like a bat."

She giggled, and Kawena smiled.

"It's happened to me over and over," Ariel continued. "I say something, and they ignore me. Then Alan says precisely the same thing, and they all leap upon the idea. It drives me mad."

Although Kawena thought that such people were not worth bothering about, she saw that Ariel was really annoyed. And she'd been so kind. "I don't see how I could help with people like that," she began.

"Oh, I don't need help with *them*," Ariel responded. "I'll show them, eventually. But it would be lovely to have a friend in the meantime. *You* listen to me."

"Of course," said Kawena. Not to attend when someone was speaking—it was graceless. "I would be honored to be your friend. But I must also pay you back for your generosity to me." Suddenly assailed by doubt, she added, "If I can recover my father's fortune."

"You will. I'm sure of it."

"How can you be?" Kawena wondered.

"There was a time in my life when I had nothing," Ariel replied. "I nearly despaired, but it all came out right in the end."

Although Kawena didn't see how this applied to her own case, she appreciated her hostess's optimism. She nodded and smiled once again.

Four

"WE ALL SHOULD GO," ARIEL TOLD JAMES AND Kawena the following evening. "The speaker is a good friend of Alan's. Or, a valued colleague, at least. And it is an unwritten law of Oxford that you help fill the seats at your friends' special lectures. With all the people you can muster."

"You'll find it fascinating," Alan added, entering the parlor in time to hear the last bit of this. "Sissingdun is discussing Sir Humphry Davy's method of passing an electric current through compound liquids to break them down into their constituent elements."

Kawena glanced at James to see if he had understood what she did not. He looked pained, and a shudder appeared to pass over his frame. It didn't look like comprehension.

"You can use the process to isolate sodium, potassium, and the alkaline earth metals," Alan continued, seemingly unaware of his audience's attitude. "Davy has also demonstrated that the hydrogen in acids can be partly or totally replaced by metals, which then reconstitute into salts and water."

James groaned audibly.

Alan laughed. "The process has many important practical applications."

"So it may," his brother replied. "But I won't understand 'em. So why must I sit there like a stuffed owl while some fellow I don't know maunders on and on about it."

"They expect us to bring our whole household," Ariel began apologetically.

"As a favor to me," Alan said at the same moment.

"Blast." James couldn't refuse his youngest brother a favor, particularly not when he was enjoying the hospitality of his house. The Gresham brothers rallied 'round when called upon. It was a knockout blow, as Alan very well knew. "Devil."

Alan merely grinned evilly back at him.

The talk was even worse than James had feared it would be. Two parts gibberish to one part schoolmasterly complacence. He couldn't believe the way people around him nodded and smiled as if each word was another pearl of wisdom. Frankly, he didn't think they understood above half of what was being said. It just wasn't possible. His only comfort was Kawena, an enticing presence next to him on the deucedly uncomfortable wooden chairs. He'd seen her dark eyes glaze with boredom a few minutes into the droning. Indeed, they'd threatened to fall closed at one point, and her shoulder had rested against his until she caught herself and jerked upright. It had been a very pleasant sensation. "Feeling sufficiently edified?" he whispered.

"My mind feels like a bit of seaweed left in the sun too long," she murmured. "Shriveled down to nothing."

James laughed, earning a barrage of glares. He was forced to subside for the rest of the oration. Half a lifetime or so, he estimated.

Afterward, there was only tea and some sickly sweet wafers. James was about to duck out a side door, brother or no, and find a pint of ale when he noticed Ariel approaching with a pretty blond. It was the same girl he'd noticed at the garden party, he realized, before that event had disintegrated into mayhem. The one he'd thought Ariel might be introducing as a potential bride. She was a taking little thing, with bright golden hair, big blue eyes, and a neat figure.

"James, may I present Lily Randall," Ariel said when they drew near. "Miss Randall, Lord James Gresham, my husband's brother."

The girl dropped a curtsy, murmuring something like, "So pleased."

James gave her a bow and his best smile. "Delighted, Miss Randall."

"You are both…" Ariel began, but broke off at the sight of something over James's shoulder. When he looked, he saw that Alan was beckoning rather urgently. "I'm sorry," said Ariel, "if you will excuse me." She rushed off, leaving the new acquaintances alone.

"Enjoy the talk, did you?" James asked the girl.

Miss Randall clasped her hands at her breast, inevitably drawing the eye to a most enticing bodice. Her sigh increased the effect. "Oh, it was perfectly splendid, wasn't it? So very deep."

It wasn't the response James had expected. "You're interested in acids and, er, hydrogen then?"

Her eyes grew even wider. James would have said that wasn't possible. "Oh, it was all far too complicated for me to understand," she assured him.

James had felt the same. But now, stubbornly, he told himself he could have followed the fellow's line of reasoning, if he'd wished to devote the time to study. "Why come to hear it then?" he asked.

"Oh, we must."

Did Miss Randall begin every sentence she uttered with "oh"? James waited for her to offer a sounder reason to sit through an incomprehensible oration. But she said no more. "So it might have been a load of hogwash, for all we know," he suggested.

She gazed up at him, blinking her big blue eyes, apparently profoundly shocked. "Oh no."

"It might have been, though. How would we know, since we didn't understand it?"

"Oh, that isn't possible…" Her soft voice trailed off.

James was seized by a desire to convince her. His reasoning was sound. You couldn't judge the merits of a discourse you didn't understand. He wanted her to admit this, to come over to his side. And he wanted to penetrate below her surface parroting of what she'd been told. "Well, it's *possible*," he argued. "He could be mistaken. There are other…theories." There always were, according to what Alan had told him about scientific investigation. "Who's to say this fellow isn't completely wrongheaded?"

Miss Randall was shaking her head. "Professor Sissingdun is the wisest man I know. Everyone at Magdalen says that his work is vitally important."

"Well they would, wouldn't…?"

"And he is my uncle." Her blue eyes seemed less liquid now, and more hawk-like.

"Ah." He'd put his foot in it. Why had Ariel abandoned him? She should've stayed at her post to guide him through the crosscurrents of Oxford society.

"And I think the fellows at the college know a good deal more about what is true than you," Miss Randall added. Her tone said that this was the deathblow to his argument.

At least I've gotten her to stop saying "oh," James thought. "No doubt," he muttered.

"I believe my mother is looking for me." With barely any acknowledgment, Lily Randall turned and walked away.

James found he didn't care very much. A little of Miss Randall's company had been quite enough for him. It wasn't the hint of steel beneath the fluttery facade. He wasn't looking for a spiritless female. No, it had been her refusal to so much as consider his point that put him off. She'd treated him like an idiot.

James looked around at the diminishing crowd. Spotting his party, he walked across the room to join them and, he hoped, convince them they had stayed quite long enough. But when he reached his brother's side, he found he couldn't get a word in. The older gentleman who'd been talking about turtles at the garden party had backed Kawena up to a wall and was rather looming over her. Alan and Ariel both looked a bit tense.

"Surely you could have *someone* send me a few specimens," the man was saying. He sounded aggrieved. "It's a simple enough request. By the word 'specimen' I mean—"

"I know what it means," Kawena interrupted. "Turtles to cut up."

The man seemed astonished to be cut off in midsentence.

"It's a very long voyage," Alan put in. "Here's my brother. He's a navy man and can tell you better than I. It takes weeks for a ship to reach Valatu, doesn't it, James?"

"Months," he replied. "Depending on the type of ship, your luck with the weather, could be the greater part of a year." Noticing Kawena's suddenly stricken expression, he added, "Might be a bit less."

"Indeed," said his brother. "So simply to send a message and receive any sort of…result would require a very long time."

"I will be back home by then," Kawena declared. It sounded as if she was convincing herself.

"Splendid, then you can send me specimens—"

"Turtles cannot stay on a ship for so long," she broke in on him again. "They would die and rot away."

He glared at her. "Perhaps you will allow me to complete a thought, young woman!" He tapped his chin with one finger. "Some specimens preserved in salt would be better than nothing," he concluded.

"I won't send turtles off to die," Kawena replied.

"Do you care nothing for the cause of science?"

"Nothing," Kawena agreed.

The older gentleman looked outraged, then resigned. He sighed and turned to Alan. "One can't expect women to understand the importance of our endeavors, I suppose. It's a great pity, but… Ah, well. Send her over to my house tomorrow afternoon.

I can, at least, question her about island fauna. She must have noticed *something*, living among them her whole life."

James started to object to his tone. Ariel opened her mouth to speak. Alan looked distinctly uncomfortable. But Kawena forestalled them all. "No," she said.

The turtle enthusiast frowned down at her.

"I do not wish to come to your house," she continued. "Or to talk to you about island 'fauna.'"

"It means simply—"

"Animals. Yes, I know. A man who visited my father used this word. He trapped many, many birds and killed them and took their skins away with him."

"Someone has been there before me?" The professor whirled on Alan. "You must *order* her to come and tell me all she knows."

James feared that his brother would retreat under the beetling eyebrows and fierce stare of a senior collegian. But happily, Alan was made of sterner stuff. "Miss…Kawena is a guest in my house. I don't command her time."

"You would let some stupid native girl's whim stand in the way of scientific—?"

"We do not 'let' our guests be insulted," said Ariel. "I think you must excuse us." Gathering her party with a glance, she headed for the door. James felt like letting loose a cheer as he followed her.

Relieved to be away from the furious old man, Kawena welcomed the soft evening air with a deep breath. It was just past sunset. The western sky still showed streamers of red and gold. She matched her steps to Ariel's.

Alan appeared at her other side. "I don't believe you have told us your last name," he said. "At least, I do not know it. And it is awkward to call you Miss…uh."

"Benson," she answered. It sounded a bit rusty on her tongue. Her father's name was seldom added to her own on the island. And she hadn't used it while traveling dressed as a young man.

"Thank you," her host said.

"I am sorry if I made any trouble for you," she told him, though she didn't know how else she could have answered the studier of turtles. Even if she'd been inclined to help him, which she emphatically was not, her mother would have forbidden it. After the bird killer, her mother had vowed that no such person would be allowed on the island again.

"Harris will get over it," Alan replied. "His temperament is quite impervious." He dropped back to walk next to his brother.

Ariel took her arm. "Are you all right?" she asked. "I'm sorry for the way he spoke to you."

Kawena shrugged. "He has nothing to do with me. But I understand better what you said about the way they treat you here."

"You'd think that intelligent, educated men would be more open-minded," she responded. "They're always talking about testing out theories and shifting their 'hypotheses' when they prove faulty. *My* hypothesis is: they put too much stock in their schooling. They've worked so hard at it, are so proud of their scholarly accomplishments. If you don't have that… stamp of approval, you're inconsequential."

Clearly, Ariel had thought a great deal about this. Because she had to live her life here among them, Kawena supposed. She was glad she didn't. "At least Lord Alan isn't like that," she offered. She'd discovered at the lecture that her host and his brother were supposed to be addressed as "lords"—another new custom to remember.

"Now," Ariel agreed. "When I first met him…" A reminiscent smile crossed her lips. "It was quite a while before he acknowledged my abilities."

There was a whole, tender tale in her expression. The glow in her hazel eyes made Kawena a bit envious. Even in the short time she'd been here, she'd observed that Ariel and her husband shared a special bond. "You're fortunate," she said.

"Yes."

That one brief word was full of love. As Ariel glanced over her shoulder at her husband, Kawena wondered whether she could hope for such a marriage. Sadly, it seemed unlikely. At home on her island, there was always a…distance between her and the young men. That was partly—no, mainly—her father's doing. He had *not* encouraged such connections. But she knew it wasn't only that. With all her father had insisted she learn and do, the island men found her unsettling, foreign in a way that put off rather than intrigued. She intimidated some, irritated others. She'd been told as much, during a fumbling, humiliating encounter at age fourteen. She felt it from her side, too. She wasn't like them.

And here, on the other side of the world, amidst the other side of her heritage, she felt even more alien. Of course, until the last few days, it had been critical to hide the fact that she was a woman.

"You're very silent," said Ariel. "Are you sure you're all right?"

Kawena nodded. "Just thinking."

"It must make your head spin, sometimes, so many new things to absorb."

These professors are fools to dismiss this woman's abilities, Kawena thought. Ariel saw right to the heart of things.

Her mind did feel muddled at times like this. Kawena was a foreigner at home, and a foreigner here. The Englishmen she'd met so far treated her as an oddity, even more than her childhood companions had done. Except Lord James. He seemed different, less rigid. Perhaps it was because he'd spent so much of his life at sea. On their recent walk along this same lane, she'd felt comfortable and stimulated and curious and...

But he—any Englishman—would expect her to live in this country, and she couldn't imagine doing that. It wasn't home, would never be. And yet, home wasn't quite home any more either, with her father gone. Add the long ocean voyage, and her life had been turned upside down. She didn't know what she thought half the time.

As they reached the house and went inside, Kawena gave herself a mental shake. Once she recovered her father's fortune, she would have many choices. That was her mission, and must be her focus. If she failed...

She wouldn't. She couldn't. The alternative was simply inconceivable.

Five

ONLY FOUR DAYS LATER, JAMES RECEIVED AN ENVELOPE franked by Nathaniel. Opening it, he was surprised and pleased to discover that his eldest brother had actually managed the thing. "Nathaniel found us an admiral who's willing to help," he told the others at dinner that evening. "He's written to a friend at the Admiralty offices to smooth my way."

"What does that mean?" asked Kawena.

"Unofficial access to navy records," he told her. "I can get a look at the addresses where they're sending half pay without filling out a pile of forms. I'll go up to London to talk this 'friend' and—"

"*We* will go," said Kawena.

James shook his head. "That won't wash. He'll talk to me, because his old friend vouched for me and asked him to, and I'm a navy man as well. But he'd balk if other people show up, particularly a lady. He won't be accustomed to dealing with females on matters such as these."

"I don't see why—"

"Aren't I right, Ariel?" James added.

His brother's wife nodded, though her bright eyes crackled with annoyance. "I'm afraid that's all too likely, Kawena."

"But it is my story," Kawena objected. "I can explain it better than anyone else."

"I'm not going to tell him your story," James replied.

"What?" She fixed him with wide dark eyes.

It was always so distracting when she did that. *It feels as if I could fall into those eyes and never come out*, James thought. Her steady—warm?—inquiring gaze scattered thoughts like petals in a stiff breeze. He gathered his. "If I go in accusing some navy man of theft, this fellow will clam up, and I won't—"

"Does your navy care nothing for justice?" Kawena asked.

"It does," James told her. "But a straight-out accusation makes the matter more complicated. A case for investigation and tribunals. He'd have to report it, and then there'd be an absolute boatload of forms, and word would get out into the ranks. My former crew would hear about it."

Kawena considered this. "And the thief would hide."

"If there is a..." James broke off at her frown. "Yes. We can report it after we get your jewels back. We'll have the evidence then, anyhow. The navy will pay attention."

She remained reluctant. "I suppose you know best how to deal with them."

"I do," James said. "You're going to have to trust me."

It was a weighted word. This time, James did lose himself in that fathomless gaze. Its combination of interest and hope was a heady mixture. He could see her uncertainty, her resistance, and then resignation. Finally, Kawena gave a small nod. It was a tiny gesture, barely noticeable, but it filled James with a fierce desire to deserve her trust. She was so lovely, and so courageous, and so alone.

A stifled gurgle of laughter broke the spell. James turned to find Ariel biting her bottom lip, her hazel eyes dancing. His brother's head was cocked, as if he'd heard some curious sound that he couldn't quite identify. They were both looking at him.

Suddenly self-conscious, James picked up his wineglass and took a decorous sip. He cleared his throat. "I shouldn't be gone above a day or two," he announced. "Where can I hire a decent horse, Alan?"

His brother replied, and the moment passed, and James put it from his mind.

∽

Lord James departed very early the following morning, striding down the lane toward Oxford to hire a mount. Kawena watched him go from her bedroom window, a tall, handsome figure, moving with purpose and lanky grace. How she wished she was going with him! Over the months of her voyage, she'd become accustomed to managing for herself, to taking action when there was a task to be done. And so, she chafed at the idea that her quest depended on him now. But she had no way of finding the crew of the *Charis* without him. She'd had to concede that.

Also, she would miss him. Over the last few days, as they'd talked and sometimes walked together, her

tug of attraction had strengthened. He had the most...
alluring sort of half smile, with one quirked eyebrow
and light dancing in his eyes. And surprising hands.
Roughened by years at sea, they had yet proved
capable of fashioning intricate little creatures from
folded paper. He'd learned it from an Asian sailor, he
said, when a great typhoon trapped their ships in port
for two weeks. A sigh escaped Kawena. You couldn't
help but imagine the delicacy of that touch transferring
into...other areas. She'd found herself wondering, all
too often, what it would feel like. They understood
each other, too, shared the same reactions, or so it
seemed to her. His absence would leave a large void
in her days.

He moved out of sight around the bend; Kawena
turned from the window. Catching sight of her reflection in the dressing-table mirror, she marveled at her
situation. Somehow, she had come to trust the man
she'd planned to expose as a villain. Perhaps more
than trust. And it had happened so quickly. Barely
a week ago, she was waving a pistol in his face, full
of righteous anger. Now, she was relying on his aid,
regretting his departure. Was she a fool?

Moving closer to the mirror to wind her long dark
braids into the knot that English fashions required,
she examined the possibility. Why had she changed?
Did she have good reasons? It was partly the man
himself. His behavior had changed her opinion. His
initial reluctance to become involved in her affairs
weighed as heavily as his eventual capitulation. He
was no smooth-tongued rogue. And then, it was partly
his family, too. Ariel and Lord Alan—particularly

Ariel—had been so kind to her and so open. Their obvious respect and love for Lord James spoke for his quality. Yes, these were people who deserved trust. She was not mistaken in that.

Downstairs, Kawena found Ariel at the breakfast table. Lord Alan, as usual, had already departed for his laboratory. Lord James's empty place was a melancholy reminder.

"It's market day in Oxford," said Ariel as she came in. "I thought we would go and look at the stalls. If you like."

Kawena nodded agreement. She was hardly likely to refuse any request from her generous hostess, and she remained eager to learn all she could about England while she was here.

They set out at midmorning, each with a basket over her arm. The July day was bright with a few high clouds scudding across the blue sky and a wind that made Kawena glad of her cloak, though sorry it was borrowed. "There has been so little rain since I have been here," Kawena remarked. "My father says...said that England is a gray, wet country where the sky drips like Niobe's rock."

Ariel laughed. "Like what?"

"Niobe was an ancient Greek. I think. Who cried all the time."

"Why?" her companion wondered.

"I don't remember. Father had so many stories; I get them confused." If she'd known he would be taken from her so soon, she would have tried harder to remember them, Kawena thought. The familiar wave of sadness washed over her. It was less now than at the beginning, when she'd come running in response to the shouting and discovered her father lying still and cold. But it was still a sharp ache.

"Well, this is the finest time of year," Ariel said. "If you'd come in November, you'd have had more than your fill of rain."

Ariel led her beyond the college buildings to a square filled with market stalls and bustling with townsfolk examining the wares. They joined the streams of shoppers and strolled up one row and down another, surrounded by color, scent, and the din of sharp bargaining. "There are so many things in England," Kawena commented.

"What do you mean?" Ariel asked.

Kawena gestured at the stalls. "Ribbons and thimbles and teapots and tools and furniture. All these 'made' things. Everywhere."

Ariel looked around as if noticing the merchandise in a new way. "You aren't used to so many."

"No." She smiled. "There wouldn't be room for all this at home. You English are so busy—inventing and building and making. I used to be amazed at all the cargos filling ships' holds, but they were nothing to this."

"You say 'you English,'" her hostess replied. "But you're part English."

"By blood, I am," Kawena agreed. "But by feeling…" She shook her head. "Perhaps if I'd visited as a child, it would be different."

"Many Englishmen who are posted abroad send their children back here to school. So they'll know the country."

"I can see why they would."

"Does it make you sad?" Ariel asked, gazing at her from under the brim of her bonnet.

Kawena thought about it. She was certainly sad about her father's death, and her connection to this country had always been through him. But mostly she was thoughtful. Her long journey had shown her so many fascinating things and ideas. "No," she said. "It's an adventure, seeing a new part of the world."

"I can well imagine."

Ariel bought a few small things, useful and frivolous. They shared a small apple pie still warm from the oven and stopped to watch a pair of jugglers keep a dizzying array of objects in the air. The sun was well past the zenith when they started back to the house.

"This was very agreeable," said Kawena as they walked. "Thank you."

"No need for thanks," her hostess replied. "It was a pleasure to have a friend along."

In perfect harmony with each other, they left the streets of Oxford behind and entered the lane that led to the house. Halfway there, Kawena's eye was caught by movement on the left, and she turned to see a dappled gray horse running across the field. The grace of its gait stopped her in her tracks. "Oh, it looks like it's floating over the grass!"

Ariel paused as well. "She's lovely, isn't she? She's our neighbor Mr. Fletcher's pride and joy."

The horse came closer. Kawena stepped toward the fence, entranced by the creature's beauty. "We have no horses at home. I'd seen pictures, but it's only since

I've been here that I've been close to them. It's strange that so large an animal can be not at all frightening."

The gray approached the fence. She seemed to examine Kawena with one liquid brown eye.

"She likes you," Ariel said. "She's never come so close for me."

"Is it all right to touch…?"

"She's quite gentle, I think."

Kawena stepped nearer and set a hand on the horse's forehead. Her caress was accepted with regal complacence.

"It's too bad we don't have an apple for her," Ariel remarked.

"They like apples?"

"Very much."

Moved by a sudden whim, the horse tossed her head and trotted off. Kawena watched her go with regret and admiration. "Do you ride horses?" she asked Ariel as they resumed their walk.

"I can," was the reply. "I'm no expert. I never rode much, growing up."

Kawena's gaze followed the gray as she pranced across the turf. A little kick of the animal's heels looked like pure joy in movement. "It must be like flying over the ground!"

"Particularly when you're thrown off," Ariel joked.

Kawena acknowledged it with a smile. "It's a wonder that such noble creatures allow themselves to be ridden." Her eyes turned back to the horse.

"You should try it. Alan could… Or James. I'm sure he'd be glad to take you riding."

Kawena found this idea quite attractive. Then she

realized that it would involve hiring mounts, another call on her hosts' purse. "I'm content just to watch," she assured her.

But Ariel wasn't listening. "We'd have to find you a habit. I don't have one."

"Habit?"

"A riding habit."

"I don't understand. Do you mean, to make a habit of riding?"

"No. The dress one wears to ride is called a habit," Ariel told her.

"Why?" Kawena frowned. "Isn't 'habit' a thing one does often?"

"Yes." Ariel looked perplexed. "That is odd, isn't it? I never thought of it before." Her frown deepened as they reached the house and went inside. "And nuns wear 'habits,' don't they? Monks, too. But they're not at all the same. Very odd. I shall ask Alan how that came to be."

Kawena had noticed that this was Ariel's solution to all intractable puzzles. "Does he know everything?" she asked, daring to tease a little.

After a moment's surprise, Ariel laughed. "He used to think so. Now that he knows better, I allow him to inform me." She set down her basket and untied the strings of her bonnet.

"That's very kind of you," Kawena said, following suit.

"Well, he does enjoy it so. I like to indulge him."

They laughed together, and Kawena felt more at ease than she had in a long, long time.

❧

Two days later, James walked down the lane toward his brother's house. His dip into the world of Royal Navy paper pushers made it seem as if he'd been away much longer. Men such as the official he'd been sent to see hated to part with any crumb of information, just on principle, and it next to killed them when matters didn't line up with their forms and procedures. And so the meeting had taken far longer than it needed to, except that apparently a ridiculous amount of time was required. He should have learned that over years of haggling for stores and new weaponry for his ship, James thought. The fellow had finally given in, as they most often did, and come across with the information James wanted. He felt that his naval career hadn't benefited from the exchange, but it hadn't been ruined either. He'd no doubt been marked down as mildly annoying, but also as someone who could get admirals to plead his case. Neither was uncommon enough to sink him.

Told that Ariel and Kawena were sitting in the parlor off the garden, James left his hat with the maid and walked down the corridor, anticipation rising. His thoughts, and even a glorious dream, had been full of Kawena as he pursued her interests in town. He was eager to see her again, share his success, see that regal turn of her head that made his breath catch.

He paused silently in the doorway to take in the lovely picture the two women made, side by side on the sofa. A man would be hard put to find a prettier pair of females—Ariel in warm hues of cream and peach, and Kawena wearing a white dress that accentuated her honey-toned skin, her hair like a raven's wing. He couldn't tear his eyes away from her. Even more than beauty, she seemed to crackle with vitality.

Though he made no sound, after a moment Kawena turned and saw him. She smiled, and James nearly stumbled as he stepped forward to give them his news. "I got a list of addresses. I'll have to go down to Portsmouth to find most of them."

"Where is Portsmouth?" Kawena asked.

"On the south coast. It's our largest naval center, and a number of my old crew members are hanging about there, waiting to join a new ship."

She nodded, looking satisfied. "We can leave tomorrow," she said.

James was startled. "Not 'we.' I shall go alone."

"No! I won't be left behind again."

"But it will be easier if I—"

"Not easier for me! I will go with you to question these men. It is my right." She sat very straight and frowned at him.

"That won't work." James was a bit tired from the ride, and thus impatient with silly obstacles. "No sailor would talk in front of you. And anyway, I won't be lumbered with a chaperone—"

"A what?"

"A lady to bear you company."

Kawena made an impatient gesture. "What lady? I traveled around the world by myself." This was not quite true. She'd had her father's old friend to help her. But she saw no need to mention that. She had Lord James now, didn't she?

James shuddered to think of all the terrible things that might have happened to her on that voyage.

Indeed, it was amazing that she'd made it safely. "You don't understand," he said. "A man and woman, unrelated, cannot travel together."

"Why?"

"It's improper."

"Why?"

"Well…" He didn't see why she had to belabor the obvious. "To stay at inns and be alone on the road…"

"Do you intend to attack me in the inn's bedchamber?" Kawena asked in an overly reasonable voice.

"What? No! Of course not."

She shrugged. "We have no problem then."

James tried to keep his tone as even as hers. "It's not me. It's a matter of what others will think, and say…"

"Who cares?" She gazed at him as if he was the one being unreasonable.

James became aware of Ariel's interested gaze. She was just watching them, back and forth, as if they were playing a game of lawn tennis, making no effort to explain the realities of life to Kawena. He turned to appeal to her. "You know very well what I mean. Tell her it's impossible."

Ariel looked torn. Finally, she nodded. "I know what it's like to be scorned, Kawena. My mother was an actress, and some hold it against me still. The proprieties are very important to many people."

"English people," replied Kawena. "I am not English. I don't intend to be English."

"Still, you may not want to give the appearance—"

"I am not an appearance. I am as I am. These 'people' may take it or leave it." Kawena crossed her arms and stared at the two of them, obdurate.

Ariel gave James a helpless glance.

"If you leave me behind, I shall simply follow you," Kawena added. "I still have my coat and trousers. I know how to get a ride on a wagon." She had no idea how she would make such a journey with no money at all. But, again, no need to mention that.

"You are a very annoying woman," said James. And she was, partly. But he was struck by the way she sat there—chin up, very straight, fierce as a young hawk. He had to admire her assurance and fire. And it would be…interesting to spend days of travel alone with her. If she cared nothing for how it looked, should he?

"Not if you remember that I am not an Englishwoman," she answered. "Then it is all perfectly logical. I am different."

"And a master of understatement," James murmured.

"I must behave as I think best. I have my own honor."

What did that mean, exactly? Unbidden, several sorts of behavior that would change a tiresome journey into a delicious ramble flashed through James's imagination. Not that she had suggested…or that he ever would… James ordered his brain to cease and desist. "Are you certain you won't be guided by…by Ariel? You have no notion how prickly—"

"No. I left my home and traveled thousands of miles for this. I will not sit here and wait. I will find the thief." Her journey had been fueled by anger and determination; they hadn't disappeared in this comfortable house.

She made it sound as if the hunt would be easy. James knew better. But he gave up the argument. "Very well."

Kawena nodded as if there had never been a doubt. "We will leave first thing in the morning."

"That we won't. If you're coming, there are more arrangements to be made. I expect it will take a day or so." Could they take the mail coach? No, he'd have to hire a post chaise for her.

"I would like to ride there on a horse," Kawena declared.

"She's never ridden," Ariel remarked, to the air, it seemed.

"You couldn't endure such a long journey on horseback," James replied.

"The horse in the field outside likes me," Kawena told him.

"I expect he may, but—"

"*She* came to my hand like a tame bird. I have given her apples."

"That doesn't mean—"

"I think it would be a most pleasant way to travel."

"How would you know if you've never ridden?"

"I can tell by looking," Kawena assured him.

"It isn't as easy as it appears," put in Ariel, at last giving him some help. "When you first learn to ride, well, you find all sorts of muscles you didn't know you possessed. And a whole new variety of aches and pains."

"And it isn't done," James added, then immediately wished he hadn't.

Kawena fixed him with her dark, flashing eyes. "I never heard that phase until I met you. Now, I seem to hear it all the time."

That isn't fair, James thought. He hadn't said it more

than…a few times. He couldn't remember. Who could think when she looked at you in that way? Or refuse her what she wanted? Even if she shouldn't… "You moved through the countryside as a boy," he managed. "Did you see any ladies careening around on horseback?"

"Careening?"

"Traveling, then. Slogging along the high road on a longish trip without a carriage. You know very well what I mean."

Kawena considered the question. She sighed. "Oh, all right. But I think it's stupid."

"You really can't learn to ride in a day," Ariel said. "It isn't possible."

This seemed to cinch the deal, though Kawena's expression promised more protests at some later time. "England has so many ridiculous rules," she said.

"It's different for young ladies," said James. He waited for an explosion, but instead got a speculative glance that was somehow more ominous. She seemed to have no notion how vulnerable she could be, away from this house and his company. Which was *not* his fault! She was looking at him as if he was the author of all the cursed rules of polite society. Hadn't he chafed against them himself, wanting only to be off to sea? Hadn't he staged a full-blown rebellion when his mother had pushed him to attend some devilish dancing class in London?

"What sorts of arrangements must be made?" Kawena asked.

Did she expect him to head right back into Oxford and engage a carriage—without so much as a glass of wine or a biscuit? It appeared that she did. James turned away.

"You must keep a careful record of all the money you spend," Kawena added. "I will repay every bit."

"Oh, certainly," James muttered. "Just consider me your bookkeeper as well as your courier and general dogsbody."

Striding out, he heard her say, "Dogsbody? What does that mean? What dog?"

He left on Ariel's peal of laughter, seeing nothing the least amusing about his ever-expanding duties on this quixotic quest.

Six

Lord James and Kawena departed two days later, climbing into a post chaise early in the morning and rattling off down the road south, to Kawena's vast relief. She'd chafed at every moment of delay, and still more at the debates that had arisen in the household. Lord Alan had very nearly convinced Ariel that Kawena shouldn't go. And when she'd taxed him with her right to decide for herself what she would do, it had appeared that he was more concerned with his brother's fate than hers. He imagined that their journey would put Lord James under some obligation to marry her, whether he wished to or not. Which was the stupidest thing Kawena had ever heard. No sane woman, or man, would decide on marriage in such a way. And so she'd told him. She'd offered to swear a blood oath never, under any circumstances, to marry his brother—any of his brothers. That had silenced him! And if she'd felt a curious relief when he'd declined her offer…well, everyone liked to be believed without the need for solemn rituals.

Kawena turned her face to the soft summer air

wafting through the coach window. She had to admit that the seats in this carriage Lord James had hired were more comfortable than the jolting wagons she'd ridden to get to Oxford. No doubt it was far more costly as well. She hadn't inquired about the amount. What was the point? She hadn't a penny.

She stared out the front window. Right in front of her eyes, lashed to a platform above the front wheels, was the small bag of necessities Ariel had put together for her journey. She'd accepted it reluctantly, adding a paltry few items of her own. It was simply ill-natured to keep protesting her hosts' kindness, but she was very weary of depending on others. She was used to making what she needed, or trading what she made for things she couldn't produce. In England, that was simply not possible. She did feel the lure of beautiful, intricate—frivolous—items. Who could resist such colors and textures and convenience? But then one needed a bag or a trunk or a room or a house to keep them safe.

Kawena looked at the iron guards that the post boys wore on their right legs, to protect them from the center pole of the carriage. They looked cumbersome and uncomfortable, and it seemed to her that a load of possessions would be rather like that. An increasing burden that pulled at you, weighing you down. "Why are they called 'boys'?" she asked Lord James. Both of them appeared to be a good deal older than she was.

He shrugged. "It's the term used."

Kawena thought it was a little insulting, but she was learning to keep some of her opinions to herself. The wiry little man riding the leader, a jaunty sprig of lavender in his hat, seemed very proud of his job. He'd told her that post chaises were called 'yellow bounders' because of their coat of yellow paint.

"I hope you are not uncomfortable," Lord James added.

Kawena turned to look at him. "The carriage is quite luxurious."

"Yes. I meant...nothing."

He was the one who looked uncomfortable, Kawena thought. She knew the situation was straining his English notions of propriety. Although he was keeping to the far side of the seat, they were quite close together in a small space. It seemed to have destroyed the ease they'd begun to develop in his brother's house.

Surely so attractive a man had been alone with women before? Her father had given Kawena the impression that sailors jumped in and out of beds all over the world. Indeed, that they thought of little else. So, Lord James must know how to cajole and please.

The idea roused a flurry of images that sent a wave of warmth through her body. She knew what went on between a man and a woman. Her mother and half sisters and their friends had talked freely, laughed and commiserated over romantic complications. No one made a secret of that part of life, as they seemed to do here. Young people slipped off together now and then before they formed their own households, and no one minded if they took care. Indeed, despite the awkwardness caused by her father's foreign notions, Kawena had managed one or two hurried couplings of her own amongst the leaves. They hadn't been terribly satisfying. She knew there was much more to be learned and appreciated. And this man so close beside her made her want to explore all those things. In great detail. Handsome, well set up, solicitous, intelligent. His air of easy command when dealing with the arrangements for their journey had called out to something inside her.

Kawena's gaze fixed on Lord James's hand, resting on his muscular thigh in its tight buckskin breeches. She remembered his fingers' cleverness in creating tiny paper birds. She could very easily reach out and place her hand over his. His skin would be warm. He might turn his palm and interlace his larger fingers with hers. And then, if she looked into his eyes, she was sure she'd find fire there. The air inside the chaise seemed to thicken. Suddenly, it was hard to breathe.

"What is it?" he said.

Uncertain, Kawena turned away from him. She couldn't say what she'd been thinking. She had made that perfectly clear in the discussions before they set off. She didn't see that it conflicted with her promise to his brother, but it was bound to outrage Lord James's English notions of propriety. He would very likely insist that they turn back, that she must stay behind while he conducted the search. She couldn't let this journey be disrupted. "Nothing," she said, keeping her eyes on the passing countryside.

Lord James started to reply, and the chaise hit a rut in the road and bounced high in the air.

Kawena's head tapped the ceiling. She grabbed for a handhold and found none. In the next instant, Lord James caught her around the waist and pulled her tight against him as he braced. She threw her arms around his chest and hung on as the wild bumping continued.

Their bodies molded together from shoulder to knee, she could feel his heart beating at an accelerated pace that matched her own. His grip on her was like a solid mooring in a storm. Kawena's nostrils filled with his clean, masculine scent. Her lips, inches from his, parted of their own volition.

Then the carriage steadied, and he let her go. Rather hastily. Kawena had to stifle a sound of protest.

"Uh," said Lord James. He cleared his throat. "Uh…a…a rough patch of road." His voice had gone thick.

Kawena nodded. Her clothes felt too hot, and even more intolerably constricting.

Her companion leaned out the window on his side and called, "Take a little care, will you, Rollins."

"Sorry, sir," came the reply from the nearest post boy. "We didn't see them ruts until we was right on top of 'em."

"Look sharper," he ordered. He ducked back inside, met her eyes, and glanced quickly away, as if he'd done something wrong.

She'd been right, Kawena thought. Any hint of… passion would jeopardize her goal. She mustn't think of how good it had felt to be in his arms, or how close—how achingly close—they had come to a kiss. Seeing that he was gripping a strap hanging beside the door, she took hold of the one on her side. She understood now why it was there. The seat might be softer, but this vehicle was far more precarious than the heavy wagons she'd ridden in on the way to Oxford. She'd been happy to see the four-horse team when they departed, but now it seemed as if the carriage whipped behind them like the tail of a kite in a stiff breeze.

Lord James appeared to be searching for words. When he finally spoke, he made no reference to the incident just past. "Ah…we'll be traveling in stages," he said. "We'll stop at posting houses for fresh teams. There'll be time for refreshment or other…needs."

Kawena was amused to see his cheek redden slightly. But if he wished to talk of commonplaces… Well, perhaps that was best. It was a way to keep other considerations at bay. "Whose horses will we use?" she wondered.

"They belong to the inns, available for hire."

"All along the roads?"

Lord James nodded. "It's an efficient method."

"So the English have set up a whole system so that people can race around the countryside like busy ants?" she said. "You like to be able to move fast." Though their roads might be smoother, she noted.

"You keep talking about 'the English' as if we belonged in a menagerie," Lord James objected.

"I am only observing customs that are new to me. It is interesting."

"Some might find your 'observations' insulting."

He was sitting as far from her as possible again. Was he angry? Well aware that she didn't catch every subtle nuance of English manners, Kawena wasn't sure. "Do you? I'm sorry."

"Well…" He paused, looking surprised. "I don't, actually. It's…rather interesting. Hah." He turned to her. "One thing I've always enjoyed about naval missions is the chance to observe the world, see how other peoples behave. 'Exotic' rules and practices. But I rarely thought to look back at my own country that way."

"Home is the way things are," she said.

"Exactly." He smiled at her, as if pleased by their fellow feeling.

"Then you travel far away and see that isn't true. It's just one way for things to be." *And very disorienting that was*, Kawena thought.

He was gazing at her as if she'd said something profound. "Some people see that," he replied after a moment. "Others decide that everyone else is misguided, or benighted, or disgusting."

"Everyone else in the *world*?" It was a ridiculous attitude.

Lord James nodded with a rueful smile. "One's own beliefs can be very obstinate things. That's why I tell you that other people might be insulted by your observations. You want to take care."

"But why would I care about such silly people?"

"I don't suppose you want to insult anyone unnecessarily. And they can make life in society difficult."

Kawena shrugged. "You worry so much about other Englishmen and what they will think."

Lord James looked pained, then thoughtful. "I suppose it might come of being a Gresham and having a family name to uphold." He nodded to himself. "One spring when I had leave, my mother insisted that I experience a bit of a London season. Said it would be good for me." His smile was fond. "I remember one particularly dull party. I was complaining to Nathaniel, threatening to chuck lobster patties at the wall in sheer frustration. He said the season was like having a barrage of telescopes focused on you every minute. Only they were in the hands of the gossips instead of enemy ships."

Once again, Kawena was moved to take his hand. She saw that there could be different reasons to want to hold onto a man. And once again, she resisted.

"Of course, Nathaniel feels it most, being the oldest and Papa's heir."

"He will be a duke?" Kawena asked.

"Yes. Years and years from now, God willing."

"But can't a great nobleman do whatever he wants?" She'd read of kings and emperors who certainly seemed to. Hadn't there been one English monarch who had six or seven wives?

"Yes and no," Lord James said. "There are standards, and expectations. Nathaniel takes them hard."

"Well, it seems stupid to me," she said. "Not your brother, but the ones looking through the 'telescopes.'"

"Isn't there disapproval on your island? Malicious gossip? Or, uh, social transgressions?" He looked genuinely curious.

The questions stopped Kawena cold. Of course there were. From disobedient children to envy, and seemingly innate meanness to verbal and physical fights, even once a murder. You could be criticized, admonished, even; in the latter case, exiled forever. She knew she was watched particularly, because of the alien ideas her father taught her.

When she met Lord James's gaze, consciousness of this in her face, he nodded and said, "It goes both ways."

"Yes. I see."

His blue eyes held hers. "I suppose we have a lot to learn from each other," he added.

Kawena flushed, from her cheeks all the way to the core of her body. It was like stepping into a circle of fire. She wanted to learn everything he had to teach, in ways that were not at all what he meant. Or thought he meant? What lay beneath his words? Because, in these foreign circumstances, she didn't know, and she looked away.

      ∽

As they pulled up at the first posting house, James said, "Don't forget that we're telling everyone you're my sister."

Kawena nodded. "I have not forgotten. Though why anyone would believe that we're related…"

It was a stretch, James admitted silently. His auburn hair and pale complexion, even roughened as it was by years at sea, were a complete contrast to her honey-toned skin and coal black hair. He was an obvious Englishman, while she… She was an enticing, utterly desirable creature…

"All this deceit," she added, with a tilt of her head. "It could make one think that Englishmen are unable to control themselves."

James felt something like a growl rise in his throat, along with an almost irresistible desire to seize her and kiss her senseless. Which would only demonstrate that her ridiculous assertion was right. And it wasn't! He could control himself. He had practically inhuman control. Hadn't he been a perfect gentleman when she was tossed into his arms like a gift from Eros himself? And hadn't he continued to be one despite the fact that the look and the feel and the scent of her, so close and yet so unavailable, were driving him quite mad?

He shoved open the carriage door and escaped the confined quarters that had become a sort of tantalizing torture chamber. He'd be shut up with her for hours more, two days most likely, as they covered the eighty-odd miles between Oxford and Portsmouth. This journey was proving to be a greater test of his resolve than most of the naval battles he'd endured. He wondered if he could hire a horse and ride beside the chaise from here? Most likely Kawena would kick up a great fuss and insist on following suit. Which was impossible. No, he was trapped. Or did he actually wish to be trapped, and this was merely an excuse to stay near her?

Seeing that the landlady had taken charge of Kawena, he stomped into the taproom. A mug of ale would be just the thing. Two would be even better. But…no. He needed all his wits about him.

The horses were changed, new post boys mounted up, and in a few minutes they set off again. Kawena's sweet smile as they turned onto the main road south nearly undid him. He nodded in return and set himself to watch the passing scenery, in which he had no interest at all. Less than that!

An hour or so later, the carriage jerked and then wobbled. When James stuck his head out to see what was the matter, he discovered that one of the traces had broken. The postilions were struggling to halt the team with the right-hand leader out ahead, reins dragging behind him.

James braced to jump down and help, but the men knew their business. In short order they had stopped the chaise and captured the unharnessed horse. Then they bent together over the traces, examining the damage.

James sighed as he went to join them. By his calculations, they were almost precisely halfway between the first posting house and the second, as far as they could be from efficient help. This was the trouble with traveling in a hired carriage. You never knew how any particular inn cared for their tack, or their horses. And even with the best, the harness got hard usage. Mishaps like this happened all the time. If he'd ridden, alone, he'd be farther along right now. He wouldn't be fighting to keep his hands off Kawena either. But would she listen to reason about this probably futile journey? No. Reason did not appear to be one of her strongest characteristics.

"Can it be mended?" he asked one of the post boys.

"Well, yes, sir. 'Course," was the reply. "But not at the side of the road, like. With no proper tools."

It was only the answer he'd expected.

Kawena appeared at his elbow, which surprised him for a moment. A genteel English girl would naturally have left this matter to him, sitting meekly in the carriage until informed of the plan for her succor. But Kawena had to have her hand in everything, of course, even when she had no hope of understanding.

Close beside him, their shoulders almost touching, she looked down at the trace. The leather had clearly stretched under constant tension, and then parted. "Couldn't we tie it together?" she said.

The postilions looked amused, and rather smug

with it. "It wouldn't hold," James replied. "Leather's too weakened. Why don't you just wait in the carriage until—"

"Not the leather," she interrupted. "If you used a length of rope, and tied a double sheet bend here and here." She indicated spots where the trace was still sturdy. "It might be good enough until we reach the next inn, don't you think?"

James was amazed to hear her name a knot often used aboard ship. What girl knew a thing like that? And why hadn't he thought of it himself? It seemed he'd been wrong to doubt her ability to reason.

"Do you have some rope?" she asked the post boys.

"In me bag," said one. "Never travel without it."

"What's a 'sheet bend'?" asked the other.

"It's a knot used for joining broken sheets—lines—on a sailing vessel," James told him. He couldn't help a perplexed glance at Kawena. How did she know about knots?

"My father equipped trading ships," she reminded him in response. "I learned a lot about how they worked."

"Did you indeed?" She was a continual surprise. A delightful one.

"I cannot actually *tie* a sheet bend," she admitted.

James burst out laughing. "I can."

The postilion fetched his bit of rope. James fixed the ends to stronger lengths of the trace with the suggested knots, which were designed to tighten when subjected to strain. He was rather pleased with the result, as he hadn't done rope work for some years. None of the party was knowledgeable enough to appreciate the neatness of it, however.

They set off again, more slowly at first, but the makeshift harness worked quite well. Gradually, the post boys risked greater speeds, until finally they were barreling along almost as fast as before. James hung on, contemplating the idea that he hadn't imagined a pretty young woman could also be so practically competent. Growing up in a houseful of brothers, he'd formed the notion that girls were delicate creatures, more likely to moan and complain about the delay or the boredom of crawling across the countryside than to offer solutions. Of course, his mother wasn't one to sit helplessly and wait for rescue, but she was…unique, in his opinion. He sometimes thought she could read minds.

James looked over at Kawena. She clearly couldn't, or she wouldn't be looking so serene. She was intelligent and levelheaded, though, on top of gorgeous and delectable. James again felt the comradeship that had surfaced between them during their time at Alan's house. "That was a clever thought," he acknowledged.

She smiled at him.

James blinked. Comrades were not dazzling, in his experience.

"It was a simple idea," Kawena replied, though she was warmed by his praise.

"But you thought of it," he said. "I didn't. And I'm the sailor."

Kawena smiled again, enjoying the effect it seemed to have on him. The desire to tease him was nearly irresistible. His reactions were…exciting. But she still worried that he'd end the journey if she gave in to her impulses. She groped for a safe topic of conversation. "You must have seen all the ports we called at on my journey to England," she said. "They seemed such amazing places. I wanted to explore every lane and market, but I had to stay on shipboard most of the time, so as not to be exposed as a female."

"Ah, I wondered how you managed that," James replied. Ships' quarters were cramped and offered very little privacy.

"The captain of the ship was an old friend of my father's. I've known him since I was a child. When he arrived at the island soon after the theft was discovered, I asked for his help."

"I'm a bit surprised he gave it." James wouldn't have taken such a passenger on his own ship. The situation was primed for complications, or worse. Of course, his had been a navy vessel, not a private trader.

"I had to persuade him, and my mother, and others. It wasn't easy."

James tried to picture the mother of any girl he'd ever met letting her sail off dressed as a grubby lad. He couldn't.

"Finally, they saw that I was going to fight for my future, whatever it took. The idea that I had lost everything worked on them."

She held her chin high and looked utterly determined. James was impressed. "So this captain kept your secret?"

"He was very kind. He gave me a cabin of my own, with a lock, and enlisted some of his officers in my cause. I suppose the crew must have figured out my secret, eventually, but they didn't speak of it. The captain was securely in control of his ship."

"As he must be."

"It was difficult, sometimes," Kawena added.

James suspected this was a considerable understatement.

"But it worked. One of the hardest things, though, was not being able to look around the ports. The bits I could see from the ship were so interesting. I had imagined that the journey would let me visit many foreign lands, as I always wished to do."

James nodded. He understood her urge to travel. It had been one of the things that drew him to the navy in the first place.

"Were you often at Madras?"

"Quite often," he answered. "It's an important naval base in that part of the world, as well as the British administrative center for southern India."

"I know many traders go there. Is it a beautiful place?"

James thought about it. "The area around Fort St. George looks rather like home. Farther out, there are native temples, which are quite a sight. They're shaped like a pyramid, but covered with rows and rows of figures..." He remembered the nature of some of those figures and stopped.

"I visited one of those in another place," Kawena responded. "I thought some of the carvings were rather like those they make on the island. They were more intricate, of course."

She spoke without a trace of self-consciousness. Remembering the very graphic male figurines he'd seen on her island home, James discovered another way that Kawena was unlike a sheltered English girl. She seemed perfectly familiar with...certain bits of anatomy, and not at all embarrassed by the idea of them. His neckcloth felt tighter all at once. "Umm, you must have sailed south from Madras," he said.

"Yes, we went down the coast of Africa, but the stops were brief. I didn't see much else until we reached the Cape colony."

"There's a lovely spot," James said.

Kawena nodded. "The cliffs rising above the sea took my breath away. And it was thrilling to think that two oceans met in the waters offshore."

What other girl would think of that? James wondered. He remembered a day of mountainous waves as his ship rounded the horn of Africa and passed from the Pacific into the Atlantic.

"The one place I got to go ashore for a while was Gibraltar," Kawena went on. "Captain Pierce thought I'd hardly be noticed among all the different sorts of people there."

James nodded. The Mediterranean base was chock-full of Italians and Portuguese and Spaniards, not to mention the Jews and the Moors. "It's almost like a masquerade ball," he commented, recalling the rainbow colors of the costumes he'd seen there. Robes and skullcaps, along with bright British uniforms and kilts.

"Like nothing I'd ever seen," she agreed. "I stood in the square and watched a British officer slouching at a corner, looking with such scorn at all the people shouting and gesturing as they bargained."

She smiled at James, and his pulse raced.

"Some bowed with one hand to their chest." She demonstrated. "There were men in turbans sitting cross-legged, selling slippers or oranges or I don't know what. The din was tremendous. I felt I'd really made it to the other side of the world at last."

How well he knew that feeling, James thought. It was part of the adventure he'd dreamed of all his life—to see places and peoples unlike his own. He seldom met anyone who truly understood it. His family didn't. They were rooted in England, in their different ways, and content to be. Even Sebastian. His cavalry regiment might be ordered abroad, and he would go full willingly, and do his duty. But he didn't hope to be shipped to the Antipodes. He didn't anticipate the call as a rare opportunity.

A great many of James's countrymen who went off to serve the empire, or themselves, in far lands kept their minds and hearts in England, he'd found. They didn't share his delight in difference. Yet here, in the form of this lovely young woman, was a kindred spirit.

He met her eyes, and saw that she recognized it, too. Similar impulses moved them, deep down. With that realization came a touch of comfort, a sharper stab of longing, and a whiff of danger. This trip was becoming more and more complicated. He really wasn't certain how he was going to get through the rest of it.

Seven

THE MAIN ROAD TO PORTSMOUTH TOOK THEM
through Winchester, and as they stayed the night in that
town, Kawena had the chance to go out and look at
the cathedral early the next morning. She'd been urged
to do so by the innkeeper, who'd told her that it was
very ancient, built in the reign of some long-ago king.

As she stood before the towering edifice, gazing up
at spires that seemed to reach the sky, an old man in
priest's garb paused beside her. "There's been a church
here since six forty-two," he said.

"Six forty-two what?" she asked.

"The year six forty-two."

Kawena worked out the mathematics of this in her
head. Lord James walked up as she completed the sum.
"More than a thousand years?" It was difficult to think
of so much time, and of all the life that had passed
before these walls.

The old man nodded like a schoolmaster pleased
with his pupil. "This present building was consecrated
in 1093, however. Saint Swithin is buried here, as well
as a number of Saxon kings."

Kawena was looking confused. James wasn't much better off. "The ones before the Norman Conquest," he ventured, and saw that this didn't help her.

"It took them fourteen years to build it," said their volunteer guide with satisfaction. "They say the stone came all the way from the Isle of Wight. Later bishops added bits on, here and there. The priory was demolished because of all that nonsense with Henry VIII." He didn't appear to approve of this revolutionary monarch.

The old man came with them as they strolled through the cathedral. James tried to hint him away once or twice, but he was oblivious. Thus, he was at Kawena's side when they stopped to contemplate a wall of carved images.

"That looks rather like a temple in India," she commented.

"India?" said the old man.

"No, it doesn't," said James, noting the stiff saints and figures praying with clasped hands. It was nothing like the twisting, posturing dancers in India, particularly not those engaged in…activities that would scandalize any local churchgoer.

"They're all in rows, one above the other," Kawena argued. "Just like—"

"Not the same," James interrupted, afraid the old priest was going to ask for details. "We must get on the road." The design did have similarities, he admitted as he pulled her away, though of course the ideas behind it were totally different. He didn't think he would have noticed that on his own.

Travel was slow that day, as they hit a long stretch

of muddy road, turned to mire by recent heavy rains. Twice the chaise bogged down, and the second time James had to join the post boys in putting a shoulder to the rear of the carriage to help the team pull it out. Kawena offered to push beside him, but there James drew the line. Some things women simply did not do. It was enough that one of them should be spattered with muck, he told her as he scraped what he could from his boots.

At last they made it through to drier surfaces and passed into Southampton, near the end of their journey.

"Is this Portsmouth?" Kawena asked, looking out over the many boats moored in the harbor.

"No. Those are mostly rich men's yachts, not navy vessels."

"Yachts?" She hadn't heard the word before.

"It's what they call pleasure craft."

"Why?"

James shrugged. "It's just the name used for boats kept for the occasional sail out into the Channel. Perhaps a run to France, now that it's open to us again."

It seemed a waste, keeping a boat as large as some of these to be used so seldom. Not even for fishing. But Lord James spoke as if it was commonplace. "Does your father, the duke, have a yacht?"

He turned from the carriage window to look at her. "No. Why would you think so?"

"I supposed he was a rich man." She'd been thinking about such matters as the trip continued, all the similarities, and differences, between them. Their backgrounds could hardly be more unlike—their families, upbringing, expectations. They might have tastes in common, but the more time she spent here, the more she saw that English society would never see them as equal. The idea was annoying, and curiously disturbing. She wondered how he saw it.

Lord James shrugged off the question of riches. "He has no interest in keeping a yacht."

"You are the only one of your family who likes boats then?"

He laughed. "On the contrary, we had a sailboat on the lake at Langford. Well, it's still there, though not used so much now. Father taught us all to sail it."

"All?"

"Me and my brothers. It's nothing like the sea, of course, but if there was a spanking wind, you could get a bit of excitement out of her. When you could manage a turn at the tiller, that is. Everyone wanted to be captain. Nathaniel finally set up a regular schedule for us to follow."

"He is the eldest," Kawena remembered. Lord James looked younger as he spoke of this. She glimpsed the grinning, mischievous boy in the man. It was easy to imagine him racing to be the first into their sailboat.

He nodded. "Not that we paid his lists any mind. Me in particular. I was out the door and onboard whenever I could manage." He laughed again. "Papa nearly beat me once for taking that boat out at night. Even after I pointed out to him that there was only a gentle breeze and a full moon to sail by."

"That must have been beautiful," said Kawena.

He stared at her briefly, as if her response surprised him. "It was." He paused, seemed about to speak, then looked away. "It wasn't as if I could be washed out to sea or shipwrecked on our own lake. I could have walked home from any part of the shore."

"You could have drowned, and no one would have known." Kawena didn't think this had been likely, but she could imagine a parent's worries.

"I can swim better than any of my brothers. Papa made sure we all could paddle from the center of the lake to land before we were allowed to take the boat out alone. I was best with the sails, too. Never got becalmed like Robert. Without the oars, the booby."

It sounded like a large lake, and all part of the duke's estate. "Langford must be a big place," Kawena remarked.

"It's a rambling old pile," Lord James replied. "Every generation seemed to want to add their own bits. Rather like that old priest was saying about Winchester."

That he could compare his home to a vast building like the cathedral told Kawena more than any wealth of detail. And he didn't seem to notice the implication. Langford must be as different as a house could be from the small, palm-thatched place where she'd grown up. She'd seen English thatched cottages along their route; their inhabitants seemed to be farm laborers, very far from the family of a duke.

And what did it matter? she asked herself impatiently. As soon as they accomplished their mission, she would be leaving, and Lord James would be reabsorbed into the life of the English nobility. It wasn't as if they'd ever see each other again.

Although, he was still in the navy. Might his

next ship not call at Valatu? But when she imagined greeting him at their small dock, welcoming him to her mother's house…the picture broke down. She couldn't make the pieces of that story fit together.

❧

They pulled into Portsmouth in the early evening, after three days on the road. Lord James engaged rooms at a fine-looking inn, and all would have been well if Kawena had not overheard him ask the landlady to give them chambers well separated from each other. He also requested that she and her maids take special care of his "sister." Kawena suspected that money changed hands then, though she couldn't see from the hallway. Very likely he was plotting to leave her here while he went out to make inquiries, she thought. Did he imagine she could be so easily fooled? But no matter. She had plans of her own.

Early the next morning, as James addressed a breakfast of fried ham and hot bread and coffee in the taproom, a slender figure entered, pausing just inside the doorway. He paid him no mind until the fellow walked right up to his table and stood, silently, rudely, right at his elbow. Then James raised his head, a sharp setdown on his tongue, only to discover that it was Kawena, back in her male costume as he had first seen her.

James half rose from his chair, jostling coffee out of his cup and nearly overturning the small table it sat upon. "What the devil?"

"I thought this dress was best for visiting sailors," she said. "They will be less likely to—"

"Have you lost your mind?" By sheer luck, the taproom was empty. But that might change at any moment. Anybody might come in and recognize her and ask why his "sister" had donned such a scandalous, shabby costume. What was he to say to that?

"Your crew won't suspect," she said. "No one did when I traveled alone."

It was true that the baggy coat hid all the enticing curves of her body. And the sloppy cloth cap covered her hair and half her forehead. When she kept her head down, the brim made it difficult to see any of her face. Still… "Go upstairs at once and put on a proper gown. The staff of the inn are bound to notice—"

"They won't say anything. I told the landlady all about it. And swore her to secrecy."

"You what?" James felt as if the floor had dipped beneath him, like a ship's deck in a big blow.

"She saw me in the corridor outside my room. She did seem shocked," Kawena admitted. "But when I explained—"

James grabbed her shoulders and pulled her closer. He resisted an impulse to shake her. "You told her about the jewels?" he hissed. The story would be all over town in a moment. Indeed, it probably already was. If one of his crew members had the blasted things, they'd be alerted, probably on a fast horse out of town already. And their trip would be wasted.

"I'm not stupid!" said Kawena, pulling out of his grasp. "I told her a sad tale, to get her sympathy."

"Tale? What tale?"

"I said that we needed to question some rough

sailors about our brother's death at sea. That we feared there might have been foul play."

"Our brother?" repeated James, bewildered.

"Our other brother."

"Other…?" Either he'd lost his wits, or there was something wrong with his hearing, James concluded.

"You're supposed to be my brother, remember?" Kawena looked impatient. "So the one lost at sea is the other—"

"Nobody was lost at sea," he interrupted, his mind struggling to catch up.

"And I'm not your sister, either."

"Shh." There was still no one about, but how long could that last?

"You are so cut up over Donald's loss—"

"Donald?" Who the flaming hell was Donald? And how had he come into this?

"Our *other* brother," Kawena repeated, with the air of one speaking to a lackwit.

"That's a Scottish name," James objected, and then shook his head. What did that matter, in this whole farrago of nonsense?

She shrugged. "I was thinking quickly. It just popped out."

"Popped." He eyed her, dazed by this new side of her character.

"So, you are prostrate with grief," she continued. "You and Donald were very close. You are too distraught to go about alone. I have to dress as a boy to accompany you as we try to discover his fate."

"Fate." This ridiculous tale made him sound like a milksop, as well as dim.

"She promised to say nothing," Kawena finished. "Shall we get moving?"

She walked out, and he had no choice but to follow. "You realize that I may meet acquaintances here? The town is full of navy men."

"All the better that you aren't out with a nonexistent sister," she retorted, striding off.

He hadn't meant to be out with anybody at all, James thought. He'd meant to slip off, leaving her at the inn, as she'd obviously divined. He should have skipped breakfast. But he'd been hungry.

At least she was keeping her head down as she walked. James recovered his wits and reminded himself that he had the list of addresses. She couldn't find anyone without him. Catching up to her, he muttered, "You will follow my lead, and keep your mouth shut. Or we will give up this job here and now."

She gave one terse nod, eyes on the pavement, looking very much like a sullen lad, actually. She slouched and sidled along, the picture of youthful reluctance. He had to admit she was rather good at playing her chosen part.

James consulted the notes he'd made during his visit to the Admiralty, and they moved off.

He began with his former first officer, as the one most likely to have kept track of the crew's movements and noticed any unusual behavior. Simmons had received his orders for a new ship and was happy with the posting, so he was pleased to see James, and even more pleased to down a tankard of ale at James's expense. He did give James a pitying glance when James suggested a reunion of the old crew, but he agreed readily enough, helping arrange it for that evening.

James bought dinner and stood drinks for the eight sailors from the *Charis* currently in Portsmouth, and was hailed as a great good fellow all round. Kawena even played a part. Explained as the son of a friend of his family looking for preferment, pushed off on him to squire about Portsmouth to see if the navy would suit, she made an occasional sneering comment that gained him instant sympathy.

When the meal was over, Kawena retreated into a dark corner and listened as Lord James skillfully guided the men into talking about their final voyage, with special attention to the stop at Valatu. Without saying so outright, he gave the clear impression that infractions and irregularities didn't matter, now that he was no longer their captain. If a man had gone ashore without his knowledge, or engaged in some dubious trading on the side, well, that was the way of the world, wasn't it? Several of the men seemed startled to hear this from him, Simmons in particular. Others, lubricated by free-flowing liquor, boasted of their exploits in various ports of call. Kawena watched their faces as they spoke and laughed, gauged their body language for hesitance or lies. Some were sly or unsympathetic or venal. Some admitted cheating natives in various exchanges, using their ignorance to come away with items worth far more than what they gave. None said anything relevant to her quest.

As the evening wore on, James would forget that Kawena was present for a stretch of time. Then the sight of the "lad" would startle him. He would become intensely aware of her legs in rough breeches and thick stockings, of the delicacy of her hand emerging from an overlarge sleeve. His heart would pound at the thought of what would happen if she was discovered, and what she must think of the profane expressions and coarse sentiments of common sailors in their cups. When the hour grew late and amorous tales began to lace the talk, becoming more graphic as one man tried to top another, he used her youth as an excuse to depart, softening the blow by paying for a final round of drinks.

"That wasn't any help," said Kawena as they walked back to their inn. She seemed unaffected by the hours in the din and smokiness of the alehouse.

James felt a spark of resentment. It hadn't been an easy thing, to act such a part with his former crewman. Simmons, certainly, had seen many of his remarks as out of character. Others had looked startled as well. Kawena had no notion of the discipline of a navy ship, and the distance and standards a captain must maintain. So she couldn't conceive of the humiliation he'd suffered by pretending not to care for these things. Still, she might have thanked him.

"I shall have to speak to some men alone," James told her. When she started to object, he held up a hand. This had become more and more evident to him as the night unfolded. "To one man on his own, I can suggest that there was a problem on the voyage and promise to keep his name out of it. In those circumstances, he will say things he wouldn't reveal before others, including an unknown 'youth.'"

Kawena had to admit there was sense in this. And so,

on the following day, James visited Simmons again, and then the rest of the men on his list, one by one. But he discovered nothing useful. Indeed, all he accomplished was to rouse concern, and some suspicion.

Back at the inn that afternoon, sharing a dinner of roast chicken and peas, they took stock, and had to acknowledge that they had made no progress. Kawena, gowned as his "sister" again, seemed thoroughly discouraged. "It did not seem to me that any of the men were lying," she said. "This task is far more difficult than I imagined."

"When you showed up waving a pistol and offering to shoot me," James replied, hoping to raise her spirits.

She didn't smile. She scarcely seemed to hear him. She sat with bent head and slumped shoulders, eyes downcast, looking more like a mournful old painting than the spirited lass who'd nearly blackened his eye. James hated to see it. His gaze followed the exquisite line of her cheek, the flutter of dark eyelashes against honeyed skin. It was like seeing a creature of leaping flame dimmed down to embers. He wanted to reignite that brightness nearly as much as he wanted to sweep her into his arms. "There are other crew members I can speak to, in London," he suggested.

She looked up. The budding hope and trust in her eyes nearly stopped his breath. What wouldn't a man do to earn such a look? To prolong and intensify it?

"We could stop there on the way back to Oxford," he offered. "Have you been to London?"

"I passed through. It was huge and very noisy. And dirty."

He couldn't argue with her. He'd often felt the

same. "The rest of my old crew is there, however." He tried to speak bracingly. "We'll head for London tomorrow. The roads will be better, at least."

She pushed a bite of chicken around on her plate. "Do you really think we will find out anything?"

"It's the only other thing to try."

Kawena nodded gloomily. James cursed himself for a clumsy fool. Why hadn't he been more optimistic? The difference between this melancholy young woman and the lively creature he'd come to know on their journey was unbearable. A memory struck him. "Do you still want to try riding a horse?"

Kawena looked up.

They'd already seen her in boy's clothes here, James noted, aware that she would insist on wearing that garb for riding. He didn't want her doing that at Alan's house, on streets and lanes where his brother's friends might see them. But here... "I'll see about some mounts," he said, rising.

"I'll get ready," she replied, color back in her cheeks.

Eight

WHEN SHE CAME BACK DOWNSTAIRS AND WAS DIRECTED to the stables, Kawena found Lord James discussing the merits of available horses with the hostler. One was already saddled. The debate appeared to be about the second choice. "Merry's a bit of a plodder," the hostler was saying, indicating a gray horse in a nearby stall. "But Rex"—he pointed to a brown animal farther down— "is overfond of a run, if you know what I mean."

"We'll take M—"

"Rex," interrupted Kawena. "I want to run. Like flying."

James tried to intervene. "You want a gentler mount for your first—"

"Rex," Kawena insisted. She'd seen plow horses in the fields. She knew what plodding looked like. And she wasn't going to be stuck shuffling along the roadway like a sack of meal slung over a donkey. After the disappointments of the interviews, she felt an urgent need to throw herself against the world.

"He ain't dangerous," said the hostler. "Just a little…frisky on occasion."

"Perfect," she pronounced. She liked the word. Frisky was exactly how she wanted to feel—the opposite of the increasing pessimism that burdened her. She met Lord James's eyes. She would *not* be fobbed off with a plodder. Fortunately, he sighed and gave in.

Rex was saddled, and Kawena lifted onto his back. As the hostler adjusted the stirrups to her feet, Lord James explained the reins and how to communicate to Rex what she wanted. Then he sprang onto the other mount and led the way out of the stable and into the lane.

It was an odd way of sitting, Kawena thought as they made their way through the streets of Portsmouth. The horse seemed much wider when you straddled him than he had looked from the ground. And his movements caused her to sway back and forth. Lord James had told her to grip with her knees, she remembered. She tried, and Rex jolted forward, nearly colliding with a woman carrying a market basket.

"Hold up," Lord James said as the woman glared at her. "We'll keep to a walk until we're farther from town."

"Walk, Rex," said Kawena. She recalled then that he'd said you tightened your knees and leaned forward when you wanted to go faster. So she did the opposite, and was pleased when the horse settled back into a walk. Riding was really quite simple, she concluded. She didn't know why people made such a fuss about it.

Lord James guided them toward the seaside, leaving the bustle of town behind. Kawena welcomed the sight of the water, even though it was not her ocean.

This one was gray and edged with small stones instead of sand. The waves hissed and clattered in quite a different voice.

"You're doing well," Lord James called.

Kawena knew that. How could she not when all she had to do was sit there? "I want to go faster," she replied.

"The trot's a bit more difficult…"

She was deathly tired of things that were difficult. Indeed, nothing in life seemed easy, just now. Surely a ride along the beach was a simple matter? All sorts of people rode, all over this country. She'd seen tiny children atop huge farm horses. Perhaps she should stay just above the beach, however, if you could even call a field of pebbles a beach. She would not have wanted to run in those stones. Rex would probably not care for it either. Kawena pulled on one of the reins, as instructed, to turn her horse parallel to the shore. "Let's go, Rex," she said, leaning well forward and pressing her knees into his sides.

He went.

And in an instant, the ride changed utterly. Rather than an easy seat, the saddle was now a precarious, jouncing perch, threatening to jerk out from under her, first one way, then another. The stirrups wanted to fly out to the side. Pounding hooves replaced her smooth progress, and the landscape streamed by in a breathless blur.

"Kawena!"

Lord James's call seemed to come from far away. She did not dare turn to see where he was. It was all she could do to hang on.

"Pull up! Pull up!" he shouted.

The reins—one pulled on them to slow down, she remembered. But her reins were clutched in her two fists, above where her fingers were twined in Rex's mane. She would have to let go to pull on them, and she wasn't going to do that. Nor did she dare loosen her knees and sit back. Crouching over Rex's neck seemed by far the better, indeed the only, choice.

Rex veered onto sand. Water splashed around them, thrown up by his pounding hooves, and for a moment, Kawena feared that he was carrying her right into the sea. Then she saw that they were on a long spit that stretched out to a great rock rearing up from the sea far ahead. Shallow waves fanned across the sand. As they passed through a dip, their passage threw up sheets of salt water, soaking her from head to foot. Stinging seawater lashed into her eyes. All Kawena could do was duck her head and cling.

Rex raced on. Time seemed to both stretch and contract, a muddle of jolts and spray and thudding hooves. He would have to stop when they reached the crag, Kawena thought. But he did not. The horse's hooves clattered onto a stony path slanting upward, and he kept right on going. The sound seemed to echo. Then Kawena realized it was another horse. Lord James was pounding along just behind her.

He didn't catch up, however, until they both emerged on top of the crag and discovered a small house tucked into a flat space there, facing the sea. Kawena had just time to glimpse it, and marvel, and then Lord James was beside her, his horse shouldering

Rex to a standstill, his hands grabbing for her reins. In a quick tussle of hooves and teeth, he brought them to a halt. "Have you lost your wits?" he shouted.

She'd been about to thank him. She changed her mind.

He jumped down, and then practically dragged her from the saddle while keeping hold of both sets of reins. Kawena felt the jar of the landing through her feet and knees. The horses danced nervously. Lord James loomed over her, pressing her back against Rex's flank. He looked furious. "Why didn't you pull up?" he said.

Kawena realized that her cap was gone. Her hair was coming loose from its tight braids; wet tendrils trailed along her cheeks. She was soaked and cold, except where Lord James's chest rested against hers. That part of her was warming. His angry face was inches away. She was interested to find that she wasn't the least bit afraid of him, despite his fit of temper. In fact, she was very much inclined to kiss him. She wondered what he would do if she did.

Rex tossed his head and stamped. Lord James jerked away, looking nearly as wild as the horse. A large wave hit the crag, shattering blue-white and throwing spray high into the air. Wisps of damp drifted over them. "We need a place to get dry," he said.

James looked to the house. It appeared to be vacant. Spotting a small stable on the right, he led the horses toward it. "Come with me," he commanded. He was still so angry with Kawena he could scarcely speak to her. Did she have any idea how close she'd come to serious injury? He had watched her almost bounce out of the saddle a dozen times. Of course she didn't. She was a heedless, headstrong hoyden.

He led the horses out of the wind and sea spray, Kawena obediently at his heels, at least. The small stable was empty and smelled of ancient manure and sour hay. "They need a rest or they'll be blown," he said. "And you can't run horses so hard and leave them wet. I'll look for something to rub them down." James thrust the reins into Kawena's hands. "Hold 'em," he commanded, biting off the words.

He strode around to the front of the house. The door wasn't locked. Indeed, it wasn't quite shut; the sea air had warped the panels. Pushing it open, he called, "Hello?" The word echoed back to him from bare walls. "Is anyone here?"

Answered by silence, he went inside. The place was clearly abandoned. There were bits of broken furniture here and there. An armchair exuded tufts of padding and a scent of mold. In a back parlor overlooking the sea, he found heavy draperies still hanging at the windows. He pulled two of them down and carried them to the stable.

Kawena had tied up the two mounts and managed to remove their saddles, which cooled his temper. He handed her a curtain and showed her how to tend to Rex. "It was very foolish of you to try a gallop," he pointed out.

"I wanted to go fast," she replied.

She appeared unrepentant. James knew it was his duty to make her regret her recklessness, but he was diverted by how appealing she looked in the dim light. Her dark hair was straggling down her back.

Like his, her hands were filthy from the dusty cloth. She had a smudge of dirt across her forehead, and yet she was lovely. Her wet clothes clung to her, outlining every lithe line of her body. Her piquant face was charmingly intent as she worked away at the rubdown without complaint. "You're shivering," he said.

"I've often been wet, but never when the water was so cold," she replied.

James was swept by a need to take care of her. "I'll see if I can make a fire, dry our clothes a bit before we head back."

"There's no one in the house?"

He shook his head. "Not for a long time, I'd say."

They finished tending their mounts. James looked for fresh water for them, and found none. He led the way back into the house, choosing the room with the largest fireplace. He gathered up some of the bits of discarded furniture. The wood was very dry. It broke easily into smaller pieces. "Pull some of the stuffing from that chair," he told Kawena, and she went to do so. Soon, he'd assembled the makings of a fire. He pried a bit of flint out of the crumbling chimney and used it with his steel knife to strike a spark. It took several tries before the puff of tinder caught. After that, it was a simple matter to coax a blaze into life.

"How clever you are," Kawena said. She held out her hands to the rising heat. Water dripped from her bulky coat onto the dusty floor. Seeing it, she slipped out of the garment and hung it from a protruding stone in the mantel. "It's true that riding makes you sore in parts you didn't know you had," she said, rubbing one exquisite flank and smiling.

James found he couldn't tear his eyes away from that moving hand. With her coat off, Kawena's boyish costume left absolutely nothing to the imagination. Her damp linen shirt clung to a pair of the loveliest breasts he'd ever seen. Her breeches outlined a lissome waist and beautifully curving hips. He wanted to push his hands through the tangle of her hair and restore the raven waterfall she'd exhibited the day they met. Of course, that would be improper. And wasn't he thoroughly sick of thinking about what was improper? It wasn't his job. Girls were supposed to think about that, weren't they? They were drilled in it, meant to remind a fellow to hold the line, rather than stand before him like some glorious sea goddess, ripe for the picking.

Kawena turned her head and looked at him. Her eyes were as dark as the ocean depths. James felt as if she could read his mind. But if she could, why wasn't she frowning at him; why wasn't she turning away? "I'll…I'll get more wood," he blurted out. Smashing up more furniture would be very satisfying.

"I will help you."

"No!" The idea had been to get away from her. "Stay here and get warm."

"You shouldn't have to do all the work," she insisted.

James gave up. "There's part of a table in the back room," he said, pointing. "I'll check upstairs."

There was nothing on the upper level, which was one large space open to the rafters, but James spent a bit of time exploring anyway. He peered out the small windows at the ends and examined the dim corners. He wouldn't return until he was back in control, he decided. Kawena could have no idea how enflaming she looked in her wet clothing. It wasn't her fault he was seething with desire. Well, it was her fault because she'd insisted on choosing that deuced horse and then gone careening off on him like an idiot. And now she was sitting there in front of the fire, oblivious to the effect she was having on him. He had to go back down. It was freezing up there.

The object of his confused emotions sat on the floor, arms around her raised knees, contemplating a blaze that had grown with the addition of several table legs. She had released the pins and braids from her hair, and it streamed down her back in a midnight-black cascade, just as he had wanted. He stumbled over nothing, flooded with the need to bury his fingers in its silken length.

"I wonder why no one lives here," she said.

"I think they ran out of water," James replied, his voice sounding thick in his ears. He sat down on the far side of the hearth. "I saw a well from upstairs, but it looked as if it had gone dry."

"Why would it?" Firelight washed her face, adding even more of a glow to her complexion.

"Springs shift sometimes."

"They must have been sad to leave such a place."

James looked around. There was nothing outside the windows but crags and the surging sea. "Do you think so? It seems rather lonely to me. And it must be bleak here during winter storms."

Kawena appeared to consider this. "Yes, I see. It is far from the town. What sort of house would you like to live in?"

"A neat little manor, I suppose." He answered without thinking. Indeed, thinking was nearly impossible with her so near. The wet linen of her shirt was next to transparent. Her breasts seemed to point at him, call his fingers to caress—

"Like your brother's?"

"What?" James blinked, tore his eyes away. He mustn't stare at her breasts. He would look at the fire. Yes. Flames. Yellow, orange, a hiss of blue.

"A house like Lord Alan's?" she added.

James turned automatically. Kawena's shirt had sagged open at the top, revealing a delicate collarbone and a stretch of pale skin that inevitably led one's eye downward—

She was gazing at him, waiting for an answer. What was the question? "Larger than that," James replied, looking hastily back at the fire.

"It seems quite large to me," she said.

James stared at the fire, forced his thoughts away from where they wanted to go and onto the dry question of houses. Alan's place was all very well for a man who was interested in little beyond working in his laboratory. "I always think of a home as having a good stretch of land," he said, somewhat at random.

"For farming?"

James nodded. Of course, that required tenants. And a manor needed a staff of servants. His father was always talking about his dependents. It occurred to James that he didn't much want a whole herd of dependents looking to him for their livelihood. What did one do, stuck on shore with a bunch of servants waiting for orders? It was like a ship's crew, he supposed. But it wasn't really. His crews looked to the navy for their pay and their future, not to him.

"Sometimes I wonder how I will live now in a little house on my little island," Kawena said. "And what I will do with my time. After I have seen so many other places…" Her voice trailed off. "Oh," she said, and pointed out the window on her side of the hearth.

James looked, and saw the sand spit they'd crossed to reach this place being engulfed by the rising tide. He sprang up and went to the glass. The water was running fast and already looked too deep to cross safely. A curse escaped him; he should have thought of this. What sort of seaman was he? Kawena's seductive nearness had addled his wits. "There's another reason why the place was abandoned," he said. "Storms probably ate away at the beach. We won't get off this rock until the tide turns."

Kawena came to stand next to him and watch the racing water. Their shoulders touched, warm under the cold of wet clothes. She didn't move away, though. Instead, she leaned closer. "That will be hours."

Six or more hours. And then it would be night. Was there a decent moon? Intoxicated by the feel of her arm against his, James couldn't remember.

Kawena turned toward him. Her lips were inches away, which didn't seem to embarrass her at all. James couldn't stop himself. He kissed her.

It was fully as exciting as he'd imagined. After an instant's surprise, her mouth answered his, softening under his urging. James forgot every scruple as she relaxed against him, slipping her arms around his waist, pressing closer. His hands slid down the curve of her back and cupped the bottom so lusciously outlined in her boy's breeches. He felt as if they struck flame where they touched, as if steam ought to be rising from their damp garments. His body responded with alacrity, straining to get closer still. Why were they clothed? He wanted to rip off his shirt, hers. He wanted to sweep her feet from under her, ease her to the floor and take possession of her beautiful body.

She was under his protection, declared a vastly annoying inner voice. He had undertaken to escort her on this journey, to keep her safe. This blaze of passion was anything but that.

James started to draw back. Kawena leaned in and renewed the kiss, tightening her grip. She wasn't finished kissing him. His touch had set her alight. It was hard to catch her breath. The feel of him against her was thrilling, rousing a demanding ache, more intense than anything she'd ever felt. She wanted more. Now.

She moved her lips as he had, and the kiss deepened. Kawena grasped fists full of linen shirt and pulled him nearer as she arched up. Her knees wanted to give way. She curled one leg around his.

"We shouldn't…" Lord James panted when the searing kiss ended, even as his hands tightened, molding her to him.

"Why shouldn't I kiss you if I want to?" Kawena murmured.

"*You* kiss *me*?"

Her father was gone, taking his lectures with him. She was far from home. She might never make it back there. Her mother had always said that a woman should discover what she wanted, and then set out to get it, Kawena slid one arm around Lord James's neck and pulled his head down for another kiss. She wanted this. She hooked her leg more firmly and strained against him.

When he pulled up the back of her shirt, she did the same to his. When he stepped back to yank off his boots, she followed suit. She protested when he strode from the room, but he was back in a moment with the remaining curtain from the back parlor. He tossed it down before the hearth, and then hesitated. Kawena responded by skimming out of the rest of her clothes. She faced him, smiling, the fire warm on her back, and reached out to run her hands over his bare chest.

Lord James groaned. In one swooping motion he discarded his own breeches and bore her down to the floor, placing her gently on the drapery. Then he knelt over her, gazing down as if stunned. *A beautiful man*, Kawena thought. The auburn hair on his body glinted in the firelight. His form was finely muscled, his face a chiseled oval.

"Are you sure?" he said.

She didn't bother to speak. She simply reached out and ran her fingers lightly up and down the obvious evidence of his arousal. He gasped and trembled. Kawena enjoyed that reaction so much that she continued her attentions until he caught her wrist and stopped her.

She met his gaze. His eyes burned as blue as driftwood fires.

He lay down beside her and used his hands and lips to coax and tease and titillate. Kawena had thought she was aroused, but she discovered that she'd had no notion of the possible heights of desire. He kissed her and caressed her until she thought she would expire from sheer need. And when the ache exploded into fulfillment, she almost thought she had. He held her as she rode the waves of sensation. Only then did he enter her, and she had the thrill of his climb to the same peak and shudder of release. She held him as he had her, their hearts pounding in tandem, their breath loud in the deserted dwelling, her spirit soaring with delight.

Afterward, they lay before the fire, sated. His body shielded her from the cold air of the room, and his hand ran through her long hair. Kawena let out a luxuriant sigh. "That was splendid," she said.

Lord James laughed a little. "You aren't sorry?"

"No. Why should I be? At home, all the women my age have done this. Most have families by now."

His hand in her hair went still. He coughed, then cleared his throat. "I…of course I will offer…that is…I hope you will do me the honor of becoming my wife."

"What?"

"In these circumstances, there is no other…" He cleared his throat again, as if something was caught in it. "I want to assure you… Naturally, I will not hang back or fail in my duty to…to make things right."

Kawena grimaced. It was as his brother had said. She could almost hear Lord Alan listing all his reservations about their journey. What they all seemed to fear so much had occurred, and now Lord James believed he had to pay for indulging his desires. She heard it in the tone of his voice, felt it in the tension of his body. He thought he was trapped. It was stupid, and insulting, and somehow quite melancholy, too. Ignoring the latter emotion, Kawena turned and rose on one elbow to stare down at him. "No," she said. "Why would you think I wanted to do that?"

He looked confused. "Well, it's…we… You said that other women from your home had families by this—"

"I only meant that I am of an age to decide for myself what I want. Which I did. And that is that."

He didn't seem to believe her. "I don't think you understand the consequences of…of what we have done."

Kawena noticed that they were both streaked with dust from the ancient drapery beneath them. It would have been funny, had she been in the mood to laugh.

"People will talk," Lord James added.

"English people seem to be much too fond of talking. About things that are none of their affair. Let them talk all they want. I won't be here to hear them."

She saw relief in his face and looked away before his expression revealed any more. She turned and lay back down, now feeling the hard floor below the cloth. She watched the flames leap. She'd taken what she'd wanted. There was nothing to regret. She didn't regret it! She groped for the feeling of sated delight that she'd basked in only moments ago. But she couldn't quite get it back.

Nine

JAMES WOKE TO DARKNESS, WONDERING WHY WAS HE was warm on one side and freezing on the other. The coals of a fire gleamed before him. Moonlight shone through bare windows, enough to show him the empty room and the naked woman curled against his chest. It all came back to him then, in a jumble of emotion—the ride, the crag, the bout of passion with the visitor he was supposed to be shepherding around the countryside. He'd let himself be swept away by circumstance, and desire.

He looked down at Kawena, her breath soft in sleep. Her skin gleamed faintly in the firelight, and a tumble of dark hair hid her face. It would take a stronger man than he was to have resisted such beauty and spirit when she'd been so willing, so…insistent.

He hadn't taken advantage of her. He knew people would say so, and part of him wanted to argue that, of course, he had. That was said to be the way of the world. Men seduced when they could; women fell into their traps. But Kawena had been too involved in the dance, too enthusiastic, to credit it. She'd wanted him, as he had assuredly wanted her. Still wanted her with an intensity that shook him. She'd pursued when he would have drawn back. Remembering the way she'd touched him, it was all he could do to keep his hands off her now.

Yet there was nothing of the loose woman about her. What a stupid phrase that was, to be sure! She was an intoxicating mixture—forthright, passionate, and surprising. She hadn't been embarrassed, and then she hadn't been ashamed. Not in the least. She was like no woman he'd ever met or imagined.

She stirred, and a fall of raven hair slid off her shoulder. Desire shot through James, sharp and hot. Would she come to regret what she'd done when she woke? Would she turn shy and distant? Even accusing? No, she would be…just herself. She wasn't a person much plagued by regrets, as far as he could judge. He resisted his urge to brush back those dark tresses so he could see her face.

As for his offer to make amends by marrying her—the idea had seemed to make her angry. James realized that, beneath his relief at her refusal, he was a bit piqued by this reaction. He had birth, decent manners, money. He'd been told often enough that he was pleasant to look at. Did all this merit instant rejection? Not that he planned so…precipitous a match. It would never work out between them. But to be so summarily rejected stung a little. And Kawena didn't understand the consequences of her actions. Society would ostracize her for giving in…

Then he remembered. She could snap her fingers at society, because she wouldn't be living in it. She'd be thousands of miles away from the gossips, immune to their power. She wasn't a creature of the world where he'd grown up. Any more than he was of hers. So… all was well then. Things had worked out for the best. Why didn't he feel better about that?

He was shivering from the icy air at his back. James eased away from Kawena and rose. He folded the drapery over her, then put on his riding breeches, still damp and clammy. On his way to find more wood to build up the fire, he checked the tide. It had turned. With the light of the half moon, they could probably make it back to town now. But wasn't it best to wait for dawn? He didn't know the road well, and they might attract slightly less attention if they returned when the inn was awake and busy. Perhaps they could even slip up to their rooms undetected? He could hope.

When he returned with more scraps of furniture, Kawena was awake. She gazed up at him from her drapery cocoon, dark eyes unreadable. James took his time placing the wood on the coals, blowing on them to help the wood catch. He wished she would speak so he needn't be the one to set the tone for this awkward conversation. At last, she did.

"I'm very thirsty," she said.

Beset by equal parts of relief and disappointment, James said, "So am I. And the horses, I'm sure. I'll search, but I don't think there's any fresh water here."

"If only we were like those turtles."

"Those…?" Had he heard her correctly? It didn't seem possible that, lying there sleepy-eyed and gloriously disheveled in the firelight, she'd mentioned turtles.

"The sea turtles," she added. "That annoying old man said they can drink seawater and get rid of the salt."

She surprised a laugh out of James. "He did, didn't he?"

"It would be a very helpful skill to have. For the horses, too."

"Yes."

"Are you laughing at me? Why?" She rose up on one elbow and eyed him.

"I was just admiring the sharpness of your memory. I'd forgotten about the turtles."

"But it was a very interesting thing to know."

"I can't argue with that."

"You could if you wished to."

She moved, and the drapery slid half off her breasts. At that moment, James could not have argued that his name was Gresham. He might not even have remembered it.

Kawena waited. When he said nothing, she went on. "Well, if there is no water, we should go back to the inn. The tide must have turned by now?"

Maddeningly, the drapery lingered just at the point...

"Hasn't it?"

"What?" James felt the flush that warmed his cheek. He had no idea what she'd asked.

"The tide? Is the path clear?"

"Oh. Yes, nearly. It's still going out."

She sighed. The drapery rose and fell, but did not slip any farther. "So we should go, I suppose."

It didn't sound like a question. Or a conclusion. James had never strained so hard to catch the nuance buried in a few words. "We must. But it might be best to wait for first light." He didn't go into his reasoning on this point, as he had forgotten it.

Kawena sat up and stretched. The drapery fell away. She lifted her heavy hair and pushed it back over her shoulders. The movement arched her breasts so invitingly that James's breath caught. His body's instant response was almost painful. Then she smiled at him, eyes sultry, and said, "We have time then."

After that, he was incapable of a single thought. He shed his breeches as fast as humanly possible. And then he held her in his arms again and reveled in her eager welcome. Together, they dove headlong into the realm of trailing fingertips and parted lips and tangled limbs, where nothing was more complicated than how long they could prolong their mutual pleasure and how deeply they could savor its exquisite conclusion.

෴

Much later, Kawena stirred in James's embrace. Sitting up, she stretched again, looked around the room, then rose and walked over to a patch of white on the floor. She picked it up and started wiping the streaks of dust from her body. James so enjoyed the sight that he didn't notice at first what she held. Then it hit him, and he jerked upright. "Hold on, that's my neckcloth!"

"Yes," Kawena agreed. "I thought we would want to keep our shirts clean." She looked at the dusty floor. "Well, as clean as we can." Continuing her rough ablutions, seemingly unabashed by his appreciative gaze, she looked out the window. "The sun is coming up." Finished with the swatch of linen, she offered it to him and began to collect her scattered clothes.

His once-crisp neckcloth, limp and dirty in his hand, James was conscious of a sharp pang of regret. Their idyll was over. It was time to come back down to Earth. To make certain she understood the harsh English realities, he said, "You know that we can't tell anyone what…happened here?"

"Happened?" Kawena repeated.

What would Alan and Ariel say to him if they learned of it? He knew his brother loved and respected him, and there was growing affection between him and Ariel. He couldn't bear the thought of disappointing them. "We'll need a story for the innkeeper."

"A story. Like a fairy tale?"

She sounded curious, and perhaps…amused? That couldn't be right. "I've told you that people will talk, disapprove. They would treat you badly." She needed to understand. He couldn't bear the thought of her being hurt, insulted.

"Yes, I remember. We will tell whatever story you wish."

It seemed almost as if she was humoring him. She must acknowledge that he knew more about his own country than she did.

"We could simply tell them the truth," Kawena continued. "Part of the truth," she amended at his change of expression. "That Rex ran away with me, and we were trapped by the tide before we noticed."

It seemed easy when she put it that way. "I suppose."

"We can tell how we burned old furniture to keep

warm," she said, growing more enthusiastic. "And how very thirsty we became. The poor horses, too. My father always said a good story should be specific."

She spoke as if he was foolish, a man with foibles to be indulged. She had no idea what she was dealing with. She'd never seen the old biddies look down their aristocratic noses at girls whose transgressions were far more trivial than their…exquisite indulgence. She didn't know what it meant to receive the cut direct or be pursued by leering men who took one slip as an excuse to take intolerable liberties.

James's fists clenched. He started to explain it to her, then realized that she wouldn't listen. She'd only find him funnier than ever. And so why should he care? He wouldn't be subject to the same strictures. Fellows weren't. He could spread the story far and wide, if he liked, and get off scot-free. Indeed, he'd be envied, congratulated by sniggering acquaintances, encouraged to share titillating details.

On a wave of revulsion, James felt, for the first time in his life, how truly unfair that was. He'd noted it vaguely before. It was a staple of his upbringing. Girls were held to a different standard. Reputation was their job, their doom to tend and polish like some fragile heirloom. Now, faced with the threat to Kawena, he silently rebelled. They had both indulged. Why should they be regarded differently for the same actions? More, he was an Englishman; he knew the rules and had broken them. If anyone should pay, it should be him. She came from quite a different society. She should not be blamed.

James realized that Kawena was looking at him

quizzically. She hadn't the slightest notion what he was thinking.

He would simply have to be mindful for her, he concluded. Yes, she would soon be off to realms where the old biddies were a distant irrelevance. But she could be treated badly in the meantime, an intolerable thought. James met her twinkling eyes and vowed that would never happen.

❧

They started off early the next morning for London, to find the remaining members of the *Charis* crew and complete their mission. The road to the capital was better than the one from Oxford, so they barreled along at a rapid pace. Conversation was more stilted, however, and Kawena found this both irritating and unsettling. The night at the abandoned house seemed to sit between them on the seat, inserting itself into the most innocuous sentences. It complicated every accidental bump of shoulder or brush of hands, so as the miles passed, the atmosphere in the carriage grew fraught.

With each passing hour, she understood more of how her mother had felt dealing with her father, reaching toward him across a gulf of preconceptions and habits. The idle hours of the journey gave their voices in her head free rein—Papa's carping, Mama's impatience. In all their years together, the disputes had never ended. The smallest things had reignited them in one or the other, and then they would be off, tossing words back and forth. Perhaps they even enjoyed the verbal jostling, because she knew they loved each other dearly. In her memory, though, it seemed they said the same things over and over. The thought left Kawena uncertain, a little sad, and not nearly as assured as she chose to appear.

The encounter in that dusty room had been so glorious. Her few fumbling tries at home had been nothing like it. Indeed, she hadn't entirely understood what all the fuss was about before. This seemed a matter to celebrate, but Lord James clearly did not. Their attitudes about the relations between men and women were so different. He fidgeted beside her as if he couldn't wait for the journey to end. Was this really all about what other people would say?

She *did* understand that. At home on the island, people gossiped, argued, even indulged in long-running, spiteful feuds. But they arose from sensible things, like stealing a fishing net or acting disrespectfully or cheating in a trade. She couldn't imagine the whole of her small society banding together to condemn a couple who indulged, secretly, in a night's pleasure.

So was it only other people? Or did Lord James regret what they had done? Perhaps he still thought she meant to make some claim on him, despite her assurances. Did he dare to doubt her word? What else could she say? She would never force him into an unwanted marriage. Even if she wasn't leaving England. Even if she was a timid English woman frightened by the opinions of this hidebound society.

Only one thing was certain: their easy camaraderie was gone. The trip had become much less enjoyable. Her sadness about that grew with the miles. She'd so enjoyed his company before.

And it grew even worse as they neared London. Kawena began to feel hemmed in by the outer landscape as well as the mood in the chaise. The web of streets and buildings thickening around them was like a maze. If she was dropped into this tangle of filthy streets, how would she ever find her way out? The air was heavy with smoke and rank odors and raucous with noise. "How can anyone live here?" she wondered.

Lord James nodded. "This is a poor neighborhood, but I always feel like a caged animal in a city."

A wagon emerged from an alleyway ahead, and they had to slow to a crawl behind it. Another came up in the rear, trapping them. The street was crowded with people and carts and riders. The noise of hooves and babble of voices rose higher. "You can't get out," Kawena murmured.

"Precisely." He looked at her, and for the first time in days, they shared a companionable glance. Encouraged, she smiled. But it was as if she'd bared her teeth at him instead. He sat back and looked away.

"We'll stay at Langford House," he said to the teeming street. "I've directed the post boys there."

"Your father's house?"

"Yes. They're in the country, of course."

"Of course?"

"No one's in town at this time of year."

"There are people everywhere," Kawena pointed out. She was seized by a desire to argue with him, to rouse some emotion, make him look at her. Also, his remark was nonsensical.

"Society is away, I meant."

"These people are not a part of English society?" She gestured at the street.

"Not by some people's measure."

He wasn't going to engage with her. It only made her want to push harder. "Why not go to an inn, as before?"

James closed his lips on the true answer—because he wasn't sure how to be alone with her anymore. Fighting a constant desire to take her in his arms was wearing on him. Langford House would be...safer. It was more spacious, and there would be servants constantly about. They wouldn't be in each other's pockets as they had been for all the tantalizing hours of this journey. It would be easier to protect her as well, and it would show anyone who might wonder that she was a friend of his family, to be respected. His parents already knew about Kawena. Or, Alan did, at least, which meant the rest of the family soon would. She wasn't a secret to keep.

As they rattled over a stretch of uneven cobblestones, he became conscious of another motive, which startled and puzzled him. He wanted to show Kawena what she'd cast aside when she rejected his proposal. Which was ridiculous. He was relieved that she didn't wish to be married. He'd gone over the reasons why it wouldn't have done at all. But it rankled to be dismissed as if he was some half-pay officer with no breeding or prospects. A look at Langford House would show her... What, exactly?

Taut with bewildered frustration, James shoved the thought out of his mind. The thing was to get this job done, fulfill his promise to help, and then return

Kawena to Ariel. After that… Well, that would be after. It would be over. Whatever "it" was.

They pulled up before the splendid facade of his father's town house in late afternoon. As one of the post boys went to ring the bell, James handed Kawena down from the chaise. The feel of her fingers in his elicited memories so physically intense that he dropped her hand.

The door was opened by a footman unfamiliar to James. He had a moment's uneasiness. If they were turned away… But the fellow recognized him right enough, and after a momentary flash of surprise, quickly hidden, he ushered them inside. Kawena gazed about the lofty entry with gratifying awe. "We've come to stay a day or two," James said. "No time to send word ahead, I'm afraid."

"Yes, my lord. If you'd care to sit in the drawing room, I'll inform Mrs. Hastings."

James didn't wish to wait anywhere. He wanted to go to his customary bedchamber and sit there, alone, until he was able to clear his muddled mind. But he couldn't abandon Kawena, so he led her up the grand staircase and into the indigo silk–draped parlor where his mother received visitors.

"All this is just for your family?" she asked.

He nodded.

She wandered about the room, examining the furnishings and ornaments, looking suitably impressed. He'd accomplished that much, at least. For whatever it was worth.

When a middle-aged, black-clad woman bustled in, James recognized her face, as he had not her name.

Mrs. Hastings was one of the main housekeeper's assistants. No doubt she'd been left in London to oversee the town house while most of the servants accompanied his parents to the country. James introduced Kawena as a friend of the family. Mrs. Hastings gave no sign that she found it odd for one of the duke's sons to arrive with an unattended young lady. She merely assured them that chambers were being prepared and invited Kawena to accompany her upstairs. Ignoring Kawena's uneasy glances, James seized his opportunity and fled.

Ten

WHEN JAMES CAME BACK DOWNSTAIRS SOME TWO hours later, refreshed but conscious that he hadn't inquired about the possibility of dinner, he was startled to hear his name called in a familiar voice. He turned from the foot of the stairs to find his brother Robert looking down at him from above. "What are you doing here?" Robert asked.

"I might ask the same," he replied, not really wishing to explain his presence. "Don't you have rooms of your own in town? And aren't you always *out* of town at this season?"

Robert descended the steps with the languid grace of an acknowledged Pink of the *ton*. As always, in his next oldest brother's presence, James felt a bit shabby. Even in full dress uniform, he couldn't compete. Robert could look elegant covered in molasses and chicken feathers, as James had reason to know. Now, dressed in immaculate pantaloons, a coat that might have been an advertisement for his tailor, and a neckcloth of dizzying complexity, he was a sight to rouse sighs of envy from any aspirant to fashion.

"I do," he replied. "And I am. Certain...matters have kept me in London this summer."

"Matters?"

Robert raised one russet eyebrow. "Rather like whatever brought you here, perhaps? You hate London."

Face to face in the entry hall, the brothers eyed each other. His greater height ought to give him an advantage, James thought. But Robert's assurance more than overcame that factor. The friendly rivalry that had always bubbled amongst their crew of six brothers surfaced. They were at an impasse. Then, to his surprise, Robert conceded a crumb of information. "I stopped by to look for a book in Papa's library," he said.

This made no sense. Robert didn't read. It was one of the things they had in common. James wondered if this was some sort of diversion, and what Robert could really be up to.

"I thought he might have a copy of Rolfe's *History of the Assyrian Empire*, but it appears I was mistaken."

"History of the...what?" These were not words he would ever have expected to hear from Robert's lips.

"We need a citation," Robert added absently, tapping his fingers on the curving banister.

James hadn't seen his brother since Nathaniel's wedding some weeks ago. Could he have gone mad in that short period of time? "What the devil are you talking about?"

Robert acknowledged his bewilderment with a half smile. "I'm involved in a...contest of sorts. With a certain young lady."

"A contest that includes history books and...what was it, Assyrians? What the deuce is an Assyrian?"

"They were an ancient people. Byron mentions them in one of his poems." To James's utter astonishment, he proceeded to recite a few lines. "'The Assyrian came down like the wolf on the fold, And his cohorts were gleaming in purple and gold; And the sheen of their spears was like stars on the sea, When the blue wave rolls nightly on deep Galilee.'" He shrugged. "Pathetic doggerel, she calls it. Can't say I disagree."

James realized that his mouth was hanging open. He closed it. But he remained incapable of speech.

Robert laughed. "I don't wonder you're surprised," he said. "I often am myself. I'm attempting to prove that I'm not a useless fribble, you see."

"To this 'young lady'?"

Robert nodded.

"Why?" James knew that Robert attracted plenty of female attention, with scarcely any effort. He'd seen girls fluttering 'round his brother at the *ton* parties he'd been harried into attending.

"Why indeed?" was the incomprehensible reply.

"I never knew you to take so much trouble for a girl."

"Perhaps I never encountered such a challenge."

That sounded like nonsense. Robert had never appeared interested in meeting any challenges, particularly over a woman. Lounging and primping and ironic amusement were more his style.

"But you haven't said what you're doing here," his brother added, clearly changing the subject. "Are you preparing to go to sea again?"

"Er, no. I'm…helping out a…family friend." It sounded weak in James's ears. Actually, he was surprised that Robert hadn't yet gotten the news about Kawena's arrival. The family grapevine was usually much faster than that. Preternaturally fast, in fact.

"Friend?" he echoed.

"Hello?"

James turned to find Kawena standing on the stairs above them. Robert raised his eyebrows and said, "Ah."

James wanted to tell him that there wasn't any "ah" involved. But that wouldn't have helped. Nor would it have been quite true.

Kawena looked down at Lord James and a man who must be one of his brothers. The latter gazed back at her with alert curiosity. Lord James seemed uncomfortable, and Kawena earnestly wished herself elsewhere.

She was overwhelmed by this huge house and its silent-footed servants. Sitting upstairs in the opulent bedchamber assigned to her, she'd heard no sounds at all. The din of London was erased inside these walls, which should have been pleasant, but was in fact rather eerie. Mrs. Hastings had been kind enough, but distant, perhaps disapproving. Kawena hadn't been able to read her expression. The reception here had been so different from Ariel's easy welcome. She had been made to understand, without a word being spoken, that it wasn't the usual thing for her to arrive with only Lord James. This must be a taste of the censure Lord James had threatened. And while she didn't truly care what Mrs. Hastings thought of her, she didn't like feeling at a disadvantage, and she resented being stowed out of sight like surplus cargo.

Uncertain if she was supposed to wait for a summons before leaving the bedchamber, she had muttered and paced. Finally, she'd had to escape the hushed, solitary elegance. Why couldn't they have gone to an inn? Only as she gazed down at the two men in the entryway did it occur to her that inns cost money. She hadn't considered Lord James's purse. This thoughtless lapse made her flush with embarrassment and feel even more off balance.

"This is my brother Robert," Lord James said. "Robert, this is Miss Kawena Benson, a…a friend of Ariel's."

"Ah, Ariel's," he replied, as if this explained something.

Why had he called her that? This wasn't part of the "story" they had agreed to tell. Now she would be expected to know things about Ariel, to provide a history of acquaintance that she did not possess. And why did Lord James look so unhappy? Was it this new brother? Kawena examined him. He was slighter than the ones she'd met so far, with a narrower face and paler coloring; his hair was closer to red than auburn. His clothes had a subtle cut and drape that suggested both care and expense. Even an outsider like Kawena could tell he was very fashionable. She wondered if he was one of the dandies her father had mocked.

Lord Robert offered her a beautiful bow. "Delighted to meet you."

After a long moment, Kawena remembered to curtsy. People actually did this. She'd seen it during her journey. When her father had explained the gesture years ago, with a very amusing demonstration, she hadn't taken it seriously.

"I'm sad to say that I haven't heard from Ariel or

Alan lately," Robert added. He walked gracefully up the stairs and offered Kawena an arm. "You must tell me all about yourself."

"We're on our way out," said Lord James.

"Indeed? Where to?"

Kawena watched Lord Robert glance from her to his brother. His expression conveyed polite skepticism, as if silently noting that they wore no hats or other outdoor garments.

"In a moment," Lord James amended.

He didn't wish to talk to his brother, Kawena thought. Or, he didn't wish her to talk to him. Why not?

Lord Robert ignored him. "Surely you have time for a bit of conversation?" he asked Kawena.

"No!" said Lord James.

Abruptly tired of catering to his moods and of trying to figure out what silly story he wanted to tell this time, Kawena took the offered arm. Lord James had been impossible since their…interlude by the sea. It wasn't fair. She realized that she'd rather enjoy making him as uncomfortable as she'd been feeling. And she was not going to be dragged off again without consultation. "Of course," she said.

Lord Robert led her back to the drawing room. "Ring for some Madeira," he said to Lord James. "And perhaps…" He looked at Kawena. "Are you hungry?"

Kawena nodded. She'd been hoping there was some sort of dinner in the offing.

"I expect Mrs. Hastings could conjure a few sandwiches."

With a thunderous glance, Lord James went to ring the bell.

"Splendid." Lord Robert sat down beside her on a sofa, looking very much in charge. "Now, tell me all."

Kawena glanced at her traveling companion. He appeared to be sulking. That was it. She'd had enough. "I'm not really a friend of Ariel's," she said. "I met her when I tried to shoot Lord James." Of course she hadn't planned to actually fire the gun, but she enjoyed the astonishment on her listener's face almost as much as the chagrin on Lord James's. There was an art to telling a story, after all. "I thought he had stolen my father's treasure, you see."

"Treasure," echoed Lord Robert, his blue eyes alight with interest. "This sounds like quite a tale."

"There is no tale," interjected his brother. "It was a mistake. And I would appreciate it if you would not—"

The footman appeared. Lord Robert requested the wine and sustenance with assured charm, then turned back to Kawena.

"Well, he did convince me that he had not taken it," she continued. "Eventually. But it looked very bad. His ship was the only one that had visited the island at the time it went missing, you see."

"Island?" prompted Lord Robert.

"My home."

"Ah, you met at one of James's far-flung ports of call?" He looked back and forth between them speculatively.

"We never met. My father would not have allowed it."

"Miss Benson's father, a respectable Englishman, had settled there," put in Lord James. "In the South Seas."

The word "respectable" rankled a bit. Did he

imagine she required his endorsement? "I had to track down the thief, of course," Kawena added.

"Did you?" Lord Robert appeared to be fascinated by the idea.

She looked at him. "Of course. No one else was going to do it."

"Why shouldn't she?" put in Lord James, unexpectedly belligerent.

"Why not indeed?"

"So we are questioning the ship's crew to find the one responsible," Kawena finished.

"James's ship. You and he." He cocked his head at her, blandly affable.

"Correct." Kawena had no idea what he really thought. She didn't think she cared. She was weary of puzzling over these Englishmen. And very hungry indeed.

The footman returned with a tray. Kawena quickly devoured several small sandwiches and drank a glass of wine, conscious of Lord Robert's speculative gaze. His brother was irritatingly silent.

When the plate was empty, Lord Robert said, "I know a young lady who would be most interested to meet you. I think you would like her as well. Why don't you both come along with me to a gathering at her house tonight?"

"A lady?" Kawena looked down at her rumpled gown. Lord James had made it very clear that ladies would be the ones most likely to disapprove of her. And the English seemed positively fanatical about proper dress. It was one thing to twit the Gresham brothers, another to venture into the perilous waters of "society."

"Out of the question," Lord James declared. "We're not in town to make visits."

"It wouldn't be a formal call," his brother said. "More of a family occasion. The hostess is a second cousin of ours. A connection of Mama's, that is. It would be a chance for Miss Benson to see a bit of London."

"She doesn't like London."

The fact that he was right did not make his arrogance any more palatable. And perhaps there were parts of the city that she would like. How did he know?

"You have something else to do this evening?" Lord Robert asked.

"We don't need anything else to do."

It was too much. The appearance of his brother seemed to have turned Lord James into a tyrant. She would not have decisions made for her in this high-handed way. "I'd be happy to go," said Kawena.

Lord James turned on her. "You will do no such thing!"

"I beg your pardon. You do not dictate my choices. I'm sure Lord Robert will escort me if you don't wish to go."

"You're not going out alone with Robert!"

The latter was watching them with what appeared to be rapt fascination. Kawena did not point out that she had been going all sorts of places alone with *him*, Nor did Lord Robert, though she suspected that he wanted to.

"We are here to catch a thief, and for no other reason," added Lord James. "We have no time for visits."

"You were planning to question someone tonight?" Kawena asked.

"No, but—"

"Then I don't see why we should not—"

"You will do as I say!"

Kawena sprang to her feet. "Can we go right now?" she said to Lord Robert.

He checked the mantel clock and nodded amiably. "I'll tell the footman to find us a hack."

"I suppose I have to put on a bonnet."

"Not necessary for an evening party."

"Oh, good," Kawena replied, moving toward the drawing room door.

Lord James blocked her path. "I do not think this is a good—"

She put a hand in the middle of his chest and pushed. He jerked away as if her touch burned. Hurt by this excessive reaction, Kawena jostled past him and strode out.

⁂

In the end, they all three crowded into a cab. Distracted by the feel of Kawena's shoulder pressed against his, James didn't hear the address Robert gave the driver. Indeed, as they rattled off, he was plagued by an unfamiliar anxiety. Although his mother was the kindest of women, she had some really prickly relations, and he feared that this lady they were going to see might be rude to Kawena. A great many society matrons would be—an unknown young woman showing up uninvited, accompanied only by him and his brother. Kawena had no idea how unpleasant such society people could be. Though when he came to think of it, the high sticklers weren't likely to be in town at this time of year. James sat back in the seat, somewhat relieved.

He couldn't figure what game Robert was playing. His next oldest brother had a chancy sense of humor. Some of his pranks were hilarious; some were excruciating. Mostly, it depended on which side of the joke you found yourself inhabiting, of course. In this case, it seemed to him that they were instruments for bedeviling the mysterious young lady who was fond of Assyrians. And who knew how she would take it? Or what she would do when she discovered the jape. God only knew what lay in store for them, and how he would manage to shield Kawena from harm.

He was well aware that he'd made a muddle of it so far. Sparks had practically shot from her eyes when he suggested—all right, insisted—that they stay at home. The words hadn't come out right. He'd meant it for the best, for her own good. But it had emerged like an order from the quarterdeck.

He simply didn't know how to be with her now. He wanted to protect her, and to drag her into his arms and kiss her senseless. He wanted to force her to be sensible and to throw all caution to the winds. He wanted to offer her every measure of respect, and he…simply wanted her. Desperately. To top it off, her reactions were unpredictable. How could he save her if he never knew which way she would jump? Her presence, especially so intoxicatingly near, was twisting him into knots.

James noticed that they'd left London's fashionable precincts. "Where the deuce are you taking us?" he asked his brother.

"It's over near Russell Square. A most respectable address, I assure you."

James didn't care for his tone. Robert sounded amused and self-deprecating and...altogether unlike himself. "Exactly what relation is this we're going to see?" he finally thought to ask.

"Aunt Agatha."

"What?" James sprang upright and bumped his head, quite hard, on the hackney's ceiling. Bouncing off it, he fell back into his seat. The carriage rocked on its aged springs.

"All right in there?" inquired the driver from his outside perch.

"We're fine," responded Robert.

James goggled at him. "We're going to call on the dragon who stuck her parasol right through Sebastian's kite when it came too near her? The one who told Mama we were as uncivilized as a pack of wolves?"

"We *did* stage that...unsuccessful footrace in the long gallery," Robert pointed out. "We almost knocked her down the back stairs."

James rubbed his skull and muttered, "How could anyone know the servants had waxed *half* the floor?"

Robert laughed at the memory. "She's not as intimidating as you remember."

"No one could be," James said.

"Who is this?" asked Kawena.

"Oh, my God," said James. Aunt Agatha would annihilate them with one scorching look. If she found out anything about their plan, she'd call them benighted fools. And what might she say to Kawena?

"Who?" repeated Kawena.

"She's one of our mother's cousins, though we called her Aunt," James replied. "Out of respect for her…manner."

"We couldn't quite call her 'Cousin Agatha,'" Robert agreed. "She wasn't anything like our other cousins. And she's about the same age as Mama."

"Not really?" James had trouble putting the two in the same category.

"She's very pleasant when she's not being plagued by a raging pack of boys," Robert said. "In fact, she's charming."

The carriage turned and slowed, moving past a large, imposing building.

"The British Museum," Robert told them.

"How do you know that?" James wondered.

"Aunt Agatha's husband was a well-known scholar," his brother continued without acknowledging the question. "He chose to live out here to be close to the collections."

"Collections of what?" James's harried brain managed a connection of sorts. "Assyrians?"

"Objects to do with Assyrians," Robert replied.

James thought he looked positively furtive. Which was unprecedented. Robert never looked furtive.

"What are Assyrians?" asked Kawena, frowning over the word.

"What in God's name are you up to?" James demanded.

Robert met his eyes, and James tried to interpret his expression. He simply didn't look like himself. Was that uncertainty in his most assured brother's eyes? It couldn't be.

"It's a simple matter, I promise you. I truly think that…the Jennings will like Miss Benson. And she them."

"Yes, but why would you care about that?" James wondered. As far as he could recall, Robert was not in the habit of arranging cordial introductions to benefit other people. Not that he *wouldn't*, if you pressed him, and reminded him—several times. But he was usually far too occupied with his own amusements.

"It's…kind to connect people who may become friends," said Robert.

"Kind? What sort of mischief are you making here?"

"Do you think me unkind?"

It seemed a sincere question. Meeting his brother's—slightly worried?—gaze, James found himself speechless.

Robert gave him a wry smile. He put a hand to his immaculate shirtfront and bowed his head. "I swear to you that I am not making mischief. On my word of honor."

James had to be content with this—or, more correctly, confused by it—since the cab stopped just then before a large redbrick house. It stood in a prosperous-looking square, the center lush with plantings washed gold by the long summer twilight.

Robert paid off the driver and went to knock on the front door. They were admitted at once and conducted upstairs. James eyed the large slab of stone hanging at the head of the staircase. It depicted an animal, a lion he thought, with the head of a man wearing a tall pointy crown over an elaborate curled wig. Or perhaps it was his own hair. But who had hair like that? The image's expression seemed distinctly disapproving. James felt as if its eye followed him as he climbed. What kind of household had Robert brought them to?

There were other unusual ornaments in the drawing room—a wicked-looking spear over the mantel, an array of clay tablets incised with what looked like chicken tracks, mounted on the opposite wall. The sofas and chairs were quite conventional, however. A dozen or so people stood and sat about chatting. Mostly older and dowdily dressed, they reminded James of Alan's colleagues. At least their lack of evening dress would cause no comment here. Indeed, fashion seemed an unlikely topic in this room. Robert had been honest in that, at least.

The woman who stepped forward to greet them was tall and sturdily built, with sharp blue eyes and an aquiline nose, her dark hair gathered into a knot at her neck. It took a moment for James to recognize Aunt Agatha. He hadn't seen her in years. Then something about the tilt of her prominent chin did the trick.

"Aunt Agatha, this is Miss Kawena Benson, a… friend of the family," said Robert. "And perhaps you remember my brother James?"

Their hostess nodded in response to their bow and curtsy, "The naval officer, isn't it? Miss Benson. How do you do?" She seemed unfazed by the arrival of strangers.

"I thought the evening would interest them," Robert continued.

This was going too far. "What sort of evening is it?" asked James. "Is there going to be a lecture?" He ignored reproachful glances from both his companions.

Aunt Agatha gave him a sharp look, a little like those she'd bestowed on impertinent boys in his memories. "We are marking my late husband's birthday by gathering to celebrate his legacy," she answered.

"He was an authority on the Assyrians," added Robert quickly. "Most particularly on their language, which was called Akkadian."

James rolled his eyes, waiting for the full brunt of his brother's prank to fall upon them, but nothing happened other than Aunt Agatha saying, "You are welcome to join us." More bewildered than ever, James allowed Robert to lead them over to a knot of people in the corner. At the edge of the group, not really part of it, stood a tall young woman with black hair and pale skin. She held herself very straight, and her face echoed the beauty of the antique cameo fastening the neck of her pearl-gray gown. James might have put her down as the meek daughter of the household, but then he met her eyes. Their intense blue suggested that a fiery spirit burned behind her serene facade.

Robert gave her a graceful bow. "Miss Jennings, may I present Miss Kawena Benson and my brother, Lord James," Robert said. He nodded to his companions. "This is Miss Flora Jennings, Aunt Agatha's daughter."

"Flora?" James connected the name, if not the face, to an errant memory. "Wasn't it you who pushed that beastly Teddy Raines into the lake after he stole my boat and smashed it into my head?"

"I can't abide bullying," she replied coolly.

"He was a great hulking fellow of nine or ten,"

James recalled for the others. "I was six or so, I suppose." He smiled at Miss Jennings. "You can't have been much older, but you gave him a splendid shove. I seem to remember that he screamed like a stuck pig."

"As if he could have drowned in water up to his knees," she replied, a smile lightening her expression. She looked much less reserved when she smiled.

"Miss Benson is from the South Seas," Robert said, with something of the air of a cat dropping a mouse at Flora Jennings's feet.

The smile faded. "Indeed?"

James wondered what his brother had done to offend this young woman? Or, perhaps offend wasn't right. She seemed extremely wary, however.

"I thought you two would get on, as you're both…"

Flora Jennings raised her dark brows and waited. *Robert usually shows far more finesse than this*, James thought.

"Fascinating," Robert finished adroitly. "And you were bemoaning the fact that you have so few women friends."

Miss Jennings stiffened as if he'd insulted her. "Bemoaning! I never did any such thing."

"You did, when you were talking to your mother at the Manelcto concert."

The girl's pale cheeks reddened slightly. "Do you make a habit of listening to private conversations?"

"It was an accident. I was just coming to ask if you wanted some lemonade."

James watched their eyes lock. They seemed to have forgotten there was anyone else present. Belatedly, James finished making the connection. He'd been uncharacteristically slow. This was the young lady Robert was trying to impress, the object of his "contest." And she was the reason they were here. Not as a prank, but as a…gift? A diversion? Why Robert should have fixed upon a young woman so unlike his usual flirts remained a mystery.

Miss Jennings blinked and turned to Kawena. "What brings you to England from so far away?" she asked, polite rather than warm.

"I'm hunting a thief," Kawena replied.

The other woman looked startled.

"It might be best not to repeat the story in public," James suggested. You never knew what connections might stretch out from a room full of strangers.

Kawena gave him a sharp glance.

"I can fill you in later," Robert offered.

"I have no interest in prying—"

"Flora, my dear," interrupted an old man in the nearby group. "Who was that fellow who first deciphered the royal names from the cuneiform?"

"Niebuhr," said Robert.

"Grotefend," corrected Flora.

"Yes, yes, that's the one," replied the old man, nodding happily and returning to his conversation.

"For some reason, Lord Robert pretends an interest in my father's work," Flora told the others.

"I'm not pretending! How many times must I say it?"

"Until you tire of the game, I suppose."

Robert's hands flexed—closed, open. James actually felt sorry for him. "Shall we get a glass of wine?" he asked him.

Robert drew in a breath, recovered some of his customary aplomb, and nodded. "May we bring something for you ladies?"

"No, thank you," said Miss Jennings. Kawena shook her head.

The two young women watched the brothers walk away, their expressions remarkably similar.

"Did Lord Robert ask you to speak to me?" said Flora Jennings without turning.

"I met him for the first time today," replied Kawena. "Hardly an hour ago, in fact. Speak to you about what?"

"His imaginary interest in…" She made a weary gesture at the room. "All of it."

"Is there some reason that you don't believe he is sincere?" Kawena had been struck by the interplay between Lord James's brother and this coolly attractive woman. Perhaps her disputes with Lord James were not so unusual? Maybe the English enjoyed sniping at each other? Made an art of it? Did that explain things about her father and mother?

"Men like him are never sincere."

"Like him?"

Miss Jennings finally turned to look at her. Her eyes were a fiery blue. It was a powerful gaze. "Pinks of the *ton*. Their lives are devoted to amusement and frivolity. And the latest fads and fashions, of course."

"I don't understand the expression. Why do they call them pink?"

The other woman blinked. "I…I don't know."

"They wear pink clothing perhaps?"

Miss Jennings choked out a laugh. "No. That is, I

have never seen... It's just a bit of slang. I have no idea where it originated."

Kawena nodded. She was more interested in the subtleties of relationship than in oddities of language. "People sometimes change, I suppose? Perhaps he is no longer so...pink?"

"He'd like me to think so," Miss Jennings muttered darkly.

"Why would he?"

"That's the question, isn't it?"

It seemed to Kawena that there was an obvious answer. "If he likes you...?"

"Likes!"

"Why shouldn't he?"

"We have nothing in common. I do not frequent the exalted circles into which he was born. I have no interest in flirtation, and I certainly will not be seduced."

Her eyes flashed with conviction. Kawena knew enough not to suggest that her reaction was a bit extreme. And the mention of seduction cut rather too close.

"But why are we talking of Lord Robert?" the other continued. "You must tell me more about yourself. What thief are you hunting? What is your home like, so very far away?"

Kawena obliged by describing the island and her father's arrival there. She also gave a few details of her quest for the jewel thief, as there was no one nearby to eavesdrop just now. Miss Jennings seemed fascinated.

"You are quite intrepid, aren't you?" she commented when Kawena finished.

"Sometimes I am," she agreed. "But I worry I will never find the one who took my father's treasure."

"I hope you will. But even having tried is inspiring. I should be proud to have acted so decisively."

She smiled at Kawena, and they exchanged a most cordial look. Kawena felt that they really could be good friends, given an opportunity. But just then Mrs. Jennings came to fetch Flora, leading her off to a group on the other side of the room. Lord James walked over to take her place.

"Your brother and Miss Jennings are…?" Kawena didn't know what word to use.

"I have no idea," he replied. "She's not his type at all. I can't think what he's doing."

"Seduction?" wondered Kawena. The word had stuck in her mind.

He started as if she had jabbed him with a fishhook. "Of course not! Robert would never contemplate such a thing."

The word did not apply to her either, Kawena thought. She had done as she pleased, not been lured into…whatever the English thought that word implied.

"The cuneiform is sadly fragmentary on this point," said someone behind them. "I don't believe it is possible to determine a reference."

"I suppose he's gone mad," continued Lord James. "Like the rest of us."

"The rest of whom?" inquired a cool voice. Flora had returned as they talked.

"Are all the duke's sons quite irritating?" Kawena put in, resenting his characterization of her, and their quest, as "mad."

"Well, I haven't seen Randolph or James since I was a child." Miss Jennings eyed their companion as if trying to make a quick judgment. "Nathaniel is rather stuffy, I think. Sebastian thinks far too much of himself. Alan's not bad; his scientific work is impressive."

"And Robert?" asked Lord James.

Flora's gaze found him across the room. "An enigma."

"But you like puzzles," he found himself pointing out. And then wondered where that had come from.

The glance she gave him was wide and startled. Kawena was nearly as surprised. Just when she thought him incapable of noticing what was going on right before his eyes, he said something that showed he was very aware indeed.

Eleven

LORD JAMES SPENT THE NEXT TWO DAYS VISITING former crew members around London. He did not allow Kawena to don her boy's clothes and accompany him, reminding her that his men would talk much more freely to him alone. Although she suspected his preoccupation with scandal was also involved, she had to admit the logic of this and stay behind. She spent the time wandering around his family's huge house, occasionally speaking to a servant, looking at its furnishings, and going slowly mad from an unsettling combination of boredom and hope. She tried books from the library, a newspaper she found in the entry hall, but nothing held her attention for long. Finally, she took to pacing long corridors like a restless ghost, to work off some of her impatience.

And in the end, it was all for naught. "It was the same as in Portsmouth," Lord James told her on the second evening. "No one seemed to know anything. I sailed with these men for years, most of them. I'm well acquainted with their quirks and eva-sions, and I didn't spot any lies. I even tried another visit to that fellow at the Admiralty, but he had no more information."

Kawena sat on the drawing room sofa with her hands folded tightly in her lap. She was afraid that if she moved, she would fly into a thousand pieces. This was it. This was failure.

"I don't know what more I can do," he went on. "I simply don't believe that any of my crew took those jewels. Sailors live in very close quarters on shipboard, you know, even the officers. And a voyage has long, boring stretches. They notice anything unusual, and they talk about it. Someone hiding a treasure... I simply can't see it."

Her lower lip was threatening to tremble. Kawena bit it, hard, to hold back any hint of tears. That would be too humiliating.

Lord James glanced at her uneasily. "I'm very sorry. But...I've done what I promised. I don't see what else... We'll head back to Oxford tomorrow."

There had to be something. But Kawena couldn't think of a next step.

"I'll see about a post chaise," he said, sounding increasingly uncomfortable. "Are you...have you heard what I said?"

"Yes," said Kawena. Unable to bear the pitying, uneasy look in his eyes, she sprang to her feet and rushed out of the room.

In her borrowed bedchamber, she paced some more. She couldn't accept the idea that her quest was over, ending in disaster. Yet she'd tried every idea. She'd used up all her resources, including the amount of help Lord James was willing to offer. Having sat with him and some of his crew in Portsmouth, she believed what he said about his men. He did know them. However…her father's hoard had been taken. If not by someone on the *Charis*…

Kawena had questioned everyone at home. More importantly, her mother had done the same. And people on Valatu did not lie to her mother. They might wish to. They might plan to. But she had an uncanny ability to detect falsehoods. Indeed, she had uncovered a number of petty sins during the hunt for the jewels. They were not there.

But where in the wide world were they? And what was she going to do?

Kawena strode from one side of the luxurious bed-chamber to the other, feeling like the caged tiger she had seen during her long voyage here. She supposed that Lord James's family would lend her money for the passage home. Or…why pretend? It would not be a loan, but a gift. And they wouldn't care. The sum would be nothing to them. They would give it to her, care-lessly, kindly, and she would fade into their memories to become an amusing story, part of the Gresham family lore. The idea grated on her sensibilities. She would never see Lord James again, and he wouldn't care a whit. She would make her way back to a small life on the island. Her mother would see that she had a place there, as a dependent. Although she missed her family, the prospect did not appeal. It felt stark and empty.

The hour grew late, but Kawena knew that sleep was impossible. She didn't even try getting into bed. Her mind insisted upon going over and over her situation, as if repetition might produce a solution.

It did not.

She paced some more. Movement was a little better than stillness. It was the illusion of action, at least. It used some of the pent-up energy that made her want to run and flail and shout with frustration.

She was still at it when the first light of dawn showed at the windows. Although she was finally a little tired, Kawena still couldn't rest. She left her chamber, craving more space, and wandered the house again. She was up before the few servants who cared for this huge dwelling that was used for only months out of the year. She strode through room after room. She would never fit into this kind of life, she thought. The · place was oppressive—windows shrouded by layers of draperies, walls crowded up against other grand houses, with closed gardens and fenced squares. Barrier after barrier between the people and the outdoors. She found it hard to breathe here, sometimes.

Kawena came to a door at the end of a hallway in the back of the house. Her feet had led her here, unthinking. She opened it and went through, into a small parlor papered in stripes of cream and deep green. The draperies and carpet were the same dark green, and shelves held a collection of books, ornaments, and odd little items. Kawena had discovered that this was the duchess's private parlor, told by a young maid who seemed almost afraid of the place. She'd dared to sit here, even though it felt like a kind of trespass. The room had an air of ease and contentment that she hadn't found in other parts of the house.

She went over to stand before the arrangement of six small portraits on the far wall. When she'd asked the maid, she'd told her that these were the Gresham brothers, each painted at the age of five years. It was easy to pick out Lord James from among them. Though the boys all resembled one another in coloring, they had their unique looks. What was it like to be the mother of such an array of sons, the mistress of all this? she wondered. And the duchess had charge of several other big houses, too, she'd heard. It seemed to her as if it would be more burden than gift.

Kawena walked the perimeter of the room, absently running her fingers along the shelves and chair rail in the growing morning light. She looked at the informal clutter of objects the duchess had chosen to put here. She could like the person who accumulated and arranged this collection, she thought. But it was unlikely she would ever get to meet her.

The sun climbed a bit higher, and an errant sunbeam lanced through the half-open draperies and struck the upper corner of the room, gilding it with light. The sudden illumination caught Kawena's eye, and what seemed a familiar shape held it. There was something tucked away on the highest shelf, half-hidden by a row of books. Frowning up at it, Kawena moved closer. It couldn't be, but…

She fetched the chair that sat before the writing desk and set it below the shelves. Climbing onto it, she reached up. Her fingers were still inches below the object. From this nearer distance, she could see that it was imperative she get her hands on it.

She examined the shelves. They were thick and solid, built into the wall, immoveable. Clearing a space on the one just above the chair, she pulled back her skirts and placed one foot onto the painted wood. Gripping a higher shelf with both hands, she stepped up until she was standing on the shelf. Carefully, she reached again.

This time, she got it.

Taking care not to fall, she lowered herself to the chair, and the floor. She took her prize over to the window. The small, squat wooden figure had a large head and a greatly exaggerated male organ. About six inches tall, it was a type of carving produced on her island, mostly for sale to foreign traders. And she'd noticed as soon as she lifted it that it was far heavier than it ought to be.

Her heart beating fast, Kawena turned the figure over and ran her fingers around the base. There was an almost invisible crack; she could feel it. She needed a tool. With growing urgency, she scanned the room. There was a bronze letter opener on the desk. In the next moment, she was inserting the tip into the crevice in the wood. It resisted. She wiggled and pried until, slowly, the crack widened, revealing the outlines of a square plug. She twisted and pushed harder until at last the bit of wood popped out. Beneath it was a cloth bag, stuffed in the figure's hollow interior. Kawena pulled it out and untied the drawstring. Inside nestled her father's hard-won hoard of jewels, glinting up at her like laughing eyes, and like salvation.

Amazement and relief made her knees weak. Letting the wooden plug drop, she half fell into an armchair, clutching the bag close. The treasure had been here, right here, all this time. She'd found it. She'd succeeded—just when she'd given up believing that she could. Her long voyage had been worth it. Everything was all right. Except...

Outrage brought her bolt upright in the chair.

Lord James had lied to her! He *was* the thief. He'd hidden the jewels right here in his house, his family's house. He'd humored and cajoled her, gone through the pretense of talking to his crew, when all the time he'd known he had them. Perhaps he'd exulted in that knowledge, enjoyed deceiving her...

But even in her fury, logic brought Kawena up short. That, and her observations of Lord James over these last weeks. Would any thief, even the most daring, bring her here and leave her alone to explore the house, when she might do exactly as she had done and find his hiding place? There had been no need to come here. She need never have entered the place. It was stupid, and even if Lord James had somehow been able to disguise his thieving nature, she knew he wasn't stupid. She looked down at the bag of jewels in her hands. It made no sense.

Kawena sprang to her feet. She snatched up the now-empty figure and stalked out into the corridor, down it, and up a flight of stairs. A left turn, another hall, and then a closed door, which she pounded on with the carving before shoving the panels open and striding through. The door swung shut with a click behind her.

Inside a bedchamber less opulent than the one she'd been given, Lord James sat up in bed, blinking. She rushed over to him and thrust the figure at him. With her other hand, she shook the bag of jewels, making them rattle. "They were right here all the time!"

"What? What are you doing in my room?"

"Right here, all the time," she repeated, louder. "The jewels were right here!"

Lord James caught her wrist and pushed the wooden figure away from his face. His fingers were like steel bands, his strength irresistible. Belatedly, it occurred to Kawena that it might not have been wise to confront a wily thief alone, in his bedchamber, with only his family's servants to witness anything he might do. She yanked her arm free and stepped back.

He appeared to be still shaking off sleep. "You shouldn't be in my room," was all he said.

Kawena moved farther toward the door. But she still wanted answers. She still couldn't believe that this man was a consummate deceiver. "I found my father's jewels inside this figure in your mother's parlor," she told him. She held up the carving and the bag.

He stared. She watched comprehension, and then astonishment, cross his face. They looked unfeigned. "That thing? I sent that to Mama as a joke, months ago." He rubbed a hand through his hair, blinked again. "I send her odd bits and pieces from all my ports of call. She likes to get some sense of what I'm seeing."

"But how did you get this?" Kawena demanded. She shook the figure again. "There is no way you could have—"

"Well, I didn't steal it! You may be sure of that."

"No one would have given it to—"

He held up a hand. The sleeve of his nightshirt slid down to bare a muscular forearm. "Wait."

Impatiently, Kawena did so.

Lord James frowned. "I must have bought it. I buy

trinkets wherever the ship stops. I don't even think about it anymore. It's a habit."

His puzzlement seemed genuine. Kawena relaxed just a little. "No one would have sold you this at the trading center on Valatu. Not with my father's jewels hidden inside. It would never have been on the shelves. My brother would never have——"

"Wait," he said again. He frowned as if working through a knotty problem. "It was a boy," he said finally. "I'm remembering now. I thought nothing of it at the time." He threw back the coverlet and started to rise, giving Kawena an enticing view of his bare legs beneath his nightshirt. She remembered those legs quite vividly, in far more pleasant circumstances. He pulled the coverlet back up.

"I'd come to make the final payment," Lord James went on. "After all the supplies we'd ordered had been delivered to the ship. And the man I'd dealt with before wasn't there."

"My brother," said Kawena.

He nodded. "As I know now. There was only this boy around the place. He assured me I could leave the coin with him. I was in a hurry, and he kept on chattering——"

"Atui," concluded Kawena. "My brother's oldest son. He talks before he thinks. He would surely have been instructed to fetch my brother for any business."

"Well, he didn't," said Lord James. "He just talked in a funny sort of half English."

"He's very smart," said Kawena.

"I'm sure he is. And enterprising. He tried to sell me all sorts of things. I expect he'll be taking over the trading one day. And do well at it."

"This figure," she said, holding it up again.

"Right. I'd seen some of...those. Crew members had bought them from canoes that came up to the ship, and I thought my mother—"

"Would find it funny," Kawena supplied with a spark of resentment.

"Well, in a way." Lord James looked a bit sheepish. "So I told him I'd take one. This boy looked, and at first found nothing. Then he ran into the back and brought that figure out. He must have asked a small sum, or I would remember. I'm sure I readily gave it. It was over in a moment. I bought some other things as well. As I said, I always do. There was nothing memorable about the transaction." He sounded defensive. "I sent that off to my mother with the next courier we encountered."

"And Papa had an apoplexy when he found it gone," Kawena said sadly. "So he couldn't tell me what had happened." She bit her lip.

"There were some coconut-shell carvings," Lord James added. "I'm not sure where they've gotten to. I have chests of things from my voyages. They store them in the attic at Langford." He moved as if to get out of bed again, then stayed put. "You will say I should have thought of this, but how could I possibly have imagined that—"

"Papa would leave his treasure sitting out in plain sight?"

"Well, yes."

She nodded. It did seem like a foolish thing to do. But her father was not a fool.

"I suppose it might have been to throw people off

the scent," he suggested. "People on the island must have known he had the gems. And not every single one can be honest."

"No." Kawena could think of several islanders she would not have trusted with secrets.

"They wouldn't have thought to search for them in such a place."

Kawena nodded. There was also the fact that her father's office at the trading center had been sacrosanct. Indeed, it was usually locked up. But Atui got into everything, and he was notorious for not "hearing" rules. He couldn't have had any notion what he'd done. He'd probably been proud of himself for making a sale.

"The important thing is, you've recovered your inheritance."

"Yes." Kawena sighed with relief, both at this happy truth and the fact that Lord James had not turned out to be a thief. She hadn't been wrong about him. She'd known she couldn't be. Yet... She realized that she'd been holding the carving by its most prominent feature, conveniently placed like a handle. Laughing, she held it up to share the joke with Lord James.

The burning look she got in return sent a flush of heat along her skin. He was so close, really, in the tumbled bed, his bare chest enticing through the open neck of his nightshirt, his auburn hair tousled. They were alone, together, in a house that still slept. Her fingers tightened on the carving.

Lord James's eyes were so very blue, like the ocean off the edge of a reef. She had a sudden intensely tactile memory of his hands on her, his lips driving her wild.

Kawena stepped nearer, holding his gaze, setting the figure and the bag of gems on the small table beside the bed. She reached out and ran her fingers lightly along his collarbone, and down.

"We can't," he murmured, his voice hoarse. "Not here." He didn't draw back, however.

Kawena began to unbutton her gown.

"We can't," he repeated, with somewhat less conviction, she thought. "The servants…"

She shrugged off that concern, and her dress. It fell into a puddle of fabric at her feet.

"You mustn't." His tone was clearly halfhearted this time.

The cumbersome English undergarments took a little longer. *Probably some of the disapproving gossips he was always talking of invented these cursed laces*, Kawena thought.

Lord James groaned as she stripped off her shift. "I'm not made of stone, Kawena."

She glanced at the bedclothes, which showed a clear sign of his arousal. "Some of you almost might be." Laughing, she threw her arms around his neck and kissed him. She slid a knee up onto the ticking, ready to climb into bed.

Whatever new objection he might have been formulating sizzled to nothing. He pulled her close as she wriggled under the covers and stretched out next to him. He took her kiss and deepened it until her senses began to reel. She felt as if her skin had caught fire.

With the urgency of desire, Kawena pushed his nightshirt up along the hard muscle of his thighs, the softer skin of his ribs, caressing as she went. He drew back and yanked the garment up and off, cursing when the cuffs caught at his wrists. A button went flying as he tugged, When he threw the shirt against the wall, Kawena laughed again.

And then she couldn't laugh, or speak, or think. She could scarcely breathe as he met her pent-up longing of the last few days with a response as strong and sweet and deep. The explosive passion of their night by the sea swept through them once again, dizzying her in the delight of hands and lips and arching bodies. It built to a trembling peak, so achingly intense it seemed almost like pain, and then burst into luscious release. Kawena felt that they vibrated in perfect harmony as they rode the tide together.

It was only afterward, as they lay entwined, letting their pulses slow, their breathing ease, that Lord James said, "Oh, God."

Cuddled in the circle of his arm, Kawena found his despairing tone offensive. "You're not going to begin—"

"You don't understand what we've done."

She trailed her fingertips over his chest. "Don't I?"

He caught her hand in his. "No, you don't. Servants are the worst gossips of all, Kawena. When they discover you've been with me here, they'll call you a lightskirt. They'll tattle to their opposite numbers at Langford, and then my mother's bound to hear of it. She'll be angry. I know she would have liked you, too..." He stopped and clenched his jaw, took a breath. "I can't bear the idea that she might misjudge you—despise you."

Somewhat mollified by the concern in his voice, she considered. "Well, we must see that they don't know anything about it then. I'll sneak back to my room and—"

A light knock on the door and a rattle of the handle brought him bolt upright in the bed. "Wait!" he nearly shouted. "What is it?"

"Morning tea, sir," replied a puzzled voice from the other side of the panels.

"Just a moment!" Moving with lightning speed, Lord James leapt out of bed and started snatching Kawena's scattered clothes from the floor. He pulled her from the tumbled sheets and shoved the bundle into her arms. "Get in the wardrobe," he whispered.

"What?"

"Ssh!" He grabbed his nightshirt and pulled it on even as he pushed her toward the large walnut wardrobe against the far wall. When Kawena would have protested, he laid two fingers over her lips. Then he practically lifted her into the wardrobe and shut the doors, immersing her in darkness.

"All right," she heard him say, his voice muffled.

There were more muted sounds. Unsure whether to laugh or be angry, Kawena waited. After a few minutes, the door opened, and Lord James stood before her, looking grim. "Well, that's torn it. They'll have taken your tea as well, and found your bed empty."

Kawena stepped out of the wardrobe, holding her clothes, feeling foolish and not much liking the sensation. "I never even got into it, I was so—"

"What?" He turned so fast it startled her.

"I couldn't lie still," she explained. "Because I thought I'd failed when we couldn't—"

"Your bed wasn't slept in?"

"No." She was quite bewildered by the intensity of the question, and the sudden calculation in his eyes. "What—"

Lord James held up a hand for silence. Mildly irritated, she kept quiet.

"All right," he said after what seemed quite a time. "I'm going to tell Mrs. Hastings that you were called away late last night by an…emergency. At a…a friend's house. And you had to stay over with her." He clutched at his tousled hair. "The deuce. Who can it be? You don't know any females in London."

"Except Miss Jennings." There was something fascinating, if demented, in his utter focus on this nonsense.

"Right! Yes. Who's to say you weren't already well acquainted? And so you had to go to her at once. There was no time to pack anything—"

"Why?"

"Because you were in such a tearing hurry," he replied, as if this was utterly obvious and somehow sensible.

"No, I mean why did I have to go to her?"

"I don't know!" He looked harried. "Some…some female reason."

Kawena did laugh then, earning a frown from her endearingly obsessed companion.

"The reason is none of the servants' affair," he said, suddenly lofty.

"So you must explain the fact, but not what is behind it?" she asked. Once again she marveled at the time and effort the English put into making up stories to hide the fact that they had done what they wished to do.

Lord James ignored her philosophical inquiry. "We'll smuggle you out of the house, and you can return later—"

"But will Miss Jennings agree?"

"To what?" He appeared confused.

"To say that I stayed at her house—"

"We're not going to tell her about this." He seemed appalled that she would think so. "We're not going to tell anyone. Anything."

"Except the servants." Kawena was bemused.

"That's right." He sank into the armchair by the hearth, seemingly exhausted by his efforts at invention. "Do you want some tea?"

"No. I hate tea."

"Really?" He looked up from the pot as if this was the oddest thing he'd heard today, and Kawena nearly laughed once again.

Then their eyes caught and held.

Kawena started to lower her bundle of clothing.

"No, no, don't…"

"No one knows I'm here," she said. "We could have time to—"

He turned away like a man abandoning his heart's desire. "Get dressed. Please, Kawena. I beg you."

Taking pity on him, she did.

Twelve

KAWENA "RETURNED" TO THE LANGFORD TOWN HOUSE
an hour later, having successfully evaded observation
on the way out. She'd spent most of that time riding
around the neighborhood in a hansom cab, under the
care of a bewildered but obedient driver.

Lord James heralded her arrival with polite inquiries
about her friend, which she answered as instructed.
She was not able to tell if the footman found her story
odd. She didn't know him well enough, and he clearly
prided himself on remaining impassive at any cost.
He did have a distinctly alert air, and Kawena had no
doubt that her words would be reported to the rest of
the staff. Lord James seemed satisfied, however, and
that was enough for her.

And then the two of them were left alone again,
in the drawing room. Kawena sat down, but Lord
James hovered near the door, as if he might dart
out at any moment. "So..." he said. "All's well. Er,
mission accomplished. I suppose...you'll be going
home now."

Kawena examined his strained expression. In many

ways, this English duke's son seemed like two different men. There was the ardent lover—all skill and certainty and fiery freedom. That man entranced her. But then there was this other—the one harried and bounded by "society." He was so often irritating; he even, sometimes, seemed to disapprove of her. Yet she also pitied him, a little. He was like a fish tangled in a net. She realized that she was staring, and that she hadn't answered him. "Home," she said. A wave of melancholy washed over her at the word. She was feeling the effects of all that had occurred in the last twelve hours, she decided.

Lord James cleared his throat. "You should probably make some arrangements first." He didn't seem to wish to look at her.

"Arrangements?"

"Not a good idea to go sailing off alone with a bag full of gems in your luggage."

"I wouldn't tell anyone they were there," she pointed out.

"Of course not. But it's risky. You don't want to chance losing them again."

That would be unbearable. And she wouldn't have the protection of her father's old friend on the voyage home. Thinking of setting out on that long, solitary journey, of arriving at the island, even with the triumphant return of the treasure, made her feel desolate. Which was idiotic. She told herself that she was simply tired when she had to swallow threatened tears.

"I'll tell you what," Lord James continued. "You should meet my father's man of business. Mr. Crane knows more about how to keep the finances in tune than any six bankers. He'll be able to tell you just what to do."

"Do?"

"According to what my father and my brother Nathaniel say, a fortune needs a deal of managing."

Kawena had made no practical plan beyond recovering the jewels. She touched the pocket of her gown, where the bag currently lay. Now that she had them back, perhaps there was some better course of action than simply hiding them away again. She'd gained her fortune. She should…employ it. "All right."

"It might take a day or two to set up an appointment."

The idea that she could not embark immediately for the other side of the world was…a curious relief.

❧

James took Kawena to Crane's offices the following morning, after a day that had nearly driven him mad. At every moment, his body cried out that she was *his*, and demanded the thrill and solace of touch. At the same time, his mind insisted that he act correctly, to preserve her reputation and position, to protect her. The push and pull of these two impulses twisted him into knots, reduced him to stiff silence. Goaded beyond endurance, he retreated into the manners drilled into him in his youth. A stately formality saved him when Kawena smiled or gazed into his eyes, when she sat at his side in the cab rattling down to the City. His training demanded that he focus on the matter at hand and set aside his petty personal desires.

James had never had much to do with his father's

very superior man of business. He'd paid no heed to the ducal estates and investments, set as he was on leaving for the navy. Still, he'd met the man, and his family name got them a cordial reception and immediate admittance to the firm's premises off one of the narrow, cobbled streets in central London.

But the man who emerged from the inner offices to greet them wasn't the sober, middle-aged figure he remembered. "I'm Ian Crane," he said. "My father, whom you knew, I believe, died last winter. Please come in."

They followed him into a darkly paneled chamber, with ancient mullioned windows overlooking the narrow lane outside, and took chairs before his wide, paper-strewn desk. Ian Crane wore black, proclaiming his seriousness, but his hair was sunny yellow, and his face round and open, his eyes a guileless light blue. He looked more like one of the students in Oxford than a wily lawyer. James wondered if his father would have employed such a youth if Crane's father and grandfather hadn't served the Langfords in a similar capacity.

"You're thinking that I look rather young for my job," he said, appearing to read James's mind. "And wondering if I know what I'm doing."

"Ah." James couldn't deny it.

Ian Crane waved his embarrassment aside. "People do. My father was taken off very suddenly, at barely fifty years of age. I'd expected to become much more grizzled and wise before stepping into his shoes." His face showed good humor mixed with sadness.

"I'm sorry to hear of it," James replied. "I met him once or twice at Langford."

Crane nodded his thanks. "I can assure you that he, and my grandfather and their partners, trained me quite thoroughly. If you would prefer to go elsewhere, however…"

"No, no." James had no idea where else to go. "This is Miss Benson. A friend of mi…my family. She has recently come into a large inheritance. And she would like some advice."

"Indeed." Crane smiled and nodded at Kawena. "Inheritance in the form of lands or…?"

Kawena took out the bag of jewels and set it before him. She untied the drawstring so that he could see inside. The stones glittered, multicolored, in the lamplight.

"Ah." Crane leaned forward. "That's…extraordinary."

"My father was a trader in the South Seas," Kawena said. They had agreed on what and how much to tell Crane. "He took payment in gems, whenever he could. Or converted his profits into them."

"I see." Ian Crane reached out. "With your permission?" Kawena nodded, and he picked out a large ruby from the bag, holding it up to the light. It glowed a rich crimson. "I can't judge the quality of these," he continued. "They would need to be valued by an expert. I would suggest they be sent "

"I won't have them out of my hands," Kawena interrupted.

James could understand why she wouldn't wish to let the hoard out of her sight again. He couldn't imagine just handing them over to a stranger when they had at last been found.

Ian Crane nodded. "That you take them to Rundell

and Bridge, on Ludgate Hill near St. Paul's. They are a very reputable company. Extremely knowledgeable."

James had heard of them. He thought perhaps his father had purchased items there.

"Once you know their value, we can discuss what you wish to do."

"What would you suggest?" Kawena asked.

Crane tapped the tips of his fingers together. It seemed to James like a gesture he'd inherited along with his family's business. "I would recommend selling some proportion of the gems—the exact amount is something to discuss—and investing the proceeds in various ways. Jewels are not very liquid…" Noticing Kawena's puzzled expression, he explained. "They can't be used like money, all in a moment. They usually have to be converted into cash first, which is not always a simple matter."

She nodded her understanding. James admired the perfect curve of her cheek, the glint of lamplight on her hair. He nearly lost himself in memories of it loose and flowing down her bare back.

"You might wish to own property or other types of assets," Crane continued. "We can review an array of options."

"Yes, I see." Kawena nodded again. She glanced at James, and then away.

The change in their circumstances struck him then, as it had not, for some reason, before now. Everything was different. Kawena was no longer a waif tossed up by the ocean currents, dependent on his aid. She was a very rich woman. Her new status showed in the way Ian Crane spoke to her, to both of them. He was perfectly courteous to the fifth son of his noble employer, of course. But his attention was really concentrated on Kawena. James had become… an appendage.

The story was much the same when they reached Rundell and Bridge later that day. Crane had sent a clerk ahead to pave the way, and Kawena was received like minor royalty. They were taken to a private viewing room with a table covered in soft cloth and several comfortable chairs. They were offered refreshment and invited to sit and observe while three experts examined the jewels right before their eyes. Watching these men evaluate each gem through a lens that fitted into one eye, rather like a quizzing glass without a handle, James keenly felt his role as mere supernumerary. He might almost have been a footman, for all he was contributing. The thought rankled.

The tests were boring as well—minutes of peering at a stone, turning it this way and that to observe every angle, more minutes of note taking, and then the same all over again. Progress was painstakingly slow. And conversation was not encouraged, although other members of the firm peered 'round the door now and then, seemingly riveted by the evaluation process.

After what seemed to James like an eternity, they finished. Their verdict was favorable. The gems were of good quality. The fellow who'd been overseeing the whole congratulated Kawena and named a staggering sum as a value for the whole collection. It was not an amount they could cover themselves all at once, he intimated, but Rundell and Bridge would be happy to help her find buyers.

Kawena accepted the verdict with an almost regal calm. James watched, fascinated and strangely depressed, as she dealt with the fawning jewelers, obviously needing no help from him. She elected to sell one stone then and there, receiving a sheaf of banknotes in exchange, before tucking the others back in their cloth bag. The bowing and scraping as they departed was almost comical.

"You need a better place for those," James said as they returned to the street. "A strongbox or something. Not to mention a troop of guards." He was a bit stunned by the overall worth of the collection.

"No one knows what I am carrying," Kawena replied.

"They do in there," James said, indicating the jeweler's display window. "And at Crane's offices." He spotted a hack and flagged it down.

"You said they were trustworthy people."

"And so they are. But…people simply don't stroll around town with a fortune in jewels in their pockets."

"It isn't proper?"

He didn't understand the edge in her voice. Shouldn't she be bouncing with glee? "It isn't sensible," he replied. If they were attacked by footpads and robbed, she'd probably blame it on him. James handed her into the cab and gave the driver the address.

"Now that I have money, I'd like to get some clothes," Kawena said as they clattered through the streets toward Langford House. "So that I can return Ariel's things." She plucked at the fabric of the blue dress she wore. "And have something different to wear."

"Can't help you there," James replied. His spirits

were steadily sinking. The part of him that claimed Kawena for his own, that could barely keep his hands off her, was clamoring for action. She was drifting away from him like a vessel on a different tack, this inner voice insisted. He had to take her now, or she'd be lost to him. The urge was nearly irresistible. But not quite. His manners and training fought it to a grim standstill.

He had to get away and be on his own for a bit, to work off some of this simmering conflict. "I've never lived in London, you know. Still less purchased gowns and fripperies here." He scowled at the passing scene. How he hated this filthy, clamorous city.

"Yes," she replied.

James glanced at her. It was an odd response. He couldn't read her expression. She simply nodded, and then said nothing more for the remainder of their journey.

◦◦◦

Back in her bedchamber at Langford House, Kawena set the bag of jewels on the dressing table and sat gazing at it. Such a small thing, fitting easily into her two hands, and yet it had altered her world. The value the jeweler had named had seemed gigantic to her, but it was Lord James's reaction, quickly hidden, that confirmed the significance. If a duke's son thought she was rich, then she must actually be so. And she knew from her father, and from observations of her own in England, that this meant she would be viewed and treated quite differently.

She'd had one unsettling example already. Lord

James had fled as soon as they climbed down from the hack at the front door. Over the course of the morning, he'd become more and more prickly. And then it had seemed as if he couldn't get away from her fast enough. There'd been no sign of the lover in whose arms she'd found such joy just hours ago. He had been starkly and rigidly the society Englishman, the duke's son. It had seemed to pain him to look at her.

Kawena sat back in her chair. She might have the funds to make purchases, and take action, but she felt more alone than ever. Lord James was the only person she really knew in the great intimidating mass of humanity that surrounded her, and he seemed to be…not angry. That wasn't it. He was distant and… perhaps ashamed? But that didn't seem right either. She couldn't tell what he felt, just that it was uncomfortable. Remembering the way he had hustled her out of the house this morning, sneaking and creeping in fear of being caught by servants, she put her head in her hands.

It was illogical, and unfair. She'd recovered her fortune, done exactly as she'd set out to do. And here at the moment of triumph, something very like desolation threatened. It felt like a great wave curling over her head, about to break and smash her into the sand with bone-crushing force. Kawena crouched lower, braced for disaster.

And then, between one breath and the next, she stiffened and straightened. There was no wave. She would not be engulfed. She'd been alone before, when her prospects had been much worse than they were now. She would find her way. She'd figure something out.

With that resolution, Kawena remembered Flora Jennings. Here was someone else she knew in London—or had been introduced to, at any rate. The English set such great store by introductions. She'd been impressed by Miss Jennings's intelligence and apparent strength of character. Also, she would know where to get clothes. She would go and see her and ask her.

As she hadn't removed her bonnet, it was just a matter of finding a secure place to leave the bag of jewels—she chose a small drawer with a key in its lock—and going back downstairs. Kawena found the footman standing in the front hall, as he often was when they came in and out during the day. He looked up as if expecting some instructions when she came down, and it seemed awkward to walk past him without a word. "Would you find me a cab, please?" Kawena asked.

"Just you, miss?"

"That's right."

He hesitated, then gave her a little bow. "Yes, miss."

When he returned with a hackney, Kawena thanked him and sent him away. She told the driver to take her to Russell Square. It was all she remembered of the address, but she was confident she could pick out the Jennings house once they arrived.

In the hurly-burly of the streets, with the constant shouts and bouncing of the carriage, Kawena didn't have the leisure to wonder about her welcome. But when the cab pulled up before the redbrick house that she had indeed recognized, she hesitated briefly. Then she squared her shoulders. She had come this far.

If they didn't wish to see her… She shrugged, walked up the steps, and rang the bell.

Admitted and conducted to the drawing room, Kawena discovered that Miss Jennings was out. However, her mother, sitting there alone, greeted her. "Flora will be back quite soon," she said, and offered a cup of tea as they sat opposite each other before the hearth.

"The English drink so much tea," Kawena replied before she thought.

Fortunately, Mrs. Jennings looked amused rather than offended. "We do, don't we? It's a habit we form early. You don't care for tea?"

Kawena couldn't help wrinkling her nose as she shook her head.

Her hostess smiled. "May I offer you something else? I don't imagine we'll have what you're used to. But lemonade, perhaps?"

"I am not thirsty, thank you."

The older woman nodded.

Silence descended. One was supposed to make polite conversation in these drawing rooms, Kawena remembered. "But why are they called 'drawing rooms'?" she wondered.

"I beg your pardon?"

"Do you draw here sometimes?" She looked around. There was no sign of artistic pursuits. Bits of her father's dictionary drills came back to her. You could draw on a bow as well. Or draw a mug of beer from a tap. But neither of those seemed any more apt.

"It's a shortened form of 'withdrawing room,'" Mrs. Jennings said. "A place for ladies to withdraw, ah, to."

"From what?"

"A pertinent question. The short answer is: the gentlemen. You are an interesting young woman, are you not?"

Interesting was not necessarily a favorable thing to the English, Kawena had noticed. Determined to make a better attempt at conversation, she said, "You are a relation of the Duchess of Langford?" This had been mentioned, but she didn't recall the exact connection.

"Yes, Adele and I are second cousins. We were presented in the same season, and were good friends long ago. But then she married Langford, while I chose Henry."

"Mr. Jennings was a great scholar." *Perhaps this was the trick of polite conversation,* Kawena thought. *Repeat information you already know.*

"It was his passion for learning that struck me, at first," the older woman agreed. "He was mad to discover and explore. It was inspiring, and rather thrilling."

Kawena could understand that. She enjoyed the reminiscent love in her hostess's eyes.

Mrs. Jennings sighed. "But he didn't belong to fashionable circles, or care a whit about them. And so I drifted away from old friends. And now he's gone, long before I expected he would be."

It was sad, Kawena didn't know what to say.

"Leaving me wishing I hadn't been such a coward," said the older woman, as if speaking to herself.

"You do not seem like a coward," Kawena observed, mystified. The Gresham brothers had described quite the opposite sort of person.

"I was." The older woman looked into the distance; she seemed to be lost in her own musings. "I didn't have the strength of my own…not convictions. Choices. Once I married, I felt I didn't fit with my former friends. In houses like Langford, for instance. It was mostly in my head, I see now, but I was angry whenever I ventured into society, always expecting to be snubbed. Ready to fight back. It was…fatiguing. So I stopped visiting. And now we are left alone, and I have put my Flora in an ambiguous position."

"Ambiguous? I have not heard that word."

"Not one thing or another," the older woman replied absently. "Not part of a recognized social set."

"This is important?" It sounded rather like some of the things Lord James had told her.

Mrs. Jennings looked up, blinking as if recovering herself. "I beg your pardon. I don't know why I began talking of this. I was thinking when you came in, and I… But you can have no interest in my history."

"I do," said Kawena. "I am 'ambiguous' myself." She had not had a single label for her place in England before.

Her companion examined her. "Yes, I see."

"So I would like to know why it worries you. For my own sake."

"Clever as well as interesting," Mrs. Jennings murmured. "Well, Miss Benson, it is a state that can make a girl vulnerable, you see."

Kawena cocked her head. "'Vulnerable'? In danger, you mean?"

"I suppose that sounds silly to you. But spiteful gossip can be very unpleasant, and it certainly limits one's…opportunities."

"What sort of opportunities?"

"Chances for a happy life." Her hostess grimaced. "I worry about Flora's future. She knows only our old friends. She is not invited anywhere. And then she will go about town all alone."

"Should she not? I came here in a cab."

"Young ladies customarily take a servant when they go out. Flora frequents quite poor neighborhoods, too."

Best not to mention that she'd sailed around the world alone dressed as a boy, Kawena thought.

"Of course, her charitable work is terribly important," Mrs. Jennings continued. "But there was nearly an open scandal there a few months ago. Though it had nothing to do with Flora, it still could have been disastrous to her prospects. But she will not listen to my objections." Shaking her head, she broke off.

In the ensuing silence, Kawena didn't know how to respond. But she did see that Lord James was not alone in his concern about gossip. Mrs. Jennings seemed such a solid, sensible person. Perhaps he wasn't being as silly as she'd thought.

"I beg your pardon," the older woman said again. "Do tell me about your home. I am so very interested."

Clearly the previous subject was closed. Kawena obligingly described the island and her father's trading endeavors until Flora came in. Her mother rose at once. "I have letters to write," she said. "I'll leave you young ladies to talk." Kawena had the feeling she wished she hadn't said so much to a stranger.

Flora sat down and looked at Kawena. Her greeting had been cordial enough, but she appeared curious as to why Kawena had called.

"I found the…thief," Kawena said, then hesitated.

She hadn't told the whole story at their first meeting, and she was uncertain how much to reveal now. Lord James's family would no doubt hear it, since the carving had been sitting in their house all these months. But Flora was not a Gresham. They might not wish the world to know. "And recovered my fortune," Kawena added.

"That's splendid." Did the very self-possessed Miss Jennings look a little wistful?

Kawena moved right to the point. "I should like to purchase some English gowns. And I hoped you might know where I could do so."

Flora shrugged. "If you want a fashionable wardrobe, I can't really help you. I have no interest in the latest styles, and can't afford them anyway." She indicated her dark blue gown as if it demonstrated these points.

Kawena thought that she might like ensembles more colorful and daring than this. But Flora Jennings had an air of distinction. "Your dress is very fine," she replied.

"It is well made," the other acknowledged, looking pleased.

"I don't understand fashion or society," Kawena added. "And I don't know if I'm much interested." Although she didn't know that she wasn't, either. It was like exploring a new bit of the island; you couldn't decide until you'd absorbed it all.

"What intelligent person could be?"

"Do you think I'm intelligent?" Kawena replied. "In the English way, I know only what my father taught me."

"As do I."

"But yours was a great scholar."

Flora nodded. "Yes, so I can interpret Akkadian cuneiform tablets. But I'm not a very good dancer. And I can't embroider or play the pianoforte or…flirt with young gentlemen."

"Like Lord Robert."

"No one is like Lord Robert," Flora murmured. "He is an utter anomaly in my life."

"A what?" Here was another new word. They came thick and fast in this household.

"Something unusual, unprecedented." Flora looked off into the distance. "Like a comet that streaks through the sky once in your lifetime, and then is gone."

"I can't be so intelligent, after all. I don't understand what you mean."

"Neither do I," said Flora. She stared at the wall as if she could see right through it.

"Do you *want* to embroider?" Kawena wondered. She had seen this activity on her travels and thought it looked remarkably tedious.

Flora Jennings burst out laughing. "No. It's a dead bore. Dancing, though…"

"I love to dance," agreed Kawena.

Miss Jennings gave her a frankly friendly look. "I can recommend the dressmaker I use, if you like. She's very skilled."

"And quick? I'm not certain how much longer I will be in town."

"I believe she keeps models made up to show. I'm sure she could alter some of them for you."

"Thank you." Kawena wondered if it was rude to depart the moment she'd gotten what she came for.

Probably. So many commonplace things were considered rude here. She cast about for a suitable remark and found only, "Where were you?"

"I spend most of my mornings at a refuge for street children."

"Street?" She wasn't certain what that meant.

"The children society leaves to beg or starve," Flora added, fire kindling in her bright blue eyes. "And to be preyed upon by the worst sort of villains."

"I don't understand."

"Poor children," Flora explained, "who have lost their parents to disease or accident and are left to fend for themselves."

"But…why?" asked Kawena.

"That's a very good question. One I cannot answer. Except to say that society seems to care very little for its most vulnerable members."

Shocked, Kawena said, "My father never told me about this."

"People don't talk about it," was the contemptuous reply. "Most of them choose not even to know about it. They look past begging children just as they do a rat or a pigeon."

"But you help them." Kawena found herself admiring this intense young woman.

Flora looked regretful. "We provide a meal or two, an occasional bed for a night, a place to recover from…difficulties. It's like trying to catch a waterfall in a bucket." Her tone made it clear that the situation galled. "There is never enough space or money or… interest to change things."

Kawena pulled out the roll of currency she received

at the jeweler's. She peeled off a twenty-pound note. "I should like to make a contribution."

Flora didn't take it. "I would be glad to have it, but you should not be advised by me. I am an interested party, and you cannot know whether I am trustworthy."

"I can judge that for myself."

Flora smiled at her. "Nonetheless, you should consult an expert."

Kawena pushed the banknote into her hands. "Lord James introduced me to a man named Ian Crane," she said.

"I've heard that name. I think his firm is used by many fine families."

Their eyes met, blue and dark brown. An unspoken sense of fellow feeling passed between them. "I'll be sorry to go back to Oxford and not see you again," said Kawena.

"You're going soon?"

"In the next few days." She needed to return Ariel's things, and also to get out of the huge, dirty city.

"I've been meaning to visit the Bodleian Library in Oxford," Flora mused. "They have several books I should consult."

"You should come with us," Kawena exclaimed.

"Us?" Flora raised her dark brows.

"I, ah, suppose Lord James will be going back also. He was staying there with his brother before."

"He began helping you with your search," Flora finished.

"Yes." The other woman's steady gaze made Kawena feel self-conscious. It was as if she could see far more than most people.

"I may very well take you up on that," said Flora. "To be honest, it would save me stage fare."

"You must come," declared Kawena.

Flora promised to let her know the following day, and they parted warmly. Kawena felt that a bond had begun to form, and that Flora Jennings might well become a true friend.

She stopped at the recommended dressmaker's on the way back, and tried on several attractive gowns. The woman and her assistant pinned and prodded and agreed to make the necessary alterations and deliver the dresses the next afternoon. Kawena decided that would do; there must be places to buy undergarments and other things in Oxford.

In the cab back to Langford House, and for a long time after she had returned, Kawena sat in her bed-chamber and thought about everything that had happened since she'd left home. She reviewed things she'd heard and facts she'd learned, certain items standing out in her mind. She thought over the course of her life so far, her father's teachings, and dreams and ambitions she'd had. She decided that she would return to Ian Crane's office by herself and have a long talk with him. It was time now to make a plan.

Thirteen

JAMES DUCKED, LUNGED, AND SMASHED HIS LEFT FIST into his opponent's ribs. The man let out an "Oof" and danced backward in the boxing ring. James followed, dodging a roundhouse right by a hair. He took a sharp blow to his bare shoulder, and then caught his sparring partner glancingly on the jaw. They moved apart again, fists upraised, sweat beading on their skins. Though not previously acquainted, they were well matched, paired up by the retired champion who ruled Gentleman Jackson's Boxing Saloon as a courteous despot.

Movement, action, had always been the best way for James to deal with upsets or confusion or the floods of excess energy that sometimes plagued him. Physical exertion cleared his mind as nothing else could do. He'd learned to box with his brothers as a youth, and it was good to see that his skills hadn't been lost. Good, too, that this civilized bout was nothing like the hand-to-hand combat of the war. It called up no bad memories. His opponent moved back in with a flurry of jabs. James dodged and responded, and they danced apart again.

Kawena had gone out somewhere first thing this morning, without telling anybody what she was up to. At this moment, he had no notion where she was, which both annoyed and concerned him. But to be with her was to want what he couldn't have. His lapse in his parents' house was not to be repeated. His mind still shied away from the fact of it.

And in any case, Kawena didn't seem to need or want his guidance now that she'd gotten what she wanted, now that she was rich. She'd sloughed him off like a tattered sail. Probably she still blamed him for the near loss of her blasted jewels. How could it be his fault that some careless boy had sold him the carving? Or that her father had hidden his fortune in such a blasted silly place? Or that it was the sort of piece that one would never mention to a young lady?

Hadn't he gone out of his way to help her search? Traveling up and down the country when he'd far rather have been doing something else? He told himself that he was glad the task was over, while uneasily aware that this was not the whole truth. Actually, he was melancholy and resentful and frustrated all at the same time. And so here he was exchanging blows with a stranger.

His attention diverted, James sustained a hard knock to the side of his head. His ears rang, and he went down on one knee under the impact. Jackson at once climbed into the ring, saying, "That's enough, gentlemen." He moved between them, although James's opponent had already stepped back. "Some good cross and jostle work," the trainer added. He put a hand on James's shoulder. "All right, then?"

James nodded, rising to his feet. Following his sparring partner out of the ring to leave room for another pair to begin, he began unwrapping the strips of cloth protecting his fists. Fingers free, he shook hands with the other man, then went to wash off the sweat.

James returned to Langford House late in the afternoon, having stopped at an inn for bread and cheese and a tankard of ale. He was tired of pick-up meals, too, and well aware that Mrs. Hastings was even more tired of providing them. She'd hinted more than once that her small staff was not equipped for sustained family visits. He would inform Kawena that they were going back to Oxford, no matter what she thought she was doing. As soon as he could find her, that is.

James realized that he was hanging about his mother's drawing room, listening for the sound of the front door like a mooncalf. With a savage gesture, he retreated to his bedchamber. But there was nothing to do there except recall the delicious, forbidden moments when Kawena had shared this bed with him—her eager lips, the tumble of her beautiful hair, the soft cries she made...

James sprang up and paced the floor, seething with desire, a growing irritation over her absence, and fear that something had happened to her. By the time he finally heard a carriage pulling up in front of the house, well after five o'clock, he was primed for an explosion.

He met her on the stairway landing above the entry hall. He started to ask where the devil she'd been, but when she looked up at him, he was momentarily silenced by the beauty of her face, the depths of her dark eyes.

"Lord James," she said with a nod. "I think it is time we returned to Oxford."

Those precise words died on his tongue. James endured a further surge of annoyance at the fact that she'd said it first. "Oh, have you taken charge of arrangements now?" he replied unreasonably.

Kawena looked startled. "It is simply the sensible thing to do."

"Are you saying I'm not sensible?" He hadn't been the one who stored a fortune in jewels in a lewd carving and then left it lying about where anyone might walk off with it. "And where have you been? You can't go wandering about the streets of London on your own."

"I wasn't wandering."

"Without a word. Anything might have happened to you. It's one thing if you wish to discard me like a used handkerchief now that you have recovered your fortune, but—"

"Discard? What are you talking about?"

He stepped closer to her. "*But* you'll have to take more care how you behave. You'll attract all sorts of attention now you're an heiress. You have to act like a young lady instead of a hoyden."

She met his eyes squarely—dark brown burning into blue. "A what?" She hadn't heard this word before. It had an odd sound. She was certain it was offensive.

"A wild, uncivilized creature, who flouts the rules of society," he replied.

They faced off, glaring, hurt and attraction simmering in their locked gazes. The air of the stairwell seemed to thicken around Kawena, making it harder to breathe.

It wasn't clear who moved first, but in the next instant they were in each other's arms, and in a kiss that made her head spin. Resentment and confusion went up like tinder in a bonfire of arousal.

Kawena's back was pressed against the wall. She wound herself around him, diving into the same delightful sensations she felt whenever he held her. His arms drew her closer still; his lips intoxicated her; she vibrated with desire. This was how they were meant to be, not sniping or treading warily around incomprehensible pitfalls. She gave herself up to the delight of it, responding in every way she knew to his ardor.

Lord James tore himself away. He pushed back from the wall, evaded her beseeching hands, and retreated to the other side of the landing. "No. No! You're not going to lure me into this again in my mother's house," he said breathlessly. He looked around as if checking for prying eyes and backed farther away from her.

"Lure you? I don't believe there was any luring required." Furious, frustrated, Kawena dug her nails into the wallpaper.

"We can't act like cats in heat in my family's home."

Kawena knew nothing of cats, but she understood an insult when she heard one. This was what he thought of her then. "Cats are quite improper, I suppose."

He ignored her, looking over the stair rail, checking whether the footman was at his post, she imagined.

"I am so very tired of that word."

Lord James glanced up. "Speak more quietly. Or come into the drawing room where—"

"No one will hear," Kawena finished for him.

"Because no one in your mother's house must know that you would kiss me." Deeply wounded, as well as angry, she put a foot on the upper stair. "We should leave as soon as possible. Miss Jennings wishes to come along with us to Oxford."

"Flora Jennings?"

"My friend, Miss Jennings." She said it in ringing tones that surely reached the lower floor. "The one who had the trouble. The one I had to go and see last night. She requires…more assistance."

"All right!"

Lord James looked hunted, which was somewhat gratifying. It helped Kawena hang on to the tatters of her pride as she started up the steps toward her bedchamber.

"I'm just not sure Alan and Ariel have room for her," he said as a parting shot.

Kawena hesitated between one step and the next. She didn't know if Flora meant to stay at Lord Alan's house. She had no right to extend such an invitation. Was she even welcome there herself, after all that had happened on this journey? Did *she* wish to continue her association with Lord James's family? Her mind a mass of confusion, she decided that it didn't matter. She could get rooms at an inn. Or elsewhere. She could afford whatever she wanted now. The thought was less comforting than she'd imagined it would be when she had only two coins in her pockets. "You object to having her in the carriage?" she replied haughtily. "I will be happy to pay for the—"

"You don't have to pay," Lord James interrupted savagely. "Everything isn't about payment."

No, it was about this infuriating thing called

propriety that reared up at the worst possible moments to blight one's life. "I'll tell her that she is most welcome then." Kawena turned her back and proceeded up the stairs.

"I'll see about a post chaise," he answered in clipped tones.

"I expect the day after tomorrow would be best," she said without looking at him. "To give Miss Jennings time to prepare."

"I am entirely at your service," he replied in a tone so biting that it might have had fangs.

"Thank you," said Kawena with the same snap.

There was a slapping sound, like a hand striking the wall. "I'm going out," Lord James snarled, and tramped down the winding stair as Kawena continued upward. From the upper corridor, she heard the front door slam.

Inside her bedroom, Kawena yanked off her stupid, constricting bonnet and threw it onto the bed. Her shawl followed. She longed for other items to hurl about, preferably things that would make loud, satisfying noises as they shattered. She nearly sacrificed a porcelain dog from the mantel, but she managed to resist. Instead, she wrote a note to Flora Jennings confirming their travel arrangement.

When it was sealed, Kawena looked at the bellpull. She knew that it would summon a servant, just as she knew that Mrs. Hastings was finding their presence irksome. Without ever saying a word, members of the small staff left at Langford House had gradually made it clear that they did not wish to wait on her. Kawena *thought* it wasn't personal, that they would have felt the same about any visitor at this unexpected time of year. But she wasn't sure.

She took the missive downstairs herself, and was lucky enough to find the footman in the front hall. He accepted the note and promised it would be delivered at once. The coin she included bought her a cheerful grin.

Kawena returned to her chamber. She was hungry, but didn't want to ask the housekeeper for a meal. Food seemed to be a particular sore point with Mrs. Hastings. More than once she'd reminded them that there was no "proper" cook on the premises. The English applied that wretched word to everything in their country, it seemed. Was there an improper cook then? Because as Kawena had pointed out to Lord James, the servants seemed well nourished, so someone must be cooking for them. He'd brushed her comment aside. Apparently, making logical arguments to housekeepers was another action forbidden by English propriety.

Kawena had a sudden vivid recollection of her mother's house, where savory tidbits would be pressed on her whenever she returned from a few hours absence. She had an established place there. No one criticized her behavior—at least, not often. It was full of people she knew and cared for, and nothing at all like this huge, echoing building peopled by strangers. A tide of bitter homesickness swept over her. It would not be resisted. Deploring her weakness, Kawena threw herself onto the bed and wept.

∽

James strode along the London streets, fuming. A stream of people trudged along with him to the east, pushing through a throng making its way west. Where could they all be going? Why didn't they just stay where they were? Then there'd be no need to jostle and mutter and consign them all to perdition.

He wondered how many of them, like him, had nowhere to go. He'd had to get out of the house, but he knew no one in London, really, had no connections in this huge, filthy city. He stopped walking; a man behind cursed as he bumped into him. There was one person…

James searched his mind for the name of the club where he was likely to encounter Robert. He'd heard it spoken of a thousand times, by several of his brothers. But he'd taken little interest in their talk of town life. It was a color. He remembered that much. Red didn't seem likely for some reason. Blue or yellow? No. White's—that was it.

James had to ask his way more than once before he found the place. But luck was with him when he inquired at the front door. His brother was indeed there, and at once invited him inside.

The clubroom was nearly empty. One or two fellows paged through newspapers, glasses of wine at their elbows. With all his fashionable friends out of town, Robert professed himself delighted to see him. "You must dine with me and perhaps have a hand of cards?"

James agreed easily to the first, his mouth watering at the idea of a juicy round of roast beef rather than grudgingly proffered sandwiches, and accepted a drink as he settled opposite his brother.

"How's the treasure hunt going?" Robert asked.

"It's over."

"What, you've given up?"

"No, Miss Benson found the jewels."

"*She* did?" Robert raised one auburn brow. "Not you?"

It was one of the things that rankled, James realized. He'd exerted himself to help her, but in the end she hadn't needed his help. Only admittance to his family home, where he—her self-appointed protector—had proceeded to risk her reputation… He made a dismissive gesture. He didn't cut a particularly heroic figure in the discovery.

"One of your crew members had them?" Robert prompted.

James shook his head. There was no hiding the truth. He could replace the figure on the shelf, but Kawena was bound to tell Ariel, and the tale would spread. Besides, why should he? So he gave Robert the whole story.

"At Langford House the whole time," his brother marveled at the end. Smiling, he added, "I remember that figure now you mention it. Mama opened the parcel in front of some high-nosed prude. She was not amused."

James emptied his wineglass.

"The prude, I mean," said Robert. "Mama found it funny—in retrospect, anyway. I caught her laughing about it."

"I should have remembered the cursed thing," James replied, the wine having some effect.

Robert shrugged. "You're always sending some

odd trinket or other. I don't wonder you'd lose track. There was the stone neck ring and the peacock fan and that terrifying female with all the arms. And the tongue."

"The…oh, Kali." He'd forgotten that statue, too. There had been many figurines over the years. James felt a bit better.

They moved into the dining room and addressed heaping plates that did indeed include a fine roast beef. James savored the excellent food and drink, and the company. This was the sort of easy fraternal occasion prohibited by his chosen life. A navy man became inured to being thousands of miles away from his family, or he quit. James's fork paused on the way to his mouth as he contemplated the latter option.

"So, is Miss Benson leaving for her home now?" Robert asked when they had made serious inroads on the meal.

"She hasn't confided her plans to me."

His brother looked up, blue eyes suddenly keen.

"She wants to go back to Oxford first," James added, trying to sound less sarcastic, more unconcerned. "She's invited Miss Jennings to tag along."

"Really?" Robert sipped his wine. "Perhaps I'll go with you as well."

"You? I thought you found universities duller than ditchwater."

"Well…I haven't seen Alan since Nathaniel's wedding." Robert twirled his glass by the stem and contemplated the ruby contents.

"Indeed. Weeks ago. And you're in the habit of visiting Alan often, I suppose."

Robert shook his head without meeting his brother's eyes.

"What exactly is going on between you and Flora Jennings?" James asked.

Robert finished off the glass in one quick gulp. "I don't know," was his glum reply.

"What do you mean, you don't know? You hang about a girl for a good long while, apparently. Learning Arcadian, for God's sake—"

"Akkadian," Robert corrected. "And you can't precisely *learn* it."

"You begin to sound utterly unlike yourself," James continued at this further piece of evidence. "And then you say you don't know why?"

"I have to make her admit that I'm not a waste of the air I breathe," Robert blurted out.

"Nobody thinks you're a—"

"*She* does. She says so at every opportunity."

James examined the handsome face across the table. Here was Robert, always the most self-assured of his brothers, a leader of fashion and a darling of society, acting like an awkward schoolboy. "Why would you care what Miss Jennings thinks? She doesn't seem to be the sort of person whose good opinion you've ever…valued."

"A nobody by the reckoning of the *ton*," Robert agreed in an odd tone of voice. "No influence, not the least bit stylish, far too serious to be considered a wit." He laughed, once again sounding quite unlike himself.

"What's wrong with you?" James asked.

Robert looked at him. "That is the question, little brother."

"I'm not your little brother; I'm three inches taller," he objected. He considered probing further, then gave it up. Robert seemed to have no notion what he was about, and he didn't have the patience for mysteries. "Come to Oxford, if you like," he said, refilling their glasses. "You're your own man."

And so was he, James thought. If he could just get a new ship, he'd sail away from all these hints and enigmas. He'd return to a world where people had clear ranks and knew how they had to behave. They did the proper thing, or they found themselves in serious trouble. Someone had once asked him why a man with four older brothers would want to place himself under other men's orders. The thing of it was, in the navy you had a clear chain of command. It wasn't a rowdy bunch of boys dragging you from one scheme to the next, or trying to argue you into three different pranks at the same time. Each man received his orders and carried them out. And then, of course, there was the sea, endlessly fascinating. He missed the sea. James sighed at the memory of its ever-changing colors and moods.

Of course, it rankled that he wouldn't captain his own vessel again for a long time. He thrust aside triumphant memories of the *Charis*. He was hardly in charge of the way his life was going now. As soon as he'd returned Miss Benson to his brother's house, he would inquire at the Admiralty again. James nodded to himself, ignoring a stab of regret at the idea of leaving her. The plum postings went to men who continually pressed their cases, so he—

"Don't you think?" said Robert.

"What?"

"Am I boring you?" his brother asked wryly. "I beg your pardon. It's an…unaccustomed role for me."

"I was just thinking about a new posting," James told him.

"Have you gotten your orders?"

"I expect them very soon," he answered, assuring himself as much as anyone.

Fourteen

In the end, they all four traveled back to Oxford together. Kawena sat with Flora in the post chaise. James and Robert rode beside it, now and then keeping pace to exchange a few words. Despite Miss Jennings's cordial company, Kawena couldn't help feeling dissatisfied by the arrangement. The trip out had been so much more…fun, exciting, adventurous. This one was… proper, she supposed. "Miss Jennings, can I ask—"

"Do call me Flora," her companion put in.

This was a sign of offered friendship, Kawena remembered. The English had rules about naming, as about everything else. "Flora," she echoed. "I wanted to talk to you about propriety."

Her companion looked surprised. "What about it?"

How to begin? Flora looked like the essence of English propriety in her neat, dark blue gown and bonnet, and yet Kawena had gathered that she was not conventional. "I understand politeness," she said, "and I believe it is important to be kind. I would always wish to be. But this idea of the 'proper' thing…it seems quite…arbitrary to me." She was rather proud of remembering that word. "And some of the rules are just silly." She held up her hands. "Why must I wear gloves when it is hot outside? My hands sweat inside them. It is very unpleasant."

Flora laughed. "You may certainly take them off here in the carriage. I won't be offended."

"But if we stop and get down, I am expected to wear them, even though they accomplish nothing." Kawena looked at the thin coverings. "I don't think these would keep my hands warm if it was cold." She pulled them off.

"No." Flora looked at her own gloves.

"But they are proper, and so considered very important."

"By some," her companion replied.

"Not you?"

Flora started to shake her head, then hesitated. "Well…yes and no."

Kawena cocked her head, inviting the other woman to explain.

"I want to do as I please," Flora went on, "but the truth is, I hate being whispered about, or mocked. Mama has always advised, since I was small, that the gossips don't tattle about what they don't notice."

Kawena remembered Mrs. Jennings's regrets. "Perhaps they wouldn't mock you."

"Society distrusts difference," declared Flora positively. "They turn on those—particularly women—whose lives do not follow certain patterns—propriety, as you say."

"People like the duke's family?" Lord James had said his mother would disapprove of their conduct in her house.

"All the *haut ton*." Flora's mouth turned down.

"But I should say the *appearance* of propriety. They define hypocrisy as discretion."

Kawena had no idea what this meant.

Flora went on before she could ask. "And so I will not put myself in their power." She looked fierce.

"But why do people waste time searching out these…missteps?" Kawena asked. "Surely they have better things to do?"

Her companion laughed. "They don't, actually. Or, they don't bother to find anything better. And so, they're bored. There's spite as well, and envy." Suddenly, she looked discouraged.

"I don't know how anyone endures, or remembers, all the rules," Kawena said. "It's like being tangled in a fishing net." She had thought this before, imagining a fish twisting and turning in the mesh.

Flora moved her shoulders as if she felt that constriction. "It's not all bad. The proprieties sometimes offer a refuge. They can protect women from insult, even attack should they come into contact with… plausible villains."

Something in her tone and expression struck Kawena. "Have you encountered such men?"

"I have. They are one important reason I try to help poor children, who are not sheltered by the rules of propriety."

Kawena had been poor, and now she was not. Did this change her relation to propriety? "How do you keep track of all the rules? It seems that every time I move, another one pops up."

"Oh, we're bred to it from time we can first walk and speak," replied Flora bitterly.

"I was on the beach naked when I began to walk," said Kawena.

Flora blinked at her, clearly a bit shocked. "Were you really?"

As Kawena nodded, she understood that even this rather unconventional Englishwoman found her background…startling. It seemed she would never fit in here, even if she wished to.

They arrived in Oxford to a warm welcome and a pleasant bustle. Ariel wouldn't hear of anyone going to an inn, even though she had to put Flora in with Kawena and Alan's two brothers in a room together. Nor would she accept any payment when Kawena drew her aside to thank her once again for her many favors. Reclaiming her borrowed gowns, she merely gave advice about where Kawena could purchase needed items in Oxford, and professed herself ready to accompany her on any shopping expeditions. Kawena let it go, privately vowing she would find a way to express her gratitude, as the group settled into the hospitable household.

"I think it must be interpreted as 'behest,'" said Lord Robert at dinner two nights later.

"Nonsense," replied Flora Jennings. "As it is near the glyph referring to King Sargon, it would obviously be 'command.'"

"No one has yet deciphered the connecting marks," he argued. "So there is no way to be sure."

Heads at the table turned from him to Flora, like observers of a lawn tennis match. The pair's dialogue had been much the same since they returned from the Bodleian Library, where Lord Alan had helped them get access to a special collection.

"My father thought the relationship quite clear," Flora retorted.

"With the studies he had at the time. But since then—"

"I will not," began Flora, holding up a warning hand, "hear my father contradicted by a mere dabbler."

Lord Robert scowled. "I think I have demonstrated that I am more than that."

His brothers looked surprised and amused, Kawena noticed. Ariel was biting her lower lip, as if to hide a smile.

"You have a certain easy facility, and for some reason you like to pretend interest."

"There's no pretense about it! I've slogged away for hours at this stuff."

Their eyes locked across the dining table. Kawena could practically feel a sizzle of connection pass between them. Then Lord James snorted, and they became conscious that everyone was looking at them. Flora flushed and looked away. Lord Robert poured another glass of wine. There was a short silence while he drank it.

"We should get ready to leave," Ariel said then. "I'm sure you'll all enjoy Professor Fiorenza's talk this evening."

James seriously doubted it. On the contrary, he was pretty certain that he wouldn't. But Ariel had been so generous with her hospitality. If she wanted them to turn out for some speech, he had to rally 'round. Particularly as she'd hinted that he—out of everyone—needed to be there.

As he'd expected, he had to jerk himself out of a nap more than once during the long oration, and he retained nothing of the subject matter. But when Ariel approached him afterward with a young woman in tow, he got an inkling of why she'd insisted he come. This must be another bride prospect. He'd nearly forgotten that matter. His joking request seemed to have been made an age ago, by another James Gresham entirely.

"Horatia, this is my husband's brother, Lord James Gresham," she said. "James, Miss Horatia Grantham."

"So pleased to make your acquaintance," said the newcomer. She was tall and lean, with gingery hair and alert blue eyes. Her face was attractive rather than pretty, lit by a lively intelligence. "I have wanted to do so ever since I heard that you are a navy man," she added.

"Have you?" said James.

"Oh, yes. I'm passionately interested in naval exploits. I have made a systematic study of the subject." She sighed happily. "Sailing thousands of miles from home, battling Britain's enemies. A band of heroes."

"I wouldn't say heroes," he murmured.

"That is because you are overly modest, like a proper naval officer."

James was startled by this characterization, which certainly did not describe most of his colleagues. He glanced at Ariel for guidance, but she just smiled and drifted off.

"I was named for Lord Nelson, of course," Miss Grantham continued. "Did you ever meet him?"

"Just once, at a staff meeting."

Miss Grantham clasped her hands together and gazed at him with delighted reverence. "What did he say to you?"

"Uh, it was more of a nod, really. I was a very junior officer, among many."

"Still, you were in his presence. The greatest hero of our time."

James might have objected that there were other candidates for that accolade. Wellington, perhaps? But Miss Grantham launched into a detailed, and extremely knowledgeable, rehash of the Battle of Trafalgar, and he was hard put just to keep up.

He might have done a better job of it if he hadn't been continually distracted by the sight of Kawena, not three yards away and attracting all sorts of attention.

She'd put on a gown he hadn't seen before—a simple fall of fabric without fussy trimmings. But the color! James supposed you'd call it orange, but the word didn't really capture the deep, rich hue of the thing. It was like no dress he'd seen before, and it suited her to a T. Her skin glowed, warm and enticing, against the cloth. Her hair shone black as a raven's wing. All in all, she looked like…well, like a tropical bird landed in a flock of pigeons.

"Don't you think?" said Miss Grantham.

James had no idea what she was referring to. "Ah, very likely," he tried. It seemed to satisfy her. She plunged on into naval strategy, while James faced the fact that he wasn't the only one who'd noticed

Kawena's beauty. She was surrounded by a circle of the younger men, and a few of the older ones as well. They were bent forward, eyeing her like... like hungry hawks, if he was to continue the bird analogy. He was seized by a desire to swoop in and scatter them.

Miss Grantham paused again, gazing up at him. He needed to say something. He was being rude. He searched for plausible words, and overheard a scrap of conversation from behind his left shoulder. "I know, such a color! Orange! But heiresses can wear whatever they like, I suppose."

James didn't catch the murmured response. But the first speaker's reply was perfectly audible. "Oh yes, my dear, vastly wealthy, like some sort of female nabob, they say."

Who said? Kawena wouldn't have. Nor any of their party, James was sure.

"No, not India," the gossipy voice continued. "Some other place." The volume sank to a suggestive murmur; he had to strain to hear. "A *native* of some kind, I understand. But she's not really dark, is she? Not that it would matter to some."

James controlled a surge of rage. However the news had gotten out—and London was crammed full of servants and shopkeepers and eavesdroppers—it was unstoppable now. He glared at the men surrounding Kawena.

"Lord James?" said Miss Grantham. "Is something wrong?"

He recalled himself. It wasn't fair to treat her this way, no matter how uninterested he might feel. "I beg your pardon. I was distracted for a moment. What were you saying? Broadsides, was it?"

From the look she gave him, it wasn't. But she forgave him and went on. He took care to listen this time. He should have turned his back on the spectacle of Kawena's admirers, but he couldn't quite manage that.

Kawena was enjoying this gathering more than any she'd attended before. She was very pleased with her new gown, and credited it with drawing the surge of flattering attention.

"What did you think of the lecture, Miss Benson?" asked the young man on her right. Ariel had mentioned his name, but she'd forgotten it in the spate of introductions that followed the talk. "Do you intend to make use of the memory techniques?" he added.

She hadn't really followed the speaker's reasoning. His plan of associating items you wished to recall with other quite unrelated things, which seemed equally difficult to keep in mind, had seemed very complicated. She shrugged. "I expect I shall just have to remember what I remember," she replied. "And what I don't...well, those things I forget."

All around the circle, gentlemen laughed heartily. "A wit, by Jove," exclaimed the one who'd asked the question.

Their response seemed exaggerated to Kawena. But perhaps they were just being kind to a stranger.

"I hope I may come to call on you," said another.

"And I," several others chimed in.

Kawena wasn't sure if she had the right to invite visitors to Ariel's home. "I'm not certain how long I'll be in Oxford," she temporized.

This roused a storm of protest, all the men insisting she must stay. Kawena began to feel hemmed in. She could scarcely see the rest of the room for the tall figures that surrounded her. Spotting Flora Jennings between two jostling shoulders, Kawena said, "Excuse me. I must speak to my friend."

Flora stood with her back to the wall, eying the chattering crowd as if someone might fly at her at any moment. "I dislike being in a room full of strangers. I never know what to say."

"Surely here you can ask about their studies?" Kawena replied. She would have thought that the scholarly Miss Jennings would be quite at home in a university town.

"Very few of them will talk seriously to a woman about their work. Were they speaking of it to you?"

"No," Kawena admitted. "They said mostly silly things. I don't know how I got in among such a crowd. The last time I came to a lecture, hardly anyone spoke to me."

"They've heard about your fortune," said Lord Robert. He'd come up behind Kawena and now lounged elegantly beside them, a glass of wine in his hand.

"You told them," Flora accused.

"I did not! What do you think me? Don't answer that." He sipped from the glass.

"But how could they know?" Kawena asked. She surveyed the people ranged before them. A great many seemed to be looking their way.

Lord Robert shrugged. "Certain kinds of news travels with astonishing speed. As fast as a horse can gallop, I suppose. Scandals, indiscretions, possession of a large fortune. James said you went to the *ton*'s favorite jeweler to discover their value, after all."

"I was told our inquiry was confidential," Kawena replied. She had no objection to the truth, but the intensity of the gazes fixed upon her was startling.

"I'm sure they meant it to be." Lord Robert finished his wine. "But a great pile of jewels...the story's irresistible."

"To those who have nothing better to do than gossip," said Flora, with a severe glance in his direction.

He turned away from her with a weary sigh. "It looks as if James is getting on with this wife prospect, at any rate."

"What?" said Kawena.

Lord Robert indicated his brother and a ginger-haired young lady, deep in conversation. "Ariel's well-known in our family for promoting perfect matches. When he first came to stay, James asked her to find him a proper English bride." He smiled as if this was amusing.

Kawena couldn't help repeating the words, "Proper English bride." They came out before she could stop them. "Proper. To marry." Immediately, she flushed at the stupidity of this, but the others didn't seem to have heard.

"I thought better of Ariel," said Miss Jennings. "You make it sound like...like picking fruit, or something equally insulting."

He had been doing this when she'd first entered the garden and pointed a pistol at him, Kawena realized. And all along, ever since.

"She promised no more than to present him to

some likely young women," Lord Robert replied. He sounded annoyed, and as if he'd had more than one glass of wine. "It's no more than is commonly done."

"In your circles," Miss Jennings retorted. "At the disgusting displays of the Marriage Mart."

Even when he'd held her in his arms, when he'd made his forced proposal to her, he'd been engaged in this hunt. He had known he wanted—told his family he wanted—someone quite different from her. She had never been part of his future. And if her plans might have started to include him…

"People have to meet," said Lord Robert. "If they keep their heads buried in dusty old books—"

"I knew you were mocking me!" Miss Jennings exclaimed.

"You put everything I say in the worst possible light." He stared at her, arms rigid at his sides. "I see there's no convincing you. It's useless to keep trying." Turning on his heel, he walked away.

Kawena was suddenly filled with a burning desire to shove propriety down Lord James's throat and let him choke on it.

"Useless, exactly," hissed Flora. "Just go."

Since he was already gone, and unable to hear this dismissal, Kawena turned to look at her companion.

"I certainly don't care." The flashing glance of Flora's blue eyes argued otherwise. She turned toward the door. "I'm going back to the house. Tell…anyone who wonders where I am."

Perhaps it was impossible to understand a people when you had not grown up among them, Kawena thought. Flora was obviously as furious as she was, but she had no idea why. But if she could understand, Kawena suspected the knowledge would be useful. She followed Flora's path toward the exit. But Lord James caught her before she reached it.

"Enjoying yourself?" he asked. The two words sounded mocking.

One sure way to outrage the dreaded propriety was to hit someone at a party. She couldn't do that. But the English used words as weapons. "Shouldn't I be?" she replied, matching his tone.

"Oh, indeed. Now that you're being lionized, there's no reason to be interested in old friends any longer."

Kawena had no notion what lions had to do with it, and in fact, only a hazy notion of what they were. A few days ago, she would have asked him. They might have laughed over the explanation. "My 'old friends' seem quite occupied with their own affairs." That was the way they did it, she thought. They never said exactly what they meant. Then if they were taxed with some insult, they could blandly deny any such intention.

"You expect they will spend every moment looking out for you, instead?"

Kawena had never realized, before this, that you could long to kiss a man, and to shake him until his bones rattled, at the very same time. She would almost have done it—the shaking part—right here in front of everybody and damn propriety, but for the distance in Lord James's eyes. They showed no sign of the fire that had burned so deliciously when he held her. The figure before her was every inch a duke's son— haughty, closed. He used his very proper manners as a barrier and a silent, unanswerable rebuke.

The ginger-haired girl he had been talking to came toward them, on the arm of a stout older man. "Lord James," she said when they were closer, "my father so wished to make your acquaintance. Like me, he is a great supporter of the navy."

She spoke as if she ruled this room. She looked utterly at home. Lord James turned automatically in response to her demand. Kawena couldn't believe that this was really what he wanted—this rigid little world. But if he thought it was…

He introduced her. She smiled.

If he thought that, someone would simply have to show him how mistaken he was.

Fifteen

ALTHOUGH ALL OF THE RESIDENTS OF ARIEL'S HOUSE were gathered at the breakfast table the following day, the meal was rendered silent by the arrival of a stack of letters. Everyone but James had a missive or two to read, and he was just as glad not to have to pretend to be in a good humor.

Alan was the first to look up from his pages. "Mama says they're going to Brighton to discover what's wrong with Nathaniel."

"Is something wrong with him?" Ariel replied, looking concerned.

"He's stopped answering letters," Robert said.

"He is on his honeymoon," Ariel pointed out.

"That didn't stop him from going up to London and spending a packet on a high-perch phaeton," Robert responded.

Alan frowned. "That doesn't sound like Nathaniel. And how do you know?"

"Lord Robert hears all the gossip," said Flora Jennings, without looking up from her own letter.

Robert glared at her before flicking a finger at

the letter before him. "Friend of mine mentioned it. Thought it was odd."

"It is, rather," agreed Alan.

"I suppose a man can buy a carriage if he wants one," said James. It came out surly, and earned him sidelong glances. He resolved to keep quiet, and not to crane his neck any farther to try to see Kawena's correspondence. She was engrossed in a thick packet on heavy paper. He'd hoped to get a look at the signature, but she was keeping it close.

Robert indicated another of his letters. "And he told Randolph that if he didn't like the breed of bishop he'd found for him, Randolph could hunt down another himself."

"Breed?" said Ariel, frowning. "What does that mean?"

"No notion," Robert replied.

"Perhaps it's some sort of joke?"

"Perhaps Violet has driven Nathaniel mad," James suggested, earning more puzzled stares from his family. But women did drive you mad. Apparently.

"She has altered her entire wardrobe," Robert said, picking up the first letter to consult it again. "Looks like quite a different creature, it seems. Prinny's been ogling her."

"The Regent? Violet?" Alan looked startled.

Flora Jennings made an involuntary sound, drawing the attention of the table.

"Is something wrong?" asked Robert.

"Not bad news, I hope?" said Ariel.

The self-assured Miss Jennings looked uncomfortable. "I had meant to return home tomorrow," she said, "but my mother writes that our cook and housemaid have contracted some sort of fever. The doctor doesn't believe it is serious, but Mama suggests that I stay away until they are recovered."

"Of course you are welcome to stay," said Ariel.

"I don't like to impose on your hospitality. And I should be at home to help."

"You can't do everything," said Robert.

Flora started to speak, then folded her lips closed over whatever retort she'd been about to loose. James didn't know what it was between these two. The woman's mere presence seemed to turn his most socially adept brother into a blunderer. It was as much a mystery as why Kawena didn't seem to be speaking directly to him any longer.

Flora rose. "I must answer her and inquire how they are doing."

Kawena folded her thick letter. "I hope you know that I am very grateful for your hospitality, and for the help in recovering my property." She included James in her look around the table. And that was all. Then she rose, taking her letter and following Flora from the room.

He should have gone off to the Admiralty days ago and lobbied harder for a new posting. Why hadn't he?

※

Kawena found Flora in the room they shared, sitting at the small writing desk with a blank sheet of paper before her. "I don't want to stay," she said when Kawena came in. "Ariel is very kind, of course, but..." Uncharacteristically, she blurted out the rest. "I don't feel comfortable making a long visit with members of Lord Robert's family. With him always *here*. Mama knows that."

Kawena sat in the armchair by the fireplace. "Perhaps I can help." When Flora turned to gaze at her, she added, "I have decided to take a house of my own in Oxford. And I would be very glad, and grateful, if you would join me for a while."

"On your own? But that isn't—"

"Proper," said Kawena, nodding. "I hoped you might help me make it so."

Flora looked both curious and puzzled. "Why?"

"Because you will know just what I must do."

"No, why get a house? Everyone expects you to go home now that you've recovered your inheritance."

Kawena looked down. Flora's blue eyes were acute. "Mr. Crane has undertaken some…business for me, which requires time to complete. I cannot go until it is done. And I find that I want to learn more about my father's country." Both things were true, and reasonable. There was no need to mention Lord James, and certainly no way to describe the jumble of feelings the wretched man roused in her.

"You would have to find an older woman to act as a chaperone," Flora replied. "I wouldn't do for that. If, that is, you care about such things."

"I intend to be a *model* of English propriety." It came out fiercely. Indeed, the intensity in her voice surprised her a bit.

Flora blinked in surprise. "You do?"

"My father would have liked that," Kawena added. She supposed he would have. Who could tell? The question had never come up between them. But she did know that there was another, younger man who was going to be shown a great deal.

This point seemed to weigh with Flora.

"And you know all about it. You could tell me how to…oh, make calls." Kawena named an activity she'd heard of, but did not precisely understand.

"You might choose someone who knows much better than I."

"No," declared Kawena. "For although you understand English propriety, you are not…dedicated to it. So you won't despise me when I make a mistake."

"Of course not!" Flora looked shocked at the idea.

"You see." Kawena nodded and smiled at her. "We might even have fun. Perhaps I shall learn English dancing after all."

Flora's expression shifted from thoughtful to almost dreamy. "You know, now and then, I find myself wishing that I was not expected to be the serious bluestocking, upholding my father's great legacy of scholarship."

Kawena nodded encouragingly. "I think your mother would like the same."

"Why do you say that?"

"She told me she was sorry she had given up going into society," answered Kawena. Somehow, it seemed important that she share this bit of conversation.

"She did?" Flora looked startled.

"I expect she would be glad for you to stay, if you were to tell her that I had asked for your help in… making my way. In the most proper manner."

Flora gave her a sharp glance. "It would be… interesting to see people other than my father's old friends." She made a quick gesture. "I have the greatest respect for them, of course. But they all see me as...one sort of person."

"When you can also be so much else," Kawena suggested.

Flora looked at her. "Perhaps. I don't know."

"Of course you can. If you wish it. Why not?" She meant to demonstrate the truth of that herself.

Flora laughed again. "You make me hopeful. And... actually"—she paused as if struck by a thought—"I might know just the woman to...lend us countenance."

Kawena frowned. "Doesn't that mean face? How could anyone lend us her face?"

"It's another way of saying chaperone."

"The English have so many ways of saying the same thing. So very many words."

"It's true." Flora examined her. "You are charming as you are, you know. There's no real need for you to learn our finicky English rules."

But there was. Someone had to be made sorry. She shook her head.

"Well then...yes. Thank you for your kind invitation. As long as my mother agrees, I accept for...a while. How long were you thinking of staying in Oxford?"

"Oh, not too long. A few weeks?" She didn't have the patience for a much longer visit. Her business would be completed soon, and her future...would be what it would be.

"Very well." Flora smiled. "Then I shall write my mother a rather different letter."

"Splendid. I'm sure she will agree. I'll set about the arrangements."

They exchanged a smile that was distinctly conspiratorial.

⁂

Kawena folded the last of her new clothing and added the garment to her new trunk. The servants arrived to take it downstairs as she was fastening the clasps. A few minutes more, and she would be off. With Ian Crane's help and Flora's shrewd advice, the details of setting up her own household had been easy. The difficulties came, rather, in the reactions of the few friends she had made in England.

Ariel had objected the most strongly, professing herself offended at this desertion. Although Kawena could tell that she wasn't actually angry, she'd also seen that her kind hostess was dismayed and would miss her daily company. Ariel's husband seemed relieved at the prospect of fewer visitors, however, which altered the balance. Lord Robert seemed suspicious about the plan, almost as if it was a trick being played on him. Though why he should think any such thing she couldn't imagine. Flora's mother had been surprisingly easy to persuade. And Lord James... Well, Lord James had been just about as annoying as a man could be. He'd criticized every decision she made, acted as if she was incapable of rational thought. And then, he'd actually gone to tea at the home of the ginger-haired girl from the party.

Kawena looked around the bedchamber one last time. She felt excited and a little melancholy and very determined. She'd recovered her inheritance; she had an exciting plan in motion under Ian Crane's direction. If she could manage this third thing… Well, they would just see. There was no need to feel melancholy. None whatsoever.

A hired carriage awaited her. Her trunk was being taken across town in a cart. Flora Jennings stood beside Ariel, her husband, and Lord James by the front door. "You really insist on going," said Ariel.

Kawena took her hands and pressed them warmly. "We will still see each other often."

"I'll hold you to that," the other woman said.

"Don't hesitate to call on us if you need assistance," said Lord Alan.

"Thank you. And for your kind hospitality."

He nodded an acknowledgment.

Kawena doubted that she would ever understand what went on in Lord Alan's complicated mind. "Where is Lord Robert?" she asked, for Flora's sake as much as anything.

"Gone back to London," Lord James answered in the clipped tone he had taken to using with her.

Flora faltered briefly as she climbed into the carriage. Kawena stepped forward to distract attention from her.

Lord James offered his hand to help her up. Like a proper Englishwoman, Kawena accepted the unnecessary aid. "I still can't see why you're setting up in Oxford," he said, holding her back from the step. "It doesn't make any sense."

He'd said this before, and apparently would say it again. Kawena did not repeat the reasons she'd given. He obviously didn't listen.

"It seems an odd thing to do with all those jewels…"

"…that you stole," she teased.

"I didn't steal them!"

"It may have been an accident," Kawena said, "but the fact is, you did." She stepped toward the open carriage door. "But you helped me find them again, and I am grateful."

"And the rest…did it mean nothing?" he said quietly.

He could say this, and still pursue his proper English bride? "What do you think it meant?" she asked.

Lord James gazed down at her, his fingers tight on her hand. His blue eyes burned into hers. Kawena's skin prickled with memories of the feel of him, the taste of him. She longed to explore those delightful sensations all over again. Except…when it was done he would be…embarrassed? Ashamed? And then he would turn away from her to his proper Englishwoman. Her anger bloomed anew. She stepped up into the carriage and sat beside Flora, pulling the door shut behind her.

Lord James reached through the open window as if he might touch her shoulder, then pulled his hand back as if burned. He moved away. The driver signaled the horses. The wheels turned, and the carriage pulled down the lane and away.

∽∾

James remained outside even after the vehicle was long gone, galled beyond bearing at her departure, and his inability to do anything about it. There was no telling what sort of trouble Kawena would get into, off on her own with only Flora Jennings, of all people, to guide her. People would misunderstand things she said, did.

They would judge her, snub her. Even riches, and the latitude wealth conferred, couldn't guarantee she wouldn't be hurt. He'd tried to tell her. But she didn't listen. She thought she knew all about the world. She didn't! His hands closed into fists at his sides.

If she met some other man that she…liked, would she offer herself as sweetly as she had to him? James was shaken by a storm of jealousy so fierce that he bared his teeth. This imaginary rival at once became the sort of blackguard who preyed on unwary females. James saw Kawena beguiled by a sneaking, insinuating rogue, used without tenderness, then despised and abandoned.

James paced his brother's lush summer garden, not seeing any of the nodding blooms. Even if Kawena escaped physical harm, the country was crawling with fortune hunters. Plausible, well-spoken fellows who flattered and fawned. She wouldn't know how to spot them. What girl did? Did she realize that all her property would pass to her husband the moment she married? Of course not. She came from a place where the women owned the houses. Before she could blink an eye, she'd be bilked out of the fortune she'd come so far to recover.

The thought of Kawena married in such a way filled him with bewildered fury. What convoluted thought process had brought him to this topic? She had no intention of marrying in England. Hadn't she told him so? Hadn't she flat-out refused *him*? She wouldn't take some other fellow.

Of course she wouldn't. Sometime, years from now, back on her island, she would no doubt have a husband and children. She would be content, happy. This picture should have been comforting, but somehow it wasn't.

Nothing made sense. She wouldn't pay him any heed. When had he been able to make her do anything?

James stopped abruptly. He was standing on the very spot where he'd first seen her, he realized. She'd lunged from behind that bush there, in her absurd boy's garb, waving her antiquated pistol and calling him a thief. The memory brought a tender smile to his face. Looking back, he suspected that sally had required every ounce of courage she possessed. But she'd been determined, and she'd done it. She had the spirit of a heroine. She'd been intrepid, gallant…adorable.

This led to other, more intimate, recollections. James stood stock-still among the flowers, both savoring and enduring reflections of the ecstasy they'd shared. She was so soft and sweet, as well as courageous. She was so beautiful, and so intractable. She was…gone.

He made himself turn and walk back to the house. This path led straight to insanity. He couldn't take it. He needed to return to a world he understood, where events were ordered and clear.

The next morning, James set off early for London, to pay another visit to the Admiralty offices. But when he inquired once again about a new posting, the naval administrator who had received him was not encouraging. "There are a great many officers eager for posts, and fewer places now that the war is over," the thin, very upright man told him.

"I know, but—"

"And many of these men rely on their naval position for their entire living, *Lord* James," the man added.

James examined him, wondering if they'd met before. He didn't think so. The fellow's face wasn't remarkable, but surely he would recall if he'd offended him at some point? No, it was more likely that word had spread through the offices about the favors he'd called in to aid Kawena. *Favors that had turned out to be totally unnecessary, in the end*, he thought wryly. It was common to use personal connections to get things done in the service, but some resented it. There were rumblings about reform. It was just his bad luck that such a one had the power to thwart him.

James surveyed the man's tight jaw and unyielding gaze. He thought of telling the fellow that his opposition would, ironically, push James into pulling more strings, even perhaps soliciting help from his father, the duke. But he stifled the impulse. It would only make matters worse. Besides, he didn't want to go to Papa about this matter. He wasn't a boy, to be begging for protection and a leg up. In the end, he indicated his understanding with a curt nod, and took himself off.

Back in Oxford the following day, he distracted himself from wondering how Kawena was getting on by starting a tally of those he might enlist in his cause. But the idea of scheming and maneuvering—not by sail and rudder, but through covert conversations and hinted favors—made him tired. It seemed alien to all the things he liked about the navy—the order and clarity and regulation. He didn't want to play politics. He hated the necessity. Yet he knew this sort of twisty plotting just got worse the higher up you rose. No one became an admiral without such skills, by all accounts. Few achieved a major command by simple ability. Years of squirming lay before him. In this moment, he thought he would rather chuck the whole thing than plunge into that.

He rose from the desk where he'd been sitting and went to look out the window. The spires of Oxford poked up beyond the trees; the garden was lush and welcoming. The scene spread before him was lovely. But…it wasn't the sea. He missed the sea. There was nothing on Earth better than standing on the deck of your own ship, feeling it respond to your orders, filling your lungs with salt air. He couldn't give that up. But what he had to do to get it… Morosely, he turned back to his list. He'd thought of no new names to add for half an hour, when Ariel entered the parlor, a welcome interruption.

"We're going out to a concert," she told him.

James stood, appreciating her fresh beauty in a pale green gown. "I suppose I must come along," he replied, not nearly as averse as he would have been if engaged in some more pleasant activity. He tried for a joking tone. "Will you be trotting out a third bride prospect? Miss Grantham was rather too…enthusiastic for my taste."

Ariel gave him a long, steady look. "As Lily Randall was too opinionated?"

James couldn't interpret her gaze. "Well, she seemed to find my views…quite irritating."

"Can you really dismiss a person after one or two conversations? Are you sure you're giving them a real chance?"

She sounded grave, and looked it. James was nonplussed. He'd never meant this "hunt" to be serious. It had started as a game, in his mind, and grown even less important as time passed. "One can learn a lot from first impressions," he attempted.

"Neither of them tried to shoot you," she replied.

"What?" Ariel was looking at him as if he was slow. "What are you talking about?"

"It's not something I can tell you. You have to figure it out for yourself."

"Figure out…what?"

Ariel turned away. "You are welcome to come with us if you wish to. There is no obligation."

James went. He didn't really enjoy himself, but the crowd and the music and even a further conversation with Miss Grantham about the Battle of Trafalgar diverted his mind from his own concerns.

Sixteen

KAWENA WALKED THROUGH THE PUBLIC ROOMS OF the furnished house she'd taken with Ian Crane's assistance. It had been described to her as comfortable rather than large—hardly more than a cottage, Mr. Crane had said. Clearly, this was an English point of view. The place had a spacious parlor, a dining room, and a study on this floor, without even taking into account the bedchambers upstairs and the big kitchen and pantries below.

What it didn't have was the sea, naturally. Here in Oxford she was miles from the sea. How she missed the sight of surging water, an endless sky. Every day of her life, before this stay in England, had featured the sound of waves. Calm or stormy, placid or wild, the ocean was in her blood. Something deep within her missed its presence all the time. This house was a fine place to pass the weeks until her plans were complete, but she knew she could never settle so far from the shore.

Kawena settled in the back of the house, on a window seat covered with cushions in several shades of blue, and gazed over the roofs of the town. She put an elbow on the sill and rested her chin in her hand.

She missed Lord James. Her dreams were filled with echoes of their intimate encounters—his lips, his hands on her body. She woke frustrated and aching, only to face a day without his companionship. With him at her side, England had been a fascinating place, full of amusing quirks and half-familiar phrases. There had always been something to discuss, opinions to compare. She'd felt like an explorer, not an alien. She'd thrilled to their kinship, as she had with no one else in this country.

Because he wasn't like other Englishmen, she decided, not the ones she'd met at least. He'd been called by the sea. He'd roamed the world, driven by the eager curiosity and thirst for experience that she knew so well. He'd visited her home. He'd had the chance to gain a new perspective on the world.

Kawena looked down. Her free hand was clenched in her lap. Because the truth was, he didn't have such a new perspective. Home from his travels, he was searching for a proper English bride.

Those three words still stuck in her throat like a bit of unchewed fruit. They stood for everything she was not, according to the infuriating Lord James Gresham. And so she knew the next step very well—to show him! She would demonstrate exactly how wrong-headed he was, and then...

Then was then. She couldn't do anything about then. Now, she must begin.

"Kawena?"

She looked up to find Flora Jennings in the

doorway, accompanied by an older woman she didn't know.

"Mrs. Runyon has arrived," Flora added.

Kawena rose and went to greet the newcomer. Flora had assured her that her mother's third cousin, Harriet Runyon, would be a good choice to chaperone them, as well as oversee a cook, a housemaid, and a boy to run errands.

Kawena surveyed the sturdy woman beside Flora. Mrs. Runyon looked to be in her midforties. She had sandy hair, regular features, and a gown that proclaimed fashionable good taste. She looked quite intelligent, with an air of brooking no nonsense that Kawena liked.

"We also have our first callers," Flora said.

Kawena immediately thought of Lord James, but her hopes were dashed by her friend's next words.

"A lady and her son who met you at a lecture." She handed over two visiting cards. "Met *you*, not me," she added with a rueful smile. "I was not mentioned when they inquired."

Kawena read the names and didn't recognize them. There had been so many thrown at her at the last event she'd attended with Ariel.

"It appears that the establishment of our new household has been noticed," Flora said. "The gossips are as efficient here as anywhere."

Kawena remembered the young men who had surrounded her after word of her newfound fortune got out. They'd been like…like flies swarming around fallen fruit. The comparison was unpleasant, yet apt, she decided. "Have the English nothing better to do than talk, talk, talk?" she exclaimed.

"We will refuse them," said Mrs. Runyon. She showed no surprise at Kawena's vehemence. "I don't think we are quite ready to receive callers. We have some plotting to do first."

She smiled. It was a rather...wily smile. Kawena could think of no other word for it.

"If I'm to be your chaperone—"

"People keep using this word," Kawena put in, "but it doesn't even sound English." The sense was clear enough, of course.

"It isn't; it's French," Mrs. Runyon replied. "It comes from *chape*, I think, a kind of protective hood. Chaperones are supposed to shelter the virtue of young ladies like a...a cozy garment."

Kawena stared at her. Her knowledge was surprising, but the dry tone she used was even more striking.

"Cousin Harriet is very well educated," said Flora with a grin. "Even better than I was."

"But I have the sense to keep quiet about it in company," replied the older woman. "Flora shoves her knowledge down unwary throats. At least, those of certain young noblemen."

Flora flushed. "I don't know what you may have heard—"

"No you don't," the older woman interrupted. "But we will discuss that later. First things first. I'll have Annie tell the callers you are not at home."

"But I am." Kawena brightened as an idea surfaced. "Do you mean I should slip out the back door to avoid them?"

Mrs. Runyon smiled. "No. We shall...tell them a lie."

"But won't they be offended if they discover that?"

The older woman held up a hand. "A social lie. Which is different from an actual lie." She went out.

"Different how?" Kawena asked. "If it is not true."

"She is my favorite relative," was Flora's odd reply.

"Are you sure she will be a proper chaperone? She seems…" It was difficult to find a phrase for what she was.

"She will be splendid. Wait and see."

She had no choice but to do so, Kawena thought. It wasn't as if she had other candidates for the position.

"All right, they've gone," Mrs. Runyon said when she returned a few minutes later. She turned to Kawena. "Tell me all about yourself. One needs full information in order to plot effectively." With a gesture, she indicated that they should sit. Such was her air of command that they all immediately did.

Kawena was growing more and more curious about this woman with each remark she made. She was also beginning to like her. She seemed very forthright for an Englishwoman. "I grew up on an island on the other side of the world," she began. "My father was English." She told the story of her journey and the jewels. Flora hadn't heard the whole before either, and her eyes widened in surprise at some points.

When she finished the tale, Mrs. Runyon nodded. "And now you are settling in England."

"No. I'm here for a few weeks more on…business. Then I shall go."

"Ah." Mrs. Runyon eyed her measuringly. "So you are not looking for a husband?"

"A proper English husband?" Kawena grimaced.

"No, I am not!" Both the others stared at her. She hadn't meant to sound bitter, or angry.

"What are you doing?" was Mrs. Runyon's mild reply.

It was a complicated question. And Flora was clearly interested in her answer as well. Kawena did not intend to reveal all her purposes to either of them. "I wish to become better acquainted with my father's...world," she said. "And to *show* the, uh, the English that I...fit here. As 'properly' as anyone." Kawena raised her chin in defiance of every one of Lord James's niggling complaints. "I shall prove that I can be a proper Englishwoman, just as...as my father would have wanted. And then I'm leaving."

"Proper," murmured Mrs. Runyon. "Someone has been throwing that word at you?"

"Throwing is a good way to say it!"

"Inevitable." When both of the young women raised their eyebrows, she added, "Miss Benson is lovely and confident and rich. Lesser mortals will always wish to...deflate such a person. As they see it. And what do they have but their petty regulations?"

"Are you a rather unusual chaperone?" Kawena asked.

"Yes, I am. But in a way that will serve you well, I think. If I came to your island, you could show me all the interesting spots and keep me out of danger, could you not?"

"Yes, of course."

"Well, I can do the same for you here, because I have made a special study of these matters."

"Special?"

"Cousin Harriet is an expert on society," Flora

offered. "The way I know cuneiform, she understands all its ins and outs."

It took Kawena a moment to remember that cuneiform had to do with Assyrians.

"I made the same choice as Agatha—Flora's mother—you see," Mrs. Runyon explained. "I married a gentleman that my family thought much beneath me. But while Agatha withdrew from society, I wormed and weaseled my way back in." She smiled at Flora. "And now, at last, Flora is going to let me use my skills on her behalf."

"On Kawena's, you mean." Flora looked startled and uneasy.

"Indeed, and yours, my dear not-exactly-cousin. Have no doubt that I can deal with your noble suitor."

"He isn't!" Flora practically squeaked.

"What is weaseled?" asked Kawena, partly to aid Flora, and partly because she was curious.

Smiling as if she understood the effort at diversion, Mrs. Runyon turned to her. "A weasel is a small animal that can wiggle into the tightest places and is known for its cunning. I found that I could get what I needed from my aristocratic relatives, as long as I had the wit to approach them just right. Some were vulnerable to flattery. Others craved amusement. A few really wanted to help. Since I have a great many of them, I never had to lean too heavily on any one person."

"And you would do this…weaseling for me?" Kawena asked.

Mrs. Runyon waved off the question. "Oh, it's all done long ago. You will simply benefit from bygone efforts."

"But why would you wish to help me? Or…are you really here for Flora?"

"You're clever. Good." The older woman gave her an approving nod. "I have often longed to aid Flora, as I said. But I find you interesting. With my own children settled happily, I'm glad to have a new…project."

Uncertain, but wanting matters clear, Kawena said, "I will bear any expense you might incur."

Mrs. Runyon interrupted with a laugh. "No need. My dear husband confounded them all by making piles of money in the India trade."

"Which made your situation much easier than my mother's," Flora pointed out.

"I know, my dear." The woman patted her hand. "All the more reason that I am determined to help you with Lord Robert. I spoke to Agatha, you know. She is quite pleased at the idea."

"I don't want any help! That is, there is nothing about him to help *with*."

"If you believe that, then you're not as intelligent as people claim."

"I am. I do. Oh, why must everyone be so insufferably silly?" Flora surged to her feet and left the room.

"Perhaps it's not the mind at fault," Mrs. Runyon mused quietly. "Perhaps it's the heart."

The next few weeks were going to be more interesting than she'd realized when she first made her plan, Kawena thought.

❧

The following afternoon, James was frowning over his list of potential helpers once again when the maid came in to announce visitors. "They asked for you particularly, Lord James, but they wouldn't give their names."

"They?"

"A man and a woman."

"And they refused to tell you who they were?"

She nodded uneasily. "They said it was important, though."

That was odd. James shrugged. Even a rude caller was better than stewing over his situation, or wondering what mischief Kawena was getting up to. "Bring them in."

"Yes, sir."

She returned with a middle-aged couple. The man, small and wiry, wore an old-fashioned skirted coat over a plain shirtfront. He had pale skin, light brown hair, washed-out blue eyes. The woman was small as well and very thin. Her gown and bonnet were the same dark brown as her hair and eyes. Both of them looked as if they had just eaten something sour.

"Good day to you, my lord," the man said. "I am Ronald Benson. And this is my wife, Maria." The latter was silent, staring at him as if her gaze could drill right through his torso. "I see you recognize the name," the man added.

"I have recently met..." James began.

"The young woman you wronged is not so friendless as you believed," the visitor interrupted.

"What?"

"We have come to remove her from your clutches." His tone was at the same time smug and accusing.

Had he actually used the word "clutches"? And

who the devil were these people? "If you are referring to Miss Kawena Benson—"

"My niece!" the fellow interrupted.

The woman's stare was unnerving. Kawena hadn't mentioned any family.

"I warn you, if you have secreted her somewhere, to be a slave to your desires, we will expose your foul scheme." The fellow scowled at him. His wife stared.

James nearly laughed. "I think perhaps you've seen too many melodramas, Mr. Benson."

"I do not attend the theater," the man replied coldly. "Now, I must insist that you take me to my poor niece. Immediately."

James wondered what Kawena would think of being called a "poor niece"? He wished he might see it. "She's no longer staying here. She may be on her way back home, for all I know." It wasn't exactly a lie. The flash of rage in the man's pale eyes told him something about the pair's true motives. "You're her father's brother then?" he continued.

"I am. My family and I are her only English relatives."

"Your family?"

He gestured at his wife. "We are blessed with four children. But we have room in our home for a poor orphan waif. We only recently received word of my addle-headed brother's death."

"Miss Benson isn't an orphan. She has a mother still."

His visitor dismissed this fact with a gesture of extreme distaste.

James began to understand why Kawena's father had settled on the other side of the world. "So you're looking for Miss Benson in order to shelter her and support her?"

Ronald Benson's pale eyes glinted, as if a curtain had been pulled back to reveal the fires of avarice, then swiftly dropped again. His wife's hands spasmed, clawlike. James was suddenly certain that they'd heard about the hoard of jewels. It had been a mistake to take them to Rundell and Bridge, he concluded, however expert the valuation. They should have found a more private expert. And yet, a man who spent his life trading in gems would probably not be able to resist gossiping. The story was just too tempting. And this Benson looked like a merchant, the sort of person who would keep an ear to the ground for such news. "Is your wife mute?" James said, playing for time.

"I beg your pardon?"

"She hasn't said a word, not so much as hello."

"She does not wish to engage in conversation with a person such as you."

James nearly asked why she'd come then. He did wish she'd stop drilling into him with her gaze. "So you intend to...?"

The caller drew himself up. "Aid my niece, of course. Young women require guidance...and protection."

To get as much money out of her as he could, James translated. All of it, by choice. He started to point out that Kawena was of age and not in need of a guardian, then changed his mind. He didn't want to tell these people anything they didn't already know. Society had a tendency to side with older male relatives who tried to take over a young woman's life. This Benson might stir up trouble in the law courts, even if his case was weak. And Chancery ate money like a ravenous heathen god.

James wondered what had happened to Kawena's pistol. He'd forgotten to ask if she'd gotten it back. He'd wager she had, though, which was a comforting thought. "As I said, she isn't here."

"It is as I feared then. You have ruined and abandoned her."

James wondered whether he'd heard that they'd stayed alone at Langford House. Another bad decision he'd made. And then there was the rest... "I did no such thing," he replied. "But if I had, I would of course be happy to make it right."

Benson didn't like that. He'd never get his paws on Kawena's fortune if James married her. No need to remember that she'd turned him down.

"You refuse to divulge her location?"

"Why would you think I know where she is?" That was weak.

"Oh, I think you know very well!"

James stepped closer, looming over the smaller man. "Are you calling me a liar?" *Splendid, James*, he thought, *resort to bullying now*.

Mrs. Benson pulled at her husband's arm. The pair moved away, but he continued to bluster. "If I find that you have deceived me..."

James retreated into the patterns of his upbringing, suddenly every inch a duke's son. "I fear I cannot spare any more time this morning," he said. He walked over and pulled the bell, waiting in icy silence until the maid came to escort the visitors out.

"You have not heard the last of this, *my lord*," Benson said as they went.

James ignored him with aristocratic thoroughness. Had the matter been less serious, he might have laughed. As it was, he waited a few minutes, to be certain the visitors were gone, then ran for his hat. On his way out, he encountered Ariel in the front hall.

"Where are you off to?" she asked.

"I have to see Kawena," he told her. "Miss Benson, that is."

She looked gratified. "You should tell Fl—her that we had a letter from Robert this morning." A smile danced in her eyes. "He's coming back to Oxford, fancy that? Oh, and the oddest thing. He says Nathaniel won some sort of race in Brighton. He's become quite the hero of the young blades. Your parents are on their…"

James didn't even hear the last part. He was already out the door.

Seventeen

OF COURSE JAMES KNEW WHERE KAWENA HAD GONE. The address of the house she'd taken was engraved on his memory, along with so many other things that he mustn't think about. But did, all the time.

He hurried through the streets of Oxford under a gray sky; banked storm clouds on the eastern horizon promised rain later on this late August day. Fifteen minutes later he stood in front of a neat little house built of brick and stone. A scrap of garden added color at each side of the front door. He plied the brass knocker and waited impatiently until the panels were opened by a housemaid. "I'm here to see Miss Benson," he said. He wished he could brush past the girl and go in. He wasn't used to having barriers set between him and Kawena, and he didn't like it.

"I'm sorry, sir, the ladies are not at home."

James's frustration mounted. "I have very important news for her. You must tell her so. I can't be fobbed off."

"They're all out shopping, sir."

It sounded like the truth. Besides, he couldn't think

of a reason for Kawena to deny him. "I'll come in and wait," he replied.

The girl looked uneasy. "Mrs. Runyon said I wasn't to admit anyone without asking her first, sir."

"Mrs.…?" He didn't recognize the name, but he had a dim memory of plans to engage an older woman to stay with Kawena and Flora, which he had approved of at the time. Now, it seemed just another annoyance placed between him and a woman who had been his constant companion for days at a time not so long ago. Seething with impatience, James pulled one of his cards from his pocket and handed it to the housemaid. "Please give that to Miss Benson and tell her that it is important I speak to her as soon as may be."

"Yes, sir." She took the card, dropped a tiny curtsy, and shut the door.

James turned away. But he couldn't quite make himself walk meekly back to Alan's. Although his mind told him there was plenty of time, that the encroaching Bensons wouldn't find Kawena's new abode all in a moment, his feelings rebelled. The thing was, he wanted to see her. She'd been part of his life for…not so very long as hours were counted, perhaps, but it seemed like forever. When she'd driven away, leaving him standing in the lane… Well, he hadn't liked it, not the least little bit—particularly with the bewildering strain that had arisen between them. He *needed* to see her, to talk to her in the old, easy way.

Restless, irritated, James strode the surrounding streets, glancing into shop windows and down narrow crossways, tracing a rough circle around the house. And finally, he had a stroke of good fortune. A female figure came out of a doorway up ahead, and he recognized the lines of her figure, the burnished black of her hair. Striding toward Kawena, James was shaken by an odd combination of relief and excitement. There she was; he hadn't lost her. She hadn't disappeared from his life. Framed by the pavement, she was a vision of loveliness on a gray day. "Miss Benson!"

Kawena raised a hand to shield her eyes from the declining sun, and there was Lord James, hurrying toward her, outlined in light, his hair gleaming copper in the slanting rays of late afternoon. Her heart seemed to turn over in her chest as he came close.

"I must speak to you," he said.

The urgency of his tone, the fire in his eyes, shook her. Every fiber of her waited to see what he would say. And then he didn't speak. He just stared at her, blue eyes burning into hers. How she'd missed him in the short time they'd been apart. She wanted to throw herself into his arms.

"I met a man who says he's your uncle."

"What?" Whatever she had expected, hoped, he might say, it was not this.

"Younger brother of your father's," he added, then frowned. "Though we'll make certain he really is, of course. Hadn't thought of that. I was in a rush to warn you."

Surprise and disappointment warred in Kawena. "My father never mentioned a brother."

"Nor would I if it was this fellow. A creeping, grasping creature. And his wife's worse. They're looking for you."

So his visit had nothing to do with the two of them,

Kawena thought. It was about some strangers. She felt no connection to the family her father had rejected. His parents had written him cruel, insulting letters.

"Or, more to the point, they're looking for your money."

He had no personal word for her at all.

"Are you listening to me?" said Lord James. "This Benson fellow means to make trouble, touting himself as the head of your family. He intends to 'guide' you in managing your fortune. Whether you want him or not."

Kawena gathered her scattered thoughts. "That's ridiculous."

Lord James shook his head. "There'll be those who think a man should be in charge. I expect you'd prevail in the end, but he could tie you up in the courts."

"He has no right!"

He shook his head. "There's right, and then there's the law, and sometimes they…don't run quite together. If you'd left the country…" He cocked his head. "I rather thought you'd go home now you have what you came for."

"I have some plans to carry out first." She would write to Ian Crane at once, Kawena concluded. The law was his business, after all. Surely he would know what to do.

"What sort of plans?"

She gazed up at the handsome face that haunted her dreams. He'd come to warn her, but not to *see* her, really. She saw no sign in his expression of the man who had held her so tenderly, kissed her until she nearly drowned in desire. Words sprang unbidden from her mouth. "How is Miss Grantham? Have you found your bride in her?"

"I beg your pardon?"

"Your 'proper English bride.' Your brother told me that you've been looking for one since you came home."

James started to ask which brother, and then realized it didn't matter. There was always some brother or other, opening his mouth and complicating his life. Many a time he'd felt that he had far too many brothers! And never so much as now. "That was a joke."

"Ariel is finding her for you," Kawena pointed out.

By which she meant that the family wasn't taking it as a joke. And he couldn't deny he'd said such a damned stupid thing. He'd never really meant to act on it. Had he? He couldn't remember now. So much had happened since he'd set foot on shore and thought of settling down. If he'd realized he'd meet a woman like Kawena... Who sounded distant and cold now, nothing like the creature of freedom and fire he'd held in his arms.

"A sweet girl who understands all about propriety."

"Damn propriety." Driven by frustration and regret and desire, James stepped forward. He needed the feel of her, the spicy scent she wore. She belonged in his arms. All his confusion would dissolve if he held her again.

"Good afternoon," said a melodious, cultured voice. "Lord James Gresham, isn't it?"

James barely heard. He reached for Kawena. There was nothing else in his world. And something tapped him—sharply—between the shoulder blades. The blow was enough to unbalance him slightly.

"Lord James!" said the same voice.

James turned and found himself facing a middle-aged woman with sandy hair and a decided air of fashion. She held a furled parasol with a sizable knob of jet on the end of the handle, clearly the source of the blow he'd sustained. In her face and stance he saw all the implacable guardians of virtue he'd ever encountered. Flora Jennings stood behind her, biting her lower lip as if fighting some strong emotion.

"How do you do?" said the older woman, as if they stood in some dashed ballroom and she hadn't just walloped him.

"This is Mrs. Runyon," said Kawena in an unsteady voice. "Who is being so kind as to chaperone us."

"I don't believe we've met," the woman replied. "But I am acquainted with your mother."

In fact, she rather reminded him of the duchess, though there wasn't the least resemblance. He couldn't quite put his finger on it. Something in the penetrating gaze.

Kawena had come back down to earth with a thud. She had been about to kiss him. Proper young ladies did not kiss gentlemen in the street in England, no matter how beguiling they were, no matter how much they wished to. Confound it. She gathered her wits. "Thank you for your warning," she said. "I will look into the...matter."

"Won't you allow me to help?"

"You must come and call on us one day," Mrs. Runyon interrupted. "Thursday, perhaps. We are just getting settled in the house, you know."

As if he cared about that, as if it was a case of

morning calls and advance appointments between him and Kawena. "Perhaps you should tell your…friend that we…" He closed his lips on the rest, fighting his anger. Because how did that sentence actually end? Tell her that they had spent the night in each other's arms? Admit the ruin that he had been trying so hard to protect her from? James shook his head. For a gentleman, the only socially acceptable response was to bow and be off. Unless he could claim a close relation, that of a fiancé, say. Which was impossible.

In that moment a great revelation came over him as an inner voice asked, "Why impossible?"

Had there been reasons? He couldn't remember any of them. When she'd walked out of his life, he'd felt like a ship in the doldrums. Nothing propelled him. Nothing seemed worth pursuing. And that was, he saw now, because he wanted only to pursue her. He just hadn't known it then. Of course there were obstacles—Kawena's views on the subject first and foremost. She'd refused him. But surely they could find a way…?

"I appreciate your news," said Kawena. "Thank you."

Mrs. Runyon and Flora simply stood there, waiting for him to go.

Impossible to speak of marriage here and now. Anyway, he had an idea that women liked a bit of romance and formality in their proposals. He'd been clumsy up to now. He hadn't known what he was doing, what he really felt, in Portsmouth. To blurt out an offer in front of this duenna, who reminded him of his mother… He nearly shuddered. Also, he needed a plan for their future. Kawena had made some scathing comments about wives who sat at home and waited for their naval husbands to return from long missions. She would never be such a meek helpmate. Thank all the gods. He had to tempt her with an existence she would savor, to woo her with a special prospect of wedded bliss. What would that mean? He needed to think.

Mind whirling with disconnected ideas, James bowed to the three women and turned away. He didn't see how wistfully Kawena watched him go.

Mrs. Runyon did. As she gathered her charges with one assured glance, she said, "You and I must have a talk, Miss Benson."

⁓

James walked for quite a while, hoping physical exertion would bring him a measure of calm. He was still thoroughly distracted when he entered Alan's house, however. He would have rushed directly up to his bedchamber, but the housemaid who let him in said, "They're waiting for you in the garden parlor, my lord."

He didn't want to chat with Alan and Ariel. But they'd been very kind and welcoming, and his training did not allow him to be rude, any more than his affection for them would have.

In the pleasant room that opened onto the lawn he found not only his hosts, but also Robert and, unbelievably, his parents. They all looked up from their comfortable seats when he entered, rendering James momentarily speechless. "What are you doing here?" he finally managed.

"We're on the way to a house party, and then on to Herefordshire for Sebastian's wedding," the duchess said, rightly taking the question as directed at the older members of the family. "Since we were passing so close to Oxford, we thought to stop for a short visit. Ariel has forgiven us for arriving on such short notice."

Alan's wife waved this aside with a smile. "It was in the letter I told you about this morning," she said to James.

He vaguely recalled hearing her mention it. Hadn't she said that Nathaniel had won a race? Which made no sense. That wasn't the sort of thing his eldest brother did.

They all smiled at him—Ariel encouraging, Robert sardonic, Alan inquiring, their father, the duke, with the lazy assurance that made him so formidable, Mama warmly affectionate. James was irresistibly reminded of a row of seabirds perched on a ship's rigging, on the watch for any tasty tidbits that might turn up. Which was idiotic. Nothing could be less like a tattered gull than his father.

Up until now, James had always been glad to see his parents. He was away from England for such long periods, it was a treat to visit with any members of his family. But just now his brain was full of chaotic thoughts about the future; he didn't wish this to be noticed or to be questioned about it. Which they would. Particularly Mama.

"We were just waiting for you before going in to dinner," Ariel said. She rose, and the others followed suit.

Seeing two of his brothers side by side with his parents, James noted, for the thousandth time, how all of them had the duke's tall, lean frame and shades of the duchess's auburn hair. Their faces were six variations on the theme of this union of a formidable pair of individuals. What did it take to sustain such a strong and happy bond for all these years? From what he'd seen of the world, it was a rare gift. He wondered if he had any hope of its like.

The duchess took James's arm as they went into the dining room. "Was there indeed a fortune in jewels in that dreadful figure you sent me? To think that it was just sitting in my parlor all this time."

James nodded acknowledgment.

"I'd like to meet the young woman who came so far to find it," his mother continued. "She sounds exceedingly interesting. Perhaps you will take me to call?"

James looked down, meeting her brightly inquiring gaze. Sometimes Mama seemed almost preternaturally knowing. She said it was a relic of rearing six enterprising boys. There was a strong possibility that this was one of those times, and that she was probing for information about him, rather than Kawena. Or both, he supposed. The duchess had never given up watching out for her sons. Her concern was a constant, like bedrock. It was comforting, occasionally onerous, and impossible to evade, short of leaving the vicinity. As he had so often done, come to think of it.

James felt the weight of that regard now, like a cross between a warm cloak on a frigid day and a debt of honor. It roused both a boy's longing for help and a man's insistence on independence. He would enjoy presenting Kawena to his parents, he realized. He was pretty sure they'd like her. The sticking point was how. He realized that he wanted to introduce her, without complications, as his future wife. He didn't want to begin with long explanations and doubts. What if he told them his plans, and then they didn't... He shied away from the thought. "Umm," he said as he seated her at the table, "I hope your journey wasn't difficult. Have you been to Brighton before?"

"Yes, James," replied his mother gently.

Well, of course she had. His parents had been to Brighton innumerable times over the years. They were invited everywhere. They—he groped for a phrase—loomed over London society. James wondered how Robert managed to exist in their shadow. But perhaps he didn't see it that way. He'd always appeared to be flourishing. Until lately, that is, when all the world seemed to be turning upside down.

James took his seat. He glanced down the table to find his mother smiling at him in that ominous fashion she had—the one that meant you'd already told her a great deal, all unaware. Randolph called it a pretense of omniscience. Only in James's experience it wasn't. A pretense. He cleared his throat.

Ariel presented her usual neat, delicious meal, along with a nice selection of wines chosen by Alan. The latter expertly carved a chicken at one end of the table, while his father produced perfect slices off a round of beef at the other. As they began to eat, the duke discussed plans for the autumn at Langford Abbey. The talk of guests coming for a shooting party and rota for the fall plowing made James a bit nostalgic.

"Of course you must invite people, if you like,"

the duchess said to Robert. "Does your friend Miss Jennings hunt?"

It was blatant provocation.

"No," replied Robert in a constricted tone.

A brief silence followed. This was one advantage of having five brothers, James thought. Sheer numbers offered many opportunities to shift attention away from his own, hopefully private, concerns.

"Have you had any news about a posting?" Robert asked him.

Five pairs of eyes turned in James's direction. Diversionary tactics worked both ways. "No. There's a great deal of competition for all the best ones."

"Well, we're delighted to have you at home for a good long while," said his mother.

"If you would like me to put in a word?" his father ventured.

James met the duke's blue eyes, struck, as always, by the vitality and power his father exuded. He was far more compelling than any admiral James had met. It was something of a marvel that he'd never been oppressive. The restraint was partly his own and partly fostered by Mama, James had concluded. Not that his parents hadn't made mistakes. James had his share of painful memories. But in every case, they'd made amends, even apologized to a child, which was most unusual as far as he could judge.

The duke raised one eyebrow and smiled at him. Like the duchess, he could give the impression that he saw right through you. Or perhaps he simply did.

James admired his father more than he could say. But somehow that was all the more reason to strike out on his own, to make his way without special favor. He knew he was lucky to have the love and support of such an illustrious family. Yet it could be a kind of burden, too. It intensified his desire to win their respect for his own efforts, not for things they procured.

"James?" said the duke.

"I'll keep on plugging away myself for a while," he replied. "But thank you."

His father nodded.

"Tell me more about Miss Benson," the duchess said. "A young woman who can make her way around the world on her own must be quite extraordinary."

"I think she is," Ariel replied.

"I'm sure James agrees," added Robert.

Trust a brother to know precisely what you didn't wish to speak of before your parents. Once Kawena accepted his offer... Then he'd talk all they liked. Perhaps he'd take her down to Langford in a week or so. That was a happy thought. But he had to say something now. "I introduced her to Ian Crane," he said. "To help her manage...things." There was Kawena's fortune, too. That was another complication to be considered.

"How kind of you," said his mother. She looked amused again.

The strain was getting to James. "Did you know Crane's father was dead?" he blurted out.

"I did," answered the duke gravely, but with a wicked twinkle in his eye.

Well, of course he did. And it was well past time to sound like something other than an idiot. James groped for a better diversion. "Any word from Sebastian?" he asked. "I haven't heard how he's getting on with the official visit. How's the lovely fiancée?"

"He's been unusually silent," acknowledged the duchess.

"I haven't had a letter in a week or so," agreed Robert.

"I hope it's going well," said Ariel.

He hadn't meant to throw Sebastian to the wolves. Well, not exactly. "We must keep an army of stationers in business, with all the letters this family writes," James joked. "Imagine if we kept them all."

"But I do," replied his mother. "Of course."

Of course she did.

"I have a box for each of you boys," she added fondly. "Every single letter."

James wondered how it would feel, when he was an old man, to read missives he'd written as a grubby schoolboy. Perhaps to a bevy of grandchildren. Rather good, actually, he concluded.

"I understand Miss Benson is settled quite nearby," his mother went on.

If he ever got old, James amended. If this dinner ever ended.

Eighteen

"Sit here by me," Mrs. Runyon said to Kawena that evening. They were alone in the main parlor of the house, a pleasant room that overlooked one of the Oxford colleges. The draperies were closed by this time, however. Flora had gone up to her bedchamber to write a letter to her mother. "And tell me about Lord James."

"About him?" With all the warnings Kawena had received about the spread of gossip, she didn't know what answer to give.

"You told me that he helped you search for your inheritance," the older woman continued, "but I hadn't quite... I suppose he is the one who plagues you with the word 'proper'?"

"How did you know?"

"My dear, seeing the two of you together, much was...obvious." Mrs. Runyon smiled. It was a reassuring smile, adding warmth to her somewhat commonplace features. "I am happy to help you, you know. Flora asked me to do so, and, also, I like you. But if I am to be of any use, it is important that I understand just what you want."

Kawena tried to wrestle her wants into one coherent, socially acceptable sentence. So many of her ideas seemed to contradict each other.

"You said you weren't looking for a husband," the older woman prompted.

"Not as they do it here!" Kawena said. "As if it was some sort of…trading enterprise, where the…the goods must be one certain type."

"The goods. Indeed." Mrs. Runyon looked amused.

"Lord James is searching for a 'proper English bride,'" Kawena blurted out. "Which he obviously believes that I am not. He is forever saying… And I don't care! Not in the least. It is a…a matter of indifference to me. If he wants some simpering miss with red hair, let him! I will never be such a person. I am myself. But it is not as if I *can't* be proper. It doesn't appear difficult. I can obey a few sil…a few rules."

Mrs. Runyon nodded as if this mishmash was perfectly clear. "So our task is to make Lord James sorry."

Kawena flushed. She did want that, but it sounded petty when stated aloud.

"And once he is?"

Kawena looked at her. She seemed to have no doubt that he would be. Which was surprising, and gratifying. Still, she wasn't sure what more to tell her.

"What are we to do with his remorse?" she added with another smile.

Although she'd known Mrs. Runyon a very short time, Kawena was coming to trust as well as like her. It wasn't just Flora's recommendation. There was something about the older woman—a solidity that reminded Kawena of her mother. How she wished for the latter's wise counsel right now! Still, she hesitated.

"I've been privy to many secrets in my life," Mrs. Runyon said. "And I've faithfully kept them all."

Kawena examined her open expression, her candid eyes. "Lord James grew up with propriety and English ways," she began, "but he dreamed of the sea, and he sailed away to become someone quite different. Only...I'm not sure he knows."

"Knows?"

"How different he has become."

"Ah."

Kawena paused for one final moment, and then made her decision. "I have a plan," she continued, and proceeded to tell her companion the whole. She withheld only the fact that she and Lord James had already made love more than once. This seemed a step too far for the ears of a chaperone.

"Hmm," said Mrs. Runyon when Kawena was done.

"But first I will show him that I can be as...as English as he thinks he is," Kawena finished fiercely.

"A novel idea."

"And whatever happens, I shall still have much more than I did when I came here." Which ought to have been consoling, but wasn't, quite.

"Yes, I see."

Having unburdened herself, Kawena suddenly wanted to escape from the older woman's keen, sympathetic scrutiny. "I think I will go to bed now." She rose and hurried from the room.

"It seems life will be rather full of Greshams for the

next little while," murmured Mrs. Runyon as Kawena
went out.

⋘∽⋙

James left Alan's house early the next morning, partly
evading his family and partly planning his approach to
Kawena. He had walked for some time, scarcely aware
of his surroundings, when he heard his name spoken.
Turning, he found Ronald and Maria Benson standing
nearby, flanked by four children who could only be
theirs. Brown-haired, pale, and dark-eyed, dressed in
brown, they were successively smaller copies of their
parents. The two tallest even shared their elders' sour
expression. The littlest looked curious.

"Lord James," said Mr. Benson, with a sardonic
twist to the name.

"Mr. Benson." James gave them a minimal bow.

"We are on our way to call upon my dear niece,"
Benson continued. "We have discovered that she is
staying nearby."

His triumphant tone grated. He'd been quick about
finding the address.

"And to give her the joy of meeting her cousins,"
Benson added, gesturing at his family.

James looked the children over again. They seemed
an unprepossessing bunch, unlikely to charm. But he
had little experience with youngsters. Maria Benson
drew the eldest girl close against her side, as if she
expected him to make a run at a chit scarcely into her
teens. It really was too much. James bared his teeth in
a predatory smile. The entire Benson clan shrank away
as if he might actually bite them. James touched the

brim of his hat and turned away. There was nothing to say to these people. The important thing was to warn Kawena of their imminent arrival.

But James had no sooner headed in the direction of Kawena's house than he heard his name again. This voice was far more familiar, however, and impossible to ignore. He turned back. "Hello, Papa." Oxford was too small a place to have a family the size of his, James thought.

Resplendent in a dark blue coat and buff pantaloons, plying a tasseled cane, the duke joined him. "A fine morning for a stroll," he commented. "I suspect it will be too hot later. Are you going this way?"

He didn't wish to take his father to Kawena's. He had to get there before the Bensons. He couldn't think of a plausible excuse to just run. James indicated a random turn.

They walked along side by side. James noticed, yet again, that he was an inch or so taller than the duke. It was a known fact that nevertheless always surprised him.

"Is something troubling you?" his father said after a while.

"What? No." James had been immersed in thoughts of how to get away without giving offense, or revealing his mission.

"Ah."

They crossed an arched bridge. A punt glided out from under it, and they paused to watch the young man at the oar guide the slender boat down the river.

"It's just…your mother had a notion that you were 'brooding' about something."

"Brooding!" James was revolted by the idea.

The duke laughed. "The word does conjure up visions of hens, does it not? But she's not often wrong."

She was usually uncannily right, in fact.

"I understand your position about the Admiralty, and indeed respect it. But if there's anything else I could help you with?"

But a thought had struck James. "Where is Mama?"

"Oh, she and Ariel put their heads together and went off somewhere. I thought it best not to inquire about their plans."

"Why?"

His father smiled at him. "One thing I've learned in more than thirty years of marriage is: don't ask questions if you don't wish to know the answers."

James puzzled over this. "But how do you know you don't want to know until you…know?" He grimaced at the stupidity of this sentence.

"That's the trick of it," replied the duke with a smile. "One learns with experience."

"By knowing things you wished you didn't?" *What sort of dire secrets would those be?* he wondered.

His father nodded. "I could tell they had some scheme in mind this morning. And no desire for my opinion of…whatever it was. In such cases, I've found that ignorance is often the better choice."

"Scheme?" James felt a brush of panic, mixed with a strong desire to delve deeper into his father's store of marital wisdom. But mainly, he was aware that they were as far from Kawena's house as one could be while remaining in Oxford. It was probably too late to warn her now.

❧

Thus, Kawena's household was surprised by the appearance of six Bensons on their doorstep a short while later. All three ladies were sitting in the parlor when Ronald Benson's visiting card was brought in. Kawena had briefly discussed her relatives' arrival with the others, and so they were generally prepared. *One never knew how people would take things, however*, Kawena thought as she awaited them.

The maid returned with what seemed at first a great many people. The man and woman looked between thirty and forty. Both were small and somberly dressed and dour. Indeed, Kawena found them almost aggressively drab, as if they disdained any form of ornament, or wished to give that impression. The four children with them were dressed similarly. They looked to range from around twelve to perhaps four years old. Kawena examined the man for any resemblance to her father. Beyond his brown hair and blue eyes, she found little. Perhaps their noses had the same curve. Papa had been much taller, his features etched by laugh lines.

"I am Ronald Benson," said the man with a nod of greeting. "Your uncle. This is my wife, Maria, and our children: Anne, John, George, and Susan."

As their names were given, each child gave a curtsy or a bow, except for the youngest, who merely grinned up at her.

Kawena introduced Mrs. Runyon and Flora, then said, "My father never told me he had a brother."

A look of distaste passed across the older Bensons' faces, as if they'd eaten something bitter and had to force themselves to swallow it. "Alas, we were... estranged," her newfound uncle replied.

If Kawena had needed any further evidence of what her father's family thought of him, she would have had it in the thoroughly unconvincing way he said "alas."

"But we are here to remedy that," the man went on.

"Are you? Please, sit down." Ronald and Maria Benson sat side by side on a sofa. In response to a glance from Maria, the children filed around and ranged themselves behind their parents in a graduated row.

"We've come to save you," Maria Benson said then.

"From what?" Kawena asked.

"You are all alone in the world," her uncle replied.

"On the contrary." Kawena gestured at her companions. Mrs. Runyon was the picture of fashionable respectability in a dove-gray gown. Flora looked equally proper. "And of course, I have my mother and aunts and other family back home."

The revulsion on the faces of the adults, and the two older children, dissipated any lingering doubts Kawena might have had. How dare they look so contemptuous of her mother? And what had these people told her cousins about her? Only the maid's entry with a loaded tray stopped her from making a very sharp remark. Kawena had to take several calming breaths before she could manage, "Would you care for some Madeira...Uncle Ronald?"

"I do not indulge in spirits of any kind," he said.

Of course he did not. *What is the opposite of the word "convivial"?* Kawena wondered. "Ah, some lemonade then? And cakes for the children?"

Sparks of enthusiasm in the younger Bensons'

eyes relieved Kawena somewhat. She didn't want to contemplate the sort of child who would spurn a bit of cake.

Ronald and Maria Benson accepted small glasses of ratafia and allowed their offspring one iced cake each.

"Are my grandparents still living?" said Kawena then.

"Alas, no."

His "alas" sounded nearly as insincere as before. "You must tell me about them," Kawena said. It was the one thing she would like to hear from him. Her father had told her so little about his family.

"Of course. They would want to be sure we gave you every assistance," he replied. He cleared his throat. "Particularly because...we have heard...talk that you have the...burden of a sizable fortune."

He really was transparent. Did he think she was a fool? "Burden?"

When she didn't deny the fact, Ronald Benson's pale blue eyes gleamed. It might have been enthusiasm, but seemed much more like avarice. Probably he was not aware that he was rubbing his hands together. "It is a great responsibility. And so we have come to offer you our help and protection."

Kawena indicated her companions again. "But as you can see, I'm not without friends. I don't require any...particular help."

"Strangers." He rejected the concept with a gesture. "Not family."

"When do you put the bone through your nose?" asked little Susan Benson. She had been staring fixedly at Kawena.

"Susan!" Her mother twisted in her seat and glared

at her. The other children shot their youngest sister sidelong glances, appalled and silently gleeful.

"I only wear it on special occasions," Kawena responded immediately. "To evening parties and balls."

Maria Benson paled, her brown eyes seeming to bulge in their sockets.

"It goes with my feather headdress and oyster-shell bangles," Kawena added. She heard a choking sound from Flora and took care not to look at her.

"Your cousin is making a joke to cover your rudeness, Susan," said Ronald Benson. "As you can see, she is completely at home in English fashions. Apologize to her at once."

As the little girl muttered an apology, Kawena noted that her uncle was not a fool. She mustn't forget that he was shrewd and persistent and poised to take advantage. Twitting him might be amusing, but he was clearly very serious about getting his hands on her fortune.

"Your family will have your best interests at heart," he said, picking up where he'd left off.

"What would those be?" Kawena wondered.

"What?" He looked momentarily confused.

"My best interests." She wanted to learn more of what he had in mind before making any move.

"Ah. To conserve capital, naturally. To invest wisely. I have had some experience along those lines and could take over...that is, I could advise you."

No mention of her wishes or her happiness or even her future. Kawena had heard enough. "My father taught me to be quite careful with money," Kawena answered, "as he always was." Until he stuffed his entire fortune into a carving, she did not add.

This clearly struck a chord. She watched Ronald Benson imagine the sorts of safeguards he would set around a girl's fortune. "But he is gone." Under Kawena's gaze, he quickly added, "Sadly."

"I have engaged an experienced man of business to oversee my affairs," she replied.

"Who?"

Kawena was satisfied that she wanted nothing to do with her newfound relations. It was time to rout them. "But as I establish myself in English society, I'm sure I would be glad to meet your friends."

She let Maria Benson contemplate the picture of a "half-breed" niece—as Kawena was certain they characterized her—making a mark among her acquaintances. Perhaps joking about bones and oyster shells. From the other's expression, it wasn't a welcome thought.

"I understand it is the custom in England for a young lady's family to 'bring her out'?" Kawena continued. "It that the correct phrase? And apparently I will need a number of new gowns, and, oh, many other things."

"You would of course bear the expense of such items," said Ronald hurriedly.

"Oh, but I think you are right about conserving capital. I would leave that to my family."

"We do not move in such circles," said Maria Benson, "and indeed have no interest in friv—"

Her husband hushed her with a gesture and a sharp look. As Maria subsided, Kawena contemplated what *she* would do to a man who tried to silence her that way. She would punch him, she decided.

"Fortunately, I have many connections in society,"

said Mrs. Runyon, every inch the *grande dame*. They had agreed that she would hold back and then speak when it seemed to her appropriate. "And I shall be happy to introduce Miss Benson."

"And how much do you intend to bilk her out of for this supposed 'service'?" demanded Ronald Benson.

The ladies were momentarily silenced by his breathtaking rudeness. Then Kawena stood, ready to have him thrown out of her house. As she started to speak, the housemaid came in again. "The Duchess of Langford and Lady Alan Gresham," she announced.

"Ah," Mrs. Runyon murmured as she rose at Kawena's side. "Just what we need." She stepped forward with a smile. "Duchess, how kind of you to call."

"Mrs. Runyon," replied the tall, elegant newcomer. "I hope you're well. I haven't seen you since the Trents' Venetian rout party, I believe."

"Very well, thank you. May I present Miss Kawena Benson? You are acquainted with Miss Jennings, I believe."

"Of course I am. How is your mother, Flora? I haven't seen her in an age."

"Quite well, thank you." Flora's smile showed glee at the unfolding scene.

"And Miss Benson, I've heard a great deal about you."

As Lord James's mother examined her, Kawena grew a bit nervous. The duchess had a penetrating gaze. The small curtsy she gave felt perfectly natural in this instance. "Hullo, Ariel," she added.

"Oh," said Mrs. Runyon, as if recalling some tedious task, "these are Miss Benson's uncle and aunt. And their whole family. They called...unexpectedly."

Kawena had to hide a smile. Her tone was such a perfect combination of rebuke and distaste. She made it sound as if their visit was a social misstep and an imposition, even though morning calls were commonplace.

The Bensons were staring, overawed, at the duchess. She looked at them, exchanged a glance with Mrs. Runyon that appeared to communicate a great deal, and sat gracefully in an armchair.

The small parlor was becoming crowded. Flora and Ariel, also exchanging speaking looks, took two straight chairs in the corner. Kawena and Mrs. Runyon returned to the smaller sofa opposite the Bensons.

"I was just telling…everyone," Mrs. Runyon said, "that Miss Benson is very fortunate in her friends. How many young women have the Duke of Langford, for example, taking an interest in their affairs?"

Without a flicker of surprise showing in her handsome face, the duchess nodded. "He is always glad to be of service to a friend of the family."

"A friend of your *son*, you mean," said Ronald Benson.

Kawena nearly gasped. Even his wife looked uneasy at this blatant discourtesy.

"I have several sons," replied the duchess in a tone that might have frozen him into a block of ice where he sat. "Are you acquainted with one of them?"

"I…no…not…but I have heard dire things about his treatment of my young relative." Even under the withering scrutiny of two leaders of the *ton*, he rallied. "And I won't let him get away with it."

The housemaid reappeared. She looked excited by all the activity and the stream of noble visitors. "Lord James Gresham," she said.

James walked into a small parlor crammed full of people, all of whom were staring at him with varying degrees of emotion. He was dismayed, but not surprised, to find his mother and Ariel among them. There was nowhere to sit.

"Aha!" said Ronald Benson.

He, at least, was negligible. James gave him his haughtiest, most discouraging gaze.

"You see?" added Benson, as if he'd proved something.

"Really, you cannot…" began Mrs. Runyon.

James didn't know if she was referring to him, but he was glad to see she didn't have her parasol.

"I see that my son has arrived to fetch us, as agreed," said his mother coolly.

He tried to look knowing, as one did when Mama sprang some idea out of the blue. She expected her offspring to be fast on their feet.

"I hope he will stay for a glass of Madeira," said Kawena.

James nearly lost the thread as he met her eyes. It was as if, suddenly, there was no one else in the room—just the two of them. His whole body came alive with wanting her. This wouldn't do. He looked away.

"Indeed," added Mrs. Runyon. "We must find a chair for you, Lord James." She fixed Maria Benson with a stern look.

The dismissal was no less strong for being unspoken. Mrs. Benson rose as if pulled by invisible strings. "Children," she said.

Kawena hoped for a moment that her newfound family would abandon their schemes after this. But it soon became apparent that her uncle couldn't give up on the money. The calculation in his expression was almost comical. "We are staying a few days in Oxford," he said.

"But it is expensive to lodge a family here!" exclaimed Maria Benson.

Her husband glared at her. They really were not very skilled at hiding their emotions. He rose. His wife and children clustered behind him. "We look forward to becoming better acquainted with our…dear niece." He sketched a bow and led his brood out without waiting for the housemaid's escort.

For a few moments, the only sound was footsteps on the stairs. It gradually died away. The front door thudded closed.

"What odd people," said the duchess then. "I beg your pardon, Miss Benson, but…"

"Odd scarcely covers it," Kawena said. "I can see why Papa settled on the other side of the world."

"I think we really will have to set my husband on them," she added. "We can't have this fellow spreading stories about 'dire behavior.'"

James shrank under his mother's speculative gaze. He waited for her to ask what Benson had meant, but for some reason she didn't. Neither did Ariel, or Flora, or the formidable Mrs. Runyon. Encircled by apparently incurious females, he stepped over to pour a glass of wine from the decanter on the tray, then subsided onto the vacated sofa.

"I'll speak to him," Mama concluded with a nod. She turned to Kawena. "But now, we finally have an opportunity to get better acquainted."

James observed Kawena's tentative smile. He wanted to sweep her up and whirl her away to some secluded spot. He wanted to observe all the proprieties in order to protect her position and earn his mother's respect and approval. And he was acutely aware that his best course of action was to sit still and keep quiet. It was one of the hardest assignments of his formidable career.

But as he listened to the ensuing conversation, it grew easier. He'd thought his mother would like Kawena, and he could see that she did. The reverse was also clearly true. Not only that, despite her unique origins, Kawena seemed to fit in the group as well as Ariel or Flora did. Granted those two weren't conventional society misses, but who cared about that? James felt a growing relief and joy as the talk ranged over plans for various future outings. Very soon, as soon as he could get her to himself for a minute, Kawena would be his, part of the family harmoniously represented here.

"You are very silent, James," said his mother after a while.

"Just listening to all you charming ladies," he replied. In a mellow glow, he raised his now-empty glass to her and smiled.

The duchess looked briefly startled. Then she smiled back with a warmth that buoyed him even further.

Nineteen

Two days later, Kawena examined her reflection in the long mirror in the corner of her bedchamber. The choice of what to wear for her first official outing in Oxford since establishing her own household had taken time and careful thought, and much consultation with Mrs. Runyon, an expert in the nuances of dress. They wanted to dazzle everyone who saw her, in an extremely proper way.

The resulting gown was a creamy white with a modest neckline and three-quarter sleeves. The cut emphasized her curves in an unexceptionable way. The color brought out the warm glow of her skin. And a lacy shawl in the same shade heightened the impression of decorum. She'd fastened a creamy rose in her black hair, which was once again in a knot at her nape. Any knowledgeable person could see that her clothes were expensive, the product of the finest modiste in town. No high stickler could find anything objectionable in its design. Kawena was satisfied that her goal had been achieved.

They were attending a concert. When Mrs. Runyon

had deplored the lack of regular assemblies in Oxford, Kawena had pointed out that she was not familiar with English dances. She hadn't been able to resist adding that if she was going to dance, she liked to be outside with a fire, and drums. Flora had laughed. Mrs. Runyon had allowed her a smile and said she was sure she needn't remind Kawena not to say so to anyone else.

She came downstairs to find the two of them awaiting her. Flora wore a new blue gown that matched the hue of her brilliant eyes. Mrs. Runyon had persuaded her to have her dark hair done in a mass of ringlets, and she looked somehow softer and more approachable than usual. Their chaperone was grand in amber silk with a magnificent India shawl. Everything about her proclaimed the woman of fashion.

The concert hall was already busy when they arrived. The singer, up from London, was much celebrated, and the university town was turning out to hear her. The rows of chairs near the front were filling, but many people lingered in the reception area, greeting friends and showing off their finery.

The Bensons must have been lying in wait, Kawena concluded, because they rushed up to her as soon as she entered. Though they were only two smallish individuals, she felt surrounded, and they positively herded her toward a less occupied corner. She couldn't refuse without undue fuss. This propriety could be such a wearisome thing, Kawena thought.

Her uncle bent close and murmured, "Rumors are flying about the size of your fortune. I really don't know what to tell people."

Kawena nearly asked, "What people?" She didn't think her uncle was acquainted with anyone in Oxford.

"We wouldn't wish to be deceptive," added his wife.

Kawena smiled and said nothing.

"There's talk of piles of jewels." The Bensons both leaned farther forward, waiting for her answer.

"My father left me some gems," Kawena conceded. It seemed to be common knowledge, after all. And she didn't think she would get away without telling them something.

"Valued at?" asked her uncle sharply.

Kawena took refuge in the woolly-headedness the English, and particularly her uncle, seemed to expect of young women. "Oh, quite a bit."

Ronald Benson's hands closed and opened in frustration. "Perhaps I should speak to your trustees."

"My…?"

He appeared to grind his teeth. "Where can I find them? Are they bankers? In the City?"

"Papa did not trust bankers," Kawena replied with perfect truth. "He said they were worse than leeches." Of course her uncle would assume that there were men somewhere controlling her money, she realized. He wouldn't be able to imagine any other arrangement. "Papa said that a skillful sea captain knew ten times as much about handling money," she added.

"Your trustees are sea captains?" exclaimed Maria Benson. "That's ridi…very odd."

She hadn't said they were, Kawena thought. Or even that they existed. But she felt uncomfortable. She didn't like to come so close to lying. "Are you very fond of music, Uncle Ronald?" she asked to change the subject.

She got no answer. The Bensons seemed to be searching the room, and in the next moment she discovered why. "Ah," said her uncle, and made a beckoning gesture. "Here is someone I wish you to meet, Kawena."

Was he aware of the distaste that tinged his voice every time he said her "foreign" first name? Surely he couldn't be. He must be making an effort not to insult her.

"This is our friend Anthony Haskins," he continued. "I commend him to you. Haskins, this is my niece."

"Miss Benson."

A gentleman of medium height and fashionable appearance bowed over her hand. With his pale blond hair dressed *a la mode* and his beautifully cut coat, he didn't look like a friend of Ronald Benson's. He had a handsome face, quite a pleasant smile, and an air of moderate consequence. Kawena put him in his midthirties.

The Bensons had recruited their own tame suitor for her hand, she realized. Thwarted in their direct approach, they'd found a coconspirator. Doubtless this Haskins had agreed to divide her fortune with them once she married him. She examined the man more closely. If she hadn't suspected a plot, she might have found him engaging. Her uncle was even more devious than she'd thought.

"Haskins has a neat little estate in Somerset," said Ronald Benson. "He and I have been working together on a canal scheme."

The man looked self-conscious. "Miss Benson will not be interested in canals. Are you looking forward to hearing Madame Santini sing, Miss Benson?"

An unusual sort of fortune hunter, Kawena thought. He had a definite charm. "Of course," she replied. "And you? Are you very fond of music?"

"I have had little opportunity to hear really good performances."

"Oh?"

"I live in the country and am most often busy with other things."

"But you would like to spend seasons in London," put in Maria Benson. "Given the *chance*."

Haskins winced at the clumsy emphasis she put on the last word. He offered Kawena his arm. "Would you care to find a seat? It looks as if they are about to begin."

After a moment's hesitation, Kawena took his arm, mostly because it was clear that the Bensons did not intend to accompany them. She also looked about until she caught Flora's eye, and summoned her friend with an unobtrusive gesture. Mrs. Runyon's expression suggested that she approved of this move.

Kawena introduced Flora, and the three of them took seats in the middle part of the hall. Rather curious about how this newcomer intended to win her over, Kawena said, "What brings you to Oxford, Mr. Haskins?"

"Ah, well, it was just an impulse."

"Perhaps you are a scholar?" Flora said. "The libraries here are very fine."

"No, indeed, anything but!"

"You don't think much of scholarship?"

"Well, it's rather a waste of time, isn't it?" the man answered.

"How so?" Flora's voice had grown distinctly cooler.

"There are so many more important things to do in the world."

Flora raised her chiseled brows. "My father was a dedicated scholar," she replied.

Haskins grimaced, and Kawena took pity on him. "You are busy managing your estate, I suppose."

"Yes." He said it with the air of a man grasping a lifeline. "And caring for my family. I have a three-year-old daughter," he continued, with the air of a man making a confession.

Had she been wrong about her uncle's scheme? "Your wife is not with you?"

"She died soon after Annie was born."

"I'm sorry."

He acknowledged this with a nod. As much as his situation, his self-deprecating expression won her sympathy. Yes, indeed, Uncle Ronald was a sly and skilled opponent.

There was a stir behind them, and Kawena turned to discover that the Gresham party had arrived and was standing in a group near the entry. The sight of three tall, handsome, auburn-haired noblemen posed next to their even more distinguished parents had riveted the crowd's attention. "He looks like a duke," she murmured.

"What?" said Haskins. "I beg your pardon, I didn't quite hear."

Kawena shook her head. Her tongue still ran

away with her on occasion, and produced comments that were not strictly proper. She didn't even know what this one meant—only that her first sight of Lord James's father had been oddly satisfying. Even in such striking company, his grace and assurance stood out. "Lord Robert is back," she said to cover her lapse.

"I see that he is," replied Flora, her voice carefully neutral.

And then Lord James's searching gaze found Kawena, and drove every other thought from her mind.

⁕

James was nearly wild with frustration. It seemed a simple thing, to manage a few minutes of private conversation with a woman he knew well. A woman he'd traveled with, talked with for hours, held in his arms, by God, and watched passion drown her... He made himself uncurl his fists.

He'd called at her house, several times, and been told she was out shopping. He didn't think it was a polite lie, and yet... Was he really so unlucky in choosing his times? And now, finally, there she was, a few yards away, and it might as well have been miles. He wanted to see her alone, not in the midst of a dashed crowd. She must understand that.

He gazed at her, sitting in one of the gilt chairs, exquisite in a pale gown with a rose in her hair. His pulse accelerated. She looked like a lily in a room full of nettles. She turned her head as if listening to the man next to her, a complete stranger. James bristled, wishing he could rush over, grab the fellow by his collar, and haul him away from her. That might relieve his feelings a bit.

"James?" A hand gripped his arm, and he turned with something like a growl.

"What the deuce is wrong with you?" asked Robert. His hand tightened on James's sleeve. "You've been as surly as a bear for days."

"No, I haven't."

"Yes, you have." His brother released him. "But you aren't going to pick a quarrel with me, so no point in trying." He turned to follow the rest of the Greshams to a row of chairs. "Are you coming to sit with Mama?"

"No," said James again. He moved in the opposite direction, his whole mind concentrated on separating Kawena from all these people. He'd been half-mad already, and actually seeing her, looking so lovely, fired his brain with memories of kissing her, making love to her. Why had it taken him so long to realize that he couldn't live without her?

He edged between two rows of chairs. He would simply sweep her up and march her out of this blasted place. Then she would have to listen to him. Who cared what a bunch of Oxford biddies thought?

His way was blocked by a line of projecting knees. Before he could shove past them, the musicians at the front struck up, and a buxom lady stepped out to face the audience. Fixed by a legion of glares and hissed protests, James was forced to drop into a vacant chair. He then had to endure a series of horrifying warbles in languages he didn't understand. Punctuated by rounds of applause that gave him a very low opinion of the taste of this audience. Several times during this torture, the unknown man next to Kawena made a pretense of craning to see better, making sure that their shoulders touched in the process. He smiled at her, too. Who did he think he was? Who, in fact, was he?

Finally, after what seemed an eternity of caterwauling, the singer wrapped it up and made her curtsy. James rose, relieved, only to have the blasted listeners stomp their feet and shout bravas until she came back for an encore. James had to wait another ten minutes before she left the dais for good, and he was free to seek out Kawena.

"Santini has a fine voice, doesn't she?" said an old lady next to him.

"I've gotten more amusement out of a pair of yowling cats," James said, earning a shocked, admonitory glare.

He slipped past her and wove through the flood of people leaving their seats on the way to the refreshment room. Unfortunately, Kawena and her escort exited at the other end of the row. James had to take the long way 'round to reach them. When at last he did, he found that they'd joined Ronald and Maria Benson, who had apparently been lurking at the back of the hall, like crows of ill omen.

With the sketchiest of bows, he met Kawena's dark eyes and said, "I'll take you for some refreshment." He tossed the unknown gentleman a glare as he offered his arm.

"Hello, Lord James," Kawena replied. "I don't believe you've met Mr. Haskins? Allow me to make a *proper* introduction. Mr. Anthony Haskins, Lord James Gresham. You know my aunt and uncle." She looked around the group. "Oh, Flora has gone to Mrs. Runyon."

The Bensons glowered at him. Haskins surveyed him with raised brows. James didn't care a whit. He and Kawena were known to be acquainted, and he was the son of a duke, by God. They couldn't stop him from talking to her. "Lemonade," he said. Whatever social skills he possessed had deserted him.

Kawena gave an odd little smile and took his arm. He swept her away at once. "Who the dev—who is that fellow?" he said as soon as they were out of earshot.

"It seems my newfound relatives are being so kind as to find me a husband," she replied.

James stopped moving, causing a lady behind them to bump into Kawena. "What?"

"I beg your pardon," she said to the stranger, stepping back to allow her to pass.

James pulled her into the refreshment room, then over into a corner where the buzz of conversation was not quite so deafening.

"A *proper* English husband," Kawena said then. She gazed up at him.

Staring into those mesmerizing dark eyes, he couldn't seem to find words. The roar of conversation receded to a muted buzz. He was aware only of her, how he ached for her. He needed to speak. Now was his chance.

"I'm sure I don't know what you mean," said Flora Jennings, popping up at Kawena's side like a cannon ball through the rigging.

"Yes, you do," answered his brother Robert, an equally unwelcome arrival at his own shoulder.

"I assure you I do not." Flora planted herself next to Kawena with the air of a female who did not intend to be dislodged. "Did you enjoy the music?" she asked her.

"Couldn't have," said James. "That load of screeching and wailing?"

"Santini is being hailed as the leading soprano of our age," said Robert. He sounded almost as irritated as James felt.

"By a raft of simpering toadies," James retorted.

"Is there lemonade?" said Kawena. "You mentioned lemonade."

The other three looked at him. James was seized by a longing for the heaving deck of his warship. There, he could simply order everyone away. He could shout, if he wanted to—which he vehemently did. He could rake the…deserving over the coals. Here in this blasted chattering hell, he could only…go and fetch the thrice-damned lemonade. Fuming, he did so.

When he came back, Alan and Ariel had joined the party. James handed off three glasses to the ladies, and kept the fourth for himself, wishing it was something far stronger.

"None for me?" said Robert. "Or Alan?"

"Get your own," James growled.

"Are we ten years old again?" murmured Alan in mild reproof.

"More like five," muttered Robert.

James wished they were. If they were children again, he could punch one of his brothers—Robert, by choice—without disastrous consequences.

Across the room, the duke and duchess observed their offspring, and the three lovely young ladies

beside them. "You're right, my dear," said the duke.
"James is clearly laboring under some...cloud."

"And Robert," she replied in a low voice.

"Not quite so much."

"Nearly," she answered. "Ah, those are the Bensons."
She indicated the couple with a subtle gesture.

The duke examined the somberly clad pair. "These
are the ogres I am expected to quash? Hardly up to my
weight, do you think?"

"He's more devious than he looks."

"He would have to be. You really think it necessary
that I intervene? James doesn't like it, you know."

"That's true." The duchess watched the group of
young people a while longer. "You're right. Let's wait
and see. The boys may manage things for themselves."

Her husband returned an admiring look.

∽

James learned that the second part of the evening
was to feature a string quartet. Knowing this would
be more than a man could bear, and aware that the
Bensons and this Haskins fellow were lurking, ready
to pounce, he abandoned good manners and pulled
Kawena away from the group. Ignoring Flora's frown
and Ariel's raised brows, he hustled her over to one
of the long windows, where some draperies offered a
thin illusion of privacy. "I need to speak to you," he
declared. "This Haskins fellow..." Wait, he hadn't
meant to begin with that.

"Do you think perhaps that is what Papa would
have wanted for me?" Kawena replied. "A proper
English husband like Mr. Haskins?"

James felt as if all his blood rushed to his head. "It's the last thing he would have wanted!"

"How can you be so sure?"

"Because…" He couldn't race off and throttle this Haskins, James told himself. Besides, Kawena was the one who mattered. "Your father left England, and never looked back, for his whole life."

"True," said Kawena, as if she was really considering his argument.

"He chose a wife who had nothing English about her."

"That is also true."

"I'm sure he didn't give a hang for propriety."

Kawena fixed him with a steady, unreadable gaze. "He kept a watch over me, and didn't let me go to the port when ships were in," she pointed out.

James silently applauded her father. Sailors on shore leave were a randy lot.

"So, you don't think I should marry a proper Englishman?" she added.

Too late, James saw the trap he'd fallen into. He'd been so bent on routing an unexpected rival that he'd paid no heed to his own case.

"If you want a husband, take me," he blurted out.

"What?"

"I…that is…I've been trying to call on you ever since… I wished to ask you to do me the honor of becoming my wife." He muttered it, not wanting to alert the people all around them. This wasn't the way he'd planned to make his offer. But he couldn't wait any longer for an opportunity, blast it.

"What?" said Kawena again.

She had to have heard him. "I'm as proper an

English husband as you'll find." It came out sounding inane, and not at all what he meant.

In a single flash, Kawena remembered sitting at her mother's feet and asking for the story of how her parents met. She'd heard it before, many times, but she never tired of the tale. Her mother always indulged her, recounting how her father had come down off his ship, looking to buy fresh food and take on water. She'd been among the group who greeted him, and when their eyes met, it was as if they recognized each other, instantly familiar strangers. Her mother had not believed in it, though. She had scoffed inside and turned away. Not until Kawena's father had let his ship sail on without him, not until he had learned the words in *her* language, not until he had knelt at her feet and declared that he could not live without her had she admitted the reality of that bond.

Kawena raised her chin as she imagined what her mother would have done if, instead, he'd said, "If you want a husband, take me." She wouldn't have bothered to listen to anything else from such a man. It had to be the most offhand, infuriating offer any woman had ever received. Had he even noticed her efforts to show him she could be as proper as any Englishwoman? Had he complimented her on her gown, or her oh-so-correct demeanor? She felt like hitting him. He'd ruined everything.

Anthony Haskins came up to them before she could muster a reply. "Excuse me, Miss Benson, your uncle wondered if you would care to go in for the next part of the concert." He looked from Kawena to Lord James.

It would have taken a dolt not to sense the tension

between them, Kawena thought. And he didn't seem to be a dolt.

"You haven't answered my question," Lord James said. He shouldered rudely forward and glowered at Haskins.

"I don't believe you asked a question," Kawena replied acidly. "Take me" was not a question. Not at all. It was a…an idiocy.

"It was…the question was…implied." His expression said he knew how foolish this sounded.

"No," said Kawena. She took Haskins's offered arm and turned away.

"No, it wasn't a question? Or, no, you won't? Or, no, you haven't answered?" Lord James looked massively frustrated at his own jumbled words.

It seemed there was nothing she could do but leave him standing there. She didn't want to. Every part of her yearned toward him, except the bit that insisted she deserved more than, "Take me." And so she went, allowing Haskins to lead her away.

Lord James followed, like a looming bank of storm clouds. He proceeded to take up a post by the wall, leaning against it and brooding over the remaining debacle of the evening. His sullen presence quite spoiled Kawena's enjoyment of the admiration she received from a variety of other young men. Her only consolation was that the Bensons soon grew as glum as the duke's son. They watched her like carrion birds whose anticipated meal was being stolen away. She would have laughed at their transparency had she been less irritated.

For his part, James was far beyond irritation. Indeed,

he was feeling nostalgic for his leaps onto the decks of French fighting ships. It would be so satisfying, right now, to pull out a cutlass and slash something. Of course he wouldn't kill anyone, here in an Oxford concert hall, but it would be a true pleasure to watch them scatter before his blade, bleating.

"A dashed fine-looking girl," said a voice on his left.

Turning, James discovered a friend of Robert's, gazing admiringly at Kawena. He'd met the man some time or other. He couldn't recall his name.

"They say you're acquainted with her?"

"They." That was the target he'd like to impale— the throng of tattling tongues that constituted "they." This mess was their fault.

The newcomer gave him a sidelong look. "Thought you might introduce me."

Across the room, Kawena laughed at some idiot's remark. James ground his teeth.

"Not your type?" said his unwanted companion, misinterpreting his expression. "Even for a fortune?"

He chuckled, and James turned on him with murder in his eyes.

The fellow took two steps back. "What the devil?"

"Find someone else to make your introductions," James growled. He knew it was rude, but he really couldn't help it. And it was far milder than what he really wanted to say.

Muttering about some people's execrable manners, the fellow backed away. The music was starting up again. James couldn't bear any more. He walked out.

Twenty

MORNING DID NOTHING TO IMPROVE JAMES'S STATE OF mind. For the first time in his life, the presence of family members grated on him unendurably. He left Alan's house and took to pacing the streets of Oxford once again, offending several distant acquaintances by failing to notice them as he passed. When someone called his name as he turned off High Street, he nearly didn't stop. But that was going too far, even in his current, desperately foul mood. He turned to acknowledge the hail, and then was very glad he'd done so. Ian Crane stood near the door of an inn, a hand raised in greeting. "Good day," the man said when James walked over.

He nodded a hello. "Crane. Have you come up to see Miss Benson?"

"Yes, I've just arrived from London. I brought some documents for her signature."

"Because of her uncle?" James felt relieved. Crane would know ways of keeping grasping fingers off Kawena's money.

"Her…? No." The man of business frowned. "Miss Benson never mentioned an uncle."

"He just turned up. When word of her fortune started to spread. Says he's her father's brother. Wanting to 'guide' her."

"Ah." Crane's expression showed that he understood the implications of that. "I'll mention it when we discuss the other business."

Which was what? James wanted to ask. Something to do with the jewels, most likely. Perhaps she was converting them into cash, or investments. She hadn't bothered to confide in him, even though he'd helped her find out how it was to be done. "All going well with that then?" he tried.

"Indeed. The purchase has gone through, after a good deal of back and forth, and the work Miss Benson ordered is in train."

What purchase? Crane seemed to take it for granted that he knew Kawena's plans. Wanting to preserve that illusion, he said only, "That's good."

Crane nodded. "It seems it can be done as quickly as she wished. I wasn't sure."

"You, ah, need…skilled workers for that, I suppose."

"The best, and I have been making inquiries about hiring…" Crane hesitated. His expression suggested that he'd realized it wasn't appropriate to discuss his client's affairs with another person, in the open street.

"Hiring…more workers," James assayed.

It was the wrong choice. The other man frowned, then put on a bland face. "Miss Benson can tell you all about that," he said. He bowed. "Very pleasant to see you, my lord."

Crane went into the inn, leaving James puzzling over the sparse information he'd gleaned. Kawena had bought something that required work. A house? Was she making repairs on a new home? And then hiring… what, staff? He'd thought she was against settling in England. Did this have to do with her daft new idea of finding a proper English husband? James clenched his fists at his sides. He would go and see her later on, once Crane was out of the way, and thrash this out. And by God, they would let him in.

Until then, sitting still was out of the question. He craved action like a parched man longs for water. Wishing there was a boxing parlor like Jackson's in Oxford, James walked on. As morning passed into afternoon, his stomach protested its emptiness. James was debating whether to head back to Alan's and forage for food or stop at an inn, when he saw Robert coming out of a taproom up ahead.

His fashionable brother looked uncharacteristically disheveled. His neckcloth was slightly twisted. The bottom button of his waistcoat was undone. Concerned, James hurried to catch up to him.

The face Robert turned toward him was fuzzily morose. "James," he said. "Hullo." He had a bottle of brandy under his arm, and he'd clearly sampled it after purchasing.

"Bit early for that, isn't it?" James asked.

"It's what I'm reduced to," Robert replied. He threw out his free arm. "You see before you the ruin of a once-contented man."

"Do I?" James was sympathetic, but also a bit amused.

His brother pulled out the bottle and started to uncork it. "Let's drink to understanding women, a fool's dream."

James put a hand over his. "No, Robert, we are not going to swig brandy from a bottle in the open street."

Robert stared at him. He looked around as if just now realizing where he was, and what he'd proposed. "Oh God." He rubbed his eyes, let out a sigh, and handed the bottle to James. "That tears it. I give up. I can't stand any more. I'm leaving."

"Back to London again?"

"No! I'm done kicking up my heels in town on the off chance... I never spend the summer in town. Nobody spends the summer in town! I'm going..." He seemed to grope for an idea. "I'm going to a house party in Derbyshire."

"Just a random one?"

"No. I'm invited, of course. Killdene Priory. Very exclusive guest list. I'm invited all sorts of places, you know. Lots of people eager to see me. And to hear what I have to say as well! Some people value my opinions. Quite a bit, actually."

"Of course they do," replied James.

"Don't humor me," Robert snapped. His fuzziness seemed to be dissipating rapidly. "It's not as if your case is any better."

This was true enough to be sobering. James frowned. At the same moment, his stomach growled loudly.

Robert laughed. "That brings us nicely down to earth, doesn't it? Shall we feed ourselves, and maybe just one tot of brandy after?"

This seemed like a capital idea. They walked along, in charity with each other again, until they found a promising inn. Inside, they ordered a substantial spread, deciding on mugs of ale rather than the brandy.

Robert raised his in a toast. "Here's to brothers. No women among us, eh?" He blinked. "Might have been easier if we'd had a few sisters to learn from."

James took a healthy swallow. "What can't you stand?" he asked, recalling Robert's earlier comment.

Robert looked at him. There seemed to be a good deal of pain in his blue eyes, which shocked James. He thought of Robert as up to anything, unflappable. He couldn't remember a time when his next-oldest brother had looked so forlorn.

"Sniping," said Robert. "Lack of faith. Indifference? Who can say?"

"Miss Jennings?"

His brother smiled thinly. "Obvious. The one thing I vowed never to be, and my stolid naval brother sees right through me. You see what she's reduced me to?" He drank. "Miss Jennings indeed. But I've had enough." He waved a hand. "Strike the colors, boys. I'm giving up."

"What did she do this time?" James inquired. He drank a bit more as well.

"Nothing. That's the point, isn't it? No matter what I try, she turns away." He cleared his throat, swallowed, sipped from his mug. "A man needs to know when he's beaten. Isn't that right, Captain?"

James felt a chill. Sympathy for Robert's plight combined with worry over his own. Kawena had turned away from him last night. She'd treated his offer of marriage as…an annoyance. That was the only word he could find for the look she'd given him. A woman wasn't supposed to be angry when you asked for her hand. Overjoyed, quietly pleased, satisfied.

Those were things a man might hope for. Regretful, embarrassed, kindly negative. That should be the bad side. Where did anger come into it? It made no sense.

The brothers drank together in silence for a time.

"What the devil's happening to us?" Robert said then. "Nathaniel's all right. His marriage seems to have turned out well, and I'm dashed glad of it. Alan and Ariel, regular turtledoves there. Couldn't ask for better. Maybe the odds are against the rest of us, eh? Stands to reason? A third of us manage happy matches. A third squeak by with tolerable results. And a third make a complete mull of it. But which are we? Sebastian's run mad. Randolph seems to have sunk into a terminal sulk."

"What?" James wasn't certain he heard right. He'd been brooding a bit. "What do you mean, Sebastian's run mad?"

"He's eloped, hasn't he?"

"Eloped? With whom?"

Robert looked at him as if he was incomprehensibly thick. "Lady Georgina, of course."

"But…he's already engaged to her. I thought he was visiting her family."

"And now they've run off together," Robert finished.

"Why would they do that? Everyone liked the match. They invited him up there."

"Nobody knows, do they?"

"You're not making any sense. He can't possibly have eloped. Sebastian wouldn't. He's a cavalry officer."

"What has that got to do with anything?"

"He likes things done in good order. He'd be worried what his colonel would say."

Robert shrugged. "Mama's had a letter saying they eloped."

"From Sebastian?" James still couldn't believe it. His military brother was like a good-natured lion. A bit lazy, perhaps, but strong and true. He simply couldn't imagine him deciding to flout convention so thoroughly, particularly when there was no discernible reason for him to do so.

"No, Lady Georgina's father. Or mother. I'm not sure. One of them."

This seemed definitive. And yet, James could not be convinced. "That's just...absurd."

Robert nodded. "As I said, he's run mad. She's sending Randolph to straighten it out."

"Who is?"

"Mama," Robert replied in an overly patient tone. "Haven't you been listening to me at all? She said it was two birds with one stone. He's a parson, after all."

"They'll hardly need a parson if they've eloped. And after all, Randolph..."

The two brothers' eyes met. Simultaneously, they burst out laughing. "Perhaps I'll pass on the house party and go on up to the Stanes' place," Robert said when he could speak again. "We're all due there for the wedding in September anyway."

"Randolph would think it was all a prank you'd arranged," James replied. A thought floated up. "It wasn't, was it? This isn't a joke?"

"No, James, it is not." Robert signaled for a refill of their mugs. "Even I have my limits."

"It's just...Sebastian's so...levelheaded. I wouldn't have thought he'd have the—"

"Imagination to elope?" finished Robert dryly. "Perhaps it was Lady Georgina's idea."

James snorted. "Don't be daft. There must be some mistake."

Robert nodded, sipping. "Mistakes all over the place lately. I've made 'em. You've made 'em."

"I haven't."

"You let Miss Benson slip out of your hands," his brother said, tipping his mug in James's direction and nearly spilling ale on his breeches.

"What do you mean by that?"

"Oh, come. I may be obvious, but you're transparent. Everyone can see that you've fallen for her."

"They can?" He'd hardly understood how much he cared for Kawena until just lately. Had it really been so obvious to his family? James thought of telling Robert about the botched proposal, even asking his advice. But Robert wasn't doing very well on the romantic front. And he had a tendency to laugh at one's social gaffes.

"Why do you think Ariel's stopped making introductions?" Robert added. "Why do you think Mama took it into her head to visit Oxford, of all places?"

"She came to see Alan."

His brother made a derisive sound. "Alan and Ariel are going to Stane Castle with the rest of us in a few weeks. No need to see them beforehand, was there?"

James drank his ale and brooded over Kawena's... refusal? Had it been? Or not? He had to see her, ask her. But how to be certain he didn't botch it again? A memory struck him. "Ariel!" he said.

Robert looked up from the depths of his own thoughts, and mug. "What about her?"

"Someone said—you?—that she helped Nathaniel and Sebastian with their…romantic difficulties."

Robert nodded. "Gave them a deal of advice," he agreed.

James rose, heartened by a new resolve. He would ask Ariel how to approach Kawena. She knew her. She knew him. Perhaps she'd also know what he should do.

"Where are you going?" Robert called as he strode off without so much as a good-bye.

❧

James found Ariel easily enough. She was home, sitting in the pleasant parlor off the garden, talking with his mother. There was no question of asking her advice in the duchess's company, however. James shuddered to think of the conversation that would result. Feeling that everything was conspiring against him, James merely greeted them and continued upstairs to his empty bedchamber.

And there, to crown it all, he discovered a letter from the official at the Admiralty, who had been so utterly unhelpful. He'd looked further into James's concerns, he said, and he regretted that it might be months before a suitable post could be found for him. James could almost hear the man's fulsome voice and thinly veiled sarcasm as he read the words. Here was a fellow who reveled in petty tyranny, like a wharf rat savoring a particularly ripe bit of refuse. He delighted in thwarting a fellow officer, because of James's noble lineage.

There was no further question. James was going to have to invoke his father's influence to get a decent berth. And once he did that, his naval career would be different. It would become a matter of favors owed and given, a political exchange. His days of standing on a deck as a simple captain were over.

James felt a great revulsion for the process, and for that future. Even though it was the way of the world, it felt underhanded and unjust. He'd never wished to be one of those complacent men, conveying promises in an exchange of glances, reveling in their supposedly secret web of advantage. If he was successful—and he imagined he would be, the duke's connections were vast—in a few years he'd be sitting in an office in London or Portsmouth, writing up orders for other men. He'd be consulting with the First Lord of the Admiralty, enduring the endless yammering of meetings and social obligations. His colleagues would know that connections rather than merit had put him there, even those who had witnessed his skills in action. That wasn't what he wanted.

James sat in his sunny bedchamber, holding the sheet of paper and experiencing a positive flood of thoughts and emotions. A shift had been building in him for some time, he realized. It had started small, with his jocular request to Ariel to find him a wife. That hadn't been so much a real wish as an indication that he wanted a change. And then he'd met Kawena. James smiled. You could hardly call it "met" when she'd popped up out of the bushes to threaten him with a pistol. Say rather that Kawena had burst into his life. Nothing had been the same since then. His vague yearning for some new direction had built into a strong current, carrying him right out into uncharted waters. And then it had left him there, drifting. Or floundering.

James nodded in the empty room. Floundering was definitely a better word for the way he'd been veering from one thing to another without a proper course. He had a sudden vision of a ship caught in irons, sails flapping uselessly.

He slapped the letter with his free hand. No more. It had taken time—not too long, he trusted—but he saw clearly now. Kawena had scorned the idea of waiting ashore while a naval husband sailed off for a mission that lasted years. And why shouldn't she? She deserved more than that. So did he, for that matter. He would fit himself into the life she wanted. The house she'd bought, or…whatever it was. He'd had ten good years on shipboard. He felt a brief qualm when he acknowledged how much he would miss the sea. But there would be many compensations for a man with a wife like her. He couldn't lose her.

James took up a pen and drafted a reply to the letter. He rather enjoyed thanking the fellow for his efforts, in terms that left no doubt of his true opinion. He informed him that they were no longer necessary. He was resigning from the navy on his own terms.

He had one more bout of uncertainty as he was sealing the missive. But he shook it off. He'd commanded his own vessel. He'd fulfilled nearly every ambition he'd had as a boy. He was ready for something new. Just as long as it included Kawena.

He swallowed. If she refused him.

James stood, letter in hand. He would not contemplate such a disaster. She'd welcomed his caresses. They'd talked and laughed together on their travels. He was...almost certain she returned his regard. James set his jaw. The letter would be his sacrifice to the gods, to show that he was utterly serious about winning her for his wife.

Twenty-one

IN HER BEDCHAMBER ON THE OTHER SIDE OF OXFORD, Kawena pounded on the coverlet, whirled and kicked a stray shoe across the room. Over and over, she was thwarted by this...properness. She was sick of the silly rules and restrictions of this country. Being in England, living in their houses, wearing their clothes, eating their food, speaking their language, she'd somehow begun to imagine that she must conform to English ways. She'd started this rigmarole about a proper husband in order to show Lord James how wrong he was. And with each step she took, it seemed she'd created more of a tangle.

Kawena felt an intense nostalgia for the moment when she'd arrived in Oxford with a pistol and demanded what she wanted. She'd gotten it, hadn't she? There'd been no talk of rules then.

She pulled the pins from her hair and let it tumble down her back, shaking her head with relief at the sense of freedom this produced. She didn't want or need England. Her future plans scarcely involved this place.

But...

She stood still, meeting her eyes in the mirror. She did want Lord James Gresham. She acknowledged it openly for the first time. At least, she wanted the man of fire and passion in whose arms she'd lain. She wanted the lively traveling companion and strong ally. The one who shared her love of the sea and thirst for exploration. In the time they'd spent together searching for the jewels, she'd fallen in love with that man. Not the… the mutterer who said, "Take me," however.

"Take me," she said aloud. "Have a biscuit. And more wretched tea. Put on your bonnet. Do not laugh too loudly."

She'd been playing this silly propriety game for him—somehow, the reasons had gotten rather muddled in her mind—but all it had produced was a lukewarm, practically insulting, proposal. And if she had to change herself in order to win him, what was that worth? Neither of her parents had asked that of the other, despite their vast differences.

Had she been going about things all wrong?

Kawena plopped down in an armchair, throwing her legs over the arm as she had been told not to do, letting her skirts ride up and slide off her knees. She imagined kidnapping Lord James, spiriting him away from stuffy rooms and oppressive rituals. They could be together as they had on the road, with no one else to please. She could find some English henchmen. "Henchmen," she said aloud, liking the word. "*Proper* English henchmen." They would throw him into a carriage and bring him to her like a gift. She would unwrap him with delight.

Feeling warmer, Kawena kicked off her shoes. If only

she could magically transport both of them across the world to her home. There would be no talk of propriety among the palms on her favorite stretch of beach. In that tiny cove, where no one had ever disturbed her, they would find clothing, and hesitations, entirely unnecessary.

Kawena closed her eyes, remembering every thrilling caress of their times together, feeling her whole body flame. She wanted him so, more than she'd ever wanted anything, perhaps. Except...

Kawena let out a great sigh and sat up. The folds of her gown fell about her bare feet. She wouldn't give up the adventure of being in charge of her own life, not even for him.

That was why the future she'd dreamed for them seemed so perfectly right. Ian Crane had told her that the work she'd ordered was nearly done. Should she simply take Lord James and show him? But then, would he be choosing *her*, or a...situation? She would never know for certain.

She sighed more softly and drooped just a little in the chair. People here had been kind to her. Mrs. Runyon had exerted herself mightily on her behalf. Flora had done her part, even though she was mired in a dilemma of her own. An English duke, whom she had barely met, had taken an interest. She rose to retrieve her discarded shoes. She needed to be very sure of her plans before she threw English propriety to the four winds.

～

When James returned from posting his letter, he found Ariel alone in the garden parlor with a book. He took it as a sign that his grand gesture had worked, that his luck was changing. "Has Mama gone out?" he asked when he entered—just to be sure.

"She's writing letters upstairs," Ariel replied.

That would keep her busy for a good while since, even with two of his brothers right at hand, there were plenty still to address. He sat down opposite his hostess. "Robert said that you gave Nathaniel and Sebastian good advice about...matters of the heart."

"Did he really? I assumed he'd forgotten all about that."

"Er...no." James didn't understand her acid tone.

"And yet, he doesn't think to..." She shrugged and shook her head. "Never mind."

James was glad to comply. "Umm, so, I wondered if you could...help me?"

"With Horatia Grantham?"

"Who?" It took James a full minute to recall the name. "Oh. Her. No, I never...she was a bit...obsessive for my taste."

"You surprise me."

Again, she spoke in a dry, satirical tone. James had never found his brother's wife so difficult to talk to before. He gazed at her, uncertain what to say.

She appeared to take pity on him. "With Kawena then?"

He nodded. "I offered for her, and she didn't answer me," James complained.

"What, not at all?"

"That wretched Haskins came up, and she didn't have a chance."

"Haskins? Who is Haskins?"

"Some fellow her uncle brought to the concert." James glowered. "And I would certainly like to know what he's up to."

"You proposed in a crowd of people at the concert?"

"I couldn't get to her before that." James felt both aggrieved and defensive. "Nowadays, she's always out, or guarded by her new duenna, and Flora. I had to take my chance. And then she started talking about finding a proper English husband, and…I lost my train of thought and blurted it out."

"What did you actually say to her, James?"

He hesitated, not wanting to confess it. But you couldn't form an effective strategy without complete intelligence. "Well…I said if she wanted a proper English husband, she should take me."

Ariel stared at him as if she couldn't believe her ears. "Take you?"

"Why the dev…deuce did someone tell her that I asked you to find me a proper English bride?" James queried. "I suppose it was Robert. Sort of thing he would do. That was just a joke, you know. Mostly a joke. It turned out to be a joke."

"You said, 'take me'?" Ariel repeated, not diverted by his counter salvo.

"Yes, all right, it wasn't the smoothest sort of offer. I was flustered."

"You must have been." Ariel seemed to be suppressing a smile, which was worse than the earlier sarcasm.

"I don't understand what she's doing," James complained. "Engaging a chaperone, dressing like a deb. Kawena never planned to stay here. And now she's bought a house."

"She's only renting it."

"No, Ian Crane said she'd bought…well, something. Sounded like it might be a house. Not here. Someplace else."

Ariel gazed at him, her head cocked to one side. "I had put you down as the most calm and practical Gresham brother, but I begin to wonder."

"I'm calm," he protested, and heard that he sounded just the opposite.

"Let us go back to the beginning," she suggested. "Kawena arrived."

James smiled, as he did every time now when he remembered that first moment. "She was wonderful, wasn't she? Jumping out of the bushes, waving her pistol."

"Yes, she was. And then the two of you went off together to search for the jewels. I expect a good deal happened on your…travels."

Her sparkling hazel eyes seemed to see right through him. James nodded, afraid she'd ask for details that he couldn't give without ruining Kawena's reputation. But she didn't.

"When did you begin to think of marriage?" she asked instead.

"Well, I, er, mentioned it early on, but she said she didn't want to marry." The freedom and dust and delights of the house by the sea came back to him in an overwhelming rush. He ached for her in every fiber of his being.

"And you were relieved," Ariel said. It didn't sound like a question.

"How did you know?" Was she some sort of seer?

"But now you feel differently?"

"Yes!" He stood, unable to be still any longer. "Everything's different now. I didn't really know her. Now that I do…we can live wherever she wants." He paced a bit. "I quit the navy," he added.

"What?" Ariel looked shocked.

"She said she'd never sit around England for years, waiting for her husband to come back from the sea."

"She wouldn't want you to give up your profession."

James dismissed this with a gesture. "I didn't wish to go on with it. In the way it would go. I've been realizing that, gradually, since I got home."

"But, James."

He turned and faced her. "So will you talk to Kawena for me?"

Ariel shook her head. "That's not what I do. I'm not an…intermediary. And, in any case, what would I say? That she should take you?"

James winced. It had been a daft thing to say. He knew that. But the knowledge was no help. "What am I to do?" he asked.

"It seems to me," began Ariel, "that someone told Kawena she isn't 'proper.' Was that you, perhaps?"

"I never said that," James protested. Under her steady gaze, he added, "I explained some English notions, here and there. Things she didn't understand. I didn't want to see her hurt or insulted. I was trying to help her!"

Ariel nodded. "And it seems she listened. She's set up a proper household. You must be very pleased."

James glowered at the colorful garden border outside the window. A bird somewhere above filled the air with annoyingly cheerful song.

"Although you don't look pleased," Ariel added.

"She isn't like...herself." James remembered the wild, laughing woman who'd spurred Rex into a gallop and then clung to his back as they thundered along the beach. Strong and at ease in her boy's clothes, her hair coming loose. She'd kissed him like... He felt a pain in the region of his heart; she was unlike anything he'd experienced before.

"How not?" murmured his hostess.

"She's...dimmed down, hidden, muted." He couldn't find a word that satisfied him. But he knew one thing. "She shouldn't be! She's magnificent just as she is. Was." James would have liked to pound something, but there was nothing to destroy in Ariel's pretty room. If he could get hold of that dratted bird.

"I'm just remembering," Ariel mused. "I read a play once about an Egyptian princess who came to visit the hero's kingdom. I forget what his country was. Not Illyria. That's one of Shakespeare's. I think it was a made-up name. But the important thing is, his people mocked her foreign ways."

"People?" replied James, bewildered by the sudden change of subject, and what this had to do with anything.

"She fell in love with the hero because he didn't mock her," she continued. "He admired her, and defended her."

James gazed at his brother's wife. What had made her suddenly go off the rails this way? He was certain it wasn't anything he'd said.

"For example, she had an asp on her crown."

"A...what?" He couldn't have heard that right.

"An asp," Ariel repeated. "It's a kind of snake, I believe. Yes! Remember, an asp killed Cleopatra in Shakespeare's play." She nodded. "Of course. Everyone knows about the asp. It just slipped my mind for a moment."

That was twice now she'd mentioned Shakespeare. What did he have to do with it? And why was it always him? "Are you feeling quite well?" he asked.

"They're very poisonous," she added.

"This princess wore a poisonous snake on her head? I dashed well think people mocked her foreign ways."

"Not a real snake," said Ariel impatiently. "A replica."

"Oh." James contemplated what still seemed an idiotic idea. "Like a pheasant wing on a hat?"

Ariel gave him an impatient look. "My point is, the hero stood up for her. Instead of telling her that she was wrong not to be like his people, he showed respect."

James took a moment to work out what she meant. "I never thought Kawena was wrong." He examined his conscience, and concluded that this was mostly— almost completely—true. "I was just afraid other people would."

"I wonder if she knows that?" Ariel replied.

"Of course she does!" But as soon as he said it, he wondered, too. And as soon as he wondered, he cringed at the idea that she might not. James remembered how happy *he'd* been to leave English social obligations and propriety behind when he went off to sea as a boy. They had this in common, as so much else. When he thought of the time they'd spent alone together, he saw that they were kindred spirits. He was suddenly desperate to tell her so. "I can hardly get near her now."

"Of course you can, if you're clever," said Ariel.

"Perhaps I'm not. Perhaps I'm a dunce." He'd certainly made a mull of things so far.

"I don't think you are." She smiled at him in a way that almost reassured. "There's another lecture tonight. We're all attending, and I'll make sure Kawena is there. Actually, Flora might be quite interested. It's something about ancient history."

James repressed a groan. "We'll be in a crowd again, just like at the concert," he objected. "We're always surrounded by a blasted troop these days."

"True. But, you know, you might want an opportunity to *show* her how much you admire her before you speak of marriage again."

James only half-heard her. His brain was buzzing with ideas about how to manage a few minutes alone with the woman he loved.

Twenty-two

JAMES FOUND HE COULDN'T WAIT FOR THE EVENING TO see Kawena. He was too eager, and knowing she was right there, a few streets away, was too tempting. He knocked on her door in the early afternoon and was admitted without question by a neat housemaid and escorted to a parlor.

Kawena sat on a sofa before long windows. Sunlight gilded her dark hair and rose-pink gown, and threw her lovely face into shadow. James might have taken a moment to savor her delicate beauty. But Anthony Haskins sat beside her, near enough to touch, though of course he wasn't. Fear and jealousy surged through James. He scarcely noticed Flora and Mrs. Runyon in the chairs opposite.

"Lord James," said Kawena.

She didn't sound pleased to see him. Or not pleased. Indeed, he couldn't tell anything at all from her tone.

Behind him, the housemaid returned with a laden tray. "Will you have a glass of wine with us?" Kawena added.

It sounded almost as if she and Haskins were

the hosts, and he an unexpected caller. But no, she hadn't meant that. It was just that he was standing there, looking at the two of them. Haskins gazed at him with bland calculation. Was it the look of a confident rival? Had he established his position with Kawena so quickly?

James's heart thumped painfully in his chest as he imagined what it would be like to lose Kawena to another man. He loved her. She was exquisite, unique, everything one could want in a woman. If he actually lost his chance with her, his future was empty.

"Would you care to sit down?" Kawena said.

Everyone was looking at him. Even the maid with the tray; he was blocking her way. James dropped into an armchair, gathered his scattered faculties. He had to be canny, strategic. He managed a smile. He accepted a glass of Madeira.

"Miss Benson and I were discussing last night's concert," Haskins remarked.

James tried to conjure the spirit of Robert; his brother always had a suave and witty comeback. Well, except with Flora Jennings, who was looking at him now as if he was some sort of odd insect. "You like sinning?" he answered.

There was a moment of shocked silence.

"Singing," James blurted. "I meant…of course… singing."

Mrs. Runyon's lips trembled. James knew a suppressed smile when he saw one. His mother had just such an expression. Flora pretended to cough. He couldn't look at Kawena.

Haskins cleared his throat. "I'm fond of music," he

said. It wasn't clear whether he was embarrassed or also stifling a laugh.

Fifty years ago you could manufacture a slight out of the merest nothing and challenge a rival to pistols at dawn, James thought. Sadly, those days were gone. Organized murder was not on the table. Instead, he was supposed make polite conversation. And nobody was giving him the least help. "Robert said the singer is all the crack. They call her"—what had his brother said—"the leading soprano of our age."

"I'm sure the world's opinion matters more to him than her talent," replied Flora tartly.

Something in James snapped. Perhaps he couldn't put a bullet through Haskins, but he could defend his brother. "Will you give over, Flora? What's Robert ever done to you? You never have a good word for him. And now you're sniping at him when he's not even here."

"I was merely stating—"

"You've chased him right out of town with your continual criticism."

Flora looked startled and self-conscious. "I have nothing to do with Lord Robert's movements. I'm sure he'll be more…at home in London."

"He's not going to London."

She looked away. "Of course. How silly of me. *Quite* the wrong season for London. No doubt Lord Robert has many fashionable invitations."

"No doubt," replied James. He wasn't going to tell her where Robert meant to go. She claimed not to care; let her wonder. It was a small satisfaction to see her frown. Mrs. Runyon's complacent expression was more mysterious.

"I should be going," said Haskins. He stood.

James wanted to leap up and cheer. Thank God Haskins was the sort of fellow who would stay his proscribed half hour and no more. James stayed put through the polite farewells and the resettling of the group.

"I ran into Crane in the street," he said to Kawena then. "He said he meant to call on you."

She nodded. "He was here this morning."

James waited, but she said no more. Once he'd known all her plans. Now, her mind was a mystery. And he had no right to make demands. This was unendurable—to be constrained to mouthing polite nothings when they had spent whole days talking freely together—and more. He couldn't say anything he wanted to say and had to think up a load of things he didn't want to say to fill an awkward silence. It was everything he hated about society in a nutshell.

James leaned forward, meeting Kawena's eyes. He had to find out something. Have some real communication with her. "Have you definitely changed your plans then?" he began. "You will stay in England?"

Kawena gazed at him. Her dark eyes were unfathomable, but James thought he glimpsed sadness there, along with a touch of impatience. "Have I?" she said.

"Crane said you'd bought a place."

She raised her eyebrows. "Did he? I had understood that my dealings with him were confidential."

That stung. "I helped you find Crane and organize your affairs." He yearned to be closer to her, to sweep her into his arms. This net of words they'd become tangled in was maddening.

"It's a very reputable firm," said Mrs. Runyon. "I think your recommendation was a good one."

James had nearly forgotten the others were there. He turned now to find the older woman eyeing him with benign expectation. Flora looked thunderous.

"I suppose your family uses them," the chaperone added.

"Yes."

Mrs. Runyon nodded. "It was kind of you to pass along the name."

James became aware of the weight of three pairs of feminine eyes. Flora's brilliant blue gaze was like a spear designed to pierce pretension. Mrs. Runyon's had a pleasant beam backed by steely assurance. He thought Kawena looked both irritated and sad; he would have done almost anything to know why.

The chaperone rose. "I fear we have an appointment in half an hour. But it was very good of you to call, Lord James."

There was nothing to say to that. James had no choice but to rise and take his leave, no matter how much he might wish to argue.

When the door had closed behind him, Mrs. Runyon said, "That young man is coming along. But he's not quite 'done' yet."

The two younger women stared, but she merely smiled in response.

⤜⤏

"Must we really go to this talk tonight?" Flora said to Kawena some hours later. Flora stood before the mirror in her bedchamber, examining the effect of a new gown they had picked up at the dressmaker.

"Ariel sent a note asking us to come," Kawena reminded her. "Perhaps the speaker is another friend of Lord Alan's." She watched Flora turn, making the ruffle at the hem of her dress bell out. "Mrs. Runyon was right. That shade of green becomes you."

Flora eyed her reflection with no sign of satisfaction. She'd been touchy ever since they'd learned that Lord Robert was going away. Any attempt to discuss that fact was dismissed out of hand, however. "She mentioned that the lecture is about ancient history," Kawena said, as if such a thing could be a treat. "Perhaps you'll be interested."

"I'm sick to death of history!" Flora interrupted. "And of pretending I can find a place in society, and of…just…everything."

Kawena sympathized. She felt rather the same. And she was aware that Flora's case was stickier than her own. *She* had an escape plan. Though there was still one large—male—obstacle to its successful completion. "If there is anything I can do," she began.

"You should get ready if we're going out," said Flora, turning away. Her tone was unmistakable. She would not discuss it.

They arrived at the lecture hall just as the event was beginning. Mrs. Runyon had delayed them for no discernible reason, which wasn't like her. Many of the rows of chairs were filled when they came in. Kawena spotted the ginger-haired woman who had been put forward as a proper bride for Lord James. She was pleased to see that the Gresham party was nowhere near her, and surprised to find the duke and duchess seated between Ariel and her husband and Lord James. For some reason, she hadn't expected them to be present. There was no sign of Lord Robert.

They found seats at the back as the speaker rose and went to the lectern. He carried a discouragingly thick sheaf of papers with him, and when he started in, Kawena resigned herself to another long stretch of boredom. She'd never heard of the people he named. She gathered that they had lived long ago, as expected from the topic of ancient history, somewhere across the Atlantic sea. Far away from her home, as well as from England.

As he droned on, her thoughts drifted. She gazed at the back of Lord James's head. He had said, "If you want a proper English husband, take me." Did he wish to marry her so she could be proper? Accepted? Did he still think he owed this...obligation to her? When she considered the way he looked at her, she didn't think so. But whenever he spoke, it seemed to be all about propriety.

She gazed at his auburn hair, the enticing span of his shoulders. It seemed so very long ago that she had clung to that strong, supple body and lost herself in a daze of pleasure. She wanted to push through these finicky rows of uncomfortable little chairs and drag him from the room so she could do it again. And again.

She'd made a mistake, she decided. She should have chosen another method to show him she was as good as any English miss. This stupid propriety just got in the way. And it was nearly as dull as the speech this fat, pompous man was giving.

Lord James started to turn. Kawena glanced away, not wanting him to catch her staring. Then she quickly looked back. Why shouldn't he see the desire that burned in her eyes? But he had already turned back again.

"The scenes of these rites were great stone temples, in shape somewhat resembling the pyramids of Egypt," the speaker said.

The image caught Kawena's attention. She'd seen pictures of these monuments. They were impressive.

"The person to be sacrificed was stretched out on a stone slab by pagan priests," he continued, "and his body was sliced open with a sacred flint knife." The speaker demonstrated on his own body, running a finger from the bottom of his waistcoat up to his breastbone. "The priest then reached in, grasped the victim's heart, and tore it out, to hold it up, still beating, before the assembled worshippers."

A chorus of gasps and exclamations from the audience seemed to gratify him. Indeed, Kawena got the impression that he had hoped to shock and revolt them. Certainly it was a grisly picture. To exhibit a beating heart; the idea was horrifying. But watching the speaker scan the rows of chairs, apparently reveling in people's discomfort, was distasteful, too.

"The organ was then placed in a bowl held by a statue of the honored god," he went on when the noise had died down a bit. "The sacrificed person's mutilated body was tossed down the temple stairs to land sprawled on a terrace at the base."

Did the man realize he was smiling? Kawena

wondered. It was a thin, rather…cruel smile. She decided to take care *not* to meet him after the lecture.

There was more history after that, but the audience remained unsettled. Whispers and shudders passed through the room. Many appeared poised, even eager, for further shocks. Others shifted uneasily in their chairs. The rest of the talk was tamer, however, back to dull recitations of battles and conquest, almost enough to lull one into daydreams again.

At last, he finished, to a smattering of polite applause. The crowd began to disperse into conversational clumps. Kawena, moving along the row of chairs toward the open space at the back of the hall, heard words like "barbarians," "primitive," and "disgusting" being exchanged. Tones varied from outrage to furtive enjoyment.

She emerged into a press of chattering people, craning a bit to see where the Gresham party had gone. Flora and Mrs. Runyon were swept away in the currents of the crowd. She moved forward until she was accosted by a pair of older women she'd met with Ariel. She couldn't remember their names.

"Miss Benson," said the taller one, "what did you think of *that*?"

Kawena remembered a bit of advice Mrs. Runyon had given her, on the subject of opinions. "It was unusual," she replied.

The other woman leaned closer, as if to confide some secret. "Do your people have such…rites?" She licked her lips on the last word.

"What?" Kawena couldn't believe her ears. "Of course not! Why would you even…?"

The first woman made an airy gesture. "You do come from a more...primitive background."

There was that word again.

"You must have seen...things," added the second woman. Her pale eyes gleamed, greedy for titillation.

She was standing far too close, and wearing far too much scent. Kawena took a step away. "Excuse me. I believe Mrs. Runyon wants me." She invoked the name of her chaperone like a shield. But she was hailed again before she reached her.

"Miss Benson," said a man.

In the next moment, she was surrounded by a circle of young gentlemen. She recognized some of them. They'd been among her admirers on an earlier occasion.

"Quite an eye-opening look into the past, eh?" he said.

She nodded. "Pardon me, but I must—"

"Not so surprising to you perhaps?"

"I don't know why you would say so," she replied in her best Mrs. Runyon voice.

"We were just hearing...er, wondering," said another of the group, "what sorts of...costumes do you wear when you're at home?"

They pinned her with speculative, lascivious gazes. Fleetingly, Kawena felt like a beached fish surrounded by sharp-beaked gulls. If only her pistol lay in her pocket, instead of a useless handkerchief. "My father preferred English dress," she replied, biting off the words. It was perfectly true that he had never abandoned his native garb, even if it had nothing to do with her habits. Jettisoning politeness, she pushed between two of the young men and away. This crowd seemed much denser than those at other events she'd attended. She was beginning to feel trapped.

"There she is," declared an elderly voice.

Kawena tried to turn away from it, but the circle of gentlemen was too near.

A wizened old woman in lavender lace moved to block her way. "Do you really wear a bone though your nose?" she asked. Leaning on a cane, she peered up at Kawena's nostrils as if trying to see how it would be done.

This question brought Kawena up short. It could have only one source. She scanned the room and, sure enough, spotted her uncle and aunt in a far corner. They were small people, and had been obscured by the crowd until now. Watching the flow of chatterers, she worked out that the people with insulting questions had drifted toward her from that direction. Her dear relatives were feeding the emotions roused by the lecture with malicious stories about her.

"Well, do you?" said the old woman. "Seems a rather disgusting idea to me. What sort of bone would you use? How do you clean it?"

Kawena ignored her and her offended huff when the old lady stalked off. She shoved past a young woman in a flowered bonnet, reeled around an animated group, moving toward the Bensons. She was going to do whatever it took to stop them. English propriety could just—what was the phrase?—go to the devil. It wasn't so much the idiotic questions, or even the way these people had started to treat her. It was their utter disrespect of her mother's life, the distortion of half—more than half—of her heritage.

"Yes, that's the girl," she heard someone murmur behind her. "Plenty of money, but I understand her parents were never really married. Her father just went through some tribal rigmarole to get what he wanted, eh?"

Kawena whirled, and found that the source of this remark was the man who'd wanted her to kill turtles. His eyes glittered with scorn. Kawena's hands curled into talons.

Before she could lunge at him, Mrs. Runyon appeared at her side. "I'm afraid we have quite a… situation developing here," she said quietly. "I'm not sure why."

"My uncle," replied Kawena bitterly. She made no effort to lower her voice. "He is behind it."

"Well, it's getting out of hand."

Kawena had never heard Mrs. Runyon sound so rattled.

"Perhaps we should go," her chaperone suggested.

"And leave them here to say whatever they like about me?"

The older woman frowned. "It's just…difficult to counter such open malice without creating an even worse scene."

"I don't care what kind of—"

"Oh, I daresay she's seen her share of sacrifices," said the turtle man, louder, looking right at her. "Perhaps even presided over them. It's what they do, isn't it? These primitives." He mouthed the last word with salacious contempt.

"Do you hunt?" replied a deep, familiar voice behind her. "Have you watched the dogs tear a fox apart?"

Kawena turned to find Lord James at her shoulder. He stood there like a guardian warrior.

"I suppose the odd dog tears out a vixen's heart," Lord James added, holding the turtle man's eyes.

There were murmurs of distaste around them. "That's quite different," the other man said.

"Is it? Have you been to a public hanging over at Newgate? Watched some poor sod flail and kick at the end of the rope?"

Someone in the crowd made a shocked sound.

The turtle man drew himself up in outrage. "You cannot compare the King's justice to the capering of a bunch of savages."

"I can compare you to a damn fool," Lord James said loudly. "I can compare the lot of you to a pack of jackals," he added, even louder.

Heads turned. People drifted closer to see what the fuss was about. The crowd around them thickened even more.

"Miss Benson comes from a society kinder than ours," Lord James continued. "They're nothing like the people that fellow was talking about tonight. They don't mock strangers like this, either. I know. I've been there."

"And brought back a tasty side piece just like her father had," sneered the turtle man.

Moving like lightning, Lord James lunged, his right fist drawing back, and delivered a roundhouse punch to the speaker's jaw. The turtle man went down like a felled tree and lay on the wooden floor, stunned. Kawena nearly cheered.

"Here now," said a man on his other side. "This isn't done. Quite improper to brawl in a—"

"Propriety be damned!" Lord James shouted.

This was the man she'd fallen in love with—strong and passionate, decisive, assured. Kawena wanted to throw herself into his arms. She would have, if the way hadn't been blocked by all these stupid people. She saw Flora gazing at Lord James with an arrested expression, Mrs. Runyon looking at once appalled and reluctantly impressed. At a touch on her arm, Kawena turned, ready to hit out herself.

"I think we should slip away before the riot starts," said the Duke of Langford in her ear. "We are rather outnumbered."

Startled, and a bit overawed, Kawena let him take her arm. Lord James pulled his mother from behind the duke and linked her arm with Kawena's free one. Then he grabbed his brother and muttered something.

Shoulder to shoulder, the two tall noblemen forged a way through the press, trailed by the rest of their party. Flanked by a duke and a duchess, Kawena watched many pairs of eyes follow their progress to the doors. The murmur of comments had risen to a roar by the time they reached them.

"Well," said Mrs. Runyon when the group paused in a quadrangle well away from the lecture hall. She loosed a long breath. "That was…" She seemed at a loss for words.

"It was inexcusable," said Lord James. "What a lot of hidebound idiots."

The duke was gazing at him. Kawena wondered if he was in trouble with his aristocratic father. And

Lord Alan had friends here who might have been—probably were—offended. Ariel was laughing, so perhaps it was all right.

"Here's what we're going to do," Lord James went on, every inch the captain of the ship. "Mama, you will go out with Ka…Miss Benson tomorrow. Shopping or some such thing. Doesn't matter. Just make certain you're seen by all and sundry. I know you can stare down the gossips."

"Can I?" said the duchess. There was an odd catch in her voice. Not an objection or a doubt. Kawena couldn't tell just what it was.

Lord James faced her, resolute. "You know you can. And I'm asking you to do it. For me."

Kawena's throat tightened with tenderness and anxiety. She loved him so much. But she didn't want to be the reason for a breach in his family.

"Then of course I shall," replied the duchess with a warm smile.

Lord James nodded, as if to a junior officer. "Papa, you will help me see what can be done about Ronald Benson."

"Indeed, I will be happy to," answered the duke. "How I despise such petty malice."

"I hope it won't be a great deal of trouble," Kawena put in. Although she adored seeing the man she loved so in command, she wasn't certain this was the way to talk to a duke.

"My dear, it will be a pleasure," the latter replied. "I won't have a…member of my family treated with disrespect."

He had such a genial, well-mannered air. Yet in

that moment, Kawena decided that he was a dangerous man to cross "I'm not a member of your family,"
she murmured.

"I suspect you soon—"

Lord James…twitched. There was no other way to
describe it.

Smoothly, in the blink of an eye, the duke changed
direction. "There's Alan to think of, you see."

"Oh, yes." Kawena felt oddly sad at the correction.

"He lives here and has friends here. We must do all
we can to keep up his reputation."

"Thank you, Papa," said Lord Alan wryly. "I
expect I shall manage. Every family has its bad apples,
after all. I shall tell everyone that we sent James off to
sea because he was mad."

"Piker," said Lord James.

"Ape," said Lord Alan.

They both laughed.

A group of people passed by the edge of the garden.
They must have been coming from the lecture, because
there were whispers and discreet pointed fingers.

"We should all go home," said Mrs. Runyon.
"And…recover."

To Kawena's chagrin, the others agreed. And Lord
James made no mention of accompanying the three
of them. She'd been sure that he would. In fact, they
parted with courteous bows and polite farewells, as
if the wearisome veils of propriety had dropped over
them once again.

"A duke's family is not at all what I imagined,"
Flora said as they walked away. She sounded deeply
thoughtful.

"If you *imagine* that was typical, you will find you're mistaken," Mrs. Runyon replied.

"But they didn't seem bothered by the…upheavals," Flora said.

"The Langfords have always gone their own way," their chaperone conceded. "And since they don't give a snap of their fingers for most people's opinion, they've usually gotten away with it."

"Have they?"

Flora didn't speak again on their short walk home. Kawena scarcely noticed. Her mind and heart were far too full.

Twenty-three

THE DUCHESS ARRIVED AT KAWENA'S HOUSE THE NEXT day at midmorning. Ariel was with her, but not Lord James. Kawena tried not to show her disappointment. She had more than half expected that he would escort them on this expedition. She'd dreamed of him through the night.

"Ariel has plotted out a plan of campaign for us," the duchess said with a smile when they had greeted each other. "The best shops and a call or two."

"The dressmaker?" Mrs. Runyon asked.

"Oh, I think so."

"But what are we to say?" wondered Kawena. "Are we to explain?"

"Nothing," declared her chaperone, who had regained all of her assurance overnight. "This morning is not about explanations or, still less, excuses. It is a… demonstration, for any who might need such a thing, that you are accepted at the highest levels of society." She offered the duchess a respectful nod. It was returned with a smile. "And that you have exquisite manners, of course, and a high degree of polish."

"Do I?" said Kawena.

Flora laughed.

"Of course you do," said Ariel.

Mrs. Runyon ran her eye over the younger members of their party. "The duchess and I will manage the conversations."

"You mean I should show my exquisite manners by keeping quiet," Kawena concluded.

"Demure would be an effective strategy after last night."

"If people ask me the same sorts of offensive questions, I don't know if I'll be able to stay silent."

"Trust us to put a stop to those," said the duchess.

"Indeed," Mrs. Runyon agreed. "You may exhibit wide-eyed astonishment. You too, Flora."

"Not even a little outrage?" replied the latter wryly.

Their chaperone shook her head. "The ideas are too ridiculous to inspire anything but amazement."

"Ariel might look pitying at their provincial ignorance," suggested the duchess.

Mrs. Runyon nodded approvingly. "We will drop a few hints about bad feeling between your father and your uncle."

"Who has found it expedient to return to London," said the duchess. "It seems his business required attention."

Kawena remembered her realization that the duke was a dangerous man. "I wouldn't want my uncle ruined or…anything of that nature. I just want him to leave me alone."

"That is the idea," answered the duchess. She looked around the group. "Are we ready to begin?"

Bonnet strings were tied. Gloves were donned. The

five ladies left the house and walked along the street toward their first objective.

"You don't think this is all…beneath you?" Flora asked the duchess as they went.

Kawena had an odd sense that the two older women grew suddenly more alert, though there was nothing in their faces or demeanor to explain it.

"A diminishment of my consequence, you mean?"

"Well…yes." Flora looked away, then back again. "You're a leading light of the *haut ton* and…" She hesitated, then went on as if compelled, talking fast. "Kawena is my friend, and I like and admire her, but as far as society is concerned, she's…nobody. I know Mama would expect you to be angry that Lord James…" She flushed and turned away again. "Never mind."

"Society is composed of individuals, you know." The duchess acknowledged Flora's discomfort by speaking gently. "With different opinions."

"Agatha never understood that," commented Mrs. Runyon.

"Mama received the cut direct from one of her oldest friends after she married," snapped Flora, eyes flashing with indignation. Kawena was glad to see her spirits restored.

"Lydia Fotheringay"—their chaperone waved the name aside—"who has the brains of a pebble and the heart of a rabid stoat."

"And the morals of a Covent Garden abbess," commented the duchess.

Ariel choked on a laugh. Flora's mouth hung a little open. Kawena simply watched them all in fascination.

There was something quite reassuring about this exchange, though she didn't understand every detail.

"I asked your parents, and you, to all my parties, and down to Langford every summer," the duchess pointed out.

"Mama thought it was pity," Flora replied.

"Well, it wasn't," the duchess said with some asperity. "I've always been very fond of Agatha. And she ought to know it."

Flora frowned at the cobbles under their feet like a person with a great deal to ponder.

Kawena watched Mrs. Runyon and the duchess exchange a satisfied look.

Ariel looked pleased as well. "Here is our first stop," she said, indicating a house just ahead.

❧

As the ladies made the rounds of shops and calls, James set off on a different errand. He was absolutely determined that the next time he asked Kawena to be his wife, she would agree. Joyfully. Ardently. He didn't think he could bear another…equivocation. Or whatever it was he'd gotten the last time. He needed a plan before he plunged in again, and the best plans were based on adequate intelligence. So he'd decided to seek advice from somebody who'd successfully passed through this ordeal and come out happily on the other side.

He found his brother Alan in his customary daytime haunt, his laboratory. The large, high-ceilinged room was filled with arcane equipment, some of which was buzzing in quite an ominous way. Two young assistants tended a twisted maze of metal tubes at the other end of the space as if it was a living creature. They were well out of earshot, and didn't even look up when James came in.

Alan waved and came over to greet him. "Need to speak to you," James said.

"Is something wrong? Have you knocked out a college dean's teeth or some such thing?"

"That fellow deserved it, after what he said!" James exclaimed. "And nothing's wrong, no. Not as such."

Alan simply waited, one eyebrow cocked in inquiry.

When it came down to it, it was difficult to begin. Despite the familial relationship, after so many years away, James scarcely knew his youngest brother. The silence stretched a little longer. Either he was going to speak or he wasn't. "I intend to ask Miss Benson to be my wife," he said finally.

"Really? You surprise me."

"I do?"

"No, James," replied Alan gently.

"Then why say…?" He sighed. "You're rather like Papa, aren't you?"

"I would be delighted to think so."

"The thing I'm trying to ask," said James, mildly aggrieved, "is: how did you do it?"

"Do what?"

"Get Ariel to marry you. I mean, obviously she did. And you seem happy as a pair of doves."

"You just ask," said Alan.

"I did, but it…didn't go well. You got it right the first time. What did you say?"

Alan looked self-conscious. "Technically, it wasn't the first time."

"Technically," James repeated. He looked around at the mass of apparatus surrounding them. Was this some scientific term? "What did you say the time it worked?"

"I'm not really certain I should share that."

"I'm coming to you as a brother in need of a bit of help," James declared.

Alan relented. "As I recall, we were having an argument about honor and intellect."

"An argument?" That didn't sound promising.

"And then I was kissing her."

"And 'then'—just like that?"

"Intellectual discussion can be quite stimulating."

It was the sort of thing his youngest brother would feel, James thought. "So you grabbed her, when you were arguing."

"I didn't grab her," said Alan indignantly. "You don't just grab a lady. If that's what you've been doing—"

"It isn't," James interrupted. "And I know that."

"I should hope so." The brothers frowned at each other for a moment, then Alan continued. "The kiss just…happened."

James nodded. He understood that.

"And her father showed up," continued Alan, "and I started arguing with him."

"There's a good deal of arguing in this tale," James objected.

His brother shrugged and nodded. "Ariel told us to be quiet. And then her father said if she was going to be kissing young men in a forest—"

"You were in a forest? What were you doing in a forest?"

"Do you want to hear this or not?"

James held up his hands in surrender.

"She said that in that case, she'd better marry them…me. And I agreed. Emphatically."

James stared at him. This wasn't what he'd had in mind when he'd asked for advice. "You agreed? So, *technically*, she offered for you?"

"It was complicated," Alan said.

James shook his head. He'd heard men talk of marriage as if it was a snare one stumbled into at the least misstep. A few unwary words, and you were caught. Here he was, laboring to tie the knot and finding it damnably difficult.

"I should get back to work," said his brother.

Dissatisfied, James left him to it. Alan had been no help at all. Besides the lack of a forest, which was irrelevant, he didn't see much chance that Kawena was going to propose to him. She'd shown no sign of it. Quite the opposite, really.

With no better goal in mind, he headed back to Alan's house. He found his father there, alone, reading a letter in the parlor. "Nathanial and Violet have left Brighton for the country," he said when James came in.

"Ah." That was too far away for consultation. He didn't have time for correspondence. And Nathaniel's offer for the earl's daughter had been quite formal, and a foregone conclusion, as James understood it.

"He's decided to keep the Phaeton," the duke continued. "Violet likes it. And so matters come to a delightfully unexpected conclusion."

An idea occurred to James. A novel, unsettling idea.

His father looked at him, hovering in the doorway.

His parents had had—still had—a long and happy marriage. That was clear to anyone who knew them. It must have begun well. His father did everything right. Why not ask him for guidance?

The duke raised his eyebrows at the continuing silence.

People did. James had heard any number of men pass along paternal wisdom over the years. Of course, their fathers weren't the Duke of Langford. James had seen so little of his awe-inspiring father since the age of sixteen. Before that…well, they'd *talked*, of course. They must have, though he couldn't remember specific conversations. He'd always dreaded the prospect of appearing foolish before him. But even this, he would risk for Kawena.

"Is there something I can do for you, James?" his father said, as if reading his mind.

"Some advice," James managed.

"Of course. I'd be only too happy. Will you sit down?"

James came farther into the room and sat. "The thing is… I mean to offer for Miss Benson."

His father nodded.

"Everyone seems to know. Robert said I'm transparent."

"I wouldn't say that. But after last night… Your regard for her was…quite apparent."

James brooded briefly over people's infernal nosiness. "I want to do it…" He nearly said properly, then veered away from that word. "I want to do it well. I want to be sure she accepts."

The duke looked surprised. "Do you have some reason to believe she won't? I would have thought…"

He stopped just when James wished he wouldn't.

James waited a moment, then confessed, "I botched it the first...times."

"You asked her and she refused?"

"She didn't refuse, precisely," said James, still smarting from that scene. "But she didn't accept either. We were interrupted."

"Ah?"

"She had time to say yes," James complained. "She could have. It was..." What was Alan's word? "Complicated."

"Was it?" His father looked fascinated, which both gratified and unsettled James. "That is a rather broad term. Complicated in what sense?"

There was nothing for it but to tell him. "She was spouting some nonsense about proper husbands, and I said if she wanted a proper husband, she should take me."

His father gazed at him.

"I know it was...maladroit." That was a word he'd heard from Robert. "I was flustered. I'm going to do better the next...the last time. She'll say yes. She has to. That's why I need advice."

"On how to propose to Miss Benson?" the duke said, with the air of a man getting his facts straight.

"Right. I thought if you told me how you did it, that might help."

"How I did it?"

"Mama accepted," James pointed out. "And you're happy."

"We are."

"So." Now that he'd gotten it all out, at last, James sat back and waited for enlightenment.

"You want to follow our…scenario?" His father appeared to find the idea inordinately amusing.

"You do everything right," James pointed out.

His father put a hand to his heart. "I'm touched."

A problem occurred to James. "Or, was it just a formality, arranged in advance, like Nathaniel's match?" It probably had been. The heir to a dukedom wasn't free to choose just any girl.

"Not like that, no," his father replied with a reminiscent smile. "Your mother never told you the story?"

James shook his head.

"I suppose it's the sort of thing girls ask about, rather than sons."

With his father's ironic tone and amused expression, James was becoming rather interested in this bit of personal history.

"We met at a house party, in the winter of 1783. It was a sort of rehearsal for Adele. She was to come out in the next London season." His smile softened. "The first time I saw her, she was wearing a broad-brimmed hat trimmed with peacock feathers, and a blue silk gown. It was a good deal harder to get close to a girl in hoop skirts, I can tell you. Her hair was powdered, so I didn't know the color at first, and she looked like an angel. I enlisted in her cadre of admirers at once. They were legion."

It was odd to think of his mother besieged by a troop of suitors. "But you cut them out," he said.

"I did my best. We danced and flirted and managed one or two brief conversations. Manners were rather different thirty-five years ago."

James couldn't ask his father to get on with it, but he wished he would come to the point.

The duke went on as if he understood without words. "One afternoon, there was a riding party. You know how your mama loves to ride."

James nodded.

"It was a large, lively group. Adele was surrounded by beaus, as usual. I was jostling in with the best of them when my horse ran mad and got away from me."

"What?" His father was a bruising rider. James had never seen him at fault on horseback.

"I found out later that one of my rivals for your mother's affections had bribed a groom to slip some nettles under the poor beast's saddle blanket."

"Low," commented James.

The duke nodded. "Lightfoot tried to scrape me off with tree branches and toss me over his head. Finally, he managed to drop me in a large—a *very* large—mud hole. We'd had a week of rain to fill it."

"You?" James couldn't picture it. His immaculate, never-at-a-loss father covered with muck?

"I fear I'm ruining my reputation with you," the duke said with a rueful twinkle. "Naturally, all of the other young men found my predicament exquisitely funny. The ladies were kinder, but far more eager to avoid the mud. Except for Adele. She rode to the rescue."

"Mama always comes up trumps."

"That she does," agreed his father. "But when she tried to help me climb out, she fell in."

"You pulled her into the mud?"

"I did not! I ordered her to stand back, to go and fetch servants to get me out. She refused to listen.

She bent over and caught hold of my hand. I tried to shake her off, of course." He shrugged. "You must understand that I was not in the best of moods at that point. Jack Stanley was using his riding crop to point out the slime dripping from my sleeve." The duke's eyes grew hooded. "He had an unexpected dip in the lake later, in his best coat."

"Mama fell in a mud hole, with all those skirts," James said.

"Right on top of me," his father elaborated.

"Was she very angry?" James had a healthy respect for his mother's wrath.

"She laughed," his father said reminiscently. "We were absolutely plastered with mud, and she laughed. And then I did, too. We laughed like lunatics for a while, the rest of the party just gaping at us. And then I got her out, which involved rather a lot of…close work. That blasted hole was deep, and slippery."

James looked away. One didn't wish to see desire burning in one's father's eyes, however glad one was for the two of them.

"We ended up in each other's arms, dripping clots of mud, and I said I adored her, and she was the only woman on earth I would ever wish to marry. And she said yes."

James appreciated his father's tender expression, but really, how was he supposed to arrange for mud holes, any more than forests? It hadn't rained here in days. He wasn't putting Kawena on a horse again, either. Or…that had worked out rather deliciously the last time. But there were no wild coastlines or deserted houses around Oxford.

"The important thing is to tell her how you feel, James."

"I feel a whole muddle of things," he complained "I don't know what half of them are."

"How you feel about her," his father amended. "You do love her?"

"Yes." That was he sure of.

"Tell her that, and why."

"Why?"

"What it is about her that you love," the duke elaborated. "The unforgettable, unique things."

James was unconvinced. "That seems rather simple." Hadn't he heard you were supposed to kneel? Why couldn't there be a set of instructions for these things, like the details in a packet of naval orders?

"Is it? What do you love about Miss Benson?"

"Just...who she is."

"Perhaps a bit more specific?"

James latched on to this idea. "You think I should make a list? Use that as a kind of...crib sheet when I speak to her?"

The duke seemed to struggle for a moment. Then he laughed. "I'm sorry," he said at once. "But, James, really, a cheat sheet? We're not speaking of an examination."

Sometimes it feels like one, James thought. You could study for those, however, tedious as that might be. Offering marriage seemed more like navigating without a compass. And he still didn't have a plan.

Twenty-four

IN HER BEDCHAMBER AT THE END OF THE DAY, KAWENA stood at the window, looking down at the scrap of garden behind the house. According to Mrs. Runyon, their campaign had done its work. Her social credit was restored. And she didn't care a whit. She was wondering where Lord James had gotten to, and what she should do next, when she was interrupted by a knock on the door. "Yes?" she said.

The housemaid looked in. "A gentleman has called for you, miss. He said it was important."

Kawena heard no more. She was already past the girl and on her way to the stairs. However Lord James began this time, she would find a way to discover his true feelings, she vowed. And at last, at last, things would be settled between them. Word had arrived that her project was complete. It was time to be on the move.

She rushed into the main parlor and found Anthony Haskins standing there, looking thoughtful, hands clasped behind his back. "You." Kawena was so disappointed that she could think of nothing else to say.

"I apologize for the inopportune hour," he replied. "I called earlier, but you were out. I felt I could not wait until tomorrow to speak to you."

He looked so very English, Kawena thought. His pale blond hair was perfectly in place. He was handsome, pleasant, and…thoroughly forgettable.

"I wanted you to know that I deplore your uncle and aunt's…behavior at the lecture last night."

"Were you there?" She hadn't noticed him. But she had been rather occupied.

"No. But I heard of it."

"I'm sure you did." Kawena knew that Oxford society had been talking of little else.

"Unconscionable," said Haskins. "I wanted to assure you that I had no hand in it, no understanding of their…methods when I accepted their offer to make an introduction. I hope you will believe me."

Kawena nodded. She realized that she hadn't asked him to sit down. You were supposed to do that. Haskins continued before she could speak, however.

"I also came to offer you the protection of my name."

"Your name?" She was briefly confused.

"I live quite retired in the country," Haskins added. "As my wife, you would have a respected position in the neighborhood. People are unlikely to have heard of any…embarrassments in your history. Or dare to mention them. In any case, they would soon be forgotten." He seemed to be reassuring himself.

"You are asking me to marry you?" Kawena was incredulous. Did English women actually listen to these smug, pompous declarations? This one was even worse than the last. She thought again of her mother and father, of the passionate gestures and sacrifices each had made in order to be together.

Haskins nodded. "We have not been acquainted long, I know. But I have formed a genuine regard—"

"For my fortune," she interrupted.

Haskins reddened. "I admit it is a consideration. I am not ashamed to be taking thought for my estate and my daughter's future. Indeed, I think it only natural. I can promise you I intend to be a good husband."

He stood before her like the very essence of English propriety—with its strengths and its limitations. He held out an idea of marriage like a cloak to protect her, to kindly, even perhaps affectionately, erase all her supposed disadvantages. Kawena could understand that for some women, this would seem a welcome refuge, with a real prospect of happiness. But to her, it felt like a cage held courteously open, with no acknowledgment that she was expected to abandon her spiky individuality as she passed through the door. In that instant, Kawena rejected the idea of propriety, once and for all. "No," she said. "I don't wish to marry you."

Haskins looked disappointed, and then, just a little, like a man reprieved. "Are, er, are you sure?"

Kawena nodded. "Thank you," she remembered to say. "But I am quite certain. You may give my uncle the news."

Haskins looked at her. "I don't think I will, Miss Benson. I believe I will pack my things and go home."

"And very soon, you will thank the gods for your narrow escape," she suggested.

He stiffened. "I would never say such a thing."

"It wouldn't be proper."

Hoskins gazed at her a moment longer, started to speak, then simply bowed and turned to go.

Kawena wished him well. She hoped he found just the sort of wife he wanted, with plenty of money, too. It simply wasn't her.

❧

"You must!" said Horatia Grantham. She leaned forward in the armchair and fixed James with a fierce gaze. *Rather like an erne spotting a raft of schooling fish, poised to dive and sink its talons into scaled flesh*, he thought. The young lady—in an agitated and exigent state—had arrived at Alan and Ariel's house just as the family had been about to sit down to dinner. She'd insisted on seeing him, so urgently that Ariel had finally summoned him to the garden parlor.

"The Admiralty promised to send someone," Miss Grantham continued. "But now he isn't coming. And on the flimsiest of excuses! The ceremony is tomorrow morning."

James started to tell her that he'd resigned from the navy, and its obligations had nothing to do with him.

"A number of sailors wounded in battle will be there," she said. "I cannot believe the Admiralty means to insult them by ignoring our arrangement."

This gave him pause. "What is it again?" He'd hadn't understood the details from her first, jumbled explanation.

"We are unveiling a cenotaph dedicated to naval heroes lost at sea," said Miss Grantham impatiently. "They promised me an admiral! I am sadly disappointed in the navy." She glared at James again, as if it was his fault.

"I'm nowhere near an admiral," he pointed out. And wouldn't be even if he hadn't resigned. "Surely there's someone else who could better—"

"I can't find anyone else!" Their visitor veered toward hysteria. "It will be a disgrace. A mockery of naval tradition." She began to cry into her handkerchief.

"Hold on," said James.

Ariel shot him a look—quizzical and encouraging.

"All right," said James.

Miss Grantham looked up, instantly recovered. "Splendid!" she said, the officer in charge once more. "You must be at Oakthorpe Square at ten tomorrow. No, best come a quarter hour early, so we can be certain… You will give a short speech praising the heroism of navy men, and pull the cloth off the monument."

"Speech," repeated James. He didn't like that part of it.

"Surely you have rallied your men before a battle?" Miss Grantham replied. "Or praised them for their actions after. You can say a few words."

"I suppose so," he grumbled.

Miss Grantham rose to go. "I do hope your whole family will attend. It would be such an honor to have the duke and duchess at our unveiling."

James frowned, wondering if this was the reason she'd turned to him for this task.

"I'll inquire," interrupted Ariel before James could speak. "I'm not certain of their plans." She looked suddenly thoughtful. "May we invite other…friends as well?"

"Of course. We hope to have a good crowd." Miss Grantham seemed eager to leave now that she'd accomplished her purpose. "I beg your pardon for calling at such a late hour," she said belatedly as she went out.

"How could you have wanted me to marry her?" said James when she was gone.

"I didn't want it," Ariel replied. "It was simply an introduction."

"More like a lucky escape," he muttered, and followed her back to the dining room.

❦

When he reached the allotted place the next day, accompanied by all of his family, of course, James found a draped monument, a platform sporting the Union Jack and, in the center of it all, a massive old artillery piece. The kind of cannon Henry VIII might have used at Flodden in the fifteen hundreds. It looked as if it might have been sitting there since then, too. That would have been all right. But a fellow stood next to it, affixing a fuse. James started over to speak to him, but was intercepted by Miss Grantham and hustled toward the platform. "People are starting to arrive," she said. "You must take your place."

"Do you mean to fire that piece?" James asked her, indicating the cannon.

"Isn't it grand? It will be the perfect punctuation to the unveiling."

"Punctuation?" Her strange choice of words sounded too much like "puncture" for his taste. "Has someone checked it over? Someone who understands artillery?"

"Of course. We have only powder in it, naturally. No ball."

"Yes, but gunpowder—"

"It's time to begin," interrupted Miss Grantham. She pushed him, rather sharply, toward the front of the platform.

James looked out over the people clustered before him. Along with the Greshams there were perhaps twenty others, many of whom had the look of old sailors. He noticed a peg leg and a missing arm among them. Off to one side, he spotted a slender figure in a worn coat and breeches, with a cap pulled well down over…her face. Kawena looked up briefly, grinned at him, and lowered her head again. James's heart began to pound, and everything else went out of his mind. What was she doing here, dressed like that? And why was he up here, so far from her?

He took a step toward her, and Miss Grantham's elbow thumped into his side, recalling him to his duties. He said a few words about the hazards of naval warfare and the stout hearts of English sailors. A rope was insinuated into his hand. He pulled, and the cloth fell to reveal quite an ornate cenotaph. He glimpsed flame in the corner of his eye, and turned to find the putative gunner setting match to fuse. "No," James cried. "That's not a good—"

The fuse hissed into the hole. The crowd waited with indrawn breath, and then the huge old gun erupted.

The noise was deafening, obviously beyond what anyone had expected. Choking black smoke poured out over the onlookers. As James leaped down to help, he saw that the ancient piece had split down one if its seams. Bits of flaming powder spit from the opening. He'd tried to tell them that modern gunpowder was much more powerful than the stuff that gun had been built for.

James ran for the gunner first. The man was flat on his back, stunned, but he didn't appear wounded. James quickly checked his limbs, found them sound, and got him up and away.

Turning, he saw Kawena leading his mother to a bench on the far side of the square. Alan was doing the same for Ariel, an arm around her waist. The duke was escorting another lady, a stranger.

James went to find the wounded sailors. The man with the wooden leg was down, his arms wrapped around his head as if to shield it. Kneeling beside him, James gently loosened them. "It's all right," he said. "All flash and no ordnance. We're all right."

The fellow let his arms fall, revealing the eyes of a man who'd faced many a broadside, and the resulting carnage, in his time.

"All's well," said James. The man pointed to his ears and shook his head. James nodded. His hearing was all right, but many would have trouble for a bit. That thing had sounded like the crack of doom.

He saw that Kawena had come back for Horatia Grantham, who'd collapsed in a heap on the far side of the platform, and was half carrying her to the benches. He went to give her a hand.

Working side by side, with the help of a few others, James and Kawena attended to each member of the crowd and found places for them to settle. The ancient gun muttered and smoked. People cried or shouted or huddled, according to their natures.

When the area was clear, and the fire brigade had

arrived to douse the cannon, James found Kawena and captured her hands. All thoughts of lists had fled from his mind, but words came spilling out. "That was…just splendid. You were splendid. I adore you, Kawena. There's no other woman like you. You're everything I could want, for the rest of my life. Please say you'll spend it with me."

Utterly unaware of people staring and whispering, James amended, "Allow me to spend it with you, I should say. Whatever your plan. I don't care."

She smiled up at him, teeth very white in a face somewhat blackened by the smoke. "Yes, I will marry you," she said.

Almost dizzy with triumph and relief, James pulled her into his arms. Pent up longing surged through him. This was right, and so intoxicating, to finally hold her again. And to know that she was his. He took her lips, reveling in her eager response to his touch, and fell into a kiss sure to drive them both mad with desire. He let his hands roam over the body that had haunted his dreams and plagued his waking hours for a seeming eternity. She pressed against him, her fingers like trails of fire along his ribs, across the fabric of his breeches. James wished their clothes to perdition.

"Disgraceful!" huffed someone. James realized he didn't care a whit.

Kawena's cap fell unheeded to the ground. Her hair escaped its pins and tumbled down her back.

"It's a woman," commented a male voice. "At least."

At last, matters grew too urgent, and too obvious. They couldn't make love in a public square, beside a fuming cannon. Slowly, reluctantly, they drew apart.

"I believe that may trump a mud hole," James heard his father say.

"In sound and fury, but not in romantic originality," replied his mother.

The duke's laugh was filled with delight.

"Shall we head for home?" said Alan. "My home, that is. Where all of Oxford will be calling in the next few days to learn what the devil happened here." He sounded resigned.

"Scientific geniuses are expected to be eccentric," replied Ariel. "It's almost required, I think."

"Is it?" But Alan sounded more amused than concerned.

Relieved, with an arm firmly around Kawena, James followed his family from the square.

Twenty-five

"I SHALL GO UP TO LONDON FOR A SPECIAL LICENSE," James said as he escorted Kawena back to her own house some time later, "so we can be married right away." Memories of Nathaniel's recent wedding surfaced. It had been…somehow satisfying to have the whole family together for the occasion. The thought made him briefly wistful. Most of them hadn't even met Kawena.

"There is one thing we must do before everything is final," she said.

"What? You said yes. That's final."

"I will explain it all in Southampton," she told him.

"Southampton? What has Southampton to do with anything?"

"You will see once we go there."

"I don't understand."

"We will travel together, as we did before."

With those words, James remembered every delicious detail of their earlier journey. They would be away from chaperones and interfering relations and…everyone.

"I will meet you where the south road leaves Oxford tomorrow morning at eight," Kawena declared. And refusing to elaborate, she walked into the house.

❧

Kawena sat on her horse at the side of the busy roadway, waiting for Lord James to appear. She wore her breeches and cloth hat once again, rather the worse for smoke, keeping her head down to hide her face. Other garb was in a bag tied behind her saddle. She was still not an expert rider, but good enough for this journey.

As she waited, she felt a curious mixture of elation and uneasiness. She was certain she wanted to spend her life with…James. James. It was time to stop adding his title now that he was to be her husband. She'd wanted to settle the future on her own terms. And so, she'd succeeded. He'd declared his willingness to live whatever life she chose. There was every reason to celebrate, no reason to worry. Yet, there were issues she hadn't completely considered until the time came for this journey.

She thought the plan she'd made would please him as much as it did her. But what if it didn't? She'd taken such care over it, looked at the details from every angle. When she'd gotten the idea of revealing it to him in a great flurry of adventure, she'd imagined the scene so innocently. The mystery, the surprise. He'd be amazed, delighted, and after that everything would fall into place, just as it should be. But now it was real, not a fantasy. There were obstacles she'd ignored in her imaginings.

There he was. She watched James ride toward her, straight and easy in the saddle, so terribly handsome. He saw her and smiled, and it was as if all the other people on the road faded into insignificance. Kawena's heart filled with joy.

He reached her, and she signaled her horse to move onto the road beside his. As they rode along together, she returned his smile.

This could be the adventure as it *should* have been, she told herself. She must make certain it was.

"So will you tell me now why we're going to Southampton?" he asked.

"To look into the future," she said.

"What, you have a fortune-teller there?" he joked. "Crystal gazing and palm reading? I daresay I could find you one closer by."

Kawena smiled as she shook her head. Her heart was beating fast. "You said…yesterday…you said whatever my plan, you would follow it."

"Fortune-teller it is, then."

"But can you really put your future into my hands?" she asked. "Without knowing what it is?"

"It doesn't matter where I am, if I'm with you."

"In England, I am expected to say that, to do that, for you." He started to speak, but she held up a hand. "And I could not."

James tried to discover, in the depths of her dark eyes, what was coming.

"I told you I could not sit in England and wait while you sailed off for years—"

"I've resigned from the navy," James interrupted.

"What?" Kawena was shocked into silence.

"Days ago. It was time to do it. I dreamed of a career in the navy, and I had one. I'm ready to move on."

Even though this made matters easier, Kawena was worried. "I don't want to be the reason that you gave it up."

"Meeting you only made it clear," he replied. "Along with other things—the slow tops at the Admiralty, seeing my family and realizing how much I've missed."

"If you regret your choice."

"What I would regret, to the end of my days, is losing you. I don't care about anything else."

She gazed into his blue eyes. "Are you really sure?"

"Completely. Though I expect I shall miss the sea."

"Oh, the sea." Kawena gave him a dazzling smile, driving all thought from his head.

✑

They didn't hurry. There was no reason to, and they shared an unspoken desire to recapture the mood of their previous travels. The day was warm, if overcast, and the breeze fresh. Their horses were content to move at a brisk walk. Kawena let the rhythm of their pace, and of occasional conversation, soothe her. Only after an hour or so had passed did she ask him, "What do you think is the most important thing in life?"

"You," said James.

She smiled. But he'd said it automatically, and she wanted a more considered response. "What if you had never met me?"

James looked over at her, and seemed to catch the gravity of her question from her gaze. He grew thoughtful. "Most important," he repeated. "I don't know how to choose one thing. I have wanted to make my family proud, to act with honor, to serve my country."

"And you have," she said. "You do."

"I hope so. After those things…" He considered. "I've always wanted to see more, experience more, to find out what's beyond that next curve of shoreline. The other side of the hill."

"I, too," said Kawena, her spirit soaring with hope. She'd made the right decision, in so very many ways.

"Not that I can't settle down," he added hurriedly. "In a house or…some such."

She smiled a secret smile and rode on.

When the sun sank toward the western horizon, throwing ruddy light into their faces, James began to wonder about arrangements for the night. He was alive with hope, and desire, but wary of making assumptions. As if reading his thoughts, Kawena said, "We should find a room for the night."

"*A* room," he echoed, to be perfectly sure.

"You should engage it," she replied, with a smile that showed she was well aware of his meaning. "I don't want to be too much noticed in these clothes."

Spirits soaring, James chose a busy inn where the hostlers scarcely had time to observe them as they took charge of their horses. He bespoke a private parlor as well as a bedchamber, and saw that their things were carried up. Calling for hot water to be fetched to the room, he went off to get a good wash elsewhere.

When he returned to their parlor, much refreshed, he found Kawena sitting at a small table before the hearth. She'd taken off her boy's clothes and now wore the sunset-orange gown that gave a seductive glow to her delicate skin. Her hair was pinned up in a sedate knot that made James's fingers itch to loosen it. It was all he could do to sit down opposite, rather than crush her in his arms.

The harried waiter who brought in a tray expressed no surprise at seeing a young lady instead of a boy awaiting dinner. James's concern for appearances eased, and then evaporated when he met her dark eyes, dancing with amusement. Kawena would live as she chose, and it was one of the things he loved most about her.

As they ate, conversation gradually died, replaced by an aura of longing so intense that James thought he would burst. He couldn't have said, afterward, what dishes comprised their dinner, what wine they drank. It seemed forever, and a moment, before Kawena rose and smiled at him. "I shall be in the bedchamber," she said.

The words, and the sultry invitation in her eyes, seared through him. He waited a few, dragging minutes, and then followed her.

By the time he traversed the short distance to their room, he was breathing like a man who'd run for miles. He opened the door and stepped in, shutting it securely behind him.

Kawena sat at a tiny dressing table in the corner, wearing a thin nightdress edged with lace. In the light of two candles, the intricate tracery lay along her skin like sea foam. Her hands were raised to take down her hair. James strode over and knelt beside her. "Let me," he said, his voice thick with longing. She let her arms drop, and now at last he could pull the pins and let her hair cascade down her back in a gleaming, ebony fall. It was one of the most beautiful things about this exquisite woman.

She turned to him, and he pulled her close in a kiss that held and held. Through the thin cloth of her nightdress her skin felt hot.

Kawena stood, pulling James up with her, their bodies pressed against each other. She pushed his coat off his shoulders and down his arms. He flung it off, then bent to yank off his boots and stockings and toss them away. Urgent now, Kawena tugged at his shirt. He jerked it up and over his head, tugging impatiently when the cuffs resisted.

Then he stood before her in only his buckskin riding breeches, muscles gilded by the candlelight. Kawena stepped closer and ran her hands over his ribs and up across his chest, delighting in the shudder of desire she evoked. She slid her arms around him and pulled his head down 'for another of the lingering kisses that set her afire. She could feel his arousal, taut and urgent. She let her hand slide downward again to the fastening of his breeches. He moaned as she loosened them, and gasped when she pushed them down to free him from their bonds.

As James rid himself of this last garment, Kawena skimmed out of her nightdress. They faced each other, naked in body and soul, in the flickering glow of the candles, and moved as one into a passionate embrace. Kawena's knees threatened to give way. She pulled him back onto the snowy bedclothes. He lifted her a little as they tumbled into bed, legs interlaced, hands and lips delectably busy.

Riding a storm of sensation as wild as any tempest at sea, Kawena cried out when he covered her lips with his own and entered her. It was like discovering fantastic new lands, and like coming home, as all her senses dissolved in a crescendo of pleasure.

Afterward, they lay entwined, pulse and breath slowly easing. "I want to lie beside you every night of my life," James said.

Kawena rested her head on his chest, listening to his heartbeat. "Yes," she said.

"I wished we could simply travel together forever," he added.

She almost spoke then. Only the strength of her past imaginings stopped her.

❧

They reached Southampton at noon on the third day. Their second day and night of travel had been as wonderful as the first, and James was almost sorry to arrive, though he was curious about what awaited them there. The sea sparkled and surged on their right, its colors changeable as small clouds passed over the sun. "The sound of the ocean is the first thing I remember," Kawena said as they rode. "And the sight of waves hitting some great rocks and the spray flying up. Even before my mother's face or my family, I think of the sea."

James gazed at her lovely profile. She seemed a different woman from the adventurer of yesterday. But then, that was the thing, wasn't it? She had so many sides. Only a few weeks ago, he'd thought of women as…all one thing. They were mothers and wives, alluring or intimidating—a…a kind of species, not vital, complex, fascinating individuals. Kawena had shown him that truth.

Kawena led the way directly to the docks and into the work area of a shipyard. Then she simply drew rein and waited. James looked around at the familiar materials and tools, until his eye was caught by a hull that had clearly been repaired and was lying in a slip, ready to be relaunched. He frowned, looked closer. It was—the *Charis*. "My ship," he said, puzzled.

"My ship," replied Kawena.

James turned to look at her. "Your—"

"I bought it from the navy."

James's reaction was all that she'd imagined when she thought of this moment. His eyes widened. His jaw dropped. For several moments, he was speechless. Finally, he stammered, "*This* is what you bought?"

"The English navy didn't want it anymore."

"I know." James swiveled back to gaze at the *Charis*. "They decommissioned her while she was still—"

"Generally sound," finished Kawena, repeating the judgment of the shipwright she'd gotten to examine the *Charis* before she bought it. "Some new planking required, recaulking and new rigging. One new mast."

James stared at her as if she was speaking a foreign language, though she knew the terms were more familiar to him than they had been to her, at first.

"I've started to get a crew together, with Mr. Crane's help," she added. "A bare beginning. Very much in need of expert advice."

James shook his head as if dazed.

"Perhaps some of your former crewmen might be interested, if any have left the navy?"

"I don't understand." James gazed at the ship with bewilderment and a kind of hunger.

Relenting, Kawena explained. "I can't live in England. I have tried it, and I am not at home here. Though I have no objection to visits, of course. I want to go back to Valatu, to see my family, but I know I won't be content to settle there either. Not after all I've seen and done. So, it seemed to me that the best plan was to sail the sea."

"Sail the—"

"To live on the sea," she added. "You had told me about the *Charis*. I asked Mr. Crane to make inquiries." She wasn't ready to say, just yet, that she had bought the ship for him. It was true, but not all the truth. "We…may perhaps do some trading. Thanks to my father's legacy, cargoes won't be absolutely necessary."

James blinked. His brain couldn't seem to keep up with events. "Live on the *Charis*?"

Kawena nodded. She reached across and took his hand. "We can't be away from the sea, James."

He slumped in the saddle, overcome. He hadn't thought he'd ever see the *Charis* again. He'd put the ship out of his mind, as much as if she'd been burned or sunk. "This is your plan? When Crane said… This is what you bought?"

He was beginning to make her nervous. She'd been so sure, after the last few days, that he would be delighted. What if she'd made a mistake? Uneasily, Kawena dismounted. "Come and look inside."

She didn't wait for him, but walked directly to the *Charis* and grabbed a line for balance as she climbed aboard. Entering the former officers' quarters in the stern, she hurried down a short corridor with small cabins on either side to the larger space at the very back of the ship. She hadn't seen the finished work herself. The captain's cabin had been thoroughly refurbished. The windows spanning the stern of the ship were sparkling clean and let in a flood of light. A larger bed had been fitted into a recess on the right and furnished with a bright coverlet. On the other side, a new polished table was bolted to the deck. There had been no need to add storage; cupboards already occupied every eligible space.

James came in and stood gazing about.

"It will make a fine place to live," said Kawena, wishing he would say how he felt. "The small cabins will do for children."

"Children!"

Her chin came up. "My mother's ancestors sailed great distances in boats far smaller than this, with their families, even their animals. My children will be at home on the sea."

James went over to run his hand across the smooth surface of the table. "The old one was a mass of nicks and scratches."

"Is that all you have to say?"

"I just can't believe you've done all this." He turned to her. "You own the *Charis*." It was as if he had to keep repeating it.

"I do," Kawena agreed. "Although it seems that, under English law, my husband will own it when I marry. We will have to talk about that."

"We'll reregister her in Valatu. She'll be all yours there, like your mother and her house."

Kawena had to swallow to ease a suddenly tight throat.

He frowned. "Does Valatu have a flag? Or a ships' registry? Never mind, we'll create them. Blue for the ocean, don't you think?"

"You'd do that for me?" she asked, her voice thick.

"It was you who thought of this scheme. A brilliant idea, may I add, which solves…everything." He threw out his arms as if to embrace the whole. "So, she's your ship, Captain." With a tender smile, he straightened and gave her a smart naval salute.

Kawena's heart melted. "I'd rather be the captain's first—and only—mate," she said.

"Done!" James laughed and pulled her close.

Epilogue

James's wedding was nothing like Nathaniel's, with pomp and ceremony and all the family in attendance. On the other hand, he suffered no brotherly pranks. And though he was a little sad to have no Greshams present, he was itching to stand on his own deck again and set sail.

So they stood up before a priest in a Southampton church with strangers as witnesses and made their vows. Kawena had no family within a thousand miles, so he couldn't complain. At least she wasn't wearing her breeches, as she'd laughingly threatened.

Their wholehearted responses more than made up for the unusual circumstances, and the toasts later in their quarters on the *Charis* were equally enthusiastic. They put out to sea on the ebbing tide that afternoon. As the sails billowed and stretched taut, his heart swelled with gratitude and excitement. Life was opening up before him. There was so much to see and do. They might face dangers, yes, but that was the spice of it. With one arm around his amazing new wife, he watched the coast of England recede, as happy as he'd ever been. That would have been quite enough, and yet he had every confidence that in the years to come, he'd be happier still.

*Keep reading for a sneak peek at the next
book in the Duke's Sons series*

LORD SEBASTIAN'S
Secret

LORD SEBASTIAN GRESHAM PULLED UP AT THE TOP OF
a steep ridge and leaned back in the saddle, giving
Whitefoot a rest from the long climb. The view from
this Herefordshire height was extensive. Before him,
the land fell away in folds to a swift river at the base
of the ridge. Green fields and pastures rolled out north
and east, and mountains loomed to the west, the edge
of the Welsh Marches. Straight ahead he could see his
destination—Stane Castle, still a distant gray pile.

Thoroughly at home on horseback, Sebastian felt
only pleasantly tired, even after the long cross-country
ride. With a smile, he remembered a story his father
the duke liked to tell, of how Sebastian's three-year-
old self had clambered onto the largest hunter in the
Langford stable and clung like a burr as he hurtled over
a five-barred gate. It had taken two grooms to remove
him, squirming and kicking and protesting that he
would ride Thunderer, he *would*. Sebastian almost
thought he remembered the incident. But perhaps it
was just from hearing the tale.

He signaled Whitefoot with his knees, and they

started slowly down the path toward the river. Sebastian took in a deep breath of the soft summer air, so different from the reek of London. The scents were unlike those around his childhood home of Langford as well. Crisper somehow, with hints of cold stone and evergreen. Georgina had said that her family's estate was at the "back of beyond." Certainly the country hereabouts seemed sparsely populated.

Sebastian fell into a daydream of his lively, golden-haired fiancée. Surely there would be many more opportunities for them to be alone out here. During the London season just past, they'd barely managed a few kisses, even though they were officially betrothed. A castle would have gardens, surely, perhaps even a maze to get lost in. With their wedding coming up in a few weeks, they ought to be allowed some freedom. Sebastian relished the possibilities this thought roused.

Whitefoot's hoof sent a shower of pebbles over the edge of a narrow slant of path, and Sebastian brought his attention back to the present. First of all, he had to meet Georgina's parents. Indeed, it was odd that he'd never encountered them, but it seemed the marquess and his wife never came to London, or even Bath, which was nearer their home. That was why her grandmother had brought her out, Georgina had explained. She'd seemed uneasy, if not positively evasive, when she mentioned her parents' distaste for society. Still, Sebastian wasn't worried. The family that had produced a charming woman like Georgina must be all right. And, without false modesty, he knew himself to be a convivial fellow. He was confident the meeting would go well. If they didn't care for society, well, he'd be happy to let them be and spend more time alone with Georgina.

The zigzag path down the ridge came out at a ford. Sebastian guided Whitefoot across the river and found a lane that seemed to lead toward the castle, perched across the valley on a spur of hill. Another half hour, and he'd be there, he estimated. There was no sign of Sykes with the carriage and his luggage, but Sebastian wasn't the least surprised. Even though he'd lingered after Nathaniel's wedding and taken his time on the ride, it would probably be a day or two before his valet arrived. The roads in this part of the country were wretched. Sebastian would make do with the contents of the portmanteau lashed to the back of the saddle until then.

The road up to Stane Castle angled across the hill under a towering stone wall. As a military man, Sebastian appreciated the opportunities it provided to rain shots down on invaders. These days, tufts of wildflowers and weeds sprouted from between the great blocks. It had been years since Stane faced hordes of Welsh tribesmen boiling out of the hills to ravage the English countryside.

He rode through an open gate and into a tunnel of stone lined with arrow slits. On the other side of the wall was a cobbled courtyard, also enclosed. Sebastian dismounted as a competent-looking groom came out to take Whitefoot. "House that way?" Sebastian asked, nodding toward an arch in the inner wall as he relinquished the reins.

"Yes, sir. Through there and to your left," the lad answered.

Sebastian strode under the arch and out into an open space. Within the encircling bastion, the castle sprawled, a jumble of a building, obviously added to by generations of Stanes. An ancient moss-covered round tower anchored one end. Closer by was a more modern wing with tall windows and graceful stonework. The hoped-for gardens spread out like green skirts around the place.

Near the center of the edifice, Sebastian spotted a wide, studded oak door, up three steps from a stretch of lawn. Taking this for the front entry, he mounted the steps. There was no bell, only an iron knocker in the shape of a striking hawk. He raised it and let it fall. The thud was surprisingly loud, as if he'd struck a great drum.

The door opened at once. Primed to face a footman or maid, Sebastian blinked at the figure who confronted him instead. The slender, dark-skinned man wore a sort of long coat or tunic of figured brocade over narrow trousers. Straight black hair framed his aquiline features and brushed the raised collar of the garment. Intelligent dark eyes examined Sebastian. The man pressed his palms together and bowed. "You must be the young lord who is to marry my host's daughter," he said. "*Namaste.*"

His voice had a lilt that Sebastian recognized. He'd heard it from travelers native to India. "Er, yes," he replied, thrown a bit off his social stride.

The man moved back to let him enter. Sebastian stepped in, and paused to let his eyes adjust to the sudden gloom as the door shut behind him. He could make out a high, paneled hall in the light from small windows near the ceiling. Much of the far end of the chamber was taken up by a huge stone fireplace. A carved stair twisted upward at the back.

"I am Anat…" began the man, and stopped as a chorus of yapping arose in the distance. "Alas," he went on. "They come. They always answer the knock."

"They?" said Sebastian. The man's tone suggested calamity.

His companion merely gestured toward the stair. The yapping rose in volume, and then a positive sea of small dogs flowed down the steps and along the stone floor. They pooled around the Indian gentleman's slipper-clad feet, barking and sniffing and panting. The man crossed his arms over his chest with a pained look. "Can you command them?" he asked. "They will not hear me."

They were pugs, Sebastian saw. Fifteen or twenty of the tiny brown-and-white lapdogs favored by many older ladies in London. He'd never seen so many together. They milled about the other man, pawing at his legs, staring upward with bulging brown eyes, drooling on his feet, and all the while yapping like… Well, like pugs.

"Please," said the other man. He looked quite distressed.

Sebastian stepped further into the hall. "Here," he said, speaking as he would have to the well-trained dogs at Langford. "Come away from there."

Floppy ears pricked. Little heads came up. The dogs' prominent brown eyes shifted to him. After a moment's scrutiny, the pugs flowed over like a school of fish to surround him and began to scratch and slaver at his riding boots. One clamped its teeth on the end of his spur and tried to chew it off. The largest reared up, threw its front paws around his calf, and began moving against the leather in a highly inappropriate manner. "Stop that at once," Sebastian said.

"My thanks are yours," said the Indian man and slipped away through a doorway beside the steps.

"Wait," said Sebastian. "Where do these dogs belong?" But the fellow was gone. Another of the pugs flung himself on Sebastian's free leg. The two dogs pumped away in unison, huffing like little steam engines.

"Hello, Sebastian."

He looked up to find Georgina poised on the stair. A beam of sunlight from above gilded her hair and illuminated her oval face. She wore a pale-blue gown, and her hand rested on the wooden baluster, delicate as a flower. She looked like a masterwork in the portrait gallery at Langford.

The dogs panted and writhed on his legs.

Sebastian was not a man to blush, but he'd never found himself in a situation quite like this. Used to obedient dogs, he was torn between reaching down and pulling the two miscreants off him, which would draw more attention to their unsavory activities, and ignoring them, which was increasingly difficult. He lifted one foot off the floor and shook it a little, trying to dislodge the wretched animal unobtrusively.

"Don't kick them," Georgina said.

"Of course not." He was appalled at the idea of kicking a dog.

"People are tempted," she responded.

He couldn't tell if she was joking. Her voice

sounded odd. She didn't smile either. Indeed, she looked somehow muted, constrained, quite unlike the elegantly composed young lady he knew from London.

"I can't call them off, I'm afraid. They only listen to my mother."

This was not the sort of reunion Sebastian had pictured. He wanted to step forward and greet her properly, perhaps even kiss her, but that was out of the question in his current plight.

"I'll get Mama," Georgina added, and hurried up the stairs and out of sight.

As soon as she was gone, Sebastian bent and grasped the offending dogs by the scruffs of their necks. He lifted them away from his legs and held them up so that he could stare at them sternly, one by one. "No," he said.

Two small tongues lolled below bright eyes, almost as if they were laughing at him. Small paws waved in the air.

He set them firmly aside. "Down. Sit."

Sebastian was used to command. Troops of cavalrymen jumped to obey his orders. Animals usually responded at once to the assurance in his voice. But this crew of canines stared at him as if he was speaking words they'd never heard before. The two primary offenders dashed forward, obviously ready to resume their assault on his riding boots. "No," said Sebastian again.

He took several steps back, nearly tripping as they flowed around his moving feet. It was a challenge not to tread on any of them. As he fended them off with gentle insistence—and an utter lack of success—he actually considered climbing onto a chair, out of their reach. Which was ridiculous. And to be found in such a position by his fiancée and her mother was unthinkable.

Georgina walked quickly along an upper hall and down another stair toward the room where her mother was most likely to be at this hour. She wanted to find her mother and get her dogs off Sebastian right away, and she also wanted to retreat to her bedchamber and hide from the scene that must result. Why had she imagined an auspicious beginning to Sebastian's visit? It had been a pretty picture—her family lined up in a smiling row, cordial greetings exchanged, offers of refreshment and easy conversation. But when had her parents had the time or interest for any of that?

She loved Mama and Papa—of course she did—but at this moment she couldn't help wishing that they were not quite so...individual. Back home after months in London among people who revered convention and cultivated elegant manners, she noticed it more than ever before. Sometimes it seemed that her parents positively dared strangers to misunderstand and mock them. If Sebastian didn't get on with her family, if he despised them... Georgina feared such a reaction, and resented the possibility for myriad reasons on both sides of the question. One thing was clear, however. She simply couldn't marry him if he did. The thought left her fiercely desolate.

Seeing him again had set her pulse pounding. All the sons of the Duke of Langford were tall, handsome, broad-shouldered men with auburn hair and penetrating blue eyes. When you added to that the muscular frame, dashing side-whiskers, and unconscious swagger of a cavalry major, the combination was potent indeed. From their first meeting, Georgina had been roused by Sebastian's bold, masculine presence.

She'd resisted, of course. Even her limited social experience had predicted that such a man would be insufferably arrogant. But Sebastian wasn't. He'd approached her with all sorts of inquiries about *her* thoughts and feelings. And then he'd listened to her answers. It was unprecedented.

Still, she'd been suspicious. There'd been something stilted about it at first. But as the season went on, it became clear that his interest wasn't feigned. Their conversations grew deeper. He'd actually asked her help in understanding a cryptic conversation at a ball, and when she'd explained, he hadn't punished her afterward by drawing away or belittling her. As some men did. Many men, really. Why did they find it so insupportable, seemingly, to be schooled by a female? But not Sebastian. She'd heard him telling a mutual acquaintance later that she had "more brains in her little finger than I do in my whole head." Georgina smiled. She'd made up her mind to marry him in that moment.

And why hadn't she already done so? She could have married in London from her grandmother's house, Georgina thought as she entered her mother's workroom. This visit might have been postponed until after the knot was tied. He'd have had to take her family as he found them then. But no. She shook her head. That wasn't enough. She wouldn't avoid, still less disown, her family. It was out of the question. If only they could, sometimes, be a bit more commonplace for an hour or two.